ROBIN MURARKA

AKIN

ROBIN
MURARKA

The imagination exceeds life,
Proving us immortal.

TABLE OF CONTENTS

PART III

PART IV

AKIN

PROLOGUE

"Long ago, Parus, there was a man named Samad. He lived in a village not unlike ours, although his village was larger and further into the desert. It was surrounded by sands as far as the eye could see.

"The village and its occupants grew up together in close proximity. It was organized by a group of elders who made decisions that affected the entire village. They relied upon a well and farmed the arid land. All were known to each other.

"Samad had a son, and his name was Ionus. Samad adored his son, much as I adore mine. Ionus was a bright little boy. His mother had died during childbirth, and Samad raised him with love in his heart.

"One morning, Samad awoke to a terrible discovery. When he opened his eyes, he felt a blade in his hand and found his hut tainted red. He crawled upon the floor, looking for his son, and when he found him, Ionus was dead in his cot, lying in a pool of his own blood.

"Samad fell backwards, sitting upon the floor silently, staring at Ionus's body. He reached out to touch his son's head, but as he saw blood on his own hand, he retracted, terrified.

"Murder was unknown in their village, and when Samad was found, he was wandering the outskirts of the town aimlessly, calling out for his son. They brought him back to the village where the elders questioned him to discover what had happened.

"And though they questioned him, his answers were confusing. His own explanation came in the description of a nightmarish vision, and he was certain he had violently taken his own son's life in the middle of the night.

"He began to speak less as the situation was investigated further, and by the end of the inquisition sat mute before the elders, saying nothing. It was decided that he should remain isolated in his hut until he was able to remember what occurred that night, and that in his odd, comatose state, he would be cared for by the remainder of the village until that happened.

"After some time, however, Samad disappeared from the village. He had vanished in the middle of the night, and though the other villagers feared his whereabouts, they worried for him, as all were kin to each other. As time passed, his hut was occupied by others, and the mysterious story of Samad and his son became eerie lore they shared late at night.

"It was later heard, however, that he had become a homeless man in a nearby city. During a trade route, one villager claimed to have seen him and questioned others about him. He discovered that Samad had the strange habit of begging during the day and disappearing at night, wandering the darkness of the desert till morning."

"What did he do in the desert, jahi?"

"No one knows, Parus. I believe he would look for his Ionus . . . that he would call out his name in the hope that he would return to him."

"Will you ever hurt me, jahi?"

"No, Parus! This is just a story, a tale. My father told it to me, just as I am telling it to you. He spoke of it while we traveled from ocean to ocean upon a caravan long ago."

"Were you scared when you heard it?"

"I was, just as you are. But it is just a story, child. A story to teach us, to entertain. I remember the caravan enjoying my father's story. One traveler in particular . . . I still recall his face."

"What about him, jahi?"

"I remember sitting in my father's embrace . . . all of us watching him, listening to him. This man was quiet . . .

calm . . . for the entirety of the trip, he spoke very little and seemed to observe everything . . . as a Saifa. But when my father spoke of Samad, his eyes began to tremble. And afterwards, I saw him weeping at the back of the caravan. It was strange to me, as I had never seen such a man cry."

"Why did he cry, jahi?"

"I do not know, child. Perhaps it was pain, or perhaps it was beauty. You will learn, as you get older, that a man can cry for both."

PART I

CHAPTER 1

THE DREAM

"Who are you?"

"..."

"Are you me?"

"..."

"Is this . . . are we lost? In Ceria?"

"Aydan."

"I am Aydan."

"This is not the lost world, Aydan."

"What is it?"

"It is something else."

"What is it like?"

"It's beautiful, Aydan."

"It feels wonderful."

"How wonderful?"

"It feels . . . safe."

"You are always safe, Aydan. But here . . . nothing obfuscates that knowledge."

Eyes. Open.

"What was that?" he thought. "Was I awake? It's the middle of the night and I can still hear their whispers."

"Whispers."

Aydan raised himself out of bed and sat upright. The moonlight shone through his doorway.

"They are loud," he thought.

He closed his eyes.

"Speak, Aydan."

"Who are you?"

"Are they demons?" he asked himself.

"Think not without speaking, Aydan."

"Are you the Kai of Ceria?"

"What are the Kai, Aydan?"

"They are," he thought. "They are pretending."

"Think not without speaking, brother."

"Brother?" he thought.

"Brother?"

"What are the Kai, Aydan?"

"The demons of the lost world . . . Ceria Kai. You are them, aren't you?"

"Why do you fear the intangible, Aydan?"

"Because you consume our spirits."

He suddenly began praying.

"Vespa . . . Vespa. Please protect me. I don't want this. Please protect me, make this a dream, make it end."

"They are right, Aydan."

"Please . . . please go away," he begged. "Don't choose me. I know of you and don't want to be chosen. Excuse me in this case . . . please leave me. Choose another."

"Brother, we may leave you tonight for your desperate fear of us. But know that we will return when a great silence surrounds you again."

"Why? Why do you have to return?"

"Because, Aydan. What they do not tell you is that we do not choose you, you choose us."

"But I didn't! I didn't choose you! I don't want you! There is a mistake! You are mistaken!"

Aydan didn't notice the people outside his room until his father entered with a fiery wick, revealing the many eyes staring at him.

"It was a nightmare, right boy? It was a dark dream, nothing more."

He turned to the others.

"It was a nightmare - you can go home. There is nothing of concern here."

"We are warned, Bethelhurst. This is a symptom of the mark. To be awoken like this, to speak to wanton spirits is indicative of the mark!"

"Go home, Mayah. Please, know that it is a nightmare. Tell them, Aydan."

Aydan nodded, petrified.

"Yes, it was a nightmare. I dreamed of the skies falling upon me and a titan crushing me. I was full of fear but I am all right now."

"Yes, such dreams frequent our line, Mayah, all. I have had such a dream as well, but it is just a dream," his father explained.

"We shall see, Bethelhurst. I won't let one marked by the Kai roam freely!" she warned.

"Go home, Mayah. It will be discussed tomorrow," another townsperson suggested.

As the crowd dispersed, Bethelhurst leaned down towards Aydan, pretending to kiss him.

"You will forget this entirely and remember only the nightmare. Do not agree, just sleep."

As the light diminished and the crowd disappeared, Aydan was alone again. His doorway stood bare for all to see, and he feared them coming back.

"Please, Vespa. Protect your son."

CHAPTER 2
AZURE SHADOWS

As sunlight crept into Aydan's room, his mind slowly awoke, unaware of the previous night's events. But just as iridescence filled his room, so did the memories, and he suddenly became worried. He felt his body jolt with a familiar feeling as a weighted, jittery sense overtook him.

"Fear, I feel it."

He knew he had heard nothing the night before, that it was indeed just a nightmare. So vivid was the nightmare now that he even envisioned the images that he dreamed. Massive clouds in the blue sky and a titan running the world, but falling, for the clouds above Aydan were too thin. And so this magnificent and ancient being fell from the skies, plummeting down right unto him, bringing the skies with him. He saw the detailed frame of the gigantic creature. And below him stood Aydan, unprepared for the end of time.

"It was just a nightmare," he smiled.

It was very early. Aydan could tell for the street outside his room was empty and everything was silent. He stood and looked out his doorway at the yellow world around him. The road was covered in a browned, golden sand which snaked around bricked, yellow houses filled with pockets of sleeping people. The sun was just awakening and was still on a narrow slant, creating black morning shadows on the dark sides of all that it touched.

"Dark sides . . ."

Aydan blurred his eyes and saw the image of a world with yellow, bright frames and darkened eyes within. Every doorway was immersed in blackness, and within slept each and every other villager. Between each house was a dim break of shadow, segregating the golden brick from its brethren.

"I can't stop it from happening, can I?" he whispered to himself.

Aydan shook his head.

"No, you cannot."

Aydan fell to the ground and hid himself from sight. He began to breathe heavily and curled himself up, leaning against the side of his wall.

"Why? Why? Why am I doing this? Please, someone, help me . . ."

He began to cry but desperately tried to keep his voice down, petrified.

"Please, god, someone, help me. Make it stop."

Aydan hit himself in the face once, then twice, and for an instant the thoughts went away. But as he looked up, hopeful, listening to himself, he once again felt those emotions, telling him stories of the shadows.

He began to heave again, covering his face in his hands.

"Oh, god. It's not going away. Oh, god."

He felt a sudden slap and fell backwards, dragged out of sight. As he looked up, he saw Bethelhurst staring at him with devastatingly menacing eyes. His father's frame seemed to fill the whole world, and Aydan cowered at the sight of this angry persona directed entirely at himself.

"Are you insane? Do you know what will happen if anyone sees you like this?" he whispered aggressively.

Aydan yelled back at his father and pushed him. "Don't hit me! You strike someone while they cry?"

Bethelhurst grabbed Aydan and muffled his mouth, holding him tightly in an anxious grip.

"Quiet! Quiet, Aydan. Please be quiet."

The huts around them still brimmed with the immature morning sun. They listened for voices, but heard nothing. The village was still sleeping.

Aydan tried to free himself from his father's hold but could not loosen his tight grasp. As he calmed, Bethelhurst let him go and shifted away, still out of sight from the outside world. They both sat on the floor of his room, seemingly out of breath.

"I don't know what's happening to me," Aydan blankly stated.

"Nothing is happening to you."

Aydan looked up at his father and smiled sardonically.

"You would like that, and I would like that, but I am thinking thoughts I can't will away."

Bethelhurst lunged at Aydan but stopped himself for fear of being seen. As he saw his father approach, Aydan cowered, immediately frightened. Bethelhurst stared outside, frozen, ensuring no one had seen or heard him.

He looked at Aydan piercingly and pointed his finger at him.

"Nothing is happening to you. We all feel . . . confused at times. This will pass. Do you understand?"

Aydan stared at his father as tears began to roll down his cheek once more. He nodded as his father approached him slowly and hugged him.

"Nothing will happen to you and everything will be fine. You just have to do as I say, boy."

Aydan hugged him back for an instant then weakly let go, wiping his face.

"You wouldn't see me in Visium, would you?"

Without thinking, Bethelhurst slapped Aydan. Aydan once again rebelled, grabbing his father's tunic.

"Don't hit me!"

Bethelhurst got up abruptly and walked out of Aydan's room, almost frightened, leaving him on the floor. Aydan felt his cheek and massaged it gently, staring blankly at his floor. His thoughts went to Jacub and the image of his last breath as he collapsed in the pit.

"Where is he now . . ." he whispered to himself, almost stuttering.

CHAPTER 3

THE AIZIK

Aydan's day was a mish mash of slow motion and hazy colors. He silently balanced the trencher with his weight as his father guided the bovin. He did not need to focus on his work, for he had been doing it all his life, and instead spent his days conversing with his father. On days like this one, he silently watched the earth split as the cutter tore through.

The noise was deafening to him but provided a consistent hum, drowning out the world. As the spike tore through, leveling bits of rock and soil, familiar crunching noises resonated loudly as if a violence was being perpetrated against the land itself.

The hum slowly filled Aydan's mind, and it began to wander far away from the site, pondering thoughts of Jacub.

Jacub had been the well-getter of the town many years ago. Aydan had always found some serenity in observing him calmly pulling the bucket up, distributing water to all the townsfolk. Aydan loved the sound of the water as the bucket landed in it and equally enjoyed seeing it poured into vessels for the people. Most engaging, however, were Jacub's slow and deliberate movements. There were so many actions Aydan would himself perform in an efficient, quickened pace, whereas as Jacub pulled the bucket up or even poured it out, he did so with slow, graceful gestures. It was within these spaces that Aydan would become entranced, as if a glazed relaxation was oozing over his mind.

He was a polite man with a soft-spoken voice. He had no family and seemed content in his role. Aydan did not know him well, and aside from his purpose as the well-getter, because of his benign existence, he wasn't a very well respected man. He wasn't included in most Aizik festivities, but it wasn't clear to Aydan whether this was of his own accord, or that of the villagers.

As he thought about it, Aydan realized that he was only a child when he witnessed what happened to Jacub.

It started with a seemingly incidental event. A little girl named Magya had approached Jacub to fill an amphora of water for her. Aydan had never noticed before, but Jacub always seemed to keep his back to the well which allowed him to see villagers as they approached him. In this case, however, Magya had asked him to fill her container while he was still helping another villager. Despite her requests, he blankly ignored her.

Aydan could see the image in his mind: the golden village, and in its center, the town well, with Jacub, the anchor of the location, a calm reliable sight that somehow made it easier to breathe. But Aydan was not there when Magya approached Jacub. He had heard the story from others, presumably embellished and distorted.

And so, as the story went, Magya began to raise her voice, even playfully singing loudly to elicit some reaction out of Jacub who still continued to ignore her. As her voice began to ring around the center circle, other villagers began to stare, observing Magya's playful nature and Jacub's odd apathy.

Aydan stared at the ground as he reflected, and noticed that he found peace in the random directions that the dirt and stones flew as they were excavated. Day after day he observed it, and because of its consistently unique reaction to the cutter, the dirt appeared very human to Aydan. It must have been such a complex creation, bonded in a thousand different ways, to have so many unique reactions to the same cutter. And to Aydan, there was something beautiful and honest about that. It made him feel serene in that despite the antagonism between him and his father and the uneasiness of the previous night's goings-on, the dirt was still true to form, unchanged by threat or addiction. It was simply as it was, unmolested by its own fears or apprehensions, still completely intact in its unique existence.

Aydan had heard, the following day, that Jacub had been taken before the Aizik Council. There, it was discovered that he had hidden a hearing condition whereby his ability to observe sound was so diminished that the world appeared quite dim to him. This sort of condition was looked down upon by the Council, for it promoted isolation which provided more opportunities for the demons to take shape, marking an individual. Such conditions were themselves considered to be an act of malice on the part of the Kai, and afflicted individuals such as Jacub were therefore in dire need of help. His concealment of the condition further exasperated the hammer, for it suggested virulent intent on his part.

Jacub was subsequently subjected to the Saghnim where he was encouraged to rid himself of the demons that had taken shape within his mind, clouding his ability to hear. The process was behind closed doors, but whispers suggested intense stimulation in an attempt to awaken Jacub's hearing. This was achieved forcibly where the afflicted had their eyes held open with sticky resin for days at a time. Other cleansing mechanisms intended to reveal the demons included various forms of physical torture, for it was widely accepted that pain was the one true purifier capable of ridding the body and mind of possession. Starvation, perversion, and the use of forced intercourse with objects and animals were also rumored. The use of sexuality in such sessions was meant to draw out the Kai where they could be witnessed, investigated, and neutralized.

In Jacub's case, however, it seemed none of the Council's efforts worked, for his hearing did not improve. As a result, he was placed within the pit to experience the Ascendance. It was understood that if an individual failed to respond to the cleansing, they would inevitably be marked by the Kai. They were therefore put in Vespa's hands and placed in Agalm's Pit within Visium to await her beckoning.

"Boy, let's take a break."

Aydan nodded.

The sun was on its final pass now, and the day had proceeded without incident. If the sun remained still and the heat maintained itself, he would not have to plough the field again, and tomorrow they would seed and muster it. He knew Bethelhurst wanted to work as long as possible to make use of what daylight was available. Bethelhurst never did accept Aydan's complaints or recommendations, and so any suggestion towards retiring home early would likely be ignored.

They both sat under a lone tree and opened their clay pots, revealing a tasty dal. Bethelhurst unwrapped a bread and broke it in half, handing one piece to Aydan. He dipped the torn end into his dal and bit into it, feeling the salty flesh of the bread laced with the green soup fill his mouth. His sweat began to dry as he ate and felt his taste buds react to the flavor with as much zeal as his throat did to the water his father had handed him a moment before. His body ached for the food, and it tasting so familiar yet new made him lose his breath. He paused to catch it and stared out at the red sun and the picture it painted before him.

Aydan had felt so strange the entire day. It was as if he was living a dream, and the colors of all that sparkled and reflected were being consumed by his eyes. He did not feel comfortable staring at the red earth before him, nor did he want to feel emotionally overwhelmed by the sharp border of the shadow of the tree. It extended far beyond the tree itself, stretched out by a dying sun, and underneath its leaves were Aydan and his father. They had eaten under this tree for years, the grass under it thinned from having been used as a permanent seat for both him and his father and other farmers nearby. It had no Kunda, yet it stood tall and did not die. Aydan felt safe in the shade of the tree, and as he felt this, an alien thought came to him. He wondered . . . what was there to be safe from?

He bit into his bread and wandered into time. He remembered Jacub's lopsided and broken face the last time he saw him. It hadn't been warped by madness like Tobias or others like him. It was as if he was aware he was dying just as he died. His skin was like stretched silk across his face, and his breaths were slow and thin, almost as if his body did not want to lose life by exhaling. He remembered staring at Jacub, hoping for some acknowledgment, that his eyes would meet Aydan's and some degree of compassion or respect would travel with him to the next world. But he just stared forward, lying on his side, inhaling ancient dust at the bottom of the pit, exhaling clean air.

Agalm's Pit was at the center of Visium. It was a large bowl-shaped hole in the earth that fully exposed its inhabitants to both the sun and onlookers. No one knew how old it was, but lore suggested it was created thousands of years ago by Vespa herself as she placed her palm into the earth, forming a divine imprint. It was said she leaned down, gleaming and massive as she floated above, pushing her divine essence into it. Only the Aizik were permitted to be cleansed within the pit, while Visium itself became a holy shrine for the world around them. The land around the pit was a center of pilgrimage, and many religious ceremonies and rituals were performed there. People flocked to Visium from all areas, and the Aizik themselves were regarded as a holy people for their correlation to the shrine. Aizik children were marked behind their necks, and as a child Aydan was often approached by outsiders while visiting Visium. It was said that Aizik children had the potential to bestow great fortune upon others.

Aydan remembered a destitute mother and desperate father kneeling in front of him with their son, placing his hand on each of their heads. He stood there, unknowingly observing them as they nearly cried. Nearby elders approached angrily and yelled at the family, forbidding them to touch the Aizik children. One elder knelt down beside Aydan and wiped his hand with her shawl, smiling at him. He smiled back and ran away.

He used to play in Visium with his cousins because it was always busy, flocked with outsiders. The pit was used more often back then, usually hosting some person or family within it. As with most things, as a child Aydan did not fully understand what the pit was. When he used to frequent Visium, he enjoyed standing on its edge, watching the people inside begging or screaming at the outsiders. He did not interact with them much, but watched as the other children taunted or threw stones at them. Sometimes the children were disciplined, but their mischief usually went ignored. He used to sit on the edge, watching whole families hold each other, crying, praying, trying to console one another. The children were always the first to stop breathing, and the parents would go numb shortly after. The children around the pit used to gather at about this time because it was then that the parents usually became quite erratic and confused. They'd often start yelling, speaking gibberish, or angrily try to claw their way out, trying to distance themselves from the view of their dead offspring. It was a spectacle the children enjoyed, and although some adults kept their distance, Aydan always noticed others that watched with a strange fixation.

"Finish your food. We'll complete the path over there and go home. If nothing happens tonight, nothing will happen at all."

Aydan heard his father and continued to eat. Nearing the end of a dal was tragic because only then did he fully appreciate how good it tasted to him. He often licked the inside of the bowl to salvage what salts he could.

He looked at his father arbitrarily, observing his scarred and unemotional face. Arguments had always ended badly between them, Bethelhurst's strength seemingly dwarfing Aydan's. He had always seemed larger as a man than Aydan even though Aydan was now almost as tall as his father. His childhood propensity to look up at him continued as he aged, however, and Aydan still felt like a little boy, completely under the mercy of Bethelhurst's opinions.

As he stared at his father's face, he thought about his smiles. It seemed he never smiled at Aydan. It was always for some outside threat or influence. He remembered how much his father smiled at Bhumia's wedding. His cousin was to be wed to a man named Gamet, and the wedding was held at the Enclosure in Visium. The Enclosure was used widely for celebrations or religious rituals reserved exclusively for the Aizik. Sometimes it was opened for royalty or special occasions to outsiders, but Aydan could only remember a few instances of this happening.

For the wedding, all the women of the families would weave a system of cloths together to form a large mat for all the guests to sit on. It was symbolic of the union of the two Kunda. After the wedding, the mat was given to the bride's family in exchange for the bride. It signified a permanent bond between the families, and since the husband received the wife as a token of this bond, the bride's family received the woven mat. The women took over a month to make it, forcing the members of both families to interact and become familiar with one another.

Aydan used to always spill food purposely on the mat. He did not know why, but it made him feel good to know his stain would forever be a part of that family's heritage.

He remembered the night of the wedding and how clear and dark the sky was. Images of the candles and the colors flashed in his mind. But more than this was the vivid memory of his father and mother, dancing with all the other wed couples, palm to palm. The "Mut-Tat" was a ritualistic dance that only married couples performed. Both the man and woman pressed their palms against each other and moved side to side, pointing their palms in unison in the direction of their steps. Aydan used to absolutely adore watching his parents do it. His mother seemed to glisten, and his father danced with a subtle confidence.

Aydan remembered being so full of peace at that moment that he looked to the stars, as if to assert that he didn't need to absorb everything around him because he was so filled with a calm confidence. The music and voices around him became a distant murmur, and he slowly drifted away. The moonlight was bright because of the empty sky, and he looked around the Enclosure, trying to see someone or something that didn't know it was being watched - serene, like him, at that moment.

He remembered that instant very vividly, for his eyes did indeed catch sight of something moving, and he still did not fully understand the meaning of what it was that he saw.

He remembered browsing the area outside the Enclosure, his eyes falling upon Agalm's Pit which was not too far away. Within it, the face of a man shined at the reflection of the moon. It was Tobias, whose entire family had been put in the pit a few days earlier. Aydan had always tried to remember why they had been placed there, but in vain.

Tobias's daughter had been the first to die. Like the others, Tobias and his wife Manna were erratic after her passing as the hunger and dehydration was amplified by grief. A few days later, Manna fell, and the day of Bhumia's wedding must have been the fifth or sixth day. Aydan was transported into the pit that night, for when he saw Tobias's face, he was no longer a man. His skin was stretched and unrecognizable as fully human, both in his behavior and demeanor. His mind had been damaged due to incessant panic, and he was no longer operating with a conscious awareness.

Despite his physical condition however, Tobias was doing something very odd. He stood, with his palms held flat in front of him, dancing the Mut-Tat, all alone. His wife and daughter both lay dead, their contorted bodies only a few feet next to him, and in his delusional state, he was reacting to the music he heard, behaving in some instinctual manner.

His steps were small and erratic, his movements frail. Aydan watched this, completely oblivious to his surroundings. He was transported only a few feet away from Tobias and could hear his footsteps and forced breathing. He could see, clearly, the melancholic smile on his face with his mouth ajar. Aydan knew that Tobias did not know his wife was not standing in front of him. It was as if he had found an image of her within his mind and transmuted her into reality so that he could see her.

Just as quickly as Aydan had noticed Tobias, he fell to the ground, out of sight. Aydan never saw him alive again, but surmised that as he lay there that night, Tobias was oblivious to the pit and probably smiled as he passed. His leg would twitch in some familiar rhythm, consuming the last impulses of life, ousting them into the dance.

After he fell, the music of the world suddenly struck Aydan, and it became deafeningly loud. He remembered covering his ears immediately with his small arms, looking around, being disoriented and confused. All the smiling faces around him terrified him to the core. He closed his eyes, absolutely petrified, trying to drown it all out, but the bright lights and loud sounds crept through, jumbling his feelings and thoughts.

As he opened his eyes, he looked up at his parents, and as he caught sight of their frames, the sounds dissolved once again. He stared at their glowing, smiling faces, dancing, as if in slow motion. As he stared at them, he started to feel an illness take shape in his stomach, and so he closed his eyes and covered his ears once more to calm his nerves.

He remembered his father's face and looked at it now, under the Gimba tree. It was unsmiling, unemotional. Decrepit almost. His father was like a stone, and he did not know if that was what it meant to be a man, for he felt unsure of his capacity to be so hard. He always thought he would never become a man because he could not envision a version of himself as strong as his father.

He imagined a rock in Bethelhurst that no water could penetrate. Despite his attempts over the years, there was no joviality between them because life had become too serious. Aydan was petrified of Bethelhurst, but it was some odd pity that held his love bonded to the man.

CHAPTER 4

THE VILLAGE AT NIGHT

"Y
ou have to be more calm, Aydan," his father advised. "We walk a thin line, you and I. We are Kunda."

They had stayed in the fields much later than usual, and it was nearing a pitch darkness in every direction.

"I'm not doing anything wrong," Aydan remarked. "I'm seeding the fields and keeping to myself. But that isn't acceptable . . . no matter what I do now, the fear will exist."

His father shook his head.

"Nothing will happen if we do what they say. It they come to us tonight, we will abide by their demands. You will do exactly what is asked of you."

"I have always done what is asked of me. Yet you still declare that I should change my ways."

"And this business last night . . . was that asked of you?" Bethelhurst asked sharply.

Aydan snickered.

"A dream! You blame me for what I do when I sleep? When I can control nothing?"

His father looked at him in the darkness.

"I have never done anything of the sort, and this is why our Kunda has survived the changes. You do what you do because you have the luxury of blasphemy. I don't."

As he spoke, his voice rose.

"And if you want to be a man, you will stop childish daydreaming that follows you into the night!"

Aydan's voice held steady as his father became agitated.

"I want to be a man, but not one like you."

Bethelhurst, upon hearing Aydan's words, approached him menacingly, screaming at him.

"Then leave, fool!"

He raised his arms and pointed into the abysmal darkness.

"Disappear from this Kunda and find your holy land! Do you think the world is beautiful, waiting for you with open arms? Seeding the fields with your father is a luxury! A blessing! Go! Find food and shelter with your priceless daydreams!"

Aydan stopped and looked at his father's face, frozen. Bethelhurst's eyes were wide with rage, his frame leaning towards Aydan, his arms pointed still into the blackness.

"Go, you ungrateful waste!"

They stood there for a few moments, locked in position, looking at one another. Aydan stared at his father and felt a sickness enter his system.

"I have nowhere to go."

His father immediately pointed his finger at Aydan's face, stepping even closer.

"That's why you will to do exactly as I tell you! For you, and for this Kunda! Do you understand?"

Aydan stared at his father, not wanting to answer. He waited, trying to rebel against Bethelhurst's demand of acknowledgment.

"Speak! Answer me, you ungrateful child!"

"Yes," Aydan, seemingly calm, muttered, "I will do as you ask."

Bethelhurst retracted his finger and started walking ahead of Aydan towards the village. Aydan waited a few moments to gather his wits. His head was buzzing, and he felt a tenseness pressing his senses, briefly immobilizing him. He tried to normalize his breathing, then followed his father.

The path they walked was treaded into the dry grass, and they barely made its outline through the moonlight. In the distance, a dim light glimmered, surrounded by a sea of blackness. Bethelhurst walked ahead, and Aydan followed. The night air was cool, as were most nights, and the world about was silent. This far from the village, nothing could be heard except for the brief instance of a breeze against one's ear.

Over the years, they had walked the same path, over and over, and the walk to and from the fields spanned almost an hour. When Aydan was younger, they were often accompanied by other villagers, but in the last few years it seemed less and less people worked them. Aydan and his father were now one of the few farming families left in the village. The walk to and from the fields had become quiet and lonely, and on this night, far from his father, surrounded by a cool darkness in every direction, he felt detached from all things living.

The light in the distance was not a welcoming sign to him, nor were his father's blunt footsteps. The temperate night that normally would be calming was piercing, for in Aydan, there was much anxiety brewing. He had not become aware of it prior, but at that moment, he realized just how deafening the angst in his heart was.

"There is no silence here. Just darkness about," he whispered to himself.

He looked down at his arms and the ground and all was painted dark by the night.

"I'm swimming in the night. Following a fish with teeth greater than mine."

His eyes stared at the ground, and his head slowly rose to see Bethelhurst a few steps in front of him, walking steadily towards the glow in the distance.

"My defa, and I don't know him. And I am petrified of him."

He stared at his father's silhouette. He walked briskly, and Aydan could tell he was very tense. He did not say a word, but Aydan knew that if Bethelhurst failed to hear Aydan's steps behind him, he would turn about and come look for him. He feared losing Aydan, and his fears fueled his rage.

Aydan suddenly felt his eyes well up as love for his father overflowed within him.

"Vespa . . . tell me. Help me. Make me strong so that I may be a man of men. Powerful and untouchable. I beg you, Vespa. Aid your son."

He gritted his teeth and grimaced at the ground, whispering with intensity.

"Make me more than I am. Make me a man."

He stumbled slightly as he felt the intensity of his words drain him. He looked up at the figure of his father once more and felt completely engulfed in hopelessness. He was consumed by confusing emotions that made him both love and hate his father and the village ahead, but all the while a weakness perpetuated itself within, and he felt completely vulnerable to the world.

"Such emotions are alien," he thought. "Why am I so overwhelmed? Why can't I just be calm?"

He grabbed his head with both his arms and squeezed, feeling his hairs pull their roots, blurring his vision.

"Why aren't you helping me?"

He released his head, and with it all the thoughts and worries dissipated, but quickly returned. He wiped his eyes and took a deep breath. He was angry now and envisioned violent thoughts with blades and axes. He caught sight of his arm and felt it was thin and frail. The weakness he perceived in his arm infected his whole body, and with it went his anger. He felt numb then, an emotionless look on his face, his mind overwhelmed by a titanic agony tearing him in every direction.

Neither Aydan nor his father spoke for the rest of the trek. Aydan noticed the color of the pale green grass in the night and how everything seemed smoothed over by darkness. He was not frightened of the blackness but knew that if his father were not with him, he would be scared. He found great open spaces only conceptually beautiful, for he always foresaw the shiny teeth of an animal leap at him from the blackness. But more than the dark, he feared the sensation of silence. And aside from his own footsteps, had he been alone that night, he would have heard nothing at all.

"What a strange world," he thought, "that I should fear the freedom of open air over the confines of the village, where as I walk Mayah is sure to be telling wretched tales of my possession to the Council."

As they neared the village, Aydan became jittery, once again filling with anxiety.

"Do you think everything will be fine?" he asked his father.

Bethelhurst turned to Aydan, the now bright glow of the town forming a line around his frame. He looked like an angel or demon, more than a man and not of this world. Aydan could not see his face at all for the light, and his voice was strong and willful.

"Nothing will happen to you, and nothing will happen to us. If they come to us, we will satisfy their queries. You had a night dream. You dreamt of titans in the clouds. It is a dream of our line."

Aydan stared at the black figure in front of him, his eyes wide and full of need.

"I am frightened," he weakly stated.

Bethelhurst approached him and placed his hand on Aydan's shoulder. Aydan could barely make out his face, but the white of his eyes became visible patches of strength.

"You are my son. You are a pillar. And nothing will harm you."

Aydan stared at his father but could not match his eyes. He looked down to his father's torso and leaned on his hand. His father retracted his arm and turned around, beginning to walk again.

"Let us go, Aydan."

Aydan regained his posture and immediately followed, this time closer to his father.

CHAPTER 5

DUSK AND BEYOND

As they entered the village, the people were loud and jovial. At first, Aydan looked about, confused, worried that it somehow had to do with him, but then realized it was Saal-Ind. He felt a sudden rush of relief believing it was possible everything would have been forgotten for focus on the festival. The tenseness in him released momentarily as he saw effigies around him and festivities abound. The light of the fires drew his gaze, and he watched the flames dance, being immersed in the lights and sounds.

Saal-Ind was the festival that celebrated the first and auspicious victory Vespa had over the demon Saal. It commemorated the changing of times, when demons that were once powerful as the gods suffered a great loss at the hands of Vespa and began to retreat into the shadows of Ceria.

Saal was a herald demon and posed as the father of the Kai. He was a dark entity who's voice was said to cause madness, echoing within the lost world. If one spent too much time in the company of the Kai, Saal would appear and utter a single word to the person, causing them to lose their humanity. His lips were said to be large and round, his face a dark black, with large hands, seated on a desecrated throne in permanent darkness. It was said the Kai were banished into darkness by Vespa, but they discovered a way to spread their malice by utilizing the power of their voices to reach out from the void.

Saal's persona unnerved Aydan. When he was a child, older boys would scare him by deepening their voices and calmly uttering vulgar notions to him. It was the calmness of their speech that terrorized him, for Saal was always presented to be a very calculating creature. It was said that after his banishment, he consumed all his rage and anger and directed it outwards through the tranquility in his voice. His calm nature was a testament to his malicious confidence, and this concept frightened Aydan.

Saal-Ind was said to be the day Vespa banished him when he was an earthbound demon and the creatures of darkness still roamed the land. An immense battle was said to have taken place, and Saal was held fast to a great tree in the center of the world which Vespa sacrificed to burn him. The tree, possessed by Diamit eons before, held its roots tight to his body as Vespa summoned forth the storms of the skies to strike it, lighting it repeatedly in a magnificent effigy.

The villagers had built effigies everywhere, burning little wooden figures of Saal. It was an important celebration for the Aizik and explained why the village had glowed so bright that night. Aydan smiled as he saw little children dressed in black running about, screaming, "Ban tor me ga!" at the fires. There was intensity in their voices, and as they loosened the hold the world had over them, they bellowed at the top of their lungs into the fires, then into the night sky. Their little bodies scurried about, and as they yelled, they flexed their arms like miniature soldiers calling out for blood. "Feast upon your heart" was said to be Saal's final scream as he burned.

It was a chaotic environment, with some groups on their knees praying, others talking and eating, while the children ran from fire to fire, filling the entire village with their frenzied calls. One group ran to a blaze near Aydan and stared into it for a few seconds, gathering their breaths. Then, as if slowed by time, Aydan watched their mouths open and their arms bend and flex as they howled into the night, yelling Saal's words as loud as they could. He stared at the leader of the group's eyes and did not see a child within, but rather a full grown man hidden in a child's body, full of a spiteful rage not unlike the demon lord himself.

Aydan looked to his father who had walked ahead, uninterested in the sights and sounds. Aydan hadn't noticed himself stopping. He felt euphoric, for his nerves had been deafening all day, filled with uncomfortable memories and a pit of fear that had grown in his belly. Now, this explosion of festivity, a hash of fluttering fires and contrasting brightness, made his irises expand and contract making him feel light headed.

He ran his hand across his brow and into his hair, still unknowingly following the group of children with his eyes until they disappeared from sight. He stared up, trying to see stars in the middle of the path, but could see nothing except the dark sky with hues of yellow seeping into his peripheral vision. Even the night sun was hidden somewhere, angularly invisible behind one of the nearby huts.

When he entered his hut, Bethelhurst had already placed the pot of water near the door and was drying himself. Aydan walked in and undressed, dipping his shirt into the pot, rubbing it all over his body. As he scrubbed, he felt the coolness pierce his senses, soothing his mind as if he hadn't bathed in years. His body was thick with sweat, and his aching muscles were sore, but the feeling of the damp cloth on his skin was a tranquilizing relief from an otherwise brutal day.

He walked to his cot, still wet, and picked up a clean tunic, gently patting himself. He placed it on the edge of the bed and sat down, facing his doorway.

As he sat, his muscles loosened for the first time all day, and he sank deep into his frame, resting his head in his hands and his elbows on his knees. He stared out blankly at the world outside, a man passing here and there, a few children running by in the other direction, and floated away.

He saw Kabal, an unfriendly neighbor that Aydan had known all his life. He always belittled Aydan's Kunda and was one of the first men to surrender his ground axe for better clothes and a position of service within the Council. He was a harsh man that appeared jovial quite often. But there was spite in his voice, and Aydan knew few men contained more potential envy in their hearts than the likes of him. His children were likewise spoiled little bastards, convinced that strength over their peers was a desirable position worthy of respect.

"A position they pursue most adamantly," muttered Aydan.

"But what is to happen to Aydan. Is everything at peace?" he whispered nonchalantly to himself.

"I don't even know how they would come, if they were to come, but perhaps that is an unreasonable expectation. Perhaps, in reality, such things only happen to people for atrocious blaspheme, not silly nightmares.

"Nightmares," he muttered once again. He thought about the night before which now seemed so long ago, separated by the elongated day. For the first time since, he questioned his words.

"Indeed . . . a nightmare? Did I see a titan, or did I construct one?"

He imagined the titan looking at him, its giant eyes gazing peacefully at Aydan as if to say, "Do I exist? Not in your sleeping dreams, my boy. And fear not purging my memory from reality, for the truth is more pious a goal than delusion."

Aydan turned his head downwards, closing his eyes, running the tips of his fingers sternly against his face, stopping at his forehead.

"If not a nightmare, then what you fool."

Bethelhurst walked in, placing a cup by Aydan's leg.

Aydan noticed it through his hands and reached down to pick it up and sip the water. Bethelhurst returned to the other room as Aydan sat there, sipping slowly, looking outside.

He did not feel like sleeping, and as the festival outside wound down, the noises became farther and farther apart, followed by the random but correlated extinguishing of flames. He lay in bed, using the others as an excuse to remain awake.

Once silence blanketed him, however, a seemingly universal stillness followed, and he felt a cold chill come over him. All were asleep or with their own, and even Bethelhurst's heavy breathing certified that Aydan's wakened mind now had no brethren.

He lay there, staring at the wall. His legs extended off his cot, and he perched on some textiles and a cushion, semi-upright. He held his arms folded in front of him and let his lids rest, closing his eyes halfway in a relaxed but completely awakened state.

"What is . . . a great silence," he whispered to himself, without conviction or force, as if speaking his thoughts just to hear them.

"Did I create that?" he muttered in response. His statements came long apart, snippets of a slow and hazy conversation taking place in his mind.

"It's quite silent now."

He smirked at his statement, revealing Aydan's smile, genuinely childlike and large, yet the creases in his face and the wrinkles in his brow hid something more familiar to an adult's trauma.

His smile dissolved slowly as he stared at the wall, listening to an uncomfortable stillness.

"It's very, very silent now."

CHAPTER 6
BEYOND

The village was quiet. Heavy breathing sounded from room to room, and in between each hut swept the dark wind, obscure like the night sun, its reflection painting the rooftops in a dark blue hue.

The night sun was mysterious to the people, and Aizik children were often frightened of it just as they feared the shadows at night. Tales of hideous rituals roamed the land in appeasement of it, the night sun being some sinister imitation of the day sun, worshipped by the wicked.

For if the sun was Vespa's glorious creation, then the night sun was something different, appearing after she departed the land. It mimicked her glorious day-bound gift at night, choosing the dark hour for its subterfuge.

Its existence wasn't the work of a devil, but some other creature, in between the plane and Vespa's abode, who's allegiance was still unknown. Such creatures existed, torn from their resting places during the great war, no longer permitted to live in the world of man, ordered by her to take their kin and vanish into the skies.

But the night sun was one such creature who could not let go of this world and tried to become something of a god himself. And in his greatest attempt, he hid between sunrises, shining as bright as he could, succeeding in only a fraction of the intensity provided by Vespa's gift.

He stared down at the world, observing the people, jealousy brooding in his mind, for after thousands of years of envious observation, resentment had begun to take shape. Rather than simply observe, the creature began to spy, becoming obsessed with the goings-on below him.

It had been reported that the night sun was sometimes seen during daylight hours, but such sightings were unwelcome, for it forebode ill will and was indicative of evil spirits trying to rise. As it became unpleasant to be the bearer of bad news, such reports became more and more scarce. It had been years since the last one, and everyone gladly accepted that Silathan was finally bound to his accursed fate.

He watched, as he did every night, the roofs of the huts that seemed to breathe in and out in a serene demeanor, like some large organism flattened against the landscape. As he fluttered across the sky ever so slowly, he observed wide-eyed every little movement, his gaze switching from branch to doorway, like a muted child.

Somewhere along the outskirts of the village, his eyes switched to a scurrying movement. To him, it appeared to be like blobs of water that moved in perfect unison despite being unattached. They looked like the creatures that inhabited the huts below, but moved as if bound together, and in the darkness of night.

They glided, quickly navigating the corridors of the town, and just as quickly as they appeared, they vanished into one of the huts. He had seen them before, and though he did not understand why, the confusion did not concern him. He was obsessed with his envy, interested only in absorbing all that he could of the world below him. The shutter of a leaf was enough to make him weep inside, and so the reasoning behind the activities of men was not of stringent interest to him.

He enjoyed the transformation, however, of the black water people. They would enter a hut as detached drops, and when they would leave, they would become one large vein, as if their purpose was to enter a hut unattached and leave a whole entity. Sometimes rogue drops meandered behind or ahead, and he wondered what exciting transmutation took place within.

He waited excitedly for the colluded water to appear on this night, wondering if the transformation would be whole or partial.

Across the horizon, a creature then caught his eye, very calmly and silently biting the grass. It was alone in the flat land, some ways from the town. He observed its snout in a magnified manner, every little nuance of movement stimulating him. The animal opened its mouth to bite into the ground, and as it bit down, the entity became overwhelmed in witnessing the earth tear under its jaw, both dirt and grass ripping away, revealing the cool ground underneath, previously unseen to the universe.

He stopped looking at the boar, savoring the moment, overwhelmed at the idea of digging into the ground, feeling the cold roots and rocks, being a part of that lovely world. He yearned to touch the gravel, to rip out grass, to shower himself in earthly things.

But such fantasies were short-lived, and as he became aware of time passing, so too did the euphoria end. He quickly looked back to the boar for more, but it was already walking away, its hooves gently clattering against the ground.

Unquenched, his gaze jumped back to the hut, hoping to catch the progression of the water.

After some time, it emerged. It was just as he had expected: a mobile band of black water led by a drop that had failed to merge with its brethren. He watched it maze through the corridors, floating just as it had arrived. Every turn it took moved him, and watching the unpredictable dance kept him enthralled.

This greatly stimulated the creature, and he felt like applauding the show that was put forth. The night had been better than most, with activities reminiscent of daylight, making him feel all the more vindicated in his decision to defy Vespa's decree so many thousands of years ago.

So immersed in his vice once again, reminiscing over his stimulation and focused away from the world, the creature failed to notice minor fluctuations of movement taking place in the long blob of moving water.

He even failed to notice a most peculiar event, for from within the water, a human finger had revealed itself, basking in his meager light.

The finger belonged to Aydan, who in a dazed state was trying to determine the nature of the liquid he found on his finger which appeared black in the night light. He knew not where he was, save a piercing headache and hands running along his body. He appeared to be in motion, laid on his back, and tried to look to the side but was surrounded by darkness. Only a thin slit of light shone through in front of him.

He tried to turn, muttering some half noise-words, but was quickly held in place by the hands. Immediately, the movement stopped.

From above, the entity caught sight of the stopped vein and watched as the leading drop moved to its brethren and appeared to bless it, striking it repeatedly with a vigorous fist.

Aydan's vision blurred, his hands and body limp, and he stared out the singular crack, connecting briefly to the night sun before darkness consumed his entire universe.

CHAPTER 7
THE ADVENT OF THINGS TO COME

"That's a . . ."

"That's a new naga."

"Yesterday."

"He smells fresh."

Aydan shifted, hearing the voice.

"Shut up."

"Go outside."

Aydan heard some scuffles, then short footsteps.

As he came to consciousness, he was struck with a foul odor that catalyzed his awareness. His eyelids were pasted together, and he gently scratched at them to remove debris and dried crusts while desperately trying to block his nose with his other hand. Each particle pulled at his skin painfully, leaving his lids scratched and bitten.

He was seated on a hard and curved surface and could sense the darkness about him. His head ached piercingly, and both the smell and thick, heated air galvanized the pain.

As he opened his eyes, he tried to come to his senses, first coming to terms with his environment. He only remembered sleeping late the night before and had no idea how he had arrived where he was. He was not worried initially, for the idea that one could fall asleep in their bed one day and wake up in a completely different place the next was too far-fetched an idea, and so he sought to reason with it.

He felt around the walls with his hands, feeling uneven rock with jagged edges. It was clearly dug out, however, for the space he was in was too arbitrary to be naturally formed. There was a flat surface on one side which he concluded was wood. As he felt around it, he found a rectangular opening in the center big enough to fit his arm through, which he did, feeling the outside surface. The air was consistently thick and murky, and aside from the wooden texture of the barrier, he could get no sense of where he was.

He pulled his arm in and leaned back against the rocky wall as if staring through the black hole opposite. He began to unknowingly breathe heavily, feeling traumatized by both the small space he was in and the underground, cavernous nature of his environment. Most devastating, however, was the trickling awareness that he had somehow been arrested and was now in the Saghnim.

The mere idea that this was possible initially bounced off him, and he once again tried to feel around, patting the ground he sat on with his hands. He could not continue, however, for the ache in his head was too harsh, immobilizing him, making even the sounds of his hands striking the floor painful.

Suddenly, a shrill wail echoed all around him, and he grabbed his head, covering his ears for the unbearable ache.

"Maniamanoo . . . naaah . . ." uttered the voice, both crying and begging in what seemed to be gibberish vocalizations of pure anguish. Aydan quickly approached the opening in the wood and pressed his lips through it.

"Please . . . please be quiet."

The voice continued to wail, interrupting Aydan, unnoticing his request.

"Mai . . . Mai . . ." it began to weep, then raised its voice, crying louder.

"Maiiiiiii . . . Mai naaaaaaaa . . ."

Aydan, still covering his ears, felt a chill run through his body upon hearing the voice again.

"Please . . . shut up," he said, louder this time.

The sobbing continued with sounds every few seconds, incoherent babblings echoing around him.

"Please, shut up!" he yelled, screaming.

It continued, cutting him like a knife.

"Shut up! Shut up! Shut your mouth! Shut your mouth, you bastard!"

As it continued disjointedly, Aydan pressed his back against the inside of his pod and once again stared forward. His eyes were wide in the darkness, and the echoing of the noises made the cavern all the more surreal.

He sat there, motionless, his palms pressed down on the ground beneath him. His vision saw nothing, yet began to shudder, and through his headache he felt faint. It was as if a tenseness had entered his brain and began to gyrate his eyeballs from side to side, moving his head along with it.

"Mata maiiii . . ." the voice echoed, crying with a pathetic desperation, reeking of hopelessness and confusion.

He leapt forward, pressing his head against the opening and screamed at the top of his lungs.

"Shut up, you fuck! Let me think! Let me think!!!"

He fell back, broken, and began to weep uncontrollably. It struck him sharply, and his entire body opened to the tears, limping his muscles, tightening his face.

His mouth opened as he cried, strings of saliva dripping from his lips as he held his face in his hands.

"Oh god . . . oh god . . ."

It was inconceivable to him, and every time the grandiose thought entered his awareness and he felt the cold hard floor under him, an intense, inescapable pain followed suit. It was as if he forgot his location, but every time he noticed the hard floor, it brought with it the rocky surface, the darkness, the smell, and the wailing creature somewhere in the shadows.

He cried hard, for the angst was overwhelming, and he dug his fingers into his skull, trying to extract it from his soul. He coughed, feeling choked, and turned to the wall, heaving, trying to vomit. He saw stars as he did, running up and down his vision as he heaved, stopping his tears and numbing his awareness.

He remained frozen in position, his palm pressed against the wall, his head hanging downwards. He was silent, and even the wailing briefly stopped.

He turned back into a seated position and leaned against the wall, his head pressed against the rocky surface.

He sat there, numb, saying nothing, doing nothing, and thinking nothing.

A rock was poking his back, and he tried to adjust himself. As he did, his palms pressed against the rocky floor, and the cold touched his flesh. He pressed them down once more, feeling the hard surface.

As he did, his face became scrunched and his eyes squinted, a lump forming in his throat.

He was in a prison, and like the worst of all nightmares, he was actually now a part of the cleansing. It was still inconceivable to him that such an age-old, mythical idea that had echoed silently in his imagination was now represented in reality. But he began to absorb the concept, for once again, he leaned down, crying, unable to fully grasp the foreboding nature of his fate, personified by the dead hardness surrounding him.

The rocky surface and weight of the wood were ugly reminders of his confinement. He struck the floor with tears pouring down his face, as if to break a hole in it, but instead made the pain worse, for the rock did not break, nor bulge, and that too suggested something very lucid about his predicament.

He slowly drifted away, for in the darkness his tears simply disappeared. And though his head wound had ceased to bleed, his body was void of all virility, forcing him away in order to heal.

He lay there unconscious, bathed in black. The foul smell was exasperated by musky, unclean air, and in the silence the creature's sobs once again resurfaced.

CHAPTER 8
TIMELESS SPACE

Aydan awoke hours later, still engulfed in darkness, unable to determine the nature of the weather or the time of day.

Though still agonizing, the head pain had lessened, and he felt around, fingering his scalp, trying to get a sense of the wound. As he finely examined it, a sting shot through him, forcing him to freeze and cope with the searing sensation.

The stench was again overwhelming, a mixture of excrement and sweat emanating from what seemed to be all around him. He felt like he was swimming in the filth, and it interrupted his thoughts with every breath.

He tried to look through the hole in the wood to see anything, but it was still pitch black. He hesitated at first, but then decided to speak, disregarding the fear of enticing the creature to begin wailing again.

"Is anyone there?" he asked through the hole.

He waited for his brief echo to subside. There was no response.

"I don't care if you can't speak . . . make a noise . . . some sound so I know you are there."

Hearing nothing, Aydan suddenly became terrified. He was struck, it seemed, through the entirety of his system, with the feeling of being stuck alone, underground, in the darkness forever. The absence of vision, along with the lack of any sound whatsoever made the entire realm feel dead, and enclosed in a little compartment was Aydan, unable to spread his arms.

The smell made it worse, as if he was in a grave filled with dead flesh, rotting from decay around him.

"Help!!! Please, someone please help! Say something! Help!" he screamed at the top of his lungs, his breathing becoming quick and sporadic, his heart beginning to palpitate heavily.

He leaned down, covering his face in his hands.

The environment was suffocating, for whether he opened his eyes or kept them closed, he saw nothing. No change in sight occurred, and along with the silence, he felt as if he was both gagged and blindfolded.

There was something unspeakably horrific about the sensation, for without any reaction from his environment, along with his confinement, he feared for the possibility that he had been left for dead and was forgotten, though still alive.

"Please, god. Calm me. I am all right. Everything is all right. Interim . . . this is temporary, and someone will be here soon. Defa will come. Food will come. Water will come. A light will approach, and I will see I am not alone. I am not alone. I am not alone."

He stopped speaking briefly and upon hearing the silence quickly continued, trying to hold onto his nerves.

"My eyes are closed, and so it is dark. It does not matter if it is bright, for I choose to close my eyes. I will sit here and wait to be freed. Someone will come."

His voice began to break, and he stopped talking.

"Don't . . . open . . . your . . . eyes . . ." he quietly commanded to himself.

"Your choice, your life. Your control. You choose . . ."

His face suddenly grimaced.

"You choose . . ."

And as if from the darkness, a voice came.

"But you did not choose to be confined to an underground grave. Who are you fooling?"

"Oh god . . ." Aydan began to sob.

He jumped forward at the wooden hole and stuck his arm through, again trying to feel around, screaming.

"Someone! Anyone! Speak to me! Talk to me! Please!"

He began to bang on the outside of the wood with his arm, through the hole.

"I can't stay here in the darkness! Please!"

He banged harder and harder, hearing the knock echo around the room.

"Please . . .

"Please!"

His voice trailed off, and he kept repeating the word in unison with his knocks, softening with his voice, bringing a rhythmic wooden banging to the place.

He sat there uncomfortably, half off his knees, his arm holding him up through the hole, knocking over and over as if just to hear it.

"It's pitch black. I am not in hell. The thick air is caused by the underground nature of this place. Light will come. I am in air, not drowning. It is air around me, everywhere, outside this hole."

He kept his eyes closed, hung his head downwards and whispered to himself, as if praying.

"The thickness is my own breathing, and the foul smell is that of a prison. No . . . no . . . not a prison. A holding cell. A room; a small room, but not too small. Someone will come into this room; it is only temporary. Only a few hours have passed. Nothing happens so quickly. Only a few hours, but in the darkness it feels like forever. Only a few hours have passed, and soon defa will come, as will someone else. Time."

He thought of the daylight and the quick passing of the sun from the east to the west and the beautiful greenery as it shimmered with different colors, green in mid-day, orange both late and early, with shadows that open in the morning and ones that close in the night.

"A day is passing over me, over my head, and though I cannot see it, it is there. The sun is shimmering."

He envisioned the sun wholly: a beautiful light, emanating a noise it seemed; a deep hum that rattled everything around it. It lit the whole sky and was looking at Aydan just as he was looking at it.

He smiled and was brought to tears with the vision.

"Oh god . . . thank you."

His head still hung low, and his palm pressed against the outside of the wood, feeling the texture gently. He remained in his euphoria, still hearing the sound of the sun, seeing the bright yellow radiate to the blue around it.

"I feel it. I feel the sun. I see you. I see it. Fill me with it. I am strong. I don't even need to be freed. I am a whole as I am, in the darkness or underground. Whether I perish here or not, I will be free. I need nothing."

He pulled his arm back through the hole and leaned down, smelling the floor like an animal, whispering to himself, still seeing the yellow sun in the watery colored sky.

"Do you think I am afraid of the filth?"

He followed the smell, and upon reaching what he felt was the most concentrated point, spat on his finger and pressed it into it. He then pressed it against his upper lip, under his nose, and smiled.

"Aaah . . ." he sighed loudly. "Do you see? I adore the smell. I love it. I am afraid of nothing."

He pressed his face against the opening with his eyes shut. He began to breathe heavily, in through his nose and out through his wide smile.

"Do you hear that? Do you hear that, you bastards?"

He began to scream, filling himself with the vision of the sun and its sound, his brain buzzing and arms tingling with a euphoric intensity.

"Do you hear that?!" he screamed at the top of his lungs.

"I need nothing from you! From people who imprison a boy for a nightmare!

"A titan! I dreamt of a titan! It fell from the skies!"

He imagined the giant figure, imposed in front of the sun, once again falling above him in a beautiful spectral of bright color.

"I see it as clear as it is dark! A forsaken titan, you bastards! Are you going to leave me here to die because I dream of titans?"

He opened his eyes and stared into the darkness through the hole.

He paused, hearing only his breathing and the beating of his heart. Even his echoes subsided.

"Let me out you bastards!!!" he suddenly screamed, banging his hands against the wood tenaciously, his eyes in the darkness spiked with both rage and desperation.

CHAPTER 9
THE FAYEM

He became aware that he was awake and opened his eyes accordingly. His cot was positioned in the center of the room, and he stepped off it, both legs in unison.

He stood up, naked, and walked out of his doorway to observe the land outside. It was still before dawn, and the reddish hue of the sun had begun to creep over the horizon. The land was still somewhat dark, but brighter than night, and became increasingly so as the sun shifted higher and higher.

Surrounding his small hut was flat land as far as the eye could see. He walked about it, circling it, taking deep breaths in the cool morning air.

Back in front of his doorway, he bent his knees and lay down, arms outstretched, face down in the sand, and prayed.

"My Vespa, for whom I live, grant me strength for my duties on this day, grant tenacity to my fingers and virility to my knees. Make my phallus long and pointed so I may stand with pride. Bless my actions in your name, in your glory.

"Thank you for this waking day, all those before, and all those to come."

He paused and arose symmetrically, pressing both his palms against the ground, pushing himself away from it, tucking his knees in, then pressed his feet against the ground, standing up, stretching to the sky, his hands flattened together.

He was not an old man, nor a young one, and wore a bald head. His skin was void of any hair save his eyebrows and eyelashes.

He walked into his hut and picked a dried piece of meat from the counter which sat on a leaf. There were many pieces of the same tough, brown meat, and he slowly chewed it.

As he chewed, his jaw rocked from side to side, making no noise save the grinding of the flesh. He knelt down and reached into a large container on the ground, pulling water out in his palms, wetting his body.

He reached over to another container and pulled out a thick, waxy substance from it, rubbing it all over his skin.

He picked up a black rock and bronze blade, both by the wax container, and rubbed the blade against the stone, methodically sharpening it. After some swipes, he placed the rock down and drenched the blade in the water bucket, drying it by pressing his thumb and forefinger against it, tightly pulling it through.

He then pressed the sharp end against his leg and began to pull. As he did, it pulled the wax off, along with thin, new hairs. He ran it between his thumb and forefinger, just as he had dried it, flinging the residue outside. He pressed it against his leg again, pulling it up slowly, scraping more of the substance away.

The noise the blade made against his skin was loud, like tearing, and it was apparent that his flesh had grown calloused to this daily ritual. When he pressed it into his skin, it indented, and when he pulled, his arms tensed, digging the blade against his body as hard as possible without drawing blood.

Every subsequent time, he seemed to press harder, making little noises, reacting to the pain.

"Harder, every day," he told himself. As he said so, he pressed the blade again, pulling. He seemed apprehensive of the pain before it struck him, then fulfilled by it after the initial sting was over.

He closed his eyes and moaned, bringing his chin to his chest as his fingers, holding the blade between his thumb, index, and middle finger, pulled it up to his knee, finishing the fourth line, clearing a quarter of his leg of the substance.

He continued, systematically cleansing his skin of all new hairs, placing his palm in the container with the wax to rub it in new locations. He was thorough, covering even the bottom of his feet, the tops of his fingers, and the spaces in between his toes.

He proceeded to his chest and genitalia, stretching his penis out as he scraped its sides. It seemed to hurt more than other places, causing him to moan even louder, almost as if he was crying.

He paused, catching his breaths, then continued by rubbing the substance into his head and the back of his neck. He held his forehead taut with one hand and pulled the blade through and through against it, stretching the skin as he did, scraping everything away. He continued along the entirety of his head, then pulled along his flesh upwards from his neck, holding it taut with his other hand below it.

After his head was completed, he doused and washed the blade, placing it carefully beside the wax pot, by the stone. He pushed them back into a corner and positioned himself on the ground, kneeling. The residual wax began to dry and encrust on him.

He took his left hand and formed a circle with his thumb and forefinger, wrapping it around the base of his penis. He squeezed tight, grimacing again, and pulled tightly outwards, ballooning the shaft with trapped blood. As he did, he again closed his eyes and let his head hang loose, whimpering slightly at the discomfort. With every pull, he switched hands, and with every switch he became further engorged, pulling harder, as if every subsequent stretch was more crucial than the last.

He clenched his teeth together and opened his eyes, frowning downwards, eyeing his penis with a focused fury.

He began to speak with every pull, the intensity in his words highest at the start and weaker near the end, increasing in volume with every subsequent stretch.

"Harden my heart, with your brutal fist.

"Stomp on it, to strengthen me.

"Give me power, Vessspa.

"Vesssssspa.

"I am your discontent . . . released.

"Fill me with ferocity."

He yanked against his body, his arm muscles tense with force.

"Enlarge me."

He stood up, continuing to pull against himself, starting to scream with the discomfort, his face contorting as he grimaced.

"I am powerful!

"I will make you repent!"

He pointed in front of him with his right hand, angrily, still stretching himself with his left.

"You will repent!

"You will cry!"

"You will rip your heart from your chest!!!"

"And feed it to me!!!"

He quickly slapped himself in the cheek.

"Repent!"

He screamed at the top of his lungs, winding up then slapping himself again, his tugging matching in intensity.

"Repent, swine!"

He wound back again and slapped himself once more, this time making him stumble in position.

He gritted his teeth with a furor that made his face tremor and tugged on his body with both hands, yelling through his teeth, his brows frowning heavily upon his tenacious eyes.

"Repent!!! Repent!!! Repent!!!"

He fell to his knees and hung his head down, exhausted. He breathed in and out, his body glistening in new sweat, limply sitting on the back of his feet.

He weakly pulled the bucket of water to himself and reached in, cupping some in his hand, sipping it.

His glans was red with tension, which he drenched with water. He then began to quietly wash his entire body of the dried wax.

He proceeded to rub a salt bar all over himself. Every spot of skin it touched caused him intense pain, and he grimaced, but did not moan as he had earlier.

He stood up tall and washed his body once more, cleansing the dried salt from his skin. He lifted a cloth from the side and patted his body dry along with his face and head.

He wrapped an off-white rectangular fabric around his waist which extended down to his feet. He pulled a sleeveless tunic over his head, also of the same color and fabric, which extended down past his waist, covering the top of the wrapped cloth.

He then proceeded to wrap a blue, rectangular textile around his body and shoulders, hanging the excess down his back, making his torso seem large and squared.

Finally, he reached over and picked up a small white cloth which he opened and pulled over his head. Before covering his mouth, he placed two morsels of dried meat on his tongue and began to chew, then pulled it down fully. It extended under his tunic and covered his head completely. It was an off-white mask with two holes roughly cut through the eye sockets.

He seemed different now, an avatar of sorts, his black eyes the only visible part of his face, and proceeded out of his hut into the desert, still chewing the meat noiselessly.

The sun was hot, but the ground was not yet glazed with heat, for it was still early. His sandals gritted against the stony sand and sunk into deeper parts, covering his toes in a thin milky coating of dust.

Along the path, there were random shrubs and the rare waterhole surrounded by greenery that quickly dispersed a few feet away.

He walked briskly, his breaths timed to his steps, and he did not waver in his direction, it seemed, because he had walked the path many times before. Despite this fact, however, his imprints disappeared every day, and no trail was created, for the dynamic nature of the desert held no memory of his presence.

CHAPTER 10
BARE

"The Fayem! The Fayem approaches!"

A thin, undernourished man, naked save a tattered cloth around his waist, stood at the opening of a cave, screaming in the sunlight.

It was early afternoon and the sun was shining brazenly down from the heavens, the heat on the ground just now starting to reflect the full force of its rays.

He ran into the cave and continued to yell, terribly excited.

"The Fayem!"

He began to laugh.

"The Fayemmmmmmm. Hahaha!"

Aydan awoke abruptly at the noise, hearing the running of footsteps and excited screaming. He lunged at the hole, yelling.

"Water! Bring me water! I am dying!"

"The Fayem, nagas! Hahahaha! Bloody hides!"

As Aydan heard the yelling, his desire for light and sound vanished along with his fear of being buried alive or forgotten forever. Even the fear of the unknown that lay ahead took shelter from the malevolent thirst in him that ached his throat through and through.

The thin man, having run deep into the ancient cave, stopped, cupping his hands around his mouth.

"You are in trouble now, nagas! Hahaha!"

He then turned and ran very quickly back the way he came.

"Bring me water, you bastard!"

Aydan's voice, trembling for the anxiety in his heart, revealed both a terrific fear of being in the dark along with the burning need to quench his thirst.

Outside the cave, the man in the blue scarf approached, walking down a sandy hill, his eyes calm and intense, mirroring his walk. The thin man stood at the mouth, becoming increasingly submissive as the Fayem approached, his eyes and head naturally looking and moving downwards as if the man in blue was a bright light that stung him.

The Fayem stopped, staring down at the thin man who was now hunched over in a subservient position, staring at the other man's feet. His hand was on his forehead, connecting his brow with his fingers, covering most of his vision, bestowing respect upon the man.

The Fayem placed his hand on the thin man's shoulder, looking at him.

"Have you given them water?" he asked.

"No, Fayem. No," the thin man replied.

The Fayem stared at him intensely as he spoke.

"Good. Take me inside."

The thin man briefly nodded and ran to the mouth of the cave where a fire was burning. He grasped a wooden stake from it and lifted it up, using it as a torch. The man in blue followed him at a slight distance, barely visible in the light as they entered deeper into the cave.

The thin man navigated the dark corridors of the cave which were smoothed by centuries of use. Inscriptions were etched into the ground and walls, revealed by the light he held. As they walked further, the inscriptions faded into darkness, revealing new ones the deeper they went. They were not of a consistent type, both in their symbolic shapes and the clarity and depth with which they were inscribed.

Aydan, holding onto the hole with both hands, staring into the blackness, frozen with angst, began to see a shimmer of light emanating some distance away, the first light he had seen in what seemed to be forever. Despite his fear, he pressed his face hard against the hole, trying to shower it in color. His thirst had become deafening, and he was convinced that water was only a few moments away. The light, it seemed, was joy for him, and he basked in it.

The thin man appeared first, followed by the large frame of the Fayem, who in the shadows seemed like some royal visitor from a beautiful palace. However, despite his thirst and euphoria, the sight of the white mask the Fayem wore turned something inside Aydan's stomach, and he felt a shudder of fear.

The thin man took the torch and lit another one that was seated in a hole in the rock, placing the one he held into another hole. The entire cave then seemed like some eerie pit with shadows dancing in the fiery light.

In the center of the cave, there was a very smooth rock that was big enough to sit on. Surrounding it was stained brown sand and rock. Aydan saw other eyes perk up from within other holes in wooden doors, a circular prison of what seemed to be five to six cells. The cells were holes dug into the cave enclosed with wooden barriers, all having uneven rectangular openings near the top.

Aydan reached out with his hand and spoke.

"Please . . . water."

The Fayem looked at him and approached, picking up a bucket near the rock. He carried it over and knelt in front of Aydan's cell.

"How is your head?"

Aydan looked up at the mask and could not see the man's eyes. He was like a ghoulish phantom that somehow knew his language. His voice was deep and raspy like an ageless deity, a quintessential representation of the male form.

"It hurts. But I'm very thirsty."

The Fayem reached into the water, drenching his fingers, then brought them out, placing them at Aydan's mouth.

"Drink."

Aydan looked at him briefly then began to suck on the man's fingers, rolling his tongue around them, trying to gather as much fluid as he could.

"Again?"

Aydan nodded and began to cry.

The man reached into the bucket and placed his dripping hand in front of Aydan again. Aydan sucked, his crying becoming worse. The man stared at his face.

"Again?"

Aydan stared at the man, tears on his cheeks, and disappeared into the darkness.

The Fayem got up and motioned to the thin man. He ran to the bucket and took it from cell to cell, pouring one ladle into the palms of the prisoners who appeared to know the ritual. They held their palms out and pulled them back carefully, drinking every drop.

When he reached Aydan's cell, Aydan followed suit. The feeling of the liquid on his palm was like nothing he had ever experienced, the weight of the fluid representing something more precious than life itself. He slowly and meticulously pulled his arm in, sipping the water, engorging his mouth in its wetness.

After all had drunk, the thin man left, and all eyes were upon the Fayem. He removed his blue dressing and stood in the center of the cave in his mask, tunic and skirt, sharpening a rock upon another one. He held a small round stone in his right hand and caressed it slowly with the side of the blade of another rock which was sharp and elongated, exactly like a knife. Its handle was worn and bore inscriptions, also worn.

One of the other prisoners began to cry loudly, almost wailing.

In the darkness of the cave, out of sight somewhere within the passage, sat the thin man. He held his knees in his arms and rocked back and forth, listening to the wailing. His eyes were closed in the blackness, deep in the cave's tunnel.

The Fayem placed the round stone on the ground and held the dagger tight in his fist. He approached a cell in the cave and knelt down. Aydan could not hear what he was whispering, but all the other inmates became silent as he did so.

He stood up and began to kick the wooden jammer out of position. With every stomp, Aydan became agitated, for the man was a lumbering beast in this small environment, and the violence with which he kicked the door seemed to foreshadow an even greater brutality to come.

As he succeeded in dislodging the wooden stake, the inmate within held the door in place. Aydan could see his eyes looking up at the Fayem, filled with fright.

"Please . . . please. Please . . . please . . . please, master, lord."

The man spoke very softly, and his voice seemed to reach into Aydan's chest, tightening around his heart. He spoke with an accent, and through his voice, Aydan could sense that as he spoke, he meant every word, bestowing upon the wretched creature that was the Fayem all the glories of heaven for his fear.

The Fayem knelt down and stared at him.

"You are my favorite, Samaye."

He yanked the door open, reaching in, grabbing Samaye's leg and pulling him out. Aydan unknowingly began to press his nails into the door to his cell, pushing his face against the opening, staring tensely at what unfolded before him.

The Fayem was strong in his movements and flung Samaye upon the rock in the center of the cave. His eyes widened as he lay there, his hands stretching out in front of him, thinned from malnutrition, trying to grasp the round rock. His eyes were welled with tears, though he did not seem to cry.

The Fayem raised his tunic and disrobed Samaye. He held the knife down against Samaye's back with one hand and used the other to guide himself. He leaned down, pressing himself into Samaye. He closed his eyes as they touched, and Samaye closed his, moving his head downwards, grunting and moaning in pain.

"I will purge the demons from you," whispered the Fayem through his ghastly mask.

Aydan watched in horror as he thrust against him, Samaye's body rigidly hammering against the rock, his weak hands now scraping against the sand on the ground. He hadn't opened his eyes since the Fayem first touched him.

The Fayem ran the knife along his neck and pulled Samaye's head upwards with it.

"Open your eyes, boy."

The way in which he said "boy" reminded Aydan of his defa, sending a sick feeling through his body. As Samaye heeded the Fayem's request, Aydan stared at his eyes, wide and white, speaking of the sort of trauma one does not reason with.

"I . . ."

Samaye began to speak, as if to no one. His words shuddered if landed upon while being thrust, his tone monotonous, as if a meditation of sorts.

"I . . . apologize . . . sir.

"For I cannot . . . appease your anger towards . . . me.

"San . . . san . . . mi . . . tha . . ."

The Fayem smacked the back of his head.

"None of that now. Focus on the darkness within you."

Samaye continued.

"Koona . . . sina . . . san . . . san . . ."

The Fayem grabbed the back of his head and leaned upwards, pressing himself hard against him, causing Samaye to grit his teeth and let out a painful grunting moan. He pressed Samaye's head down along the boulder's curvature and began to thrust even harder, banging Samaye's jaw against the rock inadvertently.

"Mi . . . tha . . . koona . . ." Samaye whispered to himself.

As he continued his prayer, the Fayem began to sweat and arch his back outwards, pressing his hands against Samaye's back, his mouth opening.

"Do you accept the grave nature of your sins?" the Fayem yelled.

Samaye did not respond.

The Fayem struck the back of his head and yelled once more.

"Do you accept the nature of your sins?!"

Samaye spoke, drool from his mouth falling upon the floor.

"Yes . . . I do."

"Are you a sinner?"

Samaye began to sob.

"Yes, I am."

The Fayem began to tense.

"Do you submit to Aizik rule?"

"Yes, I do."

"Say it once more!!!"

"Yes, I do."

"Louder!"

Samaye took a breath in and yelled, unemotionally.

"Yes, I do!"

The Fayem abruptly breathed out, his body tensing in the opposite direction as he quickly pressed the knife against Samaye's back, drawing blood. He stared at the cut as he shuddered, holding Samaye's head with his other hand.

They both lay there, Samaye unflinching and frozen, the Fayem leaning his head down, his hands rested and supported on Samaye's back.

He pressed his finger against Samaye's open wound and drenched his thumb in his blood. Samaye tensed at the pain and tried to reach back limply, his hand resolving to fall back down half-way through his attempt.

The Fayem leaned away from him and pulled his tunic down, staring at Samaye's naked body enveloped over the rock. He kicked his side, forcing him off the rock unto the ground.

"Back to your cell, naga."

Samaye slowly got up as he limped towards his cell, a thin line of blood trickling down his leg. The Fayem too had blood streaks along the front of his thighs. He wiped his body with his tunic, absorbing the sweat and blood.

Samaye closed the door to the cell behind him and disappeared from sight.

Aydan instantly turned away from the hole and leaned against the wooden door, hiding from the light. He stared at the back wall of his cell and found the color to be utterly frightening. He longed for the darkness, but then rejected that thought too, for the quiet deadness of the cave when it was void of sound or sight was violently suffocating.

He looked out his hole and at Samaye's cell, trying to spot him. The Fayem, across the cave, sat on the rock, facing away from the cells into the dark tunnel. He appeared to be contemplating and did not move.

"Maki," he calmly called.

A pitter patter was heard, and the thin man appeared from the chasm.

The Fayem motioned to Samaye's cell with his head, and Maki ran to it, pushing the wooden stake back in place, locking it closed. From within, Samaye could be heard shuffling at the sound of the door like a wounded animal.

"Feed them."

Maki ran out of the cave and came back a few minutes later carrying a bucket with old legumes and barley in it. He went from cell to cell, tossing a handful in each.

As he reached Aydan's cell, the smell of the barley jolted his hunger into full motion and he clawed at the greens that fell from the hole. He quickly tasted rotten bits and spat them out, wriggling around any softened legume to nibble on the still edible portions. All the other inmates followed suit, and the quiet chirping of teeth against grain hummed in the cave.

Aydan looked out of the hole cautiously at Samaye's cell to see if he was eating but could not make out any movement from within. He looked at the Fayem who had begun gathering his clothes and dressing himself.

Maki ran out of the cave once more with the bucket, the sounds of his feet dissipating quietly. The Fayem took a torch off the wall and dipped it in the water bucket, extinguishing it with a sizzle. He went to the opposite side of the cave and grabbed the other one, then left. As he disappeared into the tunnel, the light began to fade, and once again they were steeped in silent darkness.

Outside the cave, Maki was covering the food bucket with a rough wooden seal just as the Fayem appeared at the mouth. He tossed the torch to the ground and stood in the shadow of the cave's hood, right at the border where the sun's rays began.

He stared at Maki and cocked his head to the side. The Fayem appeared agitated and uncomfortable.

"You . . . resemble a human.

"But you have no human characteristics."

Maki silently listened, bowed in place, some distance from the man in the mask.

"I look at you, and I see that you breathe, that you eat.

"But you are thin and despicable."

He kept staring at him, his eyes displaying that he was calculating, trying to come to some understanding of his thoughts.

"You have no family nor a desire to acquire one. Even if you had one, they would take care of you.

"You don't think . . . consistently. You have no pride.

"Pride.

"You were born without pride, Maki.

"And so, you are not a man.

"You are a Thing," he said, pronouncing the descriptor as a title of sorts.

"You are here to cower, to serve, and then you will die, and be of use to the insects.

"Do you know that, Maki?"

Maki nodded quickly.

"Yes," he said. "Yes."

The man remained silent, paused, staring at Maki. He motioned for Maki to approach, which he did, then grabbed a portion of his cheek in between his thumb and forefinger, looking down at him.

"You know that? You are content knowing the beetles will feed on your skin?"

Maki did not answer, sensing in the man's voice that he did not want one.

"What is your skin if you have no pride, no desire.

"You're a piece of filth, walking, talking, eating, breathing.

"You exist, yet you have no purpose for existing."

The Fayem appeared to be grimacing under his mask, lightly shaking his head.

"You cannot be a man, Maki. You cannot be a man if you have no purpose."

Maki reached forward with his hand and lightly touched the Fayem's.

"I serve you. I serve them."

The Fayem quickly raised his hand and smashed it against Maki's face, plummeting him to the ground, sending him cowering in a curled up ball, clutching and hiding his whole head.

The man leaned down aggressively, pointing at Maki, screaming in a thunderous voice.

"That is not a purpose! You know not why you do what you do, and so you have no purpose!"

The strength and loudness of it seemed to come from some supernatural place, for the Fayem himself, his face hidden, seemed disconnected from the source of the roar. Maki nodded profusely, uttering, "yes" over and over in a blurred mixture of terror and involuntary tears.

"Get up," the man ordered. "Get up!!!"

Maki quickly arose, bowed in front of him.

The sight of a bowed Maki further angered him, and he struck him once more, this time leaning down as the thin man fell, hitting his face against the rock, beating him, screaming.

"You are pathetic!!! Be worthy of breathing!!! You weak, weak, bastard!!!"

Maki, bleeding, fell in and out of consciousness, and the man, tense and over stimulated, breathed heavily, causing the cloth in the mask to oscillate in and out. He stared at Maki with wide eyes, herding the anger that raged behind them.

"Your only desire is to fulfill me, day after day. And you permit me beat you till you bleed through your teeth.

"You truly are a sad beast."

The Fayem pushed off the ground, standing, and looked down at the semi-conscious Maki. He then began to walk away from the cave, up the sand dune, and out of view.

Maki had leveled himself, sitting up on his knees, his body oddly leaning forward as if he was about to collapse without actually falling. He had a dazed look in his eyes, staring at nothing, with blood dripping down his mouth, creating long strings of red saliva that collected in a small puddle beside him.

CHAPTER 11
THE CAVE AT NIGHT

Aydan shuffled and awoke with a painful pressure in his stomach. He felt around for the descended patch in his cell and touched cold feces. He quickly pulled his skirt off and sat over it, defecating uncomfortably. The stench coupled with the already musky air was strong, but his senses had become accustomed to most of it.

He wiped himself as best as he could, trying to clean his hands against the rock surface near the patch, rubbing them in whatever dust and sand he could find in his cell. He wrapped his skirt back on and leaned against the wooden door, placing his nose at the hole, trying to breathe in air from the central cave.

He opened his eyes and saw nothing but darkness. He tried to look outside his cell through the hole in the door, but it too was void of any light.

Again, it was uncomfortably quiet, and the stillness, originally welcomed by his senses, drew out against him. He tightened his eyes closed to try to elicit some difference in vision between their open and closed states, but as he tried to once again look about with his watery sight, he could barely tell that his lids were ajar.

He gently closed his eyes and stretched his arm through the hole in his door, feeling the cooler air of the cave soothe his skin.

"Is anyone awake?" he asked, almost ironically.

There was no response.

"Are any of you bastards awake?" he yelled.

"Please, speak gently . . ." came a voice from the cave. It was soft, not critical, but sincere in its request.

Aydan recognized the accent and dulcet voice.

"Samaye . . . is that you, Samaye?"

"It is pronounced Soo-ma-ya in Tphetria. I am not in Tphetria, but you may try to say it, as I ask for some temporary relief."

Aydan shuffled in place, pausing.

"Are you recovered? Did you eat?"

Samaye felt around the floor limply, running his hand along small rotten bits of vegetable.

"I have eaten what I could. But the pain prevents me from sleeping."

Aydan grimaced slightly, resting his face against the barrier.

"I am sorry for your pain, Soo-ma-ya," he stated empathetically.

"Ahhh . . . how it felt to hear you say it just now . . . that is great, akin."

Aydan smiled lightly.

"Then I will try to say it as you wish, Samaye."

"Ahhh . . . once again, and it reminds me of the west . . . of the yellow sands . . . of the Meniah."

Aydan pulled his arm in and pressed his head against the hole, his face uncomfortably fitted against it. He was quiet, somehow warmed by Samaye's voice.

"Samaye, Samaye . . . does my voice bring you solace?"

Samaye closed his eyes, leaning his head backwards, soothed.

"To hear my name . . . as you say it . . . I travel to the lands of Tphetria with ease . . ."

Hearing the relief in Samaye's voice, Aydan felt encouraged.

"Tell me of your lands, Samaye . . ." Aydan asked.

Samaye thought of his homeland and hesitated. It was a natural hesitation brought about by the fear of his physical being in the present and the possibly hazardous notion of distracting himself with thoughts of home. He thought about the thick deserts, different somehow than those found in this place, and found the fondness sweet, clinching his decision to fade into a world far away from his cell.

"In Gaizun . . ." he paused, thinking of the city. "We walk from it . . . north . . . to the Sea of Thieves, akin. The largest ocean I have ever seen. Waves . . . taller than men. Able to carry whole villages in their palms. Have you ever seen such blue water?"

Aydan imagined it as best he could, envisioning an endless blue river before him that touched the sand, cool to the touch.

"I can only imagine it . . . but I feel I would drink it all."

Samaye contemplated fondling the water as he had as a child and could almost feel the dwindled waves pulsating against the back of his hand.

"Much is large in my land. The waves, beautiful and gorgeous."

He raised his hand in the air and pressed the back of it gently against his face.

"The power . . . the energy of the world, burgeoning from below, erupting. Humility in seeing it . . . I kept the memory, always."

"I have never seen water as you describe," replied Aydan.

He contemplated sitting upon such water and being carried from place to place. The thought was overwhelmingly sweet.

"I have only seen dust move like that."

"There are structures in Tphetria that have existed before our time. No one knows where they came from, akin . . .

images, portraits made in stone. They are so large . . . the largest things you will ever see. Larger than a hundred men, like ancient goliaths frozen in stone. You may stand before it and touch it and feel some relic that is beyond our understanding. They litter the land in auspicious places."

Aydan imagined great stone figures touching the sky and how magnificent it would be to sleep in their palms, hidden from all things worldly.

"To the south is a holy place call Azum. Within it, the home of the Meniah. The Meniah is the birth-place of all the people of the world - the center of life. It is forbidden to look upon it, to visit. Yet, it exists and is closed to us. But they say it is the birthplace of life, where a small leafed plant grew thousands of years ago. The first ever. And from it came all life."

"Azum," Aydan responded. "I would like to see the color of this plant. I imagine it a tender green."

Samaye was lost in memory. His eyes were open to the darkness, seeing nothing, envisioning all the colors of the west.

"They paint the Damask . . . the Meniah plant . . . portraits and symbols in the sand. I see them, akin . . . beautiful visions by different people, children. The hues are so varied . . . it encapsulates all the colors of the imagination. To look upon it would be to see everything . . . all things. A two leafed plant . . . mother to all life.

"It pains me that I have never seen it . . . been in its presence. But I have imagined it since a child. I imagine it now, akin . . . I imagine it now, and it is the most beautiful, tender thing I have ever seen."

As Aydan contemplated a small plant in the middle of the world, surrounded by sand, his thoughts flew across the infinite dunes. The piercing golden particles swam along the horizon like an ocean, layered by a blue sky and cool breeze. He was flying, and it was a dream he had contemplated his whole life. He imagined flights like a bird, into the clouds above as a child . . . the visions aided him in falling asleep. But now there was aversion to it, for wings never grew upon him, nor were the skies blue. At this moment, the world was dark, and he was buried underground. Tomorrow, he would not fly, and some inconceivable atrocity would happen, and it angered him that his imagination would once again betray him so. He felt the toughness of the rock and the wooden barrier he leaned against, and it grounded him from his dreams in such an intense manner that he was almost glad to be rid of it.

"I do not understand why you would leave such a place, Samaye . . . and come here. This land has been stained with vulgarity masked as providence since the day I was born."

Samaye shifted in his position and leaned flat against his door, his head facing the back wall. He was silent for some time.

"Samaye?"

Samaye suddenly felt like crying, holding his face in his hands. He inhaled deeply, trying to calm himself, and began to chant.

"San, san . . . mi . . . tha . . . koona . . . sina . . . akin, will you say it with me. Please, say it now . . ."

Aydan joined in, following Samaye's words as best he could.

"San . . . san . . . mi . . . tha . . . koona, sina," they both repeated, over and over. As they did, Samaye slowly calmed, his breathing becoming less sporadic but still tense.

"Mi . . . tha . . . koona . . . sina . . ."

Aydan settled in his position, repeating it with Samaye. There was no count or record of how many times, but every new beginning was soothing. The ends were tense, but replaced by the calm of a new round.

No one else spoke in the cave. It was as if only Aydan and Samaye were present, and they exchanged voices as the night progressed. It was void of all light, and the sounds of their voices and minor shuffles as they re-adjusted became sharp, their ears becoming their primary connection to the active world.

After some time, their chanting now a melodious and soothing predictability, Aydan, more relaxed, asked Samaye what the meaning of the words were.

"It is god," he responded. "It is the pattern of life, Aydan. In Tphetria, we cook, eat, bathe and work in tune with this. It is like taking one of your fingers and grouping it with another, making two. Then you take that group and group it with the previous group . . . making three. Then five, then eight. There are higher groups, but I do not know them. But this is god, Aydan . . . the ground bleeds this into plants, animals . . . even us . . ."

"That sounds nice, Samaye . . . I would like to be in a world surrounded by these patterns, as they are in Tphetria . . ."

"These are just stories to most, my brother. They are corrupt people . . . my people," Samaye explained. "I had to leave for my soul could not consume it. I could not understand it."

"What do you mean?" Aydan asked.

"The structures . . . they are created through god . . . through the groups. But it is my own family, my brethren that work as slaves. Not as family. There is a group, a powerful group . . . the Methias . . . they . . . were like us. But they adorn themselves in vanity . . . and they use god's knowledge for purposelessness. They attain their knowledge from strangers . . . strangers from far away. And they keep it hidden."

He began to cry gently.

"It hurts my heart, akin. That so many suffer for their greed. They keep the knowledge to themselves and the strangers hidden. And when I encounter the Methias in the street . . . they are like me . . . like you. Of flesh, with soulful eyes. The confusion in me is like a disease, akin."

His crying deepened, and he began to lose his breath and heave as thoughts began to consume him.

"I am . . . perplexed . . . akin . . . the man in the mask . . . the rest . . ." he struggled to say between gasps.

Aydan suddenly became concerned and called to him.

"Samaye . . . you must calm yourself. Count with me . . ."

Samaye began to cry harder, the sobs turning into grunts as the intensity of his groaning became louder and harder.

As he heard Samaye, a hollowness began to form in him.

"It . . . it is . . . akin . . . it is . . . inconceivable . . . that my brother . . . my own akin of flesh . . . would harm me so," Samaye uttered in between gasps of breath mixed with tears and grunts.

Aydan closed his eyes and pressed his palm against his door.

"My akin . . . brother . . . mewah akin . . . oh god . . ."

Samaye began to heave as if he was choking.

Aydan's face grimaced, and he too began to cry.

"You must breathe, Samaye . . . we are together, you and I."

Samaye fell to the ground and curled up, holding his stomach.

"My stomach pains . . . it hurts so tremendously. I . . . I . . . think of his smell . . . and it . . . it ills me, akin . . .

"It ills me . . . that such a terrible feeling should . . . should . . . associate itself . . . to the thought of my own brother!!!"

His gasping turned into a steady cry, weeping heavily as he began to drown.

Aydan's own chest began to tighten, feeling helpless towards his companion.

"Not everyone is our brother, Samaye..." Aydan responded after a moment. "Not everyone sees us as we wish to see them. Do you see?"

Samaye clutched his hair in his hands and wept wholly.

As Aydan listened to him, he began to contemplate that Samaye was not fooling himself into believing that the Fayem was his brother. It seemed he truly saw him as that. He cried with the deep seated pain that only betrayal could fuel, not delusion.

"Why, Samaye..." Aydan asked. "Why do you think he loves you... that he wants to... that he could? He is not your brother... he is an animal."

"Akin..." Samaye responded, crying deeply. "Do you believe he does not yearn to be loved freely and completely?"

Aydan opened his mouth to respond, but nothing came out. The gentleness of Samaye's rebuttal shattered any preparedness he had in his criticism of Samaye's perspective. The truth was, as he thought of the Fayem and all the cruelty in his nature, he could not argue that the Fayem yearned for love. As his mind contemplated it against his will, he found himself more and more convinced that this was indeed the case. And as he did, the fear and hatred became less fortified within him.

It was a feeling he was not comfortable with, and although he tried to re-envision the atrocities of the past day to re-enforce his stance, Samaye's voice, like the hand of god, ushered all arbitrary thoughts away, leaving only unpleasant truths.

"I . . . I don't understand, Samaye . . ."

Samaye sat in the darkness, holding his head in his hands. He contemplated the physical pain within him along with the confusion of the abuse. He nodded to himself.

"Akin . . . why did he manifest his hatred upon me when I have done nothing but love him?"

Samaye's words shook Aydan's head, and he burst into tears, uncontrollably crying at the thought of the sheer vulgarity of such hatred that would facilitate the abuses that Samaye had suffered.

"I don't understand, Samaye . . . I don't know . . ."

He cried like a child, not knowing where the tears were coming from.

"Why are his actions so hurtful to me, Samaye? Why do I expect more of him?" Aydan asked. He became furious and began to scream.

"He is an animal! Not a man! Not a man to do such things to you! Not a man! Why are you hurt? He is not a man, he is a beast! A demon placed upon this world with nothing like us in his chest! He is a beast! Why do you cry? Why do you cry at a bastard animal acting as such?"

"I know nothing, akin, except that he yearns for my love, just as I do his . . ." Samaye responded immediately.

Aydan slammed his hand against his door repeatedly, trying to alienate himself from Samaye's words. He believed it to be true, but loathed his own certainty of it.

Samaye lay down, curling up in his cell as tears ran down his cheek. He did not sob, for the thoughts came and went, but the confusion that remained hurt him with every emergence.

"I don't understand, akin . . . why would he hurt me so?" Samaye asked as one such emergence arrived, causing his tears to flow faster, his body tensing up.

And with every sob that Aydan heard, he understood them not to be fuel to the effect of hating the man, but attempting to understand his motivation and purpose, his capacity to hurt Samaye in such a manner while he was loved. It was the pain of confusion, almost mind-numbing confusion, brought about by his attempt to understand why one would reject the love, the real empathy, compassion and trust Samaye had so freely invested into him.

Aydan was confused by his feelings, for he resided in a realm of fear and openly accepted that none were his friends or comrades. Yet, the way that Samaye was, was of a completely different nature. He was suffering immensely and the victim of his faith in someone like the Fayem, but there was something he carried within him . . . something familiar to Aydan that he both deeply respected and desired.

There was a border, he saw. In the darkness, his senses numbed, he could almost visualize it. His world, entirely existing before this point, Aydan was alone, surrounded by teeth. Bethelhurst meant as well as he could but was never a companion of sorts, never Aydan's ally. And though he navigated the world around him successfully, the concept of an ally was unspeakably rich to him, as if seeing this border in the darkness opened up his thirst for love. It was as if he discovered a gaping hole in his stomach, and there was a vacuum there, and though he could not feel it before this moment, it had been there all along.

Aydan slammed his hand against his door, once, forcefully.

"Samaye . . ." he called out.

"Samaye!" he yelled.

"Yes."

Aydan calmed himself, choosing his words carefully.

"Are you my brother?"

Samaye began to weep uncontrollably, pressing himself against his wooden barrier, stretching the wound on his back.

"Because I . . . am your brother," Aydan continued.

Samaye placed his palm against his door, crying profusely.

"And I am going to break this."

CHAPTER 12
LORE

I n the desert, the sand reflects sunlight before the sun is ever seen. A shimmer leads to the edge of the world where some large, booming light awaits its entrance, and all those awake can sense the dawn approaching. Some wish the night to last forever with its cool stillness, for with the encroaching day arises action, and the movement of all things.

Aydan awoke, deep within a hole, sensing the glimmering sands. The air in the cave was cooler, just as it is right before the sun rages into view, and his anger had awoken with him.

Everything had been a dream up to now, but he had crossed to the other side. The life of a farmer was over for him.

The experience of Samaye's violation extended itself far beyond the reaches of the cave in Aydan's mind. It had cracked something within him; not immediately, but for Samaye's uncommon tenderness. It extended itself beyond space, and traveled time.

Everything . . . all things . . . changed. And somehow, his mother's face kept re-appearing in his head. His perception of her, of her gentleness, of her smiling and dancing. Her hair and even his own birth had been manifested, through a lack of rebellion, in support of the hypocrisy of the Aizik world.

All the moments he recollected became vulgar fictions. He remembered the first time he saw Tima and how wonderful her smiles were. She was like fresh air to him, brimming with some essence that seemed to be all he had ever needed in life. And when she was wed to an old man in another village, Aydan had become indifferent to it. It had always, and still did, strike a nerve within him, for he wondered what her life was like and contemplated the drab nature of cooking and cleaning for a man she did not love. He imagined her being taken by him, and the idea of her body being consummated by a man who would use her, touch her flesh without tenderness, was one of the most disturbing thoughts he could manifest.

But even those perspectives seemed to be from a different life. Tima could have used her spirit to break free of the nonsensical path that was laid before her. There was little hope in such a rebellion, for women were either wives, daughters or whores, but perhaps she could have forged a new destiny for herself regardless of the hardships.

As Aydan thought about it, he corrected himself. It was not a choice. It was confusing to him as to how her soul could have accepted such a mediocre fate. He imagined that perhaps she fought and rebelled and eventually did run away to some distant land dressed as a boy to live a free life, but knew that this was not true. Had she not accepted her chosen life fully and completely, news of their discord would have reached his village, for the mouths of the villagers wagged at even the slightest bit of social disharmony.

But nothing of the sort ever arose. Even now, they did not speak of him even though he had perused the festival some nights before. He was forgotten, assumed to be branded, as was the ruling of the Council, just as she was branded a wife and nothing more.

There was no way back, for there was nothing of value to him there. He contemplated earnestly the possibility of being freed and returning to his defa to resume his life, and it made him mentally ill. There was nothing of value to him.

"No attraction for Aydan's soul," he thought to himself.

All things, the only thing of importance to Aydan . . . more valuable than anything in a deeper, more sincere sense than the way fears had manifested desires in him before . . . was Samaye. He did not speak, though he yearned to hear his new friend's voice, for he wanted him to rest, to dream, to be away from this place.

And so he contemplated, with a calculating mind speeding with impulses of thought and activity, with only one question at the forefront of his vision: how to be free of this place.

What was to happen today . . . all the possibilities began to take refuge in his mind, with a hundred different destinies perpetuating themselves within him as he contemplated the best decision, word, choice and action . . . the best thing to do right now, to do in an hour, to be free of this bondage.

His eyes fluttered from side to side as one reality crashed in failure, moving unto another, living a week in a moment, every pivotal change and relevant detail quickly contemplated and calculated.

There were unknowns, but Bethelhurst was the key. He had to hope for a visit and had to manifest some tactic with his defa. If it did not happen today, that would be an unfortunate turn . . . but Aydan saw his own violation at the hands of the Fayem as simply a part of the calculation, and irrelevant to the goal.

If he was allowed to visit, Aydan would hold his hand and pull him close. He would have to choose his words carefully, not only for the thin man and the Fayem and whomever else that may be present, but other prisoners as well.

Bethelhurst would insist on solving it in some amicable manner - appealing to the Council or pleading with the Fayem - and so, Aydan would have to make his decision as clear and communicative in the first attempt. He could not rely on the freedom to argue or to discuss. Only to communicate.

It became a priority, therefore, for Aydan to fully revel in the man that was his father. He had to know him, to think as him so as to reach him and minimize risk. He was a stubborn man and would have contemplated his own course of actions in reaction to this, which Aydan admittedly theorized could be more revolutionary and spectacular than he expected. Perhaps his love for Aydan would have triggered some dormant energy within him, and he too would have realized that the Aizik way was, in finality, a betrayal to himself.

Perhaps his father had become freer in his heart for the loss of his son, and it now raged with a passion triggered in the face of injustice.

There was indeed an importance to this crisis. This was not a seemingly benign event where someone alien to their Kunda had disappeared. Aydan was Bethelhurst's son, who had slept by him night by night, under his care, in his company. The sight of his empty cot must have affected Bethelhurst profoundly, and there was a sincere possibility that his father would react to this event in an unpredictable manner.

Yet, Aydan also knew of the heavy hand his defa maintained in regards to controlling his emotions, and perhaps it would take some other stimulus, the sight of Aydan in the cave, perhaps, to overwhelm his habitual nature.

Aydan would have to look him in the eyes and transfer unto him the true nature of this place, the horror of it, and if he did so successfully, Bethelhurst's love for him would move towards action. He could envision it now: an unready nervousness in his father's eyes as he entered the cave, close to tears as he saw his son's. And hand in hand, through this small hole in the door, Aydan would whisper to him, and drive would fill his heart. He would be driven by an all-consuming urge to protect his son, just as Aydan's burned for his friend.

It all relied on Bethelhurst, and Aydan's words to him.

Outside the cave, the sun was already well underway, scorching the rocky entrance with its rays. A solitary white flier with an orange beak stood, almost symmetrically, at the center of the entrance, its clawed foot pressed against an equally white egg. It was striking down against it with a stone it held in its beak, trying to get inside.

It fluttered away cautiously, staring at its meal as an entourage of large creatures approached.

One of the men, appearing official, holding a spear, knelt down and picked up the egg, wiping it against his tunic. He placed it in his pouch and proceeded to sit on the ground in the shade, leaning against his spear.

Five others followed: another guard who enviously stared at the first one for the treat he had found, another donning a mask and blue dress, the thin man, and two others. The two others seemed to be agitated, carrying pots in their hands. One was a man and the other a fully covered woman whose only visible feature was her eyes.

The guard who sat looked at the Fayem who nodded. He then motioned to the others with his spear, pointing towards the cave. They began to walk towards the entrance but slowed as the darkness revealed itself, blocking their path. The man turned to see the two guards fidgeting with their bodies, picking or scratching. The man in the mask stood silently staring at them while the thin man stood behind him, also staring. The man looked about and saw a small fire burning with some wood and picked up a piece. He then led the way into the cave with the woman following, pot tight in hand.

From within, Aydan's ears perked to the slight sound of something subtle, and after a few moments, whilst he forgot to breathe, the sounds became louder and more certain. He immediately stared out his door into the blackness, eagerly seeking some deviation in the light level, hoping it was a sign of hope, dismissing the alternative.

The light soon shone as the entities emerged, initially too bright for Aydan to recognize. He blinked eagerly and wiped his eyes, blocking them out for a few seconds, then stared.

Surprisingly loud, a result of the unmolested emotion that impetuously burst within him, he yelled.

"Defa!"

Bethelhurst looked about, trying to find the source.

"Defa! Defa! Here . . . I am here!"

Aydan flung his hands out and waved them uncontrollably at his father.

Bethelhurst ran over to him and reached down, holding Aydan's hands in his own.

"I am glad to see you, boy . . . very glad," he stuttered. It was as if amidst great emotion, he had subdued his volume, compensating for his joy.

Aydan pulled his arm in, holding it against his face as he closed his eyes, pressing his cheek against it.

"Defa . . . defa . . .defa . . . you are here."

Bethelhurst slowly pulled his arm out and sat beside Aydan's cell.

"I have brought you some food. Give me your hand, and I will feed you."

Aydan stuck his hand out, and Bethelhurst poured some lentils in his palm. He placed it in his mouth and shivered, tasting salt.

"Please, defa, take it to my friend. He is on the other side."

Aydan pointed towards Samaye's cell.

"Samaye! Brother! Drink what my father has for you. Taste the salt!"

Samaye, still in a daze, was filled with pleasure at waking to the sound of Aydan's voice. He replied in an almost dreamlike state.

"Yes, akin . . . as you say it. Tell me what to do . . ."

Bethelhurst looked at Aydan through the small hole and frowned.

"I do not know that boy, Aydan. I have brought this for you."

Aydan smiled.

"It does not matter, defa, he is my brother. See him, he is family."

Bethelhurst placed the pot on the ground and looked at Aydan.

"You are not to make friends with these people, Aydan. You are to leave this place. I am awake at nights trying to determine how to free you of this place, and in bringing you this dal, an offering for your appetite, to give you hope, you distribute it to unknowns and invalids? What is wrong with you, boy?"

Aydan, still with a smile on his face, stared at his father as it slowly collapsed.

"The dal . . . is irrelevant, defa. I am thankful you brought it. I must speak to you."

Bethelhurst leaned forward.

"Do you know what they do here?"

Bethelhurst shook his head.

"The man in blue . . . he tortures the prisoners. I've not been his target, but he is brutal, defa. Do you see that rock behind you?"

Bethelhurst turned briefly to see it, then back to Aydan.

"It is stained with blood. And soon it will be mine. He will defile me, defa. He will torture me and worse. If you had seen what he did to Samaye, you would not be so calm in entering here."

"I am not interested in speaking of that boy. I am only interested in you, my son."

Aydan began to unconsciously dig his nails into the ground beneath him. He paused to calm himself.

"That is an example. What he will do to me may be worse. You must help me."

"I am helping you, my boy. I have approached the Council every day since your taking. I have waited since daybreak to come here today. We will find a solution. I will appeal to all I can."

Aydan shook his head.

"You don't understand . . . it does not matter what we do; we cannot rely on their good nature for providence. We must make our own, defa."

Bethelhurst shook his head.

"What are you talking about, Aydan? There are no options but appealing to those that can do something about it."

Aydan's voice began to rise.

"We can do something about it! You! Me!"

"What, boy?! What do you suggest?"

Aydan lowered his voice again, motioning to his father.

"You must return at nightfall, father. No one guards this place. Perhaps a little man named Maki, but he is easily overpowered."

Bethelhurst laughed.

"Are you mad, boy? You wish for me to sneak in here as a criminal and-"

"Not a criminal! As a free man!" Aydan interrupted.

Bethelhurst leaned in, looking sternly at Aydan.

"You are mad, boy. You cannot escape. There is nowhere to go. We must appeal to the Council. We cannot break the laws."

Aydan grabbed Bethelhurst's hand and squeezed it.

"You are not understanding, my father."

Aydan blinked nervously.

"I cannot remain imprisoned here . . . reliant on the good nature of those that would employ the man in the mask. I will not remain imprisoned here, unknowing to what hideousness await me upon his arrival. Do you understand? Because . . . I hope that you see how serious I am."

Bethelhurst stared at Aydan for a moment then yanked his arm out of the cell and leaned back.

He pointed at Aydan angrily.

"You don't tell me what to do, boy! I have worked so hard to bring you dal-"

"Fuck your dal!" Aydan screamed. "I don't need your dal, you coward! I need a father!"

Bethelhurst banged on the door.

"I am your father!!! I am doing all I can to free you! What more do you want of me?!"

Aydan reached out and grabbed his tunic, pulling him hard against the wood.

"I want you to free me. I want you to help me!" Aydan yelled, under his voice, banging his hand against his chest.

"Not in the way you want, boy. This isn't playtime anymore. Now you see what comes of your free dreaming and airy ideas. You are there, and I am here. And I still help you, because you are my son."

Aydan stared at his father's eyes, still holding onto his tunic. He slowly released him and leaned back.

They stared at each other for a few moments.

"I am not your son, you bastard coward."

Bethelhurst stared at him for a moment and abruptly picked up the pot, wrapping it back up.

"You are not my father! You are a snake! A liar! You've lied to me, you bastard man!"

The covered woman that entered with him, who up to that point had been conversing with one of the other inmates, looked towards Aydan as he cursed Bethelhurst.

"Quiet, boy! Have you no respect for your father?" she yelled at him.

"Mind your own, whore!" Aydan screamed.

She remained silent, baffled at Aydan's words. Bethelhurst turned to Aydan, equally baffled.

"Boy . . . have you lost your mind?"

Aydan smiled.

"You are . . . the most despicable creature I have ever encountered, Bethelhurst. You defend this whore against your son, your Kunda, in opposition of all you ever claimed. Loyalty? I ask you to protect me . . . to stand firm with me in the face of such tyranny, and you cower like a dog. You are a dog. You are not a man. You bring me dal and believe you have done your part . . . your part has not even begun, and you already dismiss it."

He spat against the sandy rock.

"I need a father, not you. You're not a man, you bastard. You're not of my line!"

Aydan began to yell loudly, enraged.

"You're not of my line, you bastard man! You never dreamed of titans! That is my dream! It was never of our line! I spit on you! I spit on your Kunda! You bastard human being! You're a coward! Run to your soiled hole of a life! Sow crops for these sons of whores! Sow crops for the children of this whore and love them!"

Bethelhurst began to walk away from Aydan and out of the cave, shaken.

"Leave, you coward. It is what you do best . . . what you were born to do. You will die afraid and alone, as you should, you cockroach."

As Bethelhurst left, so too did the woman follow, and soon Aydan was in the dark, still staring into the cave. He was frozen in place, his head pulsating. His words rang like bells in his head, and his body was sweating as he stared through the hole, still unable to acknowledge what just happened.

He sat back into a now familiar position against the door. His eyes were wide, and he stared into the blackness of his cell, aloof and unmoving.

"Are you there, brother?" he numbly inquired.

"I am, akin," Samaye responded.

"The salt is like poison upon my tongue, brother. Had I consumed more, I might have died."

CHAPTER 13
EXIT

Fatigue consumed him, and he remembered nothing coherently after the darkness fell. He drifted in and out of consciousness, reality becoming a fazed confusion. His enraged words to Bethelhurst had become fantastic, as if he had dreamed them while knowing they were real.

Such was the nature of grand events, he thought randomly between sleeps. That one frees themselves from some weight and are unnerved by the new world they discover. But he had not entered a new world; the old world still frightened him, and his father's back still shattered his melancholic ideals. He was guilty, even as he sat in a dark hole waiting to die . . . he was guilty for having offended his father.

He giggled at some point, contemplating how incredibly ridiculous it was that given the true nature of both their situations, Bethelhurst had the ability to cause grief within Aydan for not fully appreciating the food he had brought.

"Did you hear that, Samaye?" he asked out loud.

Samaye was once more awoken by his friend.

"Hear . . . what, brother?"

"My heart, Samaye . . . it aches with pain, not for my or your fate, but for the forgotten and pained dal my defa brought. I rejected it, and I am sure it hurts where it sits now. I see it wrapped in cloth, sitting alone, and my father stares at it, woe and sadness filling him for its unfulfilled purpose."

Samaye smiled.

"You are a very cruel man, Aydan, to have hurt such a sensitive dal."

"Yes!" Aydan yelled. "Yes, that is correct. That is exactly what I am trying to say to you. Both you and I are bathed in horror, yet my mind focuses on his back and his hurt face and most importantly, his sensitive dal . . . what a strange, twisted state of being I am in, Samaye."

"We often do not control what our hearts tell us, akin . . . though we sense when we are being deceived . . . as you are right now. Yes?"

"Most certainly," Aydan replied. "I am being deceived right now, my brother. And my birth giver is the deceiver. What roots he has implanted in my mind, to be able to cause me to suffer grief for him whilst I await the adoration of a cruel blade."

He was silent then, unaware of whether his eyes were open or closed, nothing but darkness and Samaye's voice representing all there was in the universe.

He became serious, suddenly, and closed his eyes, pensively thinking.

He imagined Bethelhurst's face and the ghostly mask of the Fayem. He imagined the interior of the cave and reached up to feel his still sore head wound. As he touched it, he grimaced, and then began to cry silently. He did not open his eyes, however, and still imagined his father's face.

The failure of his communication was beyond him; he began to accept that it would have failed no matter what he had said or done, and that all the intricate planning he had analyzed earlier that day was the result of his naive perspective of those he held close to him.

"Akin?" Samaye called out.

Aydan was silent for a moment, and then responded.

"Yes, Samaye."

"I am your brother, and I trust you," Samaye replied.

Aydan began to cry further, as if Samaye's words pierced all that he had perceived his real Kunda to represent to him. He felt tragic as woe consumed him amidst feeling overwhelmed with pure grief at the unspeakable betrayal that Bethelhurst had committed.

"You know, Samaye . . ." Aydan spoke in between calm but teary breaths, "it is not his refusal to acquiesce to my plan that hurts me. It is an old pain that has awoken in me, spurred by the graveness of this situation and how unflinchingly unheard I am by his heart."

He continued.

"Even in this place, whether it be naive or simplistic, there can be nothing wrong with the pleasure my heart seeks in sharing the taste of salts with you. That this is of priority to me, that you share in the uplifting feeling such a sensation may bestow upon you, from a hole in the middle of the earth . . ."

He began to cry deeply.

"That this that comes from my heart is made to be questioned or despised, criticized in any manner, is blasphemy. It is . . . a terrifying event . . . unholy. And this bastard father of mine, he oozes nothing but malice towards what my heart seeks to attain."

Samaye placed his hands against his door and leaned his head against it, listening to Aydan.

"There can be nothing wrong with pure intent, akin," he said.

Aydan heard him, thought, then nodded.

"There can be nothing wrong with pure intent."

Aydan began to repeat it over and over.

"There can be nothing wrong with pure intent.

"There can be nothing wrong with pure intent."

He began to speak louder, his tears stopping, his fists beginning to clench.

"There can be nothing wrong with pure intent!"

He hit his door with the side of his fist and paused. He took a deep breath in and began to scream.

"There can be nothing wrong with my intent!!!"

He banged the door hard and took a position at the rear of his hole, pressing his back against the wall opposite. He placed his feet square against the wooden barrier and took a deep breath in.

"Do you hear me, Samaye?"

He bent his knees back and struck down hard against it, causing the door to shake and echo through the cave.

"Kick your door, Samaye! Kick it!"

Samaye felt around his door and did not fully understand what Aydan meant until he heard another loud thud as Aydan's feet landed upon it again. He sat in the middle of his hole and kicked his door. It pushed him backwards, towards the wall behind him, which he then pressed his back against. He twisted his body as he felt his wound touch the rock, using his hands for leverage.

"Kick it, Samaye!"

Aydan slammed his feet against it, over and over, the soles of his feet becoming sore and pained. Samaye began to kick as well, taking longer with each kick but pressing as hard as he could.

"You bastard liar," Aydan whispered. He imagined his father's face and thought about his claim to Aydan as a son.

"Bastard!" he screamed as he kicked his door as hard as he could, hearing the wooden fibers tear from the inside. He could not feel his feet though he knew the abuses they were now suffering would cause him anguish for some time to come.

"Kick your door, Samaye! We are free if you will it with me!"

He began to kick his door quicker now, and still harder, gathering a motion in between breaths. Samaye maintained his speed and also began to hear his door buckle as he slammed his feet against it.

"Kick!!!"

Aydan's door began to stretch, and with every kick more and more fibers tore. He could feel it giving way to his pressure, enticing him to kick even harder.

"Break, you son of a whore! Break!"

Outside the cave, Maki slept, curled up on both his feet, like a bird. He rested his head on his hands, which rested on his shoulder as he stood, perched, his knees bent fully, perfectly balanced in a deep sleep.

The loud thuds from within the cave were only murmurs outside; yet the alien sounds began to prick at his sleeping mind, and it started taking notice of them.

Aydan touched the bottom of his feet and felt open wounds, torn from the door. He then heard a loud crack as

Samaye's door gave in, breaking in half. Samaye screamed in agony, immediately.

"What, Samaye? Have you broken through?"

"Akin . . . my leg is caught on the rupture in the door. I cannot move, but it is open. It is open, brother. We are free . . ."

Aydan naturally began to secrete tears as the urgency behind his kicks increased double fold.

"I am coming, Samaye. I am coming!"

He kicked and kicked, becoming angry and desperate as it seemed fiber after fiber tore but still did not collapse the door. Soon, however, a piece broke off, and he kicked around it, making the hole bigger and bigger, soon causing almost half the door to lay in tatters outside his cell.

He immediately patted the floor cautiously and began to walk on all fours, navigating outside of his cell carefully.

"Speak, brother! Speak so that I can find you!"

"I am here, akin . . . come . . . here . . . my leg is caught in the door . . ."

Aydan crawled quickly to Samaye's cell and touched his leg, for the first time feeling his warm flesh. It brought tears to his eyes, and he held onto his foot for an instant, then kissed it.

"I am here, brother."

Samaye began to weep as well, feeling the lucid warmth of Aydan's face against his skin.

Aydan felt around Samaye's leg, examining the positioning of the door. He created a visual imprint of the positioning of the sharp fibers and tore away, piece by piece, anything surrounding Samaye's leg.

"I am going to lift your leg now, and it will hurt."

Samaye held his breath as Aydan took hold of his ankle and pulled it upwards, withdrawing sharp slivers from Samaye's leg. Samaye clenched his voice and grunted, trying to keep hold of the searing pain.

Aydan slowly moved his leg to the side and placed it down. He moved into Samaye's cell and found his hand, taking hold of it, pausing for an instant. He caught his breath as he grasped tightly at Samaye.

"Are you ready, brother?" he asked after a few moments.

Samaye clenched his friend's fist in acknowledgment. Aydan wrapped his arm around the back of Samaye and began to prop him up, out of the cell, making Samaye lean on him.

Just as they stood, they paused, suddenly.

Aydan whispered into Samaye's ear.

"Quiet, brother. Something has moved."

They stood completely silent in the darkness and began to hear a slight shuffling in the cave with them.

Aydan looked about, squinting, trying to catch a glimpse of something but could see nothing. Samaye was becoming faint for his exhaustion and loss of blood but held onto Aydan for support.

Aydan leaned Samaye against the wall noiselessly and squeezed his hand, letting go. He spread his arms out in the darkness, stepping very quietly, trying to catch whatever it was that moved.

Suddenly, something jumped out and grabbed him, biting his arm. Aydan began to slam his fist down on it over and over, trying to get it to release him. It pulled him to the ground and climbed on him, hitting his head.

"Naga! Naga! Naga, naga!" the creature yelled. Aydan immediately recognized the voice of Maki and became furious. He reached back and punched Maki's face both fast and hard, causing him to fly back and hit his head against the rock in the center of the cave.

Aydan scrambled on all fours, and like an animal ran to Maki and began hitting him. He took his head and slammed it against the rock repeatedly.

"Die!!!" he screamed.

He soon stopped, feeling the motionless body of Maki, dropping his head against the ground. Aydan sat there, his hands drenched in blood, and began to cry.

"Akin . . . akin . . ."

Aydan heard Samaye's voice, and as if awoken by it, wiped his face with his arm and stood up slowly, walking cautiously in the darkness towards his friend. He wrapped his hand around his back and kissed the side of his face, then suddenly hugged him. Samaye hugged him back, and they both limped out of the cave, following the feel of the wall.

CHAPTER 14
DOMAIN

The drive to escape in any direction came naturally, and neither Samaye nor Aydan debated their destination save getting as far away from the cave as possible. It was understood that they had crossed a threshold they could not return from, and if they were re-captured by the Aizik or any group loyal to them, they would likely suffer before they died.

As they exited the mouth of the cave, it was still dark, and they had to rely on the night sun to guide their navigation. Both felt relief as their feet touched the cold sand which temporarily soothed their soles and made their distance from captivity all the more real.

As they shuffled forward, neither spoke, though Samaye grunted in pain as his leg wound bled. Every minute, gusts of wind shattered his nerves, injecting his brain with angst. The feeling of warmth they both felt being under each other's arms was comforting even though the cold of the desert chilled their flesh.

Aydan's feet, torn from the kicking, were covered with red sand that had bonded into his wounds, causing each step to hurt.

Yet the cold, pain and blood bore no relevance to their movements. They walked and walked, and Aydan kept looking back to witness the moment the cave was no longer in sight. He realized as it happened that they were lost, and that this was a comforting thought. He walked a few more steps but suddenly felt exhausted and collapsed, taking Samaye down with him.

They hit the sand and lay there in silence, breathing the air. Simultaneously, they both realized its taste, cool and clean and how different it was than the acrid air in the cave. The boundless desert on each side was a sterile blessing, and they both rested their muscles in it.

They lay there for some time, drifting in and out of consciousness, their arms still touching. Their faces lay sideways on the sand, their mouths inhaling bits with every breath in the darkness.

"We cannot sleep . . ." Aydan said.

Samaye turned and pressed his arms in the sand, pushing himself up. Aydan followed suit, helping his friend, starting their trek once again.

PART II

CHAPTER 15
THE THINGS THAT PASSED

Aydan awoke in complete silence. There was no wind and no noise. The sand was still, orange in the sun, and the morning heat was starting to manifest. Still cool, however, his skin welcomed the warmth as it was both numb and aching from events past.

He was sitting in the sand, hunched over. In his lap was his friend's head, his body outstretched in front of him. He stared at Samaye's face and began to cry, his lips breaking into a misshapen line. He ran his hand along his hair, loving the weathered nature of his skin, the position of his eyes and his gentle lips. He had never laid eyes on him in sunlight before, and it still seemed as though he was Aydan's only conduit to life.

His tears dropped onto Samaye's skin, and Aydan smudged it, wiping away dirt from his flesh, revitalizing the look of his face.

"Samaye?" Aydan gently whispered.

"Samaye . . . my only brother."

Samaye opened his eyes and looked at Aydan.

"Why do you weep, brother?" he asked.

"Where are you, Samaye?" Aydan asked.

"I am with you, Akin."

Aydan began to cry harder.

"No, Samaye . . . you are dead."

"I know, brother."

"Were you alone . . . when you left? Did you die alone, my friend?"

Samaye smiled.

"I died in your arms, Akin."

Aydan grimaced, weeping.

"But I do not remember, Samaye. I do not remember. I do not remember."

Samaye, still smiling, replied.

"It does not matter, brother. I held unto your knee and passed into the next life knowing you cared for me, Akin, as I would have you. We are brothers, and without guilt."

Aydan leaned down and squeezed the lifeless body of his friend, burying his head in his chest, crying.

CHAPTER 16
MYSTERIES IN THE DESERT

Aydan drifted in and out of consciousness randomly. Vibrant images of Samaye flashed in his dreams, shuttering against the backdrop of the warm and cold flashes of the desert against his body. He saw Bethelhurst's face, as if slowed, both crying and screaming. The thoughts of the cave and its darkness were short and extreme, disrupting the flow of time in his mind. He had spent his whole life by the Gimba tree, farming, staring at the rocky earth split in shallow graves for seeds, the crops becoming less and less dense, more and more sparse, and his gradual descent away from all things sane.

He had dreamed of voices that morning, but they were not all his creation, but from some other place, some unseen place, unlike him, reaching out to him. They called him brother, as did Samaye.

He wept as he thought of his friend, his brother, his brethren. But just as the tears arrived, so too did they stop, as he dismissed reality in favor of fatigue and deep breathing as he fell into the world of sleep. Perhaps his friend would be there in the morning, and he was mistaken.

His hands felt the sand beneath him with every temporary moment of consciousness, as if he hoped to find grass, or water, or something other than the crystalline pebbles against his fingers. He rubbed his hand in them angrily, losing all hope, unable to even wet his lips, afraid that if he opened his mouth, his tongue would shrivel up and die, taking him along with it.

He lay down, finally, feeling weight upon his body, pushing away from it, nuzzling his head in the sand. With his nose now completely blocked, he opened his lips only minimally to take in air. He tried to filter out the loose sand that came in with every breath but could taste the rocks against his tongue and even tried to chew them in some delirious state, hoping to extract flavor and juices out of them. Perhaps no one had ever tried, he thought, and he would discover something miraculous that would empower him.

He recalled something he had contemplated as a child. His eyes closed, he tried to whisper the concept, trying to resonate it within.

"If . . .

"If . . . I can sing . . . if I can sing . . . if I can sing the words . . . then I am not defeated."

He lay there, hearing them, thinking them, feeling them. He repeated, louder.

"If . . . I sing . . . if I can sing the words . . . I am not defeated."

He took a deep breath in and felt the words, like blood, coarse through his system . . . and began to scream.

"If I have the luxury of song, I am not defeated! Hear me! I am not defeated!"

He took another desperate breath in and whispered to himself.

"If I am song . . . I will never be defeated . . ."

Then the wind in the desert was all that could be heard. The miniscule crackling of fragment after fragment, pieces of orange earth dancing in the wind, running a gauntlet up and down the dunes of the dry infinite sea. They filled his hair, his ears, and piled up on either side of him. As if attracted to the fleeting warmth in his body, the little creatures that touched him lay down with him, upon him, to be close to his spirit.

His hand closed around the sand, holding it in his fist. He kept his eyes closed and began to sing.

"The world closes around me . . .

"But I am still here, I am still here."

He stopped in between every line to pause and gather energy.

"The lands swallow me whole.

"I am still here . . . I am still here.

"I am still here . . ." he whispered quietly, feeling the embrace of the dream world.

"I will always be here."

CHAPTER 17
DIVE

S till.

Perfectly still.

It was the stillness that awoke him.

His ears perked, and some vessel of awareness ran down his ear, into his mind, and began to scream as loud as it could, and his awareness was piqued.

"Hmmm . . . ?" Aydan weakly muttered in a half dazed state.

Underneath the sand, something moved, and his hand limply emerged, sensing the wind.

This piqued his awareness even more.

Half buried now, Aydan shifted, feeling his entire body ache in agony. He moaned in pain, and in doing so tore the dry calluses on his lips, sending shearing impulses of torture through his entire body.

He finally managed to prop himself upwards on one hand and sat up, his body muffled in small particles of sand.

He remained still, trying to sense something, anything, but could not. It frightened him, more than he expected it to. Gently, he tried to open his eyes, brushing caked sand away from his face, carefully freeing his eyelashes. He peeked every now and then, and seeing and hearing nothing began to push his anxious mind to bridge the gap between unease and terror, forcing him to become frantic in his effort to discover what universe he had fallen into.

As his eyes opened, he saw the red haze of an emerging dusk color in an unmistakable gradient along the sand in front of him. The sun, as if staring directly at him but gentle enough to receive a stare back, was right in front of him, flat against the horizon in perfect proportion to the world.

Aydan stared, his body hunched, and was entranced. Something was happening to him, and he could not determine what it was. A rush of emotion is how he described it to himself, too fast to be interrupted. As if insanity and reality had collided to create an absolutely pivotal moment where the universe was bending in some strange manner to kiss him.

He looked to the side and saw a leg in the sand, connected to something that was now buried by the world, and knew it belonged to his perished friend. He began to cry, for he found it to be the most beautiful and vulgar thing he had ever seen. Samaye was in darkness, gone forever with unrequited hope, yet this color upon his leg, upon the sand, and even upon Aydan, provided by the sun, kissed it all. Aydan raised his hand at the sun, trying to feel the thickness of his feeling, but felt nothing. He stared at the orange fire, and as it began to hide under the horizon, so too did he begin to feel alone and empty.

It was as if the presence of the sun introduced noise to the environment, and though this was not the case, as it vanished, Aydan felt scared at the silence he found himself drenched in. He saw Samaye's leg once again, this time void of color or light, but simply lying there, unmoving, horrific in its suggestion of what lay connected to it. It was not an object but a sign of something more terrible, some beauty lost but not simply missing now and forever, but rather defiled and broken by the world.

His dazed thoughts were disconnected, and though he contemplated how distraught he was, he simply did not have the capacity to dwell on it. The sun was gone, and whatever magnificent feeling had emerged when he awoke went with it, replaced by the real world, one he seemed to collide with in what seemed to be only unpleasant manners.

"Samaye . . ." he whispered as tears filled his eyes.

He leaned down backwards, resting his back against the ground as if lying in bed, preparing to die. He was filled with anguish at that moment, with nothing but thoughts of failure and betrayal and the woe of witnessing the loss of the soft creature that lay beside him. He had never experienced a hopelessness that had no exits and though, for a moment, he regretted leaving the cave, as he felt the cool sand under his palms, he became suddenly assured that though it ended as it did, it was eventuated in freedom.

CHAPTER 18
HEAVENS

Aydan did not know how much time had passed since last awakening. His muscle pain had grown into a searing burn, and every movement was filled with unbearable discomfort. He felt an immense lack of energy and was barely conscious enough to open his eyes to see the darkness around him.

The night was cool, and out of the corner of his eye he saw Samaye's foot. Without thinking, he reached over and pulled himself closer to his friend.

"I am coming, brother," he murmured, not knowing if he had uttered the words or simply thought them.

The arduous task of pulling himself close to Samaye proved difficult, but once he reached him, he began to slowly move sand off his body. His torso was now deep under the brown earth, and Aydan had to shift arms and angles repeatedly so as to not over-exert any particular muscle. He began at Samaye's feet, as if in a trance, and traveled down his knees. He tried pulling Samaye out using his weight, but it did not work. He continued moving the sand off his friend.

His eyes half dazed, his mouth dry and scathed, he worked diligently.

"I will not die alone," he whispered. "Not without you, brother."

Eventually, Samaye's torso became visible which energized Aydan to clear off the rest. As he did, his friend's face came into focus, and he tilted his head sideways, smiling ever so slightly, almost deliriously, as he saw it.

He pulled Samaye and placed him in a lying position within the small depression that had been created around him. Aydan stumbled upon him, pressing his head into his chest, hugging him.

He closed his eyes and held onto his friend.

"It does not matter any longer, does it brother. We are together, and I tried my best."

Under his ear, he felt Samaye's cold body, but the softness of the skin, familiar to him, soothed his worry. He hugged Samaye tighter and kept shifting his body closer, now, it seemed, uncaring for the fate that awaited him.

As Aydan hugged him, he felt something around his waist and initially dismissed it. But his curiosity, seemingly operating independent of him, kept pushing his fingers to explore the object, trying to trigger an awareness of what it was without having to think about it. His hands followed the rough material, alien to Samaye's body, and as it reached the sand and continued underneath, his confusion began to take priority.

Aydan slowly opened his eyes to look at it and saw that there was a strange strap around Samaye's waist connected to something buried in the sand.

Aydan stared at it for a few moments, trying to understand what it was, but could come to no conclusion. He pulled at it, frowning, and little by little yanked the object out of the sand.

What began to protrude confounded him.

It was an extremely large, sealed bladder. He pressed his finger against it, not registering what it was, and felt fluid within.

He raised his head, staring at it.

"What is this . . . what is this . . ." he muttered to himself.

He reached down and pulled it up to him, unsealing it over Samaye's torso. As he did, he heard a familiar pop and the swishing of liquid inside. It sent a shudder through his heart, one he could barely stomach. He closed his eyes, grimacing.

"My god . . ."

He looked down at it and felt tears begin to collect in his eyes. He pressed his mouth against it and pulled it up slightly, forcing the fluid into his mouth. It filled him, hydrating his tongue and mouth, and drop by drop slowly traveled down his throat into his system. He purposely spilled some unto his lips and gently rubbed them together.

He leaned his head down on Samaye's chest once more, closing his eyes. The sweet taste of the fluid had given him some temporary peace, and he was completely oblivious to anything beyond that satisfaction. He soon wanted more and raised himself upwards, sitting beside his friend's corpse awkwardly.

As his body reacted to the water, he hunched over with his eyes closed. His body began to spasm, and he again filled his mouth, slowly letting it travel down his throat.

It was like a sedative, he thought, for his fatigue seemed to uncompromisingly strike him, and he could barely sit upright. He quickly sealed the bladder and collapsed on the ground having had his fill.

He awoke hours later, still in darkness. He was able to push himself upright and sat in place. He was clutching the bladder and again took a mouthful of water. The moonlight was full and the ground was bright in the darkness. He stared at the bladder with disbelief, still not registering its existence. He looked at Samaye who lay there beside him and pressed his hand against his cheek. He moved some hair out of his face and stared at him.

"Samaye . . ."

It came out as a whisper, not as he intended. He cleared his throat and tried again.

"Samaye."

It felt strange to hear his own voice.

He looked at the bladder and began to examine it. It was extremely large, probably thrice the size of one he would have used in the village. It was made of some animal's flesh, but he could not tell what kind. Attached to it was a tablet with a symbol on it. He adjusted its positioning to get more light upon it and saw it to be familiar to him, which surprised him.

"Ionus . . ." he said.

It was a name used in prayers, but was also a common name given to people in the land. The symbol was that of a man's head with a line above it, symbolizing focus. The name itself alluded to a focused man.

He looked down at Samaye.

"Where did you find this, brother? And how did you carry it?"

He opened the bladder and poured some water into Samaye's mouth, pressing his jaw shut. He began to cry.

"Drink, brother. Drink and perhaps you will awaken. Drink and perhaps we will both leave this place together."

As the water began to trickle out of his mouth, down his face, Aydan clenched his eyes shut in pain.

He lay down beside his friend and cried until he could cry no more, falling asleep. He embraced Samaye, toying with the notion that when he awoke next, it would be to the rhythmic thumping of his friend's chest.

A ydan awoke with the sunrise, clutching Samaye and the bladder. His head lay on the ground, staring at Samaye's pale rib cage, shielded by the morning sun.

It took him a few moments to calmly register that the bladder was real, and as he squeezed it in his hand, hearing the fluid inside, he closed his eyes, pressing his face into Samaye's side.

His mouth still had sand in it, as did his nostrils, and as he lay there trying to hold onto some conclusive acceptance he had come to earlier, he was uncomfortably forced into a state of action.

He was aware that his body was no longer shutting down, the water inside being the fuel that had steered it away from failure. And along with the failure of his body, he had accepted the failure of all things, transcended that border as he hugged Samaye, and let go of his attachments to either hope or life.

"It was time to restart . . . begin anew. I accepted the failure of this one," he muttered, barely, thinking out loud.

He leaned his head back and looked up at Samaye's sleeping face.

He closed his eyes after a few moments, a slightly disappointed look on his face, feeling an aching hunger in his belly.

He leaned against his arm and pushed himself upwards. His muscles still stung piercingly, but his body had somehow found reserves of energy, or perhaps released them for the new-found nectar. He sat, his eyes closed, still clutching the bladder with one hand, his other touching some part of his friend.

He stood up for the first time and felt sand fall off him as if he was some giant, slumbering creature that had just risen from an epoch of sleep. His feet were torn and bruised, and the pressure he placed on them hurt considerably.

He looked down at his friend and was struck with the awareness that Samaye was no longer with him. His body was pale and scratched, and the wound in his leg seemed some strange fixture to living tissue, un-healing and open. He stared at Samaye's face which he knew only as a voice in the darkness and muted in the light. Samaye was a disjointed symbol to Aydan, bitterly echoing what could have been.

He leaned down carefully upon his palms and kissed Samaye's cheek, then began to slowly undress him, almost ritualistically, taking his tunic off, revealing his naked body. He dug a shallow depression near Samaye and gently slid him into it, then began to cover him with sand.

His muscles were tired, and he did it slowly. As he covered his friend, he mourned somewhere inside, both for the loss and his fear of being alone. Aydan did not know what lay ahead of him, and as Samaye's torso began to disappear, the unknown became his burden wholly. He could not feel sadness but rather some numb unhappiness, for as he stared at the last few portions of his friend's body, he registered the moment as something he would return to for a lack of capacity to cope with it in the present. He acknowledged it not as a decision, but something necessary to do with life.

Samaye's face was the last to fade, and Aydan paused, kissing his cheek, before covering him up entirely. As he placed sand over Samaye's eyes, he felt a hollowness within himself. It was as if up to that point, he had still believed that Samaye might have opened his eyes at any moment. But once his face was covered and no movement, no excitement or disruption ensued, though Aydan both expected and waited for it, he sat in silence, subtly disappointed.

He remained beside the grave and closed his eyes. He took a sip of water and froze sternly in place.

"I reject all that was and is. I am returning you to the earth, my friend.

"I will carry you with me.

"I reject all that was and is. I am re-born."

He placed his hand on the sand, over Samaye's buried face. He began to cry.

"I will carry you with me, brother."

He sat for a few moments longer, then arose and looked at the horizon. He tore fragments of Samaye's tunic off, wrapping them around his feet. He wrapped the rest of Samaye's blood stained cloth over his head, covering his neck, and began a trek away from the rising sun. He took one final look at the lump in the sand and proceeded to move forward, a dismal mood coating his face. He carried the bladder strapped over his shoulder and walked in steady steps. He was used to treading the desert and naturally knew how to maximize his distance with the energy he had.

He traveled away from the sun, hoping that he would stumble upon some alien township or village, one that had no knowledge of him or the Aizik. He would present himself as a traveler and hoped it would be well met.

His hunger pains came and went, and he tried not to think about food. He was in a precarious mood, concentrating on his diminishing water supply and each step he took. He knew his energies would eventually end, and so every step was a direct investment to his survival, survival being the last thing his friend had silently urged him to pursue.

Desert crossings were practiced exercises. One had to keep themselves occupied in thought, unfocused at the heat or pain, continuing to persist in order to succeed. Aydan found thoughts easily, as there was much to think about.

He pondered Samaye's body and felt resolved knowing it was truly loved as it was left. It seemed placed, Samaye's death, for he was not one for this world. His simplicity of thought was superior to those around him, yet his perpetual confusion would have cursed him till the day he died. But even as he thought this, he pondered the life they could have led, exiting the desert together, living as brothers, finding loved ones and forever supporting one another in their endeavors. It was the laughter that hurt the deepest . . . all the laughter they would no longer share, and it made his heart sink.

"Now is the perfect time to grieve," he thought. "All the grief in the world will fuel my steps and make the passing sands blink."

"But grief . . ." he thought as he felt it surge through him like knives. "It cannot be simply quantified, though I wish it could."

He paused for a moment, wondering if Samaye had just been sleeping, considering turning back. He turned around to assess the situation and saw nothing but a sea of yellow.

He resumed walking.

"Soo-ma-ya," he whispered. "How I would repeat it a thousand times if you would awaken, my friend."

Thoughts led to the cave. For the first time, Aydan reminisced about it as if it was an age ago. Like a snake in a maze it slowly unraveled his thoughts, opening up a wound in him that was Bethelhurst.

"I will never call you defa," he whispered to himself between steps. "Bastard coward. My brother died carrying water for me and you return to your tiny hut to grow crops for the bastards. You will die alone, that I promise."

It was a steady pace that was necessary to maintain movement. Each step, the more mundane and natural, like breathing, sustained transport, avoiding the needs and ringing in his body.

"Each step," he whispered, "each step . . . and forward I move.

"San, mi, tha, koona, sina . . . san, mi, tha, koona, sina . . ."

Thoughts, again, flashing to Samaye, the cave, and always arresting at Bethelhurst. There was a chasm with him, where all his thoughts stopped, discovering some new hatred for the man.

"And so you think, I should pity you? You, you is a coward through and through. I offered you bravery. I held my hand out to you, and a stranger with love in his heart took it. He took it and stood by me."

Aydan grimaced.

"You wanted me to live through it."

He stared at the bright reflection of light in front of him intensely.

"You wanted me to live through it, defa. My defa wanted me to live through it."

He stumbled to the ground on his knees and lurched forward, about to fall, staying there, frozen. His eyes were closed, and he looked downwards. His heart was sinking, surging with black pain, filling his mind and nostrils. He could feel the poison tingle his fingertips as he thought about Bethelhurst, and overwhelmed tears formed within his eyes.

"Oh . . . you pathetic excuse for a man. How could you be my father?"

He thought of Samaye.

"You bastard! You didn't give him dal! My poor Samaye . . . Samaye, Samaye, Samaye."

He began to weep and turned hoping to see Samaye following him in the distance.

"Oh, god . . ." he muttered in agony, immediately standing and resuming his walk, falling back into pace.

CHAPTER 20
RISE

The desert escape would come in the form of shrubbery and hardened land. It was never an oasis that he would stumble upon, but little bush here and there. And if he walked in the direction of these shrubs, their numbers would increase very slowly. It was hard, however, to determine the right direction to follow.

Aydan had already passed some shrubs, but then vast amounts of lifeless sand had followed indicating that they were anomalies instead of signs of arable land. But even that was unreliable, for the sporadic nature of encroaching deserts was as chaotic as that of habitable land, the barrier between the two a vast and unclear gradient of transition.

Aydan had already committed to the direction, however, and he knew that once that decision had been made, it mattered not whether he was wrong or right. He did not waste precious time debating the direction, for in the middle of the sands there was no observation to be made, save the sun.

Overall, however, he became increasingly optimistic even as his body's aches became worse. He felt that the number of little greeneries was indeed increasing, and that perhaps over some indiscriminate number of dunes, there was life.

As dusk approached, he quickened his pace, exhausted as he was, for he knew this to be the optimal time with which to invest his energies. His steps became more deliberate, and in his excitement, he even began to breathe hard. The scorching heat was dwindling, and the temperate air was perfect to sustain quickened steps. He began to think about food and the possibility of gnashing his teeth into something juicy and edible.

He paused for a moment, opened his bladder, and took a deep drink of water, deciding to fuel himself for this brief opportunity. He had only an hour or so before it was too dark to continue for the possibility of losing his direction. He remembered horrific tales of desert nomads trying to utilize the coolness of the night only to abruptly discover they had retraced their steps for the entirety of it without the aid of the sun to direct them.

"San, mi, tha, koona, sina . . ." he muttered over and over, trying to keep himself paced as he pushed forward.

It became undeniable to him now that the shrubbery was more dense. He began to stumble over hardened pieces of land, expecting his feet to sink but instead slamming against hard earth. It hurt his feet immensely but was such a positive sign that Aydan wished for more of it.

Even as darkness began to fill the sky, Aydan continued, stubbornly seeking shelter. He pushed forward, eventually finding that his feet began to sink once again. He took a few more steps, still only treading upon soft sand, and began to slow, feeling hopeless and discouraged, falling to his knees. He leaned forward on his arms, breathing heavy, and stumbled upon his back.

"I've made it. I've made it, I've made it. I'm not back in the desert. I'm not back in the sand. I will sleep and find safety tomorrow."

He pushed himself off the ground and looked about, trying to determine his position. Because he had now stopped, the risk of losing direction was too great, and he could therefore not begin walking again. He looked for anything in the distance, be it a building, fire, or even a tree. But the night sun was not bright that night, and he could see nothing but dark horizon.

He dug a slight depression and hugged his now almost empty bladder, curling up.

But sleep did not come.

"I must sleep," he whispered to himself.

He lay there, his eyes closed, and tried to lose himself. But his mind raced with worry. He worried about water and began to contemplate whether he had buried Samaye alive. His body began to shudder with every thought he opposed.

"No. No. No!" he screamed.

"Let me sleep. Please. Let me sleep. I must sleep."

"Let me ponder something beautiful," he thought.

He imagined sleeping in the palm of a giant statue like the ones Samaye had storied. He imagined nothing but the sky above him and the world far below.

"I am in . . . a statue . . ." he whispered. "Safe . . . safe . . . above everything . . .

"Touching the sky . . ."

He began to drift.

"Touching the sky . . ."

The next day, he continued his trek in a similar fashion. He awoke, fueled himself carefully and followed the sun west. He had been mistaken in his delirium the night before, for the shrubbery was certainly denser, and though he had found an isolated patch of soft desert, he was now mostly stumbling upon hard ground. It made steps painful now, for little stones began to poke at his feet which were still bloodied and unhealed.

His energy began to wane, however. It seemed as he neared perceived salvation, his body was equally eager to fade. Perhaps it was the pain in his feet that robbed him of will, but he suddenly began to tire overwhelmingly, as if he simply could not sustain moving his feet forward. He had been travelling for days without anything to eat and was drinking even less water in an effort to preserve the dwindling bladder.

With every sip, he felt discouraged, the water supply being an indirect timekeeper. He knew that he was already worn beyond reason, and once he ran out of water, close as he was, he would fall and never arise.

Earlier than expected, and missing the opportunity of dusk, he stumbled upon the ground in front of him and lost consciousness, exhausted beyond his means.

He awoke the next day, bewildered by fatigue. He had fallen upon a small stone which had pierced his lip, causing him to bleed out. He arose and extracted it, grimacing at the pain. He looked about and saw nothing but shrubs. The sun had already risen, taking position up above him.

He felt hopeless and begrudgingly arose. His feet were bloodied from stones, and he began to walk much slower than before. His feet hurt as he tried to press on, dismally low on energy.

The day wore on, and there were now lifetimes between steps. He opened the bladder and drank the last of the water.

As it emptied into his mouth and there was none left, he stared forward, anger in his brow.

He saw a tree in the distance, but did not react to it, for it seemed incredibly far away. The tree moved, and through his blurred vision, he smiled, watching it dance as if it was waving to him. He fell to his knees and watched it get bigger and bigger. His mind understood now that it was possible this was a man, running to him. But it did not matter anymore. His body had passed numbness, and his mind was now going inwards, preparing for a long dream.

The last thing he felt was the grasp of a human hand on his arm.

"What a strange feeling," he thought.

CHAPTER 21
MEAT

He awoke to a stench, and it surged into his head like a hammer, jolting him out of position, making him nauseous. He pushed himself backwards, striking his head on a ledge. He fell over, his cheek hitting the ground, unmoving. His eyes were glazed and half open as he stared at a flickering light.

A man approached him and patted his back, handing him a cup of water. Aydan drank it quickly and turned arduously to look at the man but could not focus on him.

"Please, more . . ."

The man did not react, and Aydan angrily shoved the cup to him and let out a grunt. The man grabbed the cup and ran to the corner of the room, squatting. He filled it with water, returning it to Aydan.

Aydan swallowed it whole and rolled onto his back, breathing in deeply.

He held his hand out to the man who reached out and grabbed it. Aydan enclosed the man's hand in his and held onto it tightly.

"Thank you . . . endlessly."

The man reciprocated and sat down beside Aydan. He placed his hand on his forehead and began to chant in some foreign dialect.

Aydan kept breathing and felt soothed by the man's words. He reached into his mouth with his fingers and signaled to the man that he was hungry. The man, again, quickly arose and came back with some dried flatbread. Aydan bit into it and slowly chewed, pushing dry morsels down his throat.

He could barely see the man for the darkness in the hut. There was one doorway on the other side of the room, and it was nearly completely black outside. It smelled bad, and Aydan quickly surmised that the man was quite poor. He slowly leaned up and sat on the floor, positioning himself awkwardly, still chewing the flatbread.

Now on the same level as the man, he looked at him. He was thin and wore a wrap around his waist. He did not have shoes and looked almost like an animal. Aydan smiled and thanked him again.

"Do you understand?" Aydan asked.

The man nodded.

Aydan placed his hand on the man's shoulder and sighed.

"Thank you, brother."

The man cleared his throat and began to speak with a strong accent.

"You were impolite to me."

Aydan looked up at him.

"You were impolite to me in asking for a second cup of water. You could have done so more politely."

Aydan stared at him for a moment then looked at where he had been lying.

"I . . . I apologize. I was dying of thirst."

"That is no excuse for rudeness. I have been kind to you, have I not?"

Aydan stared at the man. He swallowed.

"Yes . . . I am thankful, and I apologize for my rudeness."

The man stared at Aydan and smiled, placing his hand on Aydan's shoulder.

"I understand. You were very thirsty, and I did not respond to your request. I was surprised to see you."

Aydan felt uncomfortable and looked down, trying to gather himself.

"Please . . . give me a moment."

He rapidly felt anxious, trying to assert calmness to himself.

"You . . . understand that I was not thinking clearly."

"I understand," the man replied.

"Then why do you seek an apology?"

"I do not wish to have it between us. I felt it rude and wish to put it in the past."

Aydan looked away from the man and thought for a moment.

"I'm not able to think clearly . . . but if you feel that is best . . . I agree. I am thankful you found me."

The man squeezed Aydan's shoulder.

"I am Kaius."

Aydan looked at him.

"My name is Akin."

"Akin . . ." the man responded. "I would like to tell you about my daughter."

Akin bit into the bread and nodded at the man.

"Tell me . . . tell me about your daughter, Kaius."

The man slid closer to Akin and put his arm around him. He pointed to a corner of the hut.

"She sits there . . . do you see her?"

Akin could see nothing.

"I see nothing, Kaius."

"Move, Heina, so that our guest may see you."

Someone shuffled in the darkness and slid into the moonlight. Akin did not expect to hear anything and was unnerved when he first noticed it. She sat on the ground, a girl of a very young age, not even fully grown, with a round belly in front of her. Akin stared at her and nodded his head in greeting.

Kaius grabbed his head and turned it to him.

"You cannot speak to her, Akin."

He looked at Heina.

"She is blessed, Akin, as you can see. She is untouched, yet she carries child. Do you understand? She is impregnated by god!"

Akin stared at the man continuously. His mind buzzed with chaotic feelings, and he could not register anything in a logical manner. He chewed his bread, not fully grasping what he was hearing or seeing, but indulged the man for he sought to be heard.

"Do you understand, Akin?"

Akin nodded.

"What do you see in her?"

Akin looked at her, then back to the man.

"She is impregnated by god, as you said, Kaius."

"Yes, but do you see it? I see it . . . I see the glow about her . . . but do you see it?"

Akin looked at her, trying to witness the glow as per Kaius's desire, but saw nothing but a pregnant little girl.

"I . . . see it, Kaius. It is beautiful."

Kaius looked at him for a moment.

"You don't believe me."

Akin stared at him.

"I will show you. Heina! Lie down!"

Akin frowned as the man approached her. He pulled her tunic up and spread her legs.

"Kaius, this is not necessary," he beckoned. "I believe you, please . . ."

Kaius inserted his finger into her and looked back at Akin.

"Look! Look! Untouched! Look in the light! Untouched by mortal man! She is beautiful!"

Akin pretended to look but instead looked to the side, hearing the sound of the man's fingers in her.

"I believe you, Kaius. You need not do that any longer."

Kaius smiled large and gently closed her legs, pulling her tunic down. He slid next to her and began to whisper things into her ear, kissing her cheek repeatedly.

Akin's stomach began to churn.

"Kaius . . . if you have any more . . . bread and water . . . I would greatly appreciate it. I have not eaten in many days."

Kaius looked at Akin and smiled.

"Of course. I don't have much, but I have enough to feed you, my friend."

Akin ate two more pieces of flatbread and drank another cup of water. He strapped his bladder tight against his body and hugged it before fading into a deep sleep. He was thankful not to be able to feel the breeze of night.

He began to dream. He saw himself kneeling, hunched over the sand, the brightness of the sun searing across the sky. He was in a state of stasis; alive, but unaffected by the elements. All around him was nothing but flat sand and a gentle wind. He stared at the ground before him, wide eyed, struck with some affliction.

He looked up and saw a large object in the distance. It became bigger amidst the waves of bending vision, yet he did not move. Hours, it seemed, as he sat staring at it.

Soon, it came into focus: a huge ornamental throne made of solid stone dragged by hundreds of rugged men. They dressed the same, hunched forward against its weight, with clean, white tunics and red scarves upon them. The throne itself was magnificently large as it tore along the sand.

Akin stared at the throne and the person who sat atop it. It was a woman with golden skin, with a crown upon her head, her almost completely naked body shining against the sun. Her breasts were visible and proportional, her pelvis covered by a small ornament of pristine slivers of gold. He watched as she stared forward, sitting upright as the men pulled her along. Even as they began to reach Akin, she did not seem to notice him. The royal caravan stopped, however, just as it was passing his kneeling body.

It was as if the megalith had never existed, for no one moved or spoke. Akin looked up towards her. Her slender arms were perched upon the throne, gold and beautiful. She, herself, was of immaculate beauty, her lips and nose centered upon her slender face, her long hair tied back tight upon her head, falling straight down along her back.

Her face turned to look towards Akin, and she stood. She beckoned to him with her hand, and he arose, approaching the steps of the throne in his tattered clothes. His hair was disheveled, his face marked with stains and dirt as he walked up the stairs towards her. She stood, staring at him from the summit of the fantastic throne, holding her arms open to him.

As he reached her, she placed one hand at the back of his neck and the other upon his cheek, cradling him in her arms. Though she touched only the back of his neck, his entire body was supported, and he leaned against her hand. She turned his face to her breast and pulled him in. He cupped her breast in his lips and closed his eyes, beginning to drink.

As if detached now, Akin saw the throne from afar as his body began to rise and curl up. He was weightless in her embrace, drinking and suckling the nectar from her warm, tender breast, the most beautiful and esteemed woman he had ever encountered.

Akin awoke with a jolt. Again disoriented, he initially did not know where he was, but the smell and small surroundings reminded him, and he calmed himself, slowing his breathing.

He heard a noise somewhere in the hut and raised his head to investigate. He initially saw nothing, then heard a grunt. He frowned and sat up in place silently, wiping his eyes. In the corner of the hut he could see the top of Heina's head as it slid back and forth in the moonlight. He moved across the hut and caught a glimpse of Kaius who was lying on her, inside her. Akin stared at his face in disbelief. Kaius was ecstatic in his movements, oblivious, it seemed, to anything around him. He was speaking a foreign dialect in little bursts, half smiling, his eyes half-closed as he ran his hands along her pregnant body, pressing himself into her over and over.

Akin looked at Heina's face which was cold and unemotional. She stared at the top of the hut, silently sliding back and forth against the uneven floor.

Akin suddenly sprang to his feet and grabbed Kaius, pressing him against the wall of the hut.

"What are you doing, man?" he yelled.

Kaius remained entranced and did not even register being moved, let alone Akin's query. He reached down and began to stroke himself, continuing to speak in half-words. Akin let him go, and he fell to the ground, rubbing himself as he curled up. He then slowly slid back over to Heina and again started climbing upon her.

Akin stepped back bewildered and stumbled down, leaning against the back of the hut. He stared at Heina's face as her legs swung back and forth, hearing the sounds of their bodies slapping against each other.

He got up once more and threw Kaius off her, against the wall. He grabbed her hand and tried to lift her, dragging her haphazardly out of the hut. She did not stand and instead remained lying, unwilling to walk. Akin leaned down and looked at her in the moonlight.

"Do you understand, Heina? You come with me. You come with me?" he said as he motioned.

She stared at him but did not move or speak.

"I will take care of you. You come with me?"

She suddenly began to scream, and with her screams, Kaius came running out of the hut.

Akin looked up at him and was frozen by the look in his eyes. He struck Akin on the head, flinging him down against the sand and proceeded to drag Heina back into the hut.

He returned to Akin who was grasping his skull in the sand.

"You try to steal my love? My devout love? You try to take her from me?" Kaius screamed, threatening more blows upon Akin.

Akin looked up at him, still cowering, protecting himself with his hands. He stared at Kaius's face which was filled with some furious malcontent, previously hidden from view.

"I will go . . . Kaius . . . I am going now . . ."

Kaius kicked dirt on him and screamed.

"Go! Never return!"

He sat down beside Akin suddenly as Akin cowered defensively. He spoke extremely calmly.

"You must go now, Akin. You could not resist temptation and so you cannot witness this divine birth. You can never return here, do you understand?"

Akin nodded, still frightened of the man.

"There is a large city west of here. You will find like-minded cowards there. It is called Sumat."

The man promptly returned to the hut and left Akin on the sand. Akin's head pulsated as he sat there, frozen. He started to hear the rubbing inside once again, along with Kaius's murmurs. He looked away from the hut, fearful of triggering Kaius again, and began to crawl away, eventually standing and walking. He walked for some time in the darkness, unaware of his direction or destination, completely bewildered and numb.

CHAPTER 22

AWAKENING

Akin ran his tongue along his lip, feeling the tear. As he walked in the darkness, he used his hands to propel himself forward in awkward and unsynchronized manners.

His head pulsated with excitement though he was not excited, and he thought about nothing as he walked in a mundane, inanimate fashion.

He dropped to his knees in the darkness and pressed his hands against the cold sand on either side of him. He focused on his breathing, trying to calm himself.

"Has the world gone mad?" he asked himself quietly.

"I am mad, to close my eyes to it."

He closed his eyes tight and forced envisioning Kaius's furious face.

He suddenly opened his eyes, feeling his head gyrate.

Closing them again, he thought about the image of Heina's small, pregnant, child-like body sliding back and forth in silence against the ground of the hut, the wet sounds of his penetration resonating against the walls.

He opened his eyes and began to hyperventilate slightly, breathing heavily at a quickened pace.

"To hell with you . . . give it to me," he sternly voiced.

He closed his eyes once more and imagined Bethelhurst hitting him as a child. He imagined his small, round, black-haired head being struck by the hand of a large man and envisioned how it would fly in the opposite direction, suddenly, and how he would cower due to the shock, terrified.

He grasped sand in his fist and squeezed, still forcing Bethelhurst's face to the forefront of his mind.

He gritted his teeth and lay down on his side, curling up, still grimacing at the thought.

"Burn me . . . burn me . . . burn me, so that nothing is of surprise . . ."

Tears began to form as the hatred lifted and Bethelhurst became nothing but a man, a father, who tried his best. His thoughts flew to Kaius who he now saw as a troubled man who also tried his best, who did not know what he did. He saw

Heina's eyes in the moonlight and how she too understood his inability, choosing to stay loyal to him.

Akin suddenly opened his eyes and got up, kneeling once again. His eyes were wide and his body stiff. He slammed his fist against the sand and screamed.

"No!!!"

But the scream echoed. He looked about, still enraged, investigating but not distracted.

He looked forward once more, his eyes piercing the night.

"They . . . choose."

He began yelling loudly, banging his fist against the sand.

"They choose!!!"

His words came out estranged and elongated, more the verbalization of an old and buried knowledge, vast and powerful unlike plain speech.

He closed his eyes and let his head drop as the intensity overwhelmed him for an instant.

Again, he opened his eyes and looked forward, as if staring at something though there was nothing to see.

"The bastard chose to desert me."

He fell upon his forearms, now on all fours, breathing heavily against the sand.

"Calm, brother."

Akin paused, hearing a familiar voice.

"Say again?" he beckoned.

"Calm, brother."

Akin leaned back in place, staring forward. He sat quietly for a few moments, calmly thinking. He closed his eyes.

"You are back, demons," he smiled.

The voice laughed back.

"Yes, brother. You have returned as well."

"I hear you . . . within my mind. I hear you loud as any other."

"It is only within your mind that we would be heard, brother."

Akin smiled.

"My name is Akin."

"And you were once known as Aydan. But that is not your name."

"No, it is not," Akin responded.

"It is the name that was given to you."

"Yes, along with many other things."

"But we . . . are alien to those gifts."

"Not gifts . . . not gifts. Demands guised as adoration," Akin responded.

"But now you see . . . Akin . . . we are as familiar as your own voice."

"As familiar as the lines in my palm."

"Are we the cause of your anguish?"

"You are the cause of nothing. The world is as it is, and I am still alive. If I were to speak in my sleep, it would happen tomorrow or the day after, or the last day Aydan lived. It is always precarious to live in fear."

"You were an unwilling participant, Akin."

"Do you understand? The guilt in my heart that I feel I could never escape?"

"There is no guilt, brother. Information is what you seek."

"It is guilt, for the things I have seen and done nothing about. Tobias . . ."

He began to weep, his eyes still closed.

"Tobias danced . . . Tobias danced . . . his mouth wide like a fool in love . . ."

Akin held his hands to his face, a hole ripping through his heart as he absorbed the pure, intense pain of imagining Tobias's face in the moonlight.

"Oh god . . ."

"You are beautiful, brother."

Akin did not respond, but drowned his mind in guilt.

"Look above, brother."

Akin wiped his face and looked up at the night sun. He stared at it, blinking like a small child.

"He stares down at me."

"What is he, brother?"

"A man, perhaps. Some eye in the dark sky, looking down upon us. Knowing . . . seeing all. Seeing all."

"And did this knowing eye guide you? Did he protect you or condemn you?"

Akin kept staring up. He shook his head.

"He has done nothing. He has just watched."

"Hold sand in your hand, brother."

Akin obediently grasped a handful of sand in his hand and lifted it up.

"Things, brother. Things that do not and have not ever altered the course . . . but remain constants in this life . . . the sand, the wind . . . do you truly believe they have hearts and memory?"

Akin stared at the sand as it drizzled out of his hand.

"I believe the sand has memory. I believe the wind speaks to us. I believe the night sun watches us and holds memory of everything. It has memory of all of this and is ageless."

"Akin . . ."

"Yes?"

"Did the night sun see Aydan the last night of his life?"

"Yes. It watched and holds memory of it. It saw me . . . it saw me carried away in the night. It reflects this memory back to me."

"Akin . . . the night sun has no memory. It witnesses nothing. It is as the sand is, for it affects nothing. It is as a stone . . . a constant, dead constant."

Akin shook his head.

"It is there . . . he is there. I can feel it. I can feel him now, staring upon me."

"It grants you calm, brother. But close not your eyes to your surroundings. Look about! You are in the desert, and upon the sand. You are alone, and it is quiet. These are our environments, brother. You are alone."

Akin shook his head again, grimacing slightly.

"There is something. There is something."

He looked up.

"There is something!"

"Look upon it, Akin, and ask yourself if what you receive from the light in the sky is something you did not create within yourself."

Akin began to break up, crying in sadness.

"I am not alone . . ."

"You . . . are . . . alone."

Akin held himself, terrified with gloom.

"I am not alone . . . I am not alone . . ."

He looked about, for it was as if the wind disappeared along with all sounds and distant murmurs. The stillness may have been there all along, but not so piercing as it was at that moment.

He imagined himself in the center of the universe, a circle of night diminishing around him, and nothing else but sand. Even the temperature seemed to drop as he shivered.

He looked up at the night sun and observed, it seemed for the first time, that it just stood there, unmoving. He had always seen it look here and there, but now noticed it shimmer, just as things shimmered in the desert.

It did not move, and it did not speak, and Akin felt it to be dead.

He looked straight in front of him. In the darkness was a void in every direction. It was Akin in the middle of the unknown. No one was witnessing this moment, he thought. No one was observing it, sharing it. In all the times that passed and all the times to come, no one would ever know of this moment except him. He was the only witness.

"You . . . are alone . . ." he said to himself, his eyes still open, focused on the words as if they were in the darkness before him.

"You . . . are alone . . . Akin."

"Is it worth it, brother?"

"Is what worth it?" he asked.

"Is this moment worth it if only you are witness to it?"

Akin sat there, thinking, staring. His eyes shifted side to side, reacting to the tempo of his thoughts.

"Are you worth this moment, Akin?"

"It is my moment," he replied, breaking up.

"It is your moment, Akin."

"It is my moment," he said out loud, feeling shivers run up his spine, overtaking his body. "It is my moment, and it is glorious."

His eyes widened, and he looked down upon the sand, pressing his palm against it. He felt the grains against his skin and closed his eyes, grimacing in euphoria.

"Oh, za . . .

"This is glorious.

"I . . . see . . . things."

"What do you see, brother?"

"I see the sand, and it is an ocean. And in this ocean there is life. Little creatures swimming about. It is . . . breathing."

He lay down on his stomach, his head perched forward, staring at the brown sand in front of him.

"This sand . . ." he said, staring intently at some grains in front of him, "is old."

"How old, brother?"

"Ancient. Timeless. It has no memory, but has witnessed everything that has ever happened. And now it sits in front of me. It is . . . in front of me. And it is immortal."

He lay there, staring.

"I am . . . of life."

"You are love, brother. Love."

CHAPTER 23

WONDROUS THINGS

"**M**mmm . . . if love were alive, it would breathe between us."

Akin stirred.

"You are . . . beautiful. Sex in your breathing, that I could taste it like nectar upon my tongue . . . hearing it, feeling it . . . mmmm . . ."

The whispers were close to his ears, the quiet moaning a raspy hum. He could feel the heat of the man's breath upon his cheek as he spoke. His hand slid across Akin's neck, running along his skin. He gently pulled Akin's head into his lap, stroking his hair while he slept.

"You are a blasphemer.

"We are together.

"I will clean you."

As he opened his eyes, he saw Bethelhurst on his knees in the darkness, looking at him. His hands were clasped together in a submissive state. He felt hands upon his head and looked up, staring at a ghoulish, masked figure.

"Hello, Aydan."

The man covered Akin's mouth and nose with his hands, twisting his neck in an awkward position. Wide eyed, Akin saw dark figures in the doorway watching as he choked. Bethelhurst sat and watched, his hands still perched together, his face frightened.

Akin began to yell in muffled screams as he suffocated. His hands jolted up, trying to pry the man's grip away from him, but soon lost consciousness.

Visions flew past his mind, far above the hut, looking down upon it in the moonlight. Then, the night sun, visible and bright, loud, as if a magnificent sound emanated from it, filled his vision. It rumbled louder than anything he had ever heard before.

Akin spoke to it, staring forward, his eyes in a fixated position.

"You do not exist, do you?"

It did not respond, but continued to rumble. Akin stared at it.

"I love you and fear you . . . but you are nothing."

The rumbling intensified.

"You are nothing."

The rumbling became worse, shaking the air around him. He held his hands in front of him, his fingers apart, palms facing the night sun, and sternly looked at it.

"You are nothing."

As he ended his words, the rumbling stopped, and Akin began to fall. Through the sky he saw the ground beneath him, far away but approaching fast. The wind burned his face, and fear surged through his body.

He slowly opened his eyes. It was still night, but dawn was upon him for he could sense a creeping brightness.

He lay there, half asleep, rubbing his legs and arms, periodically trying to warm himself. He eventually rolled over and found himself sitting, his head hanging loosely down, his eyes closed.

"The . . . way . . ." he muttered.

"I am alone.

"I am alone."

He looked up at the still barely starry sky.

"I did not know . . ." he cried suddenly. "I did not know you hurt me so . . .

"But never again," he said sternly, breathing in.

"I'll not hide."

He got up and dusted his tunic of sand and looked about, trying to get a bearing of his location. He could make out the sun rising in the distance and began to walk opposite. The ground was still sandy with shrubs and stones, and he paced himself, trying to minimize his fatigue and the pain upon the soles of his feet. He thought of people and food and drink.

As he walked, he briefly wondered if the dream had been true and soon felt sure that it was. He had seen himself being carried away the night before he awoke in a cave, but it was just a dream . . . some half-true vision his wounded head had materialized. He was alone in that cocoon, just as he had been alone as he slept in his bed.

As the sky brightened, he began to cross marks made by caravans. In the distance, he could see objects moving and squinted, the blur appearing to be a group of travelers with their bovin.

He instinctually ran his hand along the back of his neck and continued walking.

Sumat. He had heard of the great Temple City through tales of tales. Culture was thick there, his own village being a frequent pilgrimage destination for aristocrats from neighboring cities, including Sumat.

As he walked, he felt his chest tighten. Encountering others would inevitably require some clandestine story. His face and feet were mangled, and there was no explanation for his tattered clothing. He could pretend to be a distant traveler, but his perfect accent would make that story inconsistent.

One fact was certain . . . he could not be Aizik. His people were known to the holy area surrounding his village, and if the mark on the back of his neck were recognized, he would attract unwarranted and superstitious attention. Strangely, what was once looked upon as an idyllic birth caste was now his primary concern. Even now, distant from all things familiar, he felt it rushing back to him as he was forced to cope with yet another unwanted relic of his heritage.

He looked about to ensure no one was in the visible distance and pulled the tunic off his head. He looked at the dried blood and sat in place thinking of Samaye. Sadness once again struck him as he considered the excitement and beauty that would have been this trek had his friend been with him. He imagined this moment and walking up to the Sumati walls with his friend, his innocence bouncing off the city in awe.

He wrapped the tunic in a ball and buried it in the sand. He pulled his hair back, pressing sand into it to try to force it down. He straightened out his tunic as much as he could and used dirt to try to clean it. He rubbed sand all over his body, exfoliating himself, and stood, shaking all the dust off. He shook his head and ran his hands through it, removing as much grit as possible.

Again, he looked around and reached behind to touch his neck. He untied the cloths from under his feet and found a way to create a veil with them, covering the back of his head and neck from the sun. He rubbed sand off the wounds and began to walk, frowning as a sharp pain shot up his leg. He walked slower but now looked more like a poor, benign traveler than he did before.

As he approached the first caravan, he was greeted by the heads of two families. Their women stood behind the animals and the children walked in tow. They had two bovin that were led by the men.

Upon meeting them, he saw that they had many bladders hoisted upon the bovin, and though his knees quaked when he greedily eyed them, he remained calm and controlled.

He smiled and greeted them, talking with them about their trip and purpose. They were visiting the city from a village to the south and intended to sell their wares of pots. If they sold well, they would try to make the trip more often and would even consider moving to the city if their success provided sufficient means for them to do so.

Akin smiled and nodded, quickly reading their expectations of him and conforming to their social structure. The women were mostly ignored as were the children, and the chatter of the men was the only talk that was loud enough to hear. Strategically, Akin found a pause in their talks and asked if he could share in their water. The men indulged him happily, stopping the caravan long enough to wait for him to refresh himself.

As he first tasted the water upon his lips, he felt his body buckle but tightened his muscles aggressively to control himself, nearly grunting. He did not want to appear destitute nor starving, and the large bladder he carried with him lent him the unique aura of a traveller. He could not drink too much, nor too little, but just the right amount a man would drink if he were thirsty from a long walk.

He closed the bladder and thanked the men, continuing to walk with them, tensing his legs with every step to nullify the pain from his soles.

CHAPTER 24
MISERY

Akin often thought about his first day in Sumat. He remembered peering at the high walls and adjacent waterway that lined the Temple City. He remembered walking through the wide gates amongst more people than he had ever seen, his clothes tattered, still reeking of excrement and blood. So many different smells and dialects whirl winded around him with animals and goods all coming and going to trade and barter.

Sumat was ruled by an Oam whose palace was shadowed by the Temple of Mala. The temple was the center of the city and stood large, looming above everything else. Only aristocrats and priests were permitted inside, and the poor hugged its steps to receive bheek. Food was not scarce but was still hoarded and controlled by the few wealthy families at the top of the hierarchy. It was distributed to the masses in minute quantities but was mostly used as currency to trade amongst each other for property or favors.

Akin had initially liked the noise of busy days. Every morning, there was a backlash upon the first peddler that began to yell, promoting his wares. Residents would scream at him from their mud-brick houses, and he would scream back, defending his right to make a living, just as the sun was transitioning from red to yellow.

Akin had never seen the Oam or his kin. The elite of Sumat, however, visited the temple regularly for blessings or prayers, some carried in jeweled and enclosed transports.

The surrounding city walls stood tall and were always guarded. A nearby river had been diverted to line the side of the city and was the source of all the water for its inhabitants. The Oam's source was at the top of the stream, and it was an offence punishable by death for anyone but his slaves to go there. Guards patrolled the river at all times ensuring that the Oam's supply was untainted by lower castes.

Every morning, people would leave the city to make their collections, bringing back containers of water for use that day. The wealthier, the higher up they were permitted to collect. Wealth determined everything relating to one's class structure, and the environment in Sumat was very different than that of Akin's village. Amongst the Aizik, a man could do any job as long as he had the tenacity to pursue it. In Sumat, he saw no choice but to sit amongst the dregs of the city and beg for shel, adding to the pandemonium.

When he first arrived, he sought to eat and drink but found people to be hostile towards him. Somehow they knew he carried no shel and ignored his requests, even if they were just queries for information. Even the family he had encountered as he approached the city seemed to change once inside, becoming more distant and uninterested in goodwill, treating Akin as a guest who had outstayed his welcome.

As that first day wore on, he became increasingly desperate in watching people eat and drink. His stomach churned, and just as the day began to end, he remembered leaving the city in anxiety. He followed the beggars to the end of the waterway and leaned down to drink. The water at that point was filthy, having been polluted with waste by those superior in position, higher upstream. He coughed at it, his throat reacting to the bitter taste of the unclean liquid, his stomach immediately feeling ill. Further away, even lower than the unknowns were the diseased and invalid, drinking the wasteful water that was being used by everyone else to not only drink but cleanse themselves.

He remembered looking out at the desert, feeling hopeless at the prospect of entering it once more, looking for a better place. He could not legitimize such a decision, both because he could not conceive of a better place and because he was terrified of the anguish he had suffered in getting to Sumat. More than all of that, perhaps, was his exhaustion, not just for poor health and hunger, but a heavy weight that seemed to be depressing his mind, robing it of tenacity.

That night, he returned to the city as darkness fell and began staring at the ground as he walked, seeking scraps of food from animals and humans alike. He fed his belly with half eaten legumes, uncooked barley and small crumbs of bread. He pressed his thumb into crevices of brick to gather food bits in his skin, licking down unsatisfying pinches of crumb and dust. He began to loathe tasting his bladder which was now filled with filthy water, laced with a foul bitterness that made him gag with every sip.

The city became quiet at night, though the streets housed various vagrants sleeping here and there. There was an ominous feeling that lined the alleys as the once loud and busy city became relatively quiet, though it felt as if underneath that stillness was vivid movement driven by drunks and thieves, iconized by dasha embers that remained burning all through the night.

Akin had felt uneasy by the sudden isolation and sought to hide himself, though the more hospitable nooks and crannies were aggressively defended by others. He eventually found a small corner between two houses and lay down using some animal feed to cushion various parts of his body that were hard against the unforgiving ground. His head ached most severely, for he was not used to being flat against the ground nor robbed of heat for the cold brick underneath. He tried using his hands to prop his head up and felt chilly as he first lay there, though after some time, the small, roughly enclosed corner slowly heated up through his warm breaths and curled body.

There was some comfort in seeing a random stranger walk by the corridor without noticing him, and he felt safe being hidden for the first time in a long time, that first night.

Every day that followed held the same ritual. He spent most of the day trying to gather enough clean food to fill his stomach, and on more lonesome and hopeless days he would join the poor in begging. He met with acquaintances, some who helped him find tailors that would mend his clothes when he needed it in exchange for work. He did not trust anyone, however, as he quietly observed small incongruities pass from person to person as each of the people he met appeared to be just as vindictive as the vendors and shoppers, ready to turn their back upon anyone if it meant more shel.

He had to change sleep locations every now and then as the dwellers of nearby houses would eventually discover him and beat him away. He tried to habituate himself to rise earlier and move out quietly so as to keep his location secret but was always eventually found out. Sometimes it would be the woman of the house in the morning and other nights it would be a drunk husband seeing Akin out of the corner of his eye. Both instances involved a brutal and angry reaction which Akin had become somewhat accustomed to. When and if it occurred, he would calmly rise and gather his belongings, moving away. If they tried to hit him, he would stare at them and attempt to steer their hands away from him as he walked off. This did not alter their behavior nor did it prevent him from being struck a lot of the time, though it did seem to surprise many who expected him to beg for mercy, which he never did.

Akin had much time to think, and as days wore on, he spoke less and less. He pondered Samaye and thought about his body, wondering how far it had decomposed under the heated desert sky. He thought about Bethelhurst and the village and seemed to fill his heart with distaste towards everything he knew, remembered, and witnessed with each passing day.

At times, it occurred to him that he never had much interest in thinking about his mother and even tried to remember her face, but the thought seemed fleeting, and he always found something more pressing to do or think about.

Sumat had been known to him as the Temple City, and even now, at this moment, as he tried to sleep, so long after his arrival here, it appeared to be something much more dirty and convoluted than he had thought possible. His last passing thought was of unknown people and places, and if there existed in the world anything as pure as its name.

CHAPTER 25
CABAL

Akin awoke upon small morsels of old grain and looked through them for something edible. He found a few pieces and wiped them against his tunic, biting into them, separating and spitting out sand and chewing the rest. He then put rotting hay aside and picked up the rest, placing it in a small woven pouch, then got up.

The sun was starting to rise, and he cautiously peered around the nearby corners to ensure no one was walking by. He noticed a man meandering drunkenly past in the distance. The wrappings around his feet indicated he was a member of Kunda Sumai. Akin stayed hidden until he was out of view and quickly dashed through the winding corridors, heading for the city gate.

It was some ways to walk, and he felt uncomfortable every morning until other city dwellers awoke, diluting his presence. Being one of the few people awake so early gave him the opportunity to scavenge the streets for salvageable hay and food. Waking early was amongst one of the many tactics a beggar could employ to improve his position, even if only marginally, and Akin's mind naturally gravitated towards discovering such loopholes in what seemed to be a saturated industry.

He always sat near the city gate, but out of view, waiting for the main flock of people to awaken and head to the river. Some days, his system would hurt terribly as he sought to relieve himself but dared not be one of the first few people to go through the gates, striking the possibility that he could be randomly noticed and interrogated by the guards. Although he could sometimes urinate in small corners when it was too much to bear, releasing his bowels was another matter altogether, and a few times when the pressure was excruciating he would defecate into his own tunic and carry it with him until he reached the river. It was a crime to do either in the streets, and although he could get away with urinating, as many people did, if he was caught defecating anywhere in the city public, the penalty could be severe.

Eventually, the city awoke and the gates burst with people going out to perform their morning duties. He never arose until a portion of the people who had first left the city returned and there was a natural two way flow. He looked around and once again dashed out of his hiding spot, joining the mass exodus out of the gates.

Every person had their duties to perform and depending on their caste did so with other members at specific locations. All the vagrants proceeded to nearly the farthest point from the city, a procession of tattered clothes and slow walking. They would all defecate together in specific areas and cover their mess with sand then proceed to the river to cleanse themselves. Akin dug a small ditch, bent down, releasing himself, then arose, covering it in dirt. He walked to the river which was some ways away and grabbed handfuls of water with which to cleanse his hair, face, arms, under arms, legs and privates. He ran his hands along his head, savoring the cool feeling of water radiating heat through his hair. It was a soothing, pleasant feeling he enjoyed and looked forward to.

He was always sure to keep his neck covered, though with the amount of oil and dirt upon their skin, it was hard to notice any specific markings or symbols on any of the poor in the city. Not only were they ignored by the people, but they had grown to ignore each other save their rivalries for food and drink.

As he walked back to Sumat, he prepared for another day of begging. Unlike the others, however, Akin repeatedly did so with some progressive creativity and the hope that some truth would come of the experience, giving him an understanding of something greater that would allow him to improve his situation. His body had become thinner, his face darker and both his beard and hair had grown long, obfuscating the Aizik boy from view.

It was a race to find a prosperous position near the temple steps, though Akin rarely engaged in it. He walked calmly through the hustle and invested in the belief that wherever he should find himself would be the best position for him that day. Even amongst the poor there were politics, with groups shunning others in order to horde bheek, an elderly group of them always occupying the closest areas to the temple aggressively.

He placed his satchel under his body and sat down, crossing his legs. He looked like an alternate version of himself, as if the boy that was Aydan had disappeared and a quiet man who looked similar to him had taken his place.

He spoke very little and had learned to pick his targets more selectively than the rest. He watched people come and go and stared at their eyes, trying to read them.

He observed a young woman dressed in clean, unscathed garments descend the temple steps, perhaps a daughter of an Iman Ir. She was not a girl, but rather a woman seeking her place amongst her peers.

He held his hands up and looked at her feet submissively.

"If the kindness in your heart matches the grace in your step, I would be a very lucky man today."

Amongst the words and beckoning of other beggars, Akin's accent and vocabulary stood out, as did his unapologetic tone, which appeared to be at an equal footing to those he begged from. Some reacted dismissively to this while others reacted otherwise, feeling uplifted by being superior to someone who appeared to have some modus of self-respect. Even his words formed a sort of poetic verse, being both whimsical and intelligent at the same time.

The woman looked at him and stopped mid-step which was uncommon for someone like her to do, but did so in trying to explore the source of the words. When she saw how he looked with his head facing downwards, she assumed he was just a clever beggar and as a reward dropped some shel in front of him and walked away.

This was advantageous to Akin. He wanted to be memorable enough to trigger a response out of those he targeted but easily forgotten and ignored when looked upon. He dared not make eye contact so as to pique the interest of others, especially the women of the elite. Improper behavior towards them was dangerous, and if he made no eye contact and did not touch them, he was safe from most prying eyes. This was their fallacy; they failed to understand that well placed words could manipulate a person far more subtly than physical control, and because of this oversight on their part, he was able to advantageously affect the corrupt aristocracy while remaining irrelevant.

He smiled to himself, acknowledging the trick he had pulled over the young woman as he pocketed his shel.

"A conditional compliment," he thought, "for if you are to have a graceful step, you must display your kindness to me."

"And," he smirked under his beard, still thinking, "if you were to give me bheek, you would affect this man, a man, a man superior to all females in this place . . . you would affect this man's day, aiding you in feeling more powerful than the many men you are surrounded by allow you to."

He looked back up, watching people as he sought his next target. It did not work much of the time, however, as it was difficult to be noticed adequately by people who were steadily walking past. He sat thinking about his mischievousness and whether it was improper to fool the girl as he did.

"I am taking advantage of her own illusions," he whispered under his breath, so quietly it was as if he simply worded it with his lips. "She tricks herself."

Akin targeted only the benign affluent and never those with real power. He never looked at or spoke to Manu priests nor the Iman Ir for they were formed of aggressive men who had the rights to do as they wished. Even their wives held an aura of cold-bloodedness that Akin viewed as inherently dangerous.

The Iman Ir were military leaders in Sumat, and though they paraded the streets in illustrious war helmets and tunics, their influence was mostly political. Their ranks were exclusive to their bloodlines, and the sons of members were guaranteed both wealth and power. Those kin that did not have the tenacity for their leadership pursued the Manu priesthood which also held a great deal of power and esteem.

As the Iman Ir and their families passed him on the steps, overflowing with wealth, Akin never pursued them. Other beggars did and were rewarded for it, for even in their inherited positions they benefited from appearing generous. The priests themselves never gave out bheek except on special occasions, and never from their own coffers, for they had access to the endless collection of shel that was tithed in the name of Mala.

The Manu priests were a dirty lot to Akin, and he felt their pious behavior was a disgusting charade given what he had both seen and heard about them. They were an adulterous lot who, though they could not marry, satisfied their urges with every female and male they could safely reach, be it a prostitute seeking absolution, a farmer's daughter who needed a blessing, or a young, homeless boy. He imagined their lustful tongues which contrasted their subdued public behavior and royal appearance.

It was at night that many of the victims would leave the temple, violated and crying as they returned home. They feasted on the poor: widows and the dejected - all targets that had no means of recourse for a lack of any sort of social footing. Every night, it seemed, Akin would try to find a location to sleep that had some view of the temple, hoping to catch a glimpse of the result of that night's debauchery. The temple was an ominous place at night, filled with the ghosts of anguish, though nothing was ever heard or observed by outsiders. Even the women and children that had survived its belly said nothing, nor were they questioned about it. The Manu priests were permitted to do as they pleased with the lower classes, and it was considered sacrilegious to maintain ill-memory of such events, let alone speak of them.

The temple loomed over the city, its steps leading to some hellish gateway laced with bright, yellow embers that were kept burning night and day. It had the mystical aura to both frighten and attract those that looked upon it for its vulgar secrecy, for the priests had absolute freedoms bestowed upon them, sexual and otherwise. They were held in the highest regard, second only to the Iman Ir who, though traditionally knelt before them in religious processions, were only facetious in their subservience. It was apparent that the priests needed the Iman Ir's sword far more than the sword needed them.

The Iman Ir formed the Sumati military leadership, and their might was enforced by soldiers from the lower class, expendable men known as the Kin Ir. Joining the Kin Ir was one of the only ways a poor man ascended his position, and though he was a permanently disposable extension of the Iman Ir, he benefited from being able to proudly walk the streets of Sumat, freely thrusting himself upon those in even worse financial positions.

Like the Iman Ir, they wore their uniforms at all times as an assertion of dominance. And though they were to be feared, their power was restricted to the lower castes. Their ascendance within the Sumati hierarchy was shallow from a grand perspective, for they were treated quite irrelevantly by the Sumati elite, just as any commoner was. The limits of their social promotion was determined not by skill or ambition, but by an arbitrary line that ensured no common man could break the ranks of an ancient and homogeneous caste system.

Being a street dweller, Akin was commonly harassed by the Kin Ir, but since he had nothing to be extorted or thieved, they mostly left him alone. Their main focus was street vendors, prostitutes and visitors to the city who were routinely pressed for extra shel or bartered favors.

As a result of their opportunities, they became some of the wealthiest of the poor, parading the streets at all hours of night, drinking and whoring, often spending their shel on women, even beating on the poor simply for the sheer freedom to do it. Akin had heard other, more elaborate stories about conspiratorial murders, rape and thievery, but had not witnessed acts of that severity. Even if such events did occur, they would have been kept secret, for the Iman Ir would be under pressure by the Oam to quell overblown acts of violence. Overall, their corruption was self-evident, but it was the way things were, just as the sex workers did what they did, as did the shop-keepers and the rest of the city's inhabitants.

Akin looked in his satchel and counted his shel. He had enough to purchase a small meal and some more hay which he would use to sit and sleep on. The sandal on his left foot was also wearing thin, and as he walked, he was able to feel little pebbles underneath his foot. If he got up to spend his shel, he would lose his position. But since he had already spent the first part of the day sitting there, begging, he decided it was time for food.

He gathered his belongings and arose. Even as he started doing so, another beggar slid into his place, pushing him out of the way. He looked at the man who looked back at Akin. There was no reaction in his face, and it was as if he was already communicating that he wanted Akin to move on so he could resume asking for bheek.

Food was cheap in Sumat for the plentiful river and all the farms that surrounded it. Even so, he had to work every day to feed himself, but spending his shel at a dasha was one of the few enjoyable moments of his day.

Dasha littered the streets as food was the main trade in Sumat. Vendors were dining experts, having owned the same dasha their entire lives, itself being passed down from generation to generation. Sumat was an old city and had generated a plethora of unique culinary traditions, each ghetto naturally adding a unique spice and flavor that had evolved over the years.

Akin had grown fond of a particular restaurant deep in the Kunda Mashaya ghetto. Kunda Mashaya was one of the vendor tribes of the city. They forced tribute from many of the families that ran businesses in Sumat and engaged in daily skirmishes with Kunda Sumai, the other tribe.

Both were unofficially empowered by the Iman Ir. Kunda Mashaya, however, being the local Kunda, was larger and more influential. Kunda Sumai was organized by foreigners that had made Sumat their permanent home. Being the foreign tribe, it was frowned upon by the local Ir, but due to their distant connections and the wealth they brought to the city, Sumai shopkeepers were privy to similar protections that were given to Mashaya.

Underneath the family associations were racial tensions that routinely exploded over mundane arguments, sometimes resulting in bloodshed that led to larger feuds.

Both groups were in unofficial partnership with various Kin Ir, often using them for tasks and jobs, and they employed the local police as much as the Iman Ir did. Like the Iman Ir, the Kin Ir were influenced to give precedence to the local tribe if given the choice, but co-existence with Kunda Sumai had become a requirement they fulfilled, even if begrudgingly so.

Kunda Sumai's territory was smaller than Mashaya, but they had access to exotic goods which made the shops they controlled extremely valuable for trade in the city. Kunda Mashaya was an ancient organization with long standing roots in and around Sumat. Their vocabulary, accents, and traditions were deeply rooted in the general ambience of Sumat, and as one entered their corner of the city, the unique smells of their dasha was always the first thing to greet them.

Akin proceeded down the Juma corridors between the mud-brick houses, navigating a path he had walked many times before, heading towards Meso, a Mashaya dasha. Even as he caught sight of it, the smells of garlic and onions made him salivate, and he didn't even notice some spit trickling down his mouth, disappearing into his beard. He approached cautiously and waited, holding shel in his hand to ensure it was the first thing they saw when they looked at him.

"What do you want?" a boy in the front of the dasha asked.

"Minari," Akin responded.

"Five shel," the boy replied casually.

Akin took out three shel and handed it to him.

"Five! Five! I said five!" the boy yelled back.

Akin looked up at him, piercing the young man with his eyes. He knew the cost of a minari was three shel.

The boy grinned slightly and turned to look inside, yelling. "Minari!"

He motioned for Akin to get out of the way of other customers and resumed watching the inside of the dasha.

Soon, the boy whistled at him and handed him his food.

Akin walked quickly, looking for a spot to sit and eat and eventually found a corner. He placed his satchel underneath him and sat, feeling the warmth of the green leaves against his palm. He slowly unwrapped them, revealing steaming hot chickpeas fried in garlic and onion. He leaned down and smelled it, closing his eyes. He bit a piece of the green leaf and placed one chickpea in his mouth, sucking the juices off it before chewing it tenderly and slowly, savoring the taste.

Akin loved minari because it was cheap, quick, portable, and he could eat the entire meal as it was wrapped in edible foliage. After picking off the chickpeas one by one, he would re-wrap the leaves with all the onion, garlic, and juices inside and lift it so that as he bit into it, the gravy flowed into his mouth. He loved hearing the crispy onions crunch inside his jaw, then taste them as they released their flavor. Even as he finished his minari, he did not feel empty or sad. It was as satisfying as he had always wished it to be and never allowed himself to feel regretful for having eaten it too fast, or in bites too big. He had begun to reject entertaining regrets about anything he did, for thoughts of Bethelhurst and his previous life made him despise the artificial feeling of self-loathing he had lived with for much of it.

He arose, licking his fingers, and picked up his satchel, proceeding to collect more shel from the rich of Sumat.

That night, Akin found a particularly comfortable little niche with a spectacular view of the temple. Not only was the temple visible, but behind him was a dark patch of crevice that snuck behind a house, putting him completely out of view. He would remain here, staring at the temple until he became sleepy. Then he would crawl into the hidden corner, safe from the elements and people alike.

He had forgotten about this place, which was quite hard to get to. It was not on the same level as the other houses and took some navigating to find. He remembered an entire family of poor had occupied it and shooed him away the second time he tried to return. But now it was vacant, and Akin wondered if they had left Sumat, found a house to live in, or were somehow in the employ of the chosen few.

"They had a daughter," he worded under his beard. "So who knows."

He stared at the temple and watched the flickering fires in the distance. It was a quiet night, cooler than usual. The serenity of it calmed him, and he pondered what Bethelhurst was doing at that exact moment. He wondered if the Council had punished his father for his escape, but felt it was unlikely.

"They knew he was an obedient man, and his own rage at my departure would convince them of his conviction," he whispered to himself.

"Obedient man," he thought. "So much so, that even as I clamored to my father in those last moments, my hand reaching out of my cell like a little boy . . . the man turned his critical gaze to me."

Akin visualized the cave's awful aura when the Fayem first lit it. A dark hue emanated from the solitary flame, barely lighting the room, casting dismal shadows in every direction. Little eyes peered out the cells, terrified of the light.

His heart sank, and hurt, reminding him of the cell to his right . . . where dear Samaye was caged . . . and the horrific abuse that was cast upon his brother.

Akin pressed his hand against his closed eyes, trying not to cry. He breathed in and out, thinking of Samaye's face as they walked out as free men that first and last night. He remembered a still image of his friend in the moonlight, more gentle and loving than his soothing voice had been in the darkness.

He stared forward sternly, thinking about Samaye's leg as it protruded out of the sand.

"Suffocated . . . perhaps? No . . ." he shook his head. "He died in my arms . . . or in my lap. He spoke to me . . . did he not?

"I do not remember."

He covered his face in his hands again, this time unable to keep the tears at bay.

CHAPTER 26

THE ORACLE

Akin woke up later than usual. The ideal little hub he had found to sleep in sheltered him from most of the sunlight, and the busy day in Sumat that had already begun.

He pressed his hand against the rough brick of the house and pulled himself up, still groggy from his long sleep.

He stood there, leaning against the wall, trying to focus himself to regain his balance. He leaned down and picked up his satchel, lost his balance, and fell back down. He sat there awkwardly and started smiling, feeling casual about his morning.

"Well, I know I will get hungry . . . so I can't sit here forever, comfortable as it is . . ." he worded with his lips.

He slid some ways forward, enough to peer down the corridor that led to the street to check for people. Sumatis were walking by every now and then, so getting out would be slightly tricky. People did not like vagrants around their homes, and Akin would have to both walk fast and time it right so that no one noticed him or where he came from.

He gathered his things and initiated bolting a few times, quickly retracting back into the crevice upon seeing someone pass by. He started smiling after the third time, finding humorous irony in the sudden appearance of people just as he started to walk.

Eventually, he felt safe and ran out of the spot, walking straight down towards the center of the city. Immediately, he heard a yell behind him.

"Dasheet!"

Akin stopped and turned, facing two smiling Kin Ir.

"Where did you come from, little man?" one man asked.

Akin stared at him and said nothing, clutching his satchel.

"It is morning, and it is a beautiful day, dasheet. Give me your shel and you can go."

Akin looked up at the man, furiously.

The man stared back at him, smiling continuously.

Akin looked down and reached into his satchel and pulled out three shel, giving it to the man.

"Is that all you have?" he asked.

Akin looked at him and said nothing.

"Fine, get out of here."

The man struck Akin on the forehead with his palm, propelling him backwards, falling on his behind.

"Go now!" he yelled at him angrily.

Akin picked up his things and turned his back, walking away.

The river was not as busy as usual, and Akin took his time washing his face and hair and drinking his fill. His thigh hurt considerably, forcing him to limp to avoid irritating the bruise. He wore a constant scowl under his beard, noticing nothing around him, firmly lost in his thoughts and feelings.

"And if I did anything . . . and if I did anything. If I did anything . . ."

He pondered what happened and initially blamed himself for sleeping later than he should have. His resolve to never let that happen again became severe, and he suddenly realized that he was condemning himself for being jovial.

"A crime . . . a fucking crime . . ." he said, frustrated under his breath. Some people at the river looked at him, then resumed their duties. He looked back and talked quieter.

"To smile . . . to smile. To smile for awakening. Is it a crime? Is it a crime? Am I a true criminal . . . is it inherently immature to let oneself go?"

He started to become frustrated and had to remind himself to be quieter as his voice started to get loud.

"Fuck this city. Fuck these people who sit by me and use the river."

He looked at them with malice in his eyes. Old people, slowly washing clothes or their curled, wrinkled flesh surrounded the waterway. He looked at their sagging skin.

"Just what have you done with your lives, your useless wasted lives. You eat and wash and go home to a poisonous life. You are poison, and you keep eating and shitting."

He stared at a middle aged woman who was eating some bread. She had no awareness of the world around her and chewed with her mouth open, oblivious to anything. There was something oddly insane building in his head as he stared at her.

"You . . . are an animal. A dog. You eat and eat . . . and shit . . . all you know is what you want. I am just a phantom in your dream."

He became numb and suddenly felt nothing. He slowly picked his things up and began to walk back towards the city, staring at the sand. The gates looked alien to him, all the motion in between them a blur. He felt like he would faint but somehow kept walking even though it seemed everyone around him was gyrating strangely.

He reached the center circle, the maza, and sat in a less visible spot, but still the best spot he could find. He held his satchel in his hand, and his stomach began to hurt. He pulled his hands up to his face and started to breathe deeply, trying to calm himself.

He stared down at the ground in front of him, focusing on some sand and pebbles.

"That I should be shamed for smiling," he said out loud.

Some men around him looked at him oddly but resumed begging from passersby.

"That it is . . . shameful . . . to release oneself of fear," he said, louder, ending his sentence angrily.

Those around him looked at him uncomfortably and avoided acknowledging his presence. A few old men began to yell at him to keep quiet. Akin looked at them and smiled.

"What have you done with your lives? You wasted old men!"

Some men arose and began to yell, threatening him. He remained seated and looked up at them, smiling slightly.

"You'll hurt me . . . for them . . . until they hurt you, for themselves."

"Stop with your nonsense or I'll teach you some manners!" one man yelled.

Akin suddenly pointed past them and yelled.

"Ir!"

They all looked back, petrified, preparing to cower back to their seats. There was nothing behind them. They looked back at a smiling Akin, furious.

"Keep your fear . . . in your heart!" he slapped his chest. "Eat it! Grow it! Procreate it!" he yelled.

Still unnerved, they sat down, one by one, staring at Akin. He pointed at them.

"But you . . . every one of you. Keep it away from me."

They all spoke amongst each other and resumed begging shortly thereafter, choosing in unison to ignore him. He did not notice, as he was staring at the ground in front of him, his body becoming limp and began to fall into a delirious state.

"Give me some shel if you adore terror," he said casually, without focus.

"Give me some shel if you want me to fear you."

He randomly continued to speak without focus. Every now and then he would say something of a similar nature, targeting it at no one. Each time he spoke, the others around him became tense, hoping he would get up and leave.

The gaps in between his statements increased as he tired.

"I am hungry . . . and I fear nothing will satisfy my hunger. So I should be hungry for what you hunger . . . then I will starve no more."

As he spoke, he failed to notice the two feet that had positioned themselves in front of him, unmoving.

He closed his eyes.

"Hunger . . . greed. Greed."

"Ir!"

Another set of feet appeared in front of him.

"Take him to my home, now."

Hands touched his shoulder, and as soon as he felt them, he quickly shook them off and tried to strike back.

The man immediately began beating Akin, kicking and punching him violently.

"Worthless dasheet! Die, you dog, die!"

As Akin began to drift away, he heard screams all around him. He could taste blood in his mouth and smiled deliriously, some trickling out of his lips.

The first thing he sensed as he came back to consciousness was a sweet smell. He savored it, welcoming the sensation of something beautiful. After a few moments, however, the positive sensations abruptly jerked him out of his delirium, and he flung his head back defensively, opening his eyes.

In front of him sat an old man. He held a flower in his hand and stared at Akin.

"Welcome to my home."

Akin looked at him, his face swollen and lip bloodied.

"I did not mean for you to be hurt, but you were speaking in dangerous tones, and I conceded to the Ir's reaction in order to ensure that you arrived here without any unnecessary attention. Do you understand my reasoning?"

Akin continued staring at him. He wiped some blood off his lip and showed it to the man.

"It is my blood though . . . isn't it . . . that you conceded to bleeding?" he said. "I've yet to see a rich man bleed . . . but my blood . . . contained in my body . . . so often visible to strangers. Isn't it?!"

He flicked his finger at the man, spraying his immaculate, white dress with blood.

"You understand that your statements are insidious, do you not? That if I were to report them to the Iman Ir, it would be the worse for you?"

Akin grinned at him.

"Worse than this? Do what you will. I was insidious in the maza . . . if your intention was to arrest me, you would have no reason to bring me here," he responded.

The man smiled slightly.

"I'll perform no sexual deeds upon you, and will fight to prevent you from performing any on me. Aside from that, you have no reason to keep me here. Reporting me will gain you nothing, else the satisfaction of knowing you killed a man," Akin stated.

He looked at the man's eyes.

"But wouldn't the satisfaction be greater knowing I am eating, breathing, and doing all the things I am doing because you spared my life? That would be under your ownership, and a boon to take with you into the next life."

The man began to laugh.

"You are brilliant!" he blurted out. "Your sense of self-preservation is amazing, and your ability to manipulate your environment is rare. You can read the wind, my friend."

Akin stared at him seriously.

"What are you going to do?" he asked.

"Do you mean, am I going to have you arrested?" the man responded.

Akin stared but said nothing.

"No, you are quite right, my young friend. I would not have brought you here if that was my intention."

He took a deep breath in and continued talking.

"I would like you to stay here . . . with me."

Akin stared at him, confused.

"You will have a place to sleep, food to eat, and you can assist me in my calling."

Akin scowled.

"I don't understand . . . I am nothing. Why do you offer me this?" he asked.

"Because you are special, my friend," the man responded.

"That may very well be," Akin responded, "but you know not my name, nor anything about me save my accent and manner of speech. Why do you offer me this?"

The man frowned and stared at Akin intently.

"You are . . . very special. Your heart speaks to you. Loudly. I wish to have access to it . . . and to cultivate it."

"My heart tells me there is something strange going on, old man. And what shall I do with that?"

The man smiled at Akin.

"Decide upon my offer, my friend . . . your heart will guide you no matter what the confusions."

Akin looked at the man and around the room. It was a multi-room house, and there was a garden outside a doorway. He stared at the flowers and greenery, momentarily immersed in one of the strangest things he had ever seen. It was lush and alive, and he could almost sense the water vapor emanating off it. He stared at it as the sun beat down against it, reflecting the dry desert they were surrounded by.

He looked back at the man and examined him. He was clearly well fed, and though he posed no obvious threat to Akin, there was no trust relayed upon him. Akin was starved and half-delirious from the day's events, and in trying to assess the odd and precarious nature of the man's invitation, he found that the quiet and empty house seemed to relax him along with the lush garden, and he was uncontrollably attracted to the fleeting promise of calm.

An external caretaker took over from within, it seemed, making the decision, prioritizing his health over what mistrust he had and how disoriented he was.

"I accept your offer. My name is Akin. But as I said, I will accept no bondage from you, old man. This is your request I am fulfilling. Be aware."

The man smiled.

"My name is Jarvis, and I am a Mahjid."

CHAPTER 27
GREEN

A kin had never been so close to a man who quietly breathed next to him. He became intoxicated with the rhythm and smell of the older man, a poor tradesman who sat in front of him, performing his hired duty.

He had a pouch on a small table near him and squeezed it, pouring some fat into a bowl. He mixed another liquid into it and began to beat it with his finger in a manner that demonstrated expertise and precision, something it appeared he had done a thousand times before. A lather fluffed up, and he placed the bowl aside. He picked up a sharp copper blade and ran it against a flat stone he carried, sharpening it further.

He dipped his hand into the lather and took out a reasonable amount, spreading it across Akin's face. He took the blade and dipped it in some water and began to scrape away at Akin's beard. It had grown unharmed for so long now that he had thick, dirty hairs all over his face and cheeks.

As the man scraped the hair away, Akin felt some pain, but it was less harsh than he had anticipated. The lather tempered right, as was the sharpness of the copper blade, and the tradesman must have been one that performed his duty upon the wealthy, requiring him to ensure a comfortable shave.

He lifted Akin's nose and shaved his upper lip gently, changing his pace quickly upon reaching more sensitive or bruised areas of the skin. Akin soon felt abandon, letting his thoughts relax and drift away as the man, who was clearly an expert, did his work.

After the shave, the man promptly departed, and Akin was left alone in the house. Guards stood at the entrance, and after walking outside, asserting to himself that he was free to come and go as he pleased, he felt somewhat calm in the isolated environment. It had been a day or two now since he had met the Mahjid and had spent most of that time sleeping. He was still not used to a bed and slept on the flat floor, curling up against rolled up pieces of clothing or some other random textile. He hid himself in between furniture when he slept, keeping a watchful eye towards the corridor that led to his room.

The first night he awoke, he was disoriented and became anxious at being indoors. It took him a few moments of pinning himself against the wall and staring at the surroundings to familiarize himself with his environment. He could not fall asleep easily after that for fear that someone would enter the room and attack him while he slept. He was afraid of waking to such terror and lay on the floor for hours on end that first night, gently flicking his bruised lip as he stared at the ground.

He reached up and felt his face which was now smooth. The last time he had felt the smoothness of his skin was in his village, perhaps that last night he slept in his bed. He looked in a mirror and saw a now weathered version of himself, his face bruised and swollen in places, but still attractive to the eye. He ran his hand along the side of his head, above his ear, observing it slide back in the mirror.

He felt uneasy looking at himself, believing that perhaps he could be the same boy he used to be. But when he looked at his lip and stepped closer, an anger filled him, and he began examining himself intently. He could feel a difference in what he saw, observing now a different man in the mirror than any he had seen before. He looked into his eyes, which looked back, and the memories of some different life to the one he identified with flew past his mind. He was a serious man now, his rested scowl unhidden by his beard. He forced a smile to see what it resembled, examined it briefly, then released the tension in his facial muscles, watching it vanish. The smile was alien to him, some artificial mimicry of something that may have existed in him but at that moment seemed disconnected and uncharacteristic.

He walked about the house, feeling objects and looking around. The most compelling feature, which he had found intriguing that first night, that still intrigued him, was how silent it was. The infrastructure kept out all of the minute city sounds, and when Akin looked out the doorways and windows that were placed in various locations around the house, he saw that they were in a relatively isolated part of Sumat. The houses here were not crammed next to each other, and Jarvis's home was located deep within an affluent area.

Akin could not decide whether the silence was calming simply because it was quiet or if it was the special nature of the structure or insulation of this particular home. That first day, half-dazed and unclear in his mind, he noticed the same attraction he had to it. It had some depressive effect on his awareness, and though it did not numb him, it seemed to slow his thoughts quite comfortably.

The Mahjid had a garden in the center of his house which the servant watered every day. Akin sat in the doorway, staring at it. He had never seen such lush greenery in all his life. The soil was completely covered in grass, like hair upon his head, and out sprung flowers and other plants, a plethora of colors and smells. Even this courtyard, which had no ceiling and was open to the air outside, was dead quiet save a small breeze that wafted through the windows and doorways.

He sat upon the floor, hugging his knees up to his body, staring at the flowers. Sometimes it appeared as if they were moving or waving, and his eyes followed, jumping from flower to flower. He lay down, keeping his body inside the house, extending the top of his head just barely into the courtyard as if he wanted to rest as close to the garden as possible without disturbing it.

Akin was fast asleep when the Mahjid returned home, daylight still peering through the windows. He approached Akin and examined him without touching, looking at his hair, his face and the stature of his body. He smiled and walked out of the room.

Akin awoke to the smell of food permeating through the house and arose, simultaneously uncomfortable at his lust for the smell while desiring it desperately. He walked from room to room until he found the Mahjid who was already lounging on a chair next to a table with food. He motioned for Akin to sit on the chair opposite him with the long, narrow table barely separating them.

Akin stared at the food, a pool of colors with fruits and legumes, cooked varieties in small pots and many different breads. It was not an epic meal, but one with a variety that would be more than enough for a whole family.

He sat down, and though the chair was shaped in a circular fashion, encouraging the person to lean back, he sat upright and looked at the food. For a moment, he contemplated it being poisoned and hesitated.

"I still find it unlikely that you would do all this in order to poison me," he commented.

The Mahjid laughed.

"That does seem unlikely, my young friend. Food is cheap in Sumat - it is of no cost to me for you to eat your fill, and so . . . the favor is negligible," he replied.

Akin broke off a piece of spongy bread that was slightly browned on one side and dipped it into a lentil mixture. He bit into it and chewed the morsel which was cooked to perfection.

He looked over the food as he ate.

"I've never eaten such prestigious food. I suppose it tastes the same every day, which is why the variety is needed."

The Mahjid also started eating and nodded at Akin.

"You are astute, Akin. There are drawbacks to being feared. The loss of creativity . . . no improvisation for fear of repercussion. No, once a meal is commended, they go out of their way to reproduce it perfectly."

"I would be bored eating this every day, Mahjid," Akin replied.

"Yet, it is unspeakably delicious at the current moment," the Mahjid replied.

Akin nodded.

"Do you believe in prophecy?" the man asked.

"The question is, do you?" Akin smirked back. "But I'm sure your own quest for truth is clouded by your need to ensure those around you believe what you need them to."

The Mahjid shook his head.

"I see there is little point in politeness with you, my friend."

Akin looked at him seriously and ceased chewing, food still in his mouth.

"You consider deceit and dishonesty politeness? I don't believe you do . . . I do not sense that you do, but you do because, like the belief in prophecy you promote in those around you, they too promote in you the notion that polite dishonesty is an austere trait."

He continued chewing.

"I do not subscribe to such a ridiculous idea, nor do I think anyone does of their own accord."

"It is of no surprise to me that you were found where you were with the ideas that you carry, young man," the Mahjid replied.

Akin looked up at him again.

"A free man, I was. And not found but invited to partake in this wonderful meal. I found myself long ago . . . it was the world that lost me. And further, do not attempt to ridicule my beliefs based in reason through subtle references to my age . . . I've contemplated paths men twice my age fear to tread."

The Mahjid raised his voice slightly.

"You have caught me again, Akin, but will you not accept that it is beneficial for you to be here rather than collecting shel in the maza? Have I not helped you in even the slightest regard?" he asked, slightly annoyed.

Akin grinned with bread in his mouth and raised his voice in perfect synchronous pitch.

"You speak as if you did so out of the generosity of your heart! I benefit because you benefit, and I should congratulate you for your self-interest? I know not why I am here, and am glad to be eating this meal . . . but I am thankful to the wind, the sand, the sun and the sky . . . not to one whose intentions are still unknown to me!"

The Mahjid sat and stared at him, a smile slowly forming along his lips.

Akin looked at him, noticing the smile, then refocused on the food. They sat there for a few moments as Akin ate while the man continued staring at him, smiling.

"Your garden is tremendous, old man. When I leave, I intend to take it with me."

"Oh! Now you utilize my eventual mortality against me by referencing my age!"

Akin smiled out of the corner of his mouth and the Mahjid began to laugh.

"And when I leave, I shall take the garden with me!" he yelled at Akin, his face red with energy.

Akin laughed slightly as well, burying it in a cough, containing all his playfulness in a smile while he chewed his food.

They continued eating, letting the high energy dissipate, relaxing themselves in silence. Though he was eager to continue eating, Akin found his stomach became full quickly, and he adjusted himself, still facing the table, staring at the garden. The day was now passing, and there was a twilight darkness easing in on the courtyard. The garden started to breathe a magical aura, creating an enchanting view of the plants in the night light. The servant had already lit torches within the house, and within the evening silence, there was an even more intense and calming atmosphere than had existed during the day.

"This is decadency . . . you know this right?" he asked the Mahjid, still observing the garden.

The Mahjid nodded, finishing off a small piece of bread.

"That I should live the life of ten men . . . such an imbalance is strange. I know this," he replied.

Akin smiled.

"Of course you do . . . you are an oracle."

The man laughed briefly.

"Indeed . . ."

Akin turned to him.

"In all honesty, you are aware that you reap off the credulity of others . . . yes?" he asked.

The man cocked his head to the side and thought about the question, still chewing.

"To some extent, yes. The arcane magics and rituals have no real effect upon the world, nor advance our knowledge of it."

He swallowed.

"However, there is a positive and sometimes necessary effect created by faith in such practices. It breeds a willingness to open one's mind to knowledge that one may otherwise be stubborn towards. For example, if a man wishes to believe his wife is unfaithful, nothing I say against it will appease him. In performing the ritual, they become convinced of whatever they sought to believe to begin with."

"But you support their motivated belief in order to receive payment from them . . . yes?" Akin asked.

The man nodded.

"Yes, but the focus is not attempting to justify their thoughts or beliefs. The skill lies in seeing who they are and the relationships they have in order to gain their trust. Once the trust is there, once they believe you are in contact with the otherworld, they will pay you for telling them what they will eat for dinner. They are mesmerized by an intuition native to all of us that I simply acknowledge and improve."

"But that cannot possibly be fulfilling . . ." Akin commented.

"It is my line . . . I was bred to be a Mahjid, like my father, and his father. We are a line of oracles . . . it is in our blood."

"But you do not see the future . . ."

The man smiled.

"If one is intelligent enough, they may see the future far better than another man can. I may climb to the top of the temple and see a horde of soldiers a distance away, then cry prophecy that the city will be attacked. In a manner, I am predicting the future, but my means are not otherworldly. It does not matter, however. These simple tricks, even if explained to these people, will appear less plausible than the idea that god speaks to me."

"You have tried explaining them?"

"Many times, in subtlety. The complexity of these techniques seems to bore people, yet they will pay a sizeable sum to watch me perform though the information I provide is freely available to them," the Mahjid replied.

"You too are strange, Jarvis. You are an oracle, yet have no faith in prophecy. Do you not fear being found out?"

The oracle laughed.

"The investments those around me have placed in my words . . . the reliance they have upon my skills as an augur . . . the time to question that is long over. If I were to go to the maza tomorrow and proclaim that god never spoke to me, they would think me insane, for their certainty that he did."

Akin shook his head.

"Do you not find it strange to be surrounded by such fools?"

"It is so normal, Akin, that your arrival here is what now appears strange to me . . . though somewhere within me, I believe this is how humans are meant to speak."

He took a sip of some heated, flavored water and leaned forward.

"I have confided in you now . . . various things . . . yes?" he asked.

Akin nodded.

"Some things, yes . . ."

"This mistrust between us. It is unpleasant. I am not saying it is required that we know everything about one another, nor be transparent in our internal feelings. However, I want you to trust that no harm will come to you and that this is now your home."

Akin stared at him, looked down, and looked back at him.

"But that makes no sense, man. How can you offer your home to me so soon?" he replied.

The man shook his head.

"That is not of consequence. It is my desire, it is truly my desire . . . I wish for you to understand this, and I ask you now; accept it as true despite your doubts."

Akin stared at him for some time, contemplating the Mahjid's words. He sat there for a few moments, as if discussing something complex with himself, then closed his eyes intensely, thinking.

"I do not trust this . . . but I look at you now. Look at me," he ordered, opening his eyes.

The Mahjid looked at him.

"Look at my eyes and understand my words," Akin continued. "Understand that I take your words into my heart . . . and I will give you that trust. I give you my trust . . . I trust you more than I trust myself in doing so."

He paused, finding his words again, then kept talking.

"I do so because I choose to trust you . . . I choose to trust your heart. If you close it to me after this . . . it will be a stain upon the world. I will never have any recourse and there is no punishment to you. Do you understand?"

The Mahjid stared at Akin intently, both frightened and stern, seemingly confused of his own feelings and the manner in which Akin was communicating to him.

"Do you understand, Jarvis?"

The man sat there, staring and thinking. His eyes shifted back and forth to thoughts and sudden tension.

He nodded.

"I understand, Akin."

Akin kept staring, considering Jarvis's response, then leaned back and looked at him. His hesitant aura changed, less isolated in some manner.

"It is done then."

He moved forward, placing his hand on Jarvis's shoulder, wearing a small smile.

CHAPTER 28
ENDLESS WATERHOLES

"You must keep your wits about you, Akin . . . I know you prefer not to lie, so remain silent. If you are asked a question, defer to me. If you are pressed and know the answer to be objectionable, refuse to answer in a diplomatic manner."

Akin nodded as a servant dressed the Mahjid. He was being wrapped in illustrious red drapery that twirled around his body from neck to toe.

Akin laughed.

"You look like a pastry, Mahjid."

The man grinned back at him and resumed instructing the servant and Akin. He motioned for the servant to leave and leaned in, still organizing his dress, speaking in a lower tone to Akin.

"This man is Iman Ir. They are an unpredictable and dangerous bloodline that has been rooted in the hierarchy of Sumati aristocracy for ages. They believe anything they want is their birthright, so you must be wary of any attention they give you. They are militants of gluttony."

Akin nodded, looking at the Mahjid's eyes, acknowledging his worry and calming him.

They were led by another servant into the main room of the house where a man sat leisurely upon a chair, leaning back, devouring fruits.

His vibrant gold helmet sat on a table beside him, a table it seemed that was brought specifically for it. It was small and circular and was sized to perfection in synchronicity with the helmet.

The man was large, and though he no longer appeared a muscular warrior, there was a foreboding presence about him, as if his stature resembled that of an angry bovin. His hands were thick, and he seemed to be of a different genetic line than the common people of Sumat.

As he saw the Mahjid, he beckoned to his servant aggressively who came forward carrying a bowl.

"Mahjid, ah Mahjid. I have brought something wonderful for you."

He leaned up and took the bowl from the servant who quickly returned to the other side of the room. He looked inside, smiling.

He looked up at the Mahjid and nodded at him, still smiling.

"You will enjoy this. Here."

He handed the bowl to Jarvis with both his hands, as if a form of offering.

Jarvis took it from him and bowed his head, sitting down across from him. He looked in the bowl.

"Yes . . . a special creature from the other side of the desert. Alive! Here, let me show you . . ."

He took the bowl back and pulled out a strange looking beast with claws and no discernable face. Akin grimaced and Jarvis squinted but held his stature. The man stared at it and grinned, making odd sounds, mocking it, then slammed it against the table multiple times, cracking its outer shell. He then grabbed it with both hands and ripped it in half while still alive, making Akin nauseous as he heard the sounds of the animal's flesh and shell tear apart. Its limbs curled in and stuttered, then released all force as it died.

The man dug two fingers into the animal's flesh and pulled out some white meat, biting into it and chewing tenderly. He handed it to Jarvis who pulled off a small piece and also chewed, closing his eyes.

The Iman Ir smiled as Jarvis chewed, looking at him.

Jarvis opened his eyes and looked at the man.

"Thank you for your offering, my Ir. It has triggered the opening of the gates, and will aid in the answering of your questions."

The man, still smiling, leaned back in his seat.

"Who is the boy?"

"I heard a voice, my Ir. It was loud and deafening, though it made no sound at all. It came to me in a dream, though I was awake. It told me of a man from a distant land who would have no memory of this world. It instructed me to feed him, to clothe him, to carry him with me wherever I went for he was to bring good fortune to those I counseled. It was said, he was a conduit of the heavens, my Ir, through no knowledge of his own."

As the Iman Ir chewed his meat, he looked at Akin inquisitively, nodding slowly, examining him.

"A special boy, ah? A special boy. I do like special boys, Mahjid."

Akin stared at the Iman Ir, who looked down at his meat.

"Does the boy know he is not to look at his Ir as he does?" he asked, threateningly.

"Yes, my Ir. He is learning."

Akin looked at Jarvis, then at the table between them to avoid the man's gaze.

The Iman Ir tossed the half-eaten corpse of the animal on the table.

"Now then, Mahjid. What can you tell me?"

Jarvis looked at his servant who brought forward a small copper bowl. He placed it in front of them. Jarvis reached into his robe and pulled out a piece of tinder and gave it to the servant who approached a torch on the wall and lit it. Jarvis placed more of the same pieces of wood into the bowl.

The material was not normal wood, but something lighter than the trees Akin had seen. They also seemed darker and of a green hue. The pieces were small rectangles and had colors painted on two sides of them.

After placing many pieces in the bowl, the Mahjid took the small torch from the servant who returned to the corner of the room. He handed it to the Iman Ir. The Iman Ir's fingers were bulbous, and the wood looked like a small, brittle object that would break in his grasp. He gently placed it in the bowl, lighting the rest of the wood.

They both stared at the fire intently. Jarvis, however, looked up at the Iman Ir in quick momentary bursts to observe him.

Jarvis closed his eyes and placed his hands on either side of the bowl.

"Your wife, Sabaye, my Ir . . ." he spoke. "She awaits you today, and so you shall visit her. The love in her heart is at its highest, and you shall enjoy her adoration."

He paused, thinking again.

"You have dreamed troubling dreams, and they will disperse in time. They reflect an old confusion, an old pain, and in experiencing them, you strengthen your resolve and connection with the spirit world. As you dream, you will open your mind to information in the past and future, my Ir. It is a blessing, not a curse."

The Iman Ir sat motionless, listening to everything the Mahjid was telling him. He stared at the fire, as if in a trance.

"The future is uncertain," Jarvis continued. "Your safety is promised, but there will be trouble between the inhabitants of Sumat. I . . . I cannot see why . . . but . . . the Ir will be the solution."

The Iman Ir slowly frowned, still listening.

"Your children will grow strong. Your women will be protected. The temple of Mala will never be challenged. It will remain a pillar of light upon the world and stand as a testament to the power of the Ir in Sumat for protecting it from eons past, to all the time to come."

"Will the troubles threaten . . . my peace?" the Iman Ir asked.

"If you allow them to enter your dreams, my Ir, if you fear them, they will awaken you at night. If you remain strong to your line, focused on your duty as protector of the Oam, you will forever be at peace."

"What of my challenge, Mahjid? I still think of her. The bitch still haunts me though I performed my duty. I tried my best, did I not?"

"You did, my Ir."

"Then why does the cunt still haunt me?"

"The Kai are mysterious, my Ir. They pursue the strongest, and it is the burden of the strongest to defend us."

Akin found himself pondering the demons that awoke him so long ago and felt uplifted upon hearing that they target the strongest. He frowned, however, upon catching the trick, for the Kai did not exist, and therefore, his dream bore no testament to his strength. He nearly grinned as the effectiveness of Jarvis's bullshit dawned upon him.

The Iman Ir swallowed.

"I . . . still have thoughts. Thoughts of our mothers . . . thoughts reserved for the whores of the temple. What am I to do? These thoughts consume me, Mahjid. Bathing with the basla, doing as I please solves nothing. The desire burns hotter within me. Even now, I am engorged."

"It is a challenge, my Ir, the truth of which-"

"But I am sick of challenges!" the Iman Ir yelled. "I wish to not be burdened by such pointless thoughts. Why does it burn within me as if I am a sinner?"

Jarvis took a deep breath in.

"It is not punishment, my Ir. Close your eyes, and think of the fire. Place your hand upon it and feel the heat. When you do so, think only of the fire, and you will feel your pain disappear. Do it, and as the pain in your hand intensifies, so too shall your inner burning disperse."

The Iman Ir did as he was instructed and after a few moments began to smile. His hand began to heat up upon the fire.

"It pains, Mahjid. But you are right. The fear disappears. I know what I must do. I know!"

Jarvis smiled at him.

"There is a sinner among us . . . that is why I have the thoughts. In not seeing them . . . it . . . poisons my mind, for I am to cleanse it. It is a basla. She . . . is a dirty one."

He wiggled his finger in front of Jarvis and Akin, then pressed it against his behind.

"I shall deal with her today."

He smiled satisfyingly.

"I understand, Mahjid."

He closed his eyes, feeling soothed.

"I know . . . what to do.

"I will visit Sabaye today and suckle upon her breast. Then, I will visit the temple to please myself, and tend to the Jasa whore. I will delay it, to enjoy the dutiful satisfaction further."

He abruptly motioned to his servant who stood on the other side of the room. The servant approached quickly, kneeled down, and placed a bag of shel on the table between them, walking back.

"Bless me, Mahjid."

The Iman Ir knelt down before Jarvis and bowed his head, holding his helmet. Jarvis placed his hand on his head.

"You are free, my Ir."

The Iman Ir stood up, placing his helmet upon his head. As he did, his body appeared to expand, his muscles tightening. He tilted his head and looked at Akin, staring. Without moving his head, he shifted focus to Jarvis, a slight grin forming along the side of his mouth. Then, he left, his servant following.

They both stood in silence for a few moments. Akin looked at Jarvis who began to suddenly breathe quick and hard, gasping for breath. He stumbled to his chair as Akin ran to support him.

Jarvis clutched his chest.

"What is wrong?" Akin asked, concerned.

"I find it . . . hard . . . to breathe . . ." he replied in between breaths.

"Would you like water? Fruit? What will ease it?"

"I am . . . I will normalize. This sometimes happens. It has happened for many years now. There is no controlling it . . . it is my heart."

He looked at Akin and placed his hand on his chest.

"My heart, Akin. It is always crying," he said, his breathing tightening.

Akin frowned and sat back, looking at him.

"I will be all right, Akin. It just takes a few moments at times."

Akin sat and stared at him, thinking. His mouth opened as if he was going to say something, but said nothing.

"This is my line, my friend," Jarvis laughed, pitiably. "To calm the hearts of monsters. My whole life spent, calming the hearts of monsters. What life awaits me after this."

"You should calm yourself, Mahjid," Akin said.

"I am tired of remaining calm, Akin," he responded, his eyes red. "Do you . . ." he smiled, licking his lips, "do you know what this man spoke of, when he spoke of his challenge?"

"No, of course not," Akin replied.

Jarvis began to laugh, uncomfortably, almost maniacally.

"When he was a young man, and I was a younger man, he visited his daughter . . . his first daughter . . . Sona . . . and was consumed with the desire to love her. Love her, he did."

Akin frowned.

"At some point, she confided in her uncle, who transferred her concern back to him. When he discovered what she had confessed, he, upon interrogation, bashed her with a stone kifri in a fit of rage. She could no longer be recognized.

"She was a child, Akin. He confided his practices, and I listened empathetically. He would kiss and suckle upon her nonexistent breasts. He would explore her body and tell her he loved her. A child . . . his child. She was beautiful. I was at her birth."

He clasped his eyes tightly, breathing in and out.

"Sona . . ." he said, tears now sliding down his face, though he did not cry.

"She was a child, Akin. A small . . . fresh mind. He came to me for absolution, and absolution I have given him ever since. Do you know . . . what I convinced him of?"

Akin stared at Jarvis.

"I . . . aided him in understanding that she was consumed by demons, and that his own fluids served as a tool with which to cleanse her with."

He smiled, looking at Akin.

"Do you understand? He believed that his sexual urges were brought about by his sensibilities about demons, and that his desires towards her were all manifestations of a dutiful need to clean her."

He clasped his eyes again, suddenly, humming an abrasive sound at himself.

He grabbed Akin's wrists and looked at him, smiling.

"Do you know?" he paused, smiling large.

"He crushed her head, and was convinced it was because the demons would not release her. That the semen did not work, and so the kifri did. It still stands in his house! Washed, cleansed of the blood and brains."

Akin had a sullen look on his face, still listening and looking at Jarvis. Jarvis's face turned to maniacal glee, and quickly but gradually his eyebrows sank, and he frowned, his mouth twisting out of shape. He stared at Akin helplessly, then leaned back weakly.

He looked down, his head gently shaking forward and back, pondering eons.

"That was so long ago, Akin, and I have breast-fed him ever since.

"My heart has deserted me, Akin, because I have deserted it . . . I have no demands to make of it."

They both sat, for what seemed to be forever, frowning and thinking in silence. They both lay back upon their seats in time, closing their eyes.

"The garden . . . does not seem so pure anymore . . . my friend," Akin said gently.

"No . . ." Jarvis replied. "It does not."

They remained in each other's company for the rest of the day, sharing their thoughts. Jarvis slowly calmed himself and kept a bowl of water beside him which he used to wet his ears and neck.

"I know not why I have such an affinity to this work," Jarvis said randomly. "I find it easy to . . . coerce . . . lead people through dark forests . . . into paradisiacal illusions that they clutch upon for dear life. It is my talent, you might say."

Akin moved to the garden as he listened, running his palm along the top of the blades of grass. His stomach was full from the random foods Jarvis's servant had brought to them throughout the day, and a calm but inquisitive demeanor seemed to permeate throughout the room.

"I heard a story . . . a long time ago," Jarvis said, visualizing the memory. "It was about a man named Pios."

"He lived in a small community in the middle of nowhere . . . somewhere in the sands, with a large family. But he became discontent with his life. One day, he left his village and was not heard from again. His wife and many children nearly starved, but the people of the village aided her, and as a group they survived. Even when the streams ran dry and there was a long drought, the families survived by digging wells and finding water deep underground.

"It was a hardship, and some men perished in their attempts, but the village was able to survive on limited stores of water. They rationed their supplies to ensure the wells did not dry and even went so far as to limit child-birth to ensure there were no new mouths to feed until food became more plentiful. Their farms shriveled up and turned into small gardens that could feed only a few people. Though this happened and people became sick, and some died, they survived.

"Years into the drought, Pios returned to the village. He bragged of a water source he had discovered deep in the desert. He claimed he drank and bathed in it, and no matter how much he used, it never dried up. He said he put his arm in it and tried to find its end, but could not touch the ground underneath.

"His skin shone as he spoke, and he smiled with a brimming confidence. He claimed to have such an abundance of water that he would often take the fluid and throw it upon the ground, watching it dissolve into the sand underneath. That the abundance was so great, he would waste it, tearing at the hearts of the dehydrated and starving villagers. He claimed to have spent much time staring at it, that even his reflection in the water was of a different nature than anything he had ever seen.

"Upon hearing his words and observing his undeniable confidence, many people in the village became enchanted. They became convinced that the waterhole was a relic of ancient magic, forgotten when the world was released to the mortals.

"When pressed for proof by others in the village, the man simply smiled at them. He stated that proof was in the faith . . . that no matter what the naysayers claimed, the possibility that such a source existed was undeniably true, and that he had discovered it. Their unwillingness to accept his gift, he attested, was an act of shameful pride, and that their hardships would continue.

"He led a group of followers into the desert - many families and their children - leaving the village half deserted. His children begged their mother to reunite with their father and return with him, but she trusted nothing he said, and refused. Those that stayed behind continued to ration their water using the wells they had created and tended to their small, limited gardens.

"As time passed, those that left the village were never heard from again. The villagers became skilled at managing their gardens and preserving their water, and their lives improved. Eventually, a man was sent out into the desert with an excess of supplies to find out what became of their comrades.

"He walked and walked and eventually discovered an ancient oasis. A dead tree loomed over a cracked depression in the ground that was now just the corpse of a small pond. Surrounding the pond were a multitude of decomposed and dried bodies, some small, some large. The man returned to the village some days later, and they all sat in silence together, mourning the dead.

"The wife cried; not for her husband, but for the villagers that followed him.

"You see, Akin, this story was shared to encourage people to value working hard over false promises, but that is not what I understood of it," Jarvis said.

"It was Pios that intrigued me, not the villagers, because as the story unfolded I was enchanted by the endless waterhole as well! I wanted to believe in it, and when it was discovered to be false, I felt a pain in my heart. To this day, I desire to believe in such a place, existing somewhere in the desert.

"I even contemplated that Pios and the others survived wholly, and that the story was ended as it was by the villagers themselves to sustain their righteousness.

"But that is not what is of consequence," he noted. "This story had a profound effect on me, for I understood that an unreasonable faith in something beautiful, good and wholesome, is more wicked than stern dedication to something ugly and distasteful, but true."

"You see, Pios condemned the naysayers for attempting to spread negativity to those who surrounded them. He critiqued them as being harbingers of faithlessness, of a lack of hope, while he attempted to provide hope to those around him."

Jarvis leaned back and stared at the ceiling, thinking.

"It became a testament to me ... that reason ... observation ... they are gifts. That those who subscribe to advantageous but unreasonable ideas will always run out of water, because there is no such thing as an endless waterhole.

"I have met so many of such kinds of people in my days, Akin. Subscriptions to fantastic ideas abound, but so clearly manifested by their own lust or greed or need because such ideas are always advantageous to them, even if they promote fear!

"I am a testament to the abundance of such ridiculousness. I am a wealthy, powerful man . . . and my purpose in this life is to assert such illusions. Such men have no faith in their own words, for no matter how badly they wish to believe something unfathomably ridiculous, some portion of their heart whispers truth to them. They require outside support to maintain faith, be it in the form of camaraderie or dominance over naysayers."

He looked at Akin, who looked back at him.

"I hold a whimsical belief in an ancient oasis somewhere in the desert. But then my heart whispers to me. It says, 'Why would Pios have returned to the village?' Then I understand."

Akin, still examining the grass, pondered Jarvis's words.

"I used to believe the night sun watched over me . . . somehow. Even though it was evil, it provided me . . . some peace. To be witnessed, observed."

The hydrated tips of the grass tickled his palm, a tender sensation he was fond of.

"Now I know that there is nothing but you and me in this room."

He paused, listening to silence.

"But even in that there is much beauty, but true beauty . . . a tangible beauty you can touch and explore. I do not know why this grass is so beautiful . . . nor why we find ourselves in this calm moment, but it is a mystery of beauty.

"I cherish exploring it," he said, staring at the green. "As you said, it is the advantageous nature of illusion that is the problem. I see this grass as beautiful and am intrigued by it, just as I am the mystery of how the Iman Ir have existed for so long."

Jarvis rested his hands in his lap, his eyes half closed as he became euphoric amidst their untainted communications.

"Every man that lies to himself stumbles in time."

Jarvis's words triggered thoughts of Bethelhurst in Akin's mind. He thought of Bethelhurst's conviction in his belief that he had loved him sincerely and with force. He imagined him coughing in his cot, an old dejected man, preparing to die.

"You brought this upon yourself, old man," he thought. "Old man indeed. You are more content perishing in such a wasteful way than to admit error. Good for you, you receive what you desire."

"More content dying in illusion, than living in truth," he said out loud.

Jarvis looked at Akin.

"Yes! Pios would rather die believing his water was limitless than live without it! Even as his mouth dried and he watched the children perish around him, he would have persisted, I am sure of it. What was it he feared, I wonder."

Akin continued playing with the grass rhythmically with his hand. He imagined Pios, seated in front of his dry pond, still seeing water underneath it, convincing himself and those around him that this was the illusion, and that the water was actually there.

"Perhaps he felt unable to succeed as a man. He felt incapable of it, regardless of what he was capable of. He was petrified of failure, perhaps, and developed a belief in something that was assured success," Akin said.

Jarvis imagined Pios's childhood, a boy being beaten mercilessly and repeatedly for small infractions that a child should be forgiven for. Rather than being educated, he was punished, retarding his ability to learn and instead relying upon fantasy to complete his tasks.

He imagined the growth of the boy, repeatedly failing and creating deceitful excuses and arguments to defend his failure . . . failures due to his now habitual inability to learn.

"Such a man can learn, can he not?" Jarvis asked unfocusedly.

Akin pressed his hand down on the grass, forcing the blades down, feeling the coolness of it surge into his skin.

"All men can learn. All men can choose to learn," he replied.

"Be still," he whispered.

The man did not respond, but stood sternly against the wall.

He quickly dashed a look out of the narrow corridor.

"He approaches, be still."

The other man did not move or speak, clasping a small blade in his hand tensely.

As a man passed by the visible portion of the alley, the man without the knife grabbed him and pulled him in, throwing him deep into the crevice. Outside, no one saw what happened, for no trace remained of him.

Deep into the darkness of the slit between two walls, with only a small amount of skylight, they pressed him unto the floor and held his mouth covered. He was obese and stared at them in fear.

The quiet man held a knife to his throat and looked at him.

"You insulted my child as he asked for an offering?" the other man asked.

The fat man shook his head desperately, murmuring. The talking man slapped him across his face.

"Quiet, mensa. That is right. You are mensa scum, and you dare refuse a Mashaya request in our own land? This is the city of Mala - did you not know that when you brought your pale family of mensa dogs here to live?"

The fat man angrily reached up to grab him but was pinned down by the quiet one who pressed the knife hard against his neck, piercing him.

The talking man smiled at the fat one.

"How does it feel to be refused a request, fat man?"

He slapped him again, then punched him in the face repeatedly. The fat man was barely conscious, but still opened his eyes halfway, staring up at them.

The talking man leaned down and whispered into the fat man's ears, holding the quiet man's shoulder with his hand.

"I will tell your family that you are waiting for them in Ceria, Sumai scum."

The fat man suddenly tried to scream as the talking man squeezed his partner's shoulder who swiftly ran the blade across the fat man's neck, opening him up to the world. He gagged and convulsed, his tongue gyrating, then lay there, dead.

The thin man ripped the fat man's blood stained tunic off and took the blade from the quiet one, carving into his chest.

"My Oam has called upon you for counsel regarding the recent unrest that has befallen the Temple City."

The man who spoke stood upright in a tunic with thick, red drapery that wrapped around his body. He was thin and bald, a minister known as the Jhazbin. He was standing upon an elevated pedestal and behind him was an even higher one. Upon it were four men who held long wooden rods in the center of which sat the Oam. He sat upon a large, square throne that remained elevated above the ground, rested upon these rods, suspended by the four men. The platform was made of a shiny, hard surface that resembled stone but was smooth to the touch and persistently cool. He wore a cap and a long beard, his hair also long, trailing behind him.

"Many days ago, a man was found dead in Kadasha. He was discovered by a child who subsequently informed the nearest Sumai leader," said the Jhazbin.

He paused, looking across all the listening faces.

"The child did not inform the local Ir first. My Oam is displeased that the child did not do so, and instead found it more attractive to circumvent the local authority in preference of rural leaders."

He continued.

"The man, his name Mastaka, was a foreigner to the city. As such, his trade was loyal to Kunda Sumai and located within the marketplace in Kadasha.

"Upon the man's chest was etched, in blood and through his flesh, the symbol of Kunda Mashaya."

The Oam blinked slowly, staring at the men kneeling below him. The Jhazbin continued.

"The discovery of his body and news of the symbol torn into his skin has spread through Kadasha and other Sumai led areas. Repeated acts of vengeance have exploded all over the city on their behalf, which has resulted in a violent segregation between the two Kunda."

After a few moments, the Oam began to speak.

"This displeases me. I have always treated the citizens of this great city with love. I wish for an end to the violence, for trade to resume, and wish to see the city reunited for the Jamali festival."

He looked at the first man on his right, a fat man in an expensive, imported, dark green garment and matching hat.

"What do you say, Pulam?" he asked.

"My Oam," he replied, "the unrest within the city is causing a great deal of loss. Trade is at a standstill, and the segregation between the two Kunda forces isolated exchanges within their respective groups. I suggest, My Oam, that you grant tax asylum upon the festival of Jamali for all those who are members of any Kunda who vow to the prosperity of the Temple City, and to unity with the other Kunda. A vow broken to My Oam is punishable by death, and the very stranglehold of prosperity that has been placed upon the citizens of the city will encourage them to participate."

"A tax asylum is not acceptable. All citizens must contribute to the temple and war house stores for the greatness of the city. Your suggestion prompts me to bribe my own citizens, like a common beggar. They must do so by choice, not through purchase," the Oam responded.

His gaze shifted to the man in the middle, an Iman Ir dressed in his official uniform, his golden helmet upon a stand beside him. There was a softer look in the Oam's eyes as he addressed the man.

"Maerus . . . what do you say?"

"My Oam, it is a matter of force. The local Ir are insufficiently motivated. The common man cannot be expected to remain in line if not governed with a stern fist. With the Ir in line, the people will happily follow. I will make an example of the Kadasha Kin Ir, those closest to where the body was discovered. The city will be, and always has been, controlled through blood, not commerce."

He looked at Pulam unemotionally then back to the Oam.

"Commerce is used to thrive, My Oam. Blood is used to survive. The people are crying for order, and I can provide it."

"And what of the crime?" asked the Oam.

"Those responsible will pay, as will their families. Such a vulgar example I will make of them that they will fear the Ir too much to bicker amongst themselves."

The Oam looked to the third man, dressed similarly decadently to Pulam.

"And you?"

He looked to the Iman Ir and Pulam briefly, then back to the Oam.

"My Oam, I am in agreement with Maerus. Force will unify the city. There is no other option."

"You have no other suggestion?" asked the Oam.

"None, My Oam. What Maerus said, I was to suggest myself. Examples must be made, and the Kin Ir must be re-affirmed."

The Oam sat there, looking at Maerus.

"Agreed. You may use limited temple reserves to reward those that aid in your efforts."

After he spoke, Maerus rose, taking his helmet and exiting to the right. As he left, so too did the other two men, following him.

The Oam briefly followed them with his eyes then focused on the minister before him.

"Send in the Mahjidi."

Akin lay weightless upon a flat cot. He had moved it into a room with a view of the sky and placed it directly underneath the skylight, staring at the blue above. His hands lay crossed across his body, and every little while a speck of cloud gradually passed by.

The entire house was quiet save the now familiar breeze that wafted from room to room. Jarvis had specified that he wanted doorways cut into almost every room to allow air to ventilate from the outside. This made the house unique amongst others for being airy both inside and out. Others of the elite, having seen it, copied his design which was now commonplace amongst expensive abodes. The poor could not do so for fear of theft, but with guards and servants, there was little concern for the wealthy.

He knew the sky he looked upon was the same color in his village, and that at that very moment, his father was probably in the fields, plowing, cursing him. He would undoubtedly be alone as the farming community was lessening, not growing, and the work would be immense. He knew his father's sweaty, tired face well and had grown up cherishing it.

"What was it he said?" he whispered to himself.

He lay there and thought.

"What . . . what a dream, your mother must have been."

He thought about Jarvis's words. It was as a dream, thoughts of his mother. It escaped him as to why he never thought of her. She was there, and then one day, she wasn't. He does not remember the day, or even if it was a gradual change. He just had memories of her, and then he had memories without her.

He couldn't even remember if, when he thought of certain events in his past, she was there in the background or not.

She used to smile, however. He remembered something like that. Did he remember that? Or was it his imagination?

He turned to his side and curled up, placing his hands flat underneath his head, supporting himself.

"Maja."

Did he call her maja? Or was it something else? He closed his eyes and tried to imagine her. He imagined her profile, a smile on her face, her defining nose and brow, wavy black hair and soft skin.

"Maja."

He frowned. He felt it incredulous that the image of his mother was just a conceptual profile. He had no idea who she was as a person, and not because of a lack of memory. His awareness of her was restricted to smiles, small words, tight hugs and kisses . . . but he had no idea what her motivation was. He knew she would have re-stated many Aizik traditions as her values, but when he thought about her eyes and her smiles, it was as if there was a person under the face of the woman, a personality he had never met.

There were small idiosyncrasies about her. She used to draw on the floor of their house using the sand. He would sit beside her as a child, and she would show him Aizik symbols used in prayer. But even when she looked at him . . . he remembered her face. It was as if there was disappointment in her eyes after she would explain it to him. She would look at him with excitement, as if he was to understand the meaning of the symbol and what it triggered in her heart, and when he simply nodded, her smile would slowly fade into an oddly cold side grin.

"Did you want me . . . did you seek a reflection of what was in your heart? Justification of it? From me? A child?" he whispered to himself, tensely.

He closed his eyes and grimaced.

"I require reflections of myself in you . . . maja."

He cringed as he said her name, feeling pain roam his mind.

"If you suffocated, maja . . . what was I to do? What could I do?"

He thought of her face once again, the smiles of glee and every moment he could remember, and image after image that flashed through his mind held some unspoken frustration underneath. It was as if the smiles themselves were expressions of anger.

His heart tore as he thought of his mother and the deep level of compassion and love he had for her. But there was a lingering question that caused even more pain. With every empathetic thought towards what tortured her, he felt betrayed and isolated, for she hid it from one who loved her so.

It was such an immense betrayal, in fact, that he could not contemplate it. Every singular recognition of a moment of her pain caused ten explosions of confusion and desire within him, a failed burning desire to be a companion to her, to aid her and provide her support and care. The definitive and immediate failure of this love he had for his maja rippled through him.

"Of course, there are no shortcomings I could have improved upon to make you trust me. What could I have done that I did not? I am, and was, your son! Why did you not open your heart to me?" he whispered loudly to himself.

His hands clasped together tightly as he lay there, curled into a ball.

"Maja . . . maja, maja, maja, maja. My maja."

He lay there silently. His mind seemed to become empty as it calmed itself. He soon fell asleep, his muscles loosening, his mouth open, making a light wheezing sound as he slept.

He was ushered out of sleep by someone sitting on the cot beside him, then a hand lightly squeezing his shoulder. He looked up to see Jarvis in his full robe, staring up at the stars.

"You still look like a pastry, old man."

Jarvis kept looking up, then looked to the wall, an unemotional look on his face.

"Let's eat," he said.

They sat across from each other on their chairs as the servant brought food out. Akin watched Jarvis intently.

"What is it?" Akin asked.

Jarvis frowned and looked towards him, but not quite at him, still in thought.

"I'm uncertain . . . something feels strange . . . about the environment," he replied.

Akin motioned for Jarvis to eat, which he did. As they both bit on some initial morsels, they inhaled and readied themselves for reflection. Conversation around mealtime was now a regular thing, and both men found it a calm way to wrestle their thoughts.

"There is something odd in the air, Akin."

He sat, perplexed, chewing on food as if it were tasteless fuel.

"I sat before the Oam as I have a hundred times before. Other Mahjidi spoke before me, spurting the same nonsensical wit, but as my turn approached, something altered within me. I stared at him and was unable to speak in straight sentences, nor with a false confidence. I told them of a bad personal omen that affected my ability to speak, but that I saw no ill future for the Oam. It seemed to bring him even greater satisfaction to know my pain existed, but that he was exempt of it."

He continued.

"As I saw the flicker of ease in his mind at my misfortune, the feeling in my gut spoke even louder. I looked up at the Untouched and knew . . . I knew his time was coming to an end."

He looked at Akin.

"What am I to do with such knowledge?"

"Accept what you know, my friend. There is no escaping what your heart tells you, no matter how practiced you are," replied Akin.

"You do not seem concerned, Akin . . . you continue to eat, and I am terrified."

"This place could never be permanent, Jarvis. Did you not see that? The corruption and hierarchies, long as they may last, are simply opportunities the weak cling to for immediate satisfaction. If it were permanent, they would not so greatly fear losing their position."

Jarvis looked at him.

"I see you . . . as an enemy at the current moment, Akin. How can that be?" he asked.

Akin looked back at him seriously and placed the bread in his hand down. He knelt down and held his palms upwards in front of Jarvis.

"If I am your enemy, kill me . . . do what you will, my friend, to ease the fear in your mind."

Jarvis stared at him incredulously.

"I . . . cannot."

He placed his hand on Akin's head.

"That would solve nothing . . . the storm is still coming. If I were to harm you, it would be to serve my own peace of mind. It will come nonetheless, will it not?" he asked.

"All wrongs are righted, my friend. I now know this to be true. There is no stopping it. All you can do . . . is choose to be right."

"I have heard whispers, Akin. Things only the unknown know. I have heard of conspiracies . . . it is given no weight in our circles, but I believe all I know to be true has led me to this realization."

He picked up a morsel of bread from a bowl. It was beautifully soft and browned to perfection. He pressed it against his lips and bit into it, staring forward. He tasted the fluffy airy bread against his tongue, coated in salt.

"The end of this is coming, Akin. My heart tells me so."

Soon thereafter, the city was ablaze with tension as the Iman Ir flexed its muscle, violently pursuing the perpetrators of the murder. They also began eyeing the Kin Ir, selecting a few to make an example of in an effort to bring them all in line. As this went on and people scrambled to avoid them, Sumai and Mashaya friction raged forward with small but intense fights breaking out over menial arguments. The resulting casualties increased on both sides, exasperating an already strained city.

The aristocracy, however, was more or less immune to the troubles suffered by commoners. Though racism became amplified, they were somehow of a different color altogether and were wholeheartedly welcomed by Sumai traders, regardless of their bloodlines. Foreign elite were rare, and though they would likely be able to frequent Mashaya dasha and stores, they too favored Sumai neighborhoods. The Mashaya clan, therefore, as a whole, suffered greatly, both economically and socially. The Sumai improved their relationship with the rich of Sumat while the Mashaya suffered a creeping form of social dejection and financial drought.

Even the fact that the Iman Ir were aggressively pursuing the Mashaya culprits agitated their situation further, making them both fearful and defensive in their own native city while the Sumai, understandably, capitalized on the situation.

Jamali soon arrived, and along with the excitement surrounding the yearly festivities, there were rumors that the Iman Ir had completed their task and had handed the culprits to the Manu priests who were going to present them to the city during the festival.

Jamali was said to be the day that the goddess Mala erupted from beneath the sands of the earth, drifting into the heavens. It was the water festival, as her departing gift was said to have been aqueous, filling the rivers and wells, breathing life to the world. It was considered a blessing to dig into the ground and discover the blue juice, a gift bestowed upon humans by Mala eons ago.

Jamali was a very holy day, and even the Aizik celebrated it. It all reminded Akin of his mother whom he thought loved the festival. But when he pondered it further, even as he readied himself for the festivities, it occurred to him that it was possible he had likened her to Mala as a child which is why it reminded him of her.

The Sumati people celebrated the festival with far more zest than his village did. Even when he was a street dweller, the day of Jamali would bring everyone together as the rich commonly joked with the poor, and all interacted more or less as equals, even if only facetiously.

Akin and Jarvis smiled at each other but talked very little as they left the house, traveling down the winding path to the maza. Already in the distance they could see and hear screaming and music as people hammered on drums and sang, throwing water upon each other.

The main festivities always surrounded the temple, and every edge of it was filled with celebration. Large groups of people stood, holding each other, singing anthems in unison. Abruptly, it would be interrupted by someone throwing a huge vat of water on the singers who then sought playful revenge.

The river was constantly used, from morning till nightfall, on the day of Jamali. After stored water was exhausted, people would travel to the river with their buckets and vats, in arms, refueling for more jovial mischief.

When they arrived, the festival was in full swing. People, both men and women, were running about, drenched, laughing and screaming. The dashas were filled with patrons as prices were cheap to accommodate the festivities, and in the jovial spirit of the city, many traders gave away free beer and food. Children scurried about everywhere, laughing and playing.

It was different here than anywhere else Akin had been. The lines between classes were shattered, and both men and women interacted with each other in what seemed a childlike furor of glee. The day was sacred to the citizens of Sumat, not so much anymore for the religious meaning, Akin thought, but because it provided them relief from the stringent restrictions of everyday life. Even he was filled with emotional joy as he watched people genuinely laugh and smile, though he felt uncomfortable at the sudden arbitrary change that he feared would eventually regress.

The main feature of the festival was to begin soon, and people had already gathered all around the maza to watch the Manu priests. Akin and Jarvis joined in the fray and stood arm in arm with random strangers, joining in the singing, letting the contagious euphoria carry them along. As the people sang in imperfect unison, Akin was again surprised at how loud it was. Every time Jamali came to Sumat, Akin felt it was louder than anything he had ever witnessed before.

Their voices resonated so thunderously, in fact, it felt as though the temple itself would collapse. People still ran about, playing with each other, and it was as if the singing gave them the peace of mind that the day would never end, that they could run about, drink and eat, with no worries of tomorrow.

Still, it was evident that some people had segregated themselves from others, isolating their brethren in certain areas and not participating in the same gallantry. It was not entirely strange, as there were always those who chose to profit from or take advantage of others during the festival, but this time it was an uncomfortable stalemate directed at members of the other Kunda. Both Sumai and Mashaya middlemen remained controlled and collected in their respective camps, prepared to retaliate in the case of any breach. The rest of the people appeared unfazed, however, regardless of their loyalties, as it was highly taboo to initiate violence on the day of Jamali, and far more preferable to the average man to just ignore their concerns in favor of celebration.

Even the leaders of each Kunda participated, albeit in a more subdued manner, while their immediate underlings stood watch.

The Manu priests soon emerged in their blue robes, wrapped from head to toe, showing only their eyes, causing the entire maza to quickly silence. They were beautiful draperies: one long, dark-blue cloth that was wrapped over and over, covering their bodies entirely. They walked slowly and deliberately down the steps as the temple servants carried huge containers of bread and vegetables. Other servants proceeded with torches and burning herbs, leaving tantalizing aromas in their wake. The priests' robes were cleaned twice a day while they bathed and replaced in their entirety a few times a year. As a result, they always maintained the same color and thick appearance which matched every other priest.

The Manu never left the temple except for religious processions, and it was as enticing for the people of Sumat to see these mysterious beings as it was to receive the bountiful offerings that the servants threw into the crowds.

All that was visible of the priests were their eyes as they quietly stepped in perfect unison with each other. As they reached the end of the temple steps and touched the maza, some people began to scream and cry, many dropping to their knees in worship, kissing the ground beneath them.

The temple itself had always stood in the center of the city, the central focus of it, and the priests were its masters. They were representatives of something powerful and mysterious to the common Sumati which made their presence something like a surreal, waking dream.

That they only made one round of the temple corners made the madness even worse as people tried to absorb as much as they could in the brief moments they had.

Akin and Jarvis mostly remained unaffected by the presence of the Manu. Although Jarvis watched with the same casual nature he always had, Akin had more disdain in his perspective as he watched people wail in despair when they neared the priests. He watched women and men cry, holding their hands together, begging for forgiveness and blessings. They kissed the ground upon where the priests had walked and smothered their faces in it, even to the point of bleeding.

As the priests walked, many people attempted to follow them, pushing through the observing crowd to circulate at the same speed. The mania was intense as people nudged against one another, trying to get to the front and move in time with the procession. It was expected, and adults were able to mostly cope with it. Children, however, were often trampled upon, and Akin could hear screaming and crying from distant parts of the crowd as the more stimulated patrons maniacally shoved through like a force of nature.

As the priests re-emerged in front of the steps, they faced away from the temple and stood in place. From the top of the stairs and within the temple emerged servants dragging along four men who had been severely beaten. Their feet dragged against the steps painting streaks of red along them as they bled out, and upon reaching the bottom of the stairs were thrown to the ground, in a pile, in front of the priests and the crowd.

Suddenly, a thunderous voice emerged from atop the steps as did a number of other voices all around the maza. As Akin looked up, he saw an Iman Ir screaming at the crowd, his body flared.

"People of Sumat!" he screamed. Akin could vaguely hear the other voices repeating similar phrases in different places.

"You asked for justice, and justice is given! My Oam has bestowed a gift upon you, the culprits of murder!"

He pointed to the pile of barely moving, naked bodies.

"Two men! Guilty of unspeakable murder upon an innocent of the Temple City! Two Ir, sworn to protect you but flaunting their oath!

"My Oam, the Untouched, has bestowed a special gift for the people of Sumat! What was once hidden within the sacred enclosure of the great Temple of Mala, now, upon his wish, shared to all its inhabitants as proof! Feast your eyes upon justice!"

His arms lowered after he finished his statement, and more servants exited the temple carrying small containers and large, odd looking devices.

Akin did not realize he was frowning as he watched the servants descend, a sick feeling entering his stomach. He leaned into Jarvis and whispered, still watching the stairs.

"Have you seen this before?" he asked.

"No," Jarvis responded.

Akin looked about, seeing people's faces as they stared at the priests. He remained fixated at moments at the faces of small children who suckled or played with their fingers as they watched intently.

Servants placed a table on one side of the priests while others positioned a larger one in front of the four prisoners who lay there, slowly squirming in a half dazed state. The servants carrying the tools placed them upon the small table, beside the priests.

One of the priests pointed to one of the prisoners. A large servant picked him up and placed him flat on his back on the larger table.

Another priest delicately approached the tools and picked up a very small copper device. It appeared to simply be a ring attached to a rod. He approached the man on the table and looked at the large servant who subsequently pinned the man's hand down.

Akin grabbed Jarvis's wrist and squeezed it.

The priest gently inserted the man's finger into the end of the device and began to twist it. As he did, the man began to scream, banging his heels against the table violently, his body contorting as his flesh began to peel away like the skin of a fruit. The device cut his skin in a very controlled manner, not ripping it off but actually peeling his finger, creating perfect rectangular pieces that hung freely from the end of the device.

Akin felt his knees buckle and was held in place by Jarvis who stared at the event, a cautious frown on his face.

As the man's screams continued, they resonated in Akin's stomach, causing a churning he could not stop. Around him, children began to cry, and he could hear vomiting. He looked around to try to distract himself, but the screaming and blue robes prevented his mind from calming itself, and as the inconsistent banging of bone against wood kept awkwardly resonating against the silence, his head began to heat up.

A well-dressed man who had emerged from the temple began to yell at the crowd.

"First the skin is cleansed of dirt! The deed seeps within, and so the flesh itself is removed!"

After the priest finished with the finger, Akin wished for it to be over, but as he stared in horror, closing in on the priest's hands, he saw him remove the ring and start on another finger.

"Oh, god . . ." he whispered, not taking his eyes off the man on the table.

The man's eyes were wide, and it was as if he was gagging for breath with which to scream. His entire body was bathed in sweat as he screamed, his hands and legs pinned down by servants.

The priest extracted the device, ripping the still connected flesh from his fingers and approached the tools. He placed it down, dripping with blood, and picked up a very small but sharp looking blade.

He then, one by one, pressed it down on the man's fingers, severing them off his hand.

"The hand that sins must be rectified!" the well-dressed man yelled. "With this, the act is undone!"

The man was barely conscious by the time the priest finished both his hands. Many people surrounding the maza had fallen to the ground, shaking, some upon their knees crying, while others watched intently. Akin stood perplexed, his eyes wandering back and forth as his head hung loosely. He was unable to focus clearly upon anything.

"I . . . I must see this, Jarvis. I must witness it," he whispered.

Jarvis, still frowning, supported his friend and looked on.

The man lay there, his bloody stripped fingers on the ground beside him. He was delirious, murmuring words with his eyes closed as his fingerless palms shook. It was clear he had tears, but they were inseparable from the sweat which was now staining the table, causing an uncomfortable squealing sound whenever he flinched.

The priest then picked up something that resembled a flower. It had sharp, pointed and narrow leaves connected to a central circle which had a rod protruding out of it, like a stem.

He approached the man and pressed the center of the flower against the man's penis. He then quickly pulled the rod, causing the blades to snap shut on the man. He screamed, and as the priest pulled roughly, tearing his manhood off, his pitch became so high it was almost inaudible. His entire glistening frame was tensed, his muscles visibly overexerted as he contracted, arching his entire body against the table. Blood began to splatter out, and the priest held the device up to show the crowd. He then opened it, and portions of the man's scrotum fell upon the ground.

"We must prevent this sinner from reproducing in the afterlife! He must be punished for his deed and prevented from perpetuating it!" yelled the well-dressed man.

All around Akin people were vomiting. The man on the table was convulsing as he bled out, losing consciousness. The priest picked up a large blade and stood in front of the man. He lifted the blade, blocking the sun from the man's face and swung it down, beheading him.

"Justice is achieved!" the well-dressed man screamed.

The audience was quiet aside from crying and illness. No one spoke, but random sounds were heard. As Akin saw the man's head roll off the table, seeing the inside of his neck, he could hold it down no longer and began to regurgitate. He knelt down in place and threw up, drenching the ground with his insides. His face tensed as he did, and he too began to cry . . . but not with sadness. It was something that resembled raw terror, loosened by his heaving, resonating out of his mind.

Through the feet in front of him, he saw the servants remove the man's body and throw it upon the ground.

"The culprit, now, the failure of your Kin Ir!"

Akin looked up at the well-dressed man and stood up, wiping his mouth, dazed. He watched the servants pick up another man and place him upon the table.

"Behold! The failure to uphold your vow to My Oam! The people of Sumat, rejoice in justice!"

As Akin saw the man squirm on the table and the blue robed priest grasp a large copper rod, he felt a surge behind his eyes. It wiped his mind of awareness, not knowing what was happening or what had happened, as if he was flung into a dream state. The colors in front of him blurred, and the world tilted as he felt his arms loosen along with his feet. As his head leaned back, beyond his control, he began to fall upon the ground and struck it like a rag doll, unconscious.

When he awoke, it was almost dark. The maza had cleared out of the dense crowd and was replaced by those walking through it, visiting one another or proceeding to a dasha. The city was now preparing for the night festival, lighting lanterns all about, the largest and most ornamental placed at the entrances of restaurants and shops.

Jarvis was dripping water on his brow, supporting Akin's head in his lap as he lay on the ground. Akin looked to the temple stairs, and no record of the priests or tortured remained save the blotchy stains that tainted the surrounding area.

He leaned up and held his head in his hands, trying to awaken out of his drowsy state.

He looked around and at Jarvis, then back to the glitter of the city around him.

"My mind feeds on their trick.

"To store it, deep down in the recesses of my memory, whispering fear to me silently, corrupting my responses."

He lifted his arm, palms up, indicating to the bottom of the stairs.

"But look! It's like a nightmare . . . that is the ruse. A waking nightmare, forced upon me. And though I am no longer aware of it, in a moment, I will become terrified again. A trap ready to spring upon my courage."

Jarvis did not speak but listened to Akin and followed his motions, looking upon everything he pointed to. He put his hand on Akin's arm.

"Come . . . let us eat and drink. It is a worthy discussion to be had," he said.

With Jarvis's help, Akin got up and stretched, still feeling wobbly. Images and sounds of the vulgarities splashed in his mind as they walked, and he felt a sinking sensation as he pondered the fate of the remaining prisoners. He felt guilty, as if he had betrayed them by trivializing their agony by not experiencing it with them and instead contemplating it from the safety of an afterthought.

"Akin!" someone screamed.

Akin turned to face Ghezem, an elder trader who had befriended him some time ago. Akin had visited his store to purchase imported bitters for digestion, and as they talked of rare desert plants, their friendship became more habitual, though still formally informal.

"Come, you bastard. Join me! The Mahjidi too!"

Akin smiled at his joviality and recognized that he was already half drunk. They both joined him, and he threw his arms around them, walking them to a large table which hosted many men, all bantering loudly and drinking.

"Here, drink this. And drink it quick. You are certainly not happy enough, my friend!"

He nearly flung a large vase at Akin, full of liquid fermented barley. Akin turned it to his mouth and drank, gulping down as much as he could. As he did, people at the table began to scream, their voices getting louder the more he drank. When he reached his breaking point, he lowered the vase and took a deep breath in, causing everyone to cheer madly.

He handed it to Jarvis who took it and drank as well, sitting down.

Akin soon felt the juice lighten his mood, and as he looked around the table, he saw the smiling red faces of Sumai men.

He turned to Ghezem and placed his arm over his shoulders, leaning on him. Ghezem looked at him peacefully and rubbed Akin's head. He paused, looking serious for a moment, eyeing the table. His head shook slightly, bobbing front to back in his stupor. He then smiled large and looked back towards Akin.

"So, my young friend . . ." He paused, took a deep breath in, and drank some beer, wiping his mouth. "Tell me . . ."

He talked very quietly.

"Tell me, Akin . . . what did you think . . . what do you think . . ."

He then suddenly raised his voice, raising his hands in the air, screaming at the whole table.

"About our wonderful festivities!"

The men screamed in approval and Akin smiled, eyeing him.

"The beer is good," he grinned.

"Ah, yes . . ." Ghezem responded. "It is delicious, but that is not what I am asking you about."

He looked around and some other members of the group were looking at him, not so much frowning as much as forgetting to smile.

He stared at Akin, not speaking, but as if he had something to say.

He then arbitrarily frowned, as if to mock a child.

"Are you not gleeful that Mastaka's killers were found?" he asked.

Akin looked at the table and smiled, then looked at Jarvis, then back at Ghezem.

"Justice . . ."

He put his hand on Ghezem's shoulder, a menacingly angry twitch growing on his drunken lip.

"Justice was served, was it not?" Akin asked spitefully.

"Ahhh!" Ghezem responded, looking across the table. The others looked back, waiting for him. He drank some more and leaned into Akin, looking at him.

"Justice . . ." he said, slightly smiling, pondering.

Akin no longer smiled, but stared at him.

"Mastaka was a good man," Ghezem said. "I don't believe he wanted to be dead."

He laughed with his comrades as he spoke, and they began to sing. As they continued, he leaned into Akin and whispered into his ear.

"I don't believe many men do."

Akin looked at him, and he no longer smiled, but stared morosely back at Akin, almost threateningly. But Akin was not threatened by it. Instead, he felt comforted by Ghezem's malevolence. Inspired, it seemed, he quickly jumped up on the table and began to sing in his Aizik accent.

Ghezem smiled and began to clap as Jarvis continued to drink quietly.

"The flower, the flower, it was all but a dream that I saw!" Akin screamed.

"The flower, the flower, its petals beautiful raw!

"I screamed to the heavens to deliver its seed!"

He paused, looking at everyone, suddenly all quiet. Then, immediately, everyone screamed in unison.

"But all I received was desert weed!"

He stomped his feet on the table as people banged on it with their hands. Another man jumped up on the table and grabbed Akin in his arms, lifting him up, squeezing him.

Jarvis looked up at Akin and began to giggle, then laugh. As he laughed louder, the rest of the table's attention was diverted to him and became dwarfed by his joviality.

He continued to laugh uncontrollably even as the man lowered Akin and Akin's face drew concern. He leaned down and stepped off the table, hugging Jarvis, who suddenly became silent.

Ghezem also looked at him with concern, frowning.

"Children . . ." Jarvis mumbled, then screamed.

"Children of god!!!"

Blurry flashes of the squirming men flashed in Akin's drunken mind. He saw them as children. He saw them as old people and spirits floating around the world.

He hugged Jarvis tighter.

Ghezem picked up his beer and turned to the those at the table and slammed it down.

"Children of god."

Everyone else repeated, slamming their cups, jugs and vases down, then drank wholeheartedly and quietly.

"Children of god," Akin whispered to Jarvis. Jarvis's eyes tensed as they watered, hearing his words, agony filling his face.

CHAPTER 30
WHISPERS IN A DISTANT LAND

In a dark room sat two men. A candle separated them, and as they faced each other, nothing was visible around them, nor behind them, save their faces, which they did not look upon. Instead, they stared at the flame.

One man wore a weathered face and was old but appeared to have a wilful demeanor. The other was a middle aged man, a stern excitement about him that turned to cold stone at a moment's notice.

They both stared at the flame in silence, though the younger man appeared impatient, looking up at the older one periodically.

"Patience, while I organize, my King," said the older man.

"My patience is at an end. I have waited years in the shadows for what you are about to tell me. Tell me . . . tell me, Havasa . . . what I must know," said the King.

The Havasa closed his eyes and breathed in silently. He then raised his hands in front of him, separating them, and drew a line in the air.

"To the east lay endless riches, my King. Subservient the people have become to the sloth of the wealthy. Rivers and streams to the Desta Ocean. Huffa may travel the length of it unhindered by the ruthless sands. And on the banks, trees upon trees."

The King's face began to glow as he heard the Havasa speak, his eyes pulsating widely on and off as thoughts flashed through his mind.

"What of war?" he asked.

"The Shek armies will soon merge with Dimas soldiery. One unified storm, under your command, will bleed into the desert, my King."

"And what of Dimas heritage, Havasa? Do they plot against the Shek King?" the King asked.

"The remaining loyal to the usurper are quiet, my King. Dislike you, they do, for your Shek heritage, not native to the Red City."

The King frowned distastefully, then smiled.

"They bow before me, do they not?"

"They do, my King," the Havasa replied.

"They are of little concern. I shall make their wives my whores and hang their children upon spears of gold for all to see."

"To fortify your position, my King, such rebellions must be purged silently. The world must see you as a magnificent ruler, as The magnificent ruler, with passion and glory. To certify one's position in your own home, my King, is beneath you. I shall tend to the loyalists."

"Will they conspire?" the King asked.

"No, my King. When I am complete, the palace of Dimas will ring praise and glory upon its new King, and the masses upon the world will hear their voices. Those unwilling to embrace the new world will vanish from memory, my King. Quickly and swiftly."

"What of the lands to the east? What of their voices?"

"The villages will fall . . . loyalty is bred into them through their pagan beliefs. We will provide them something new to worship."

The King smiled maliciously.

"The Shek King . . . will bless them, and they will receive me."

"They will receive you, my King. Examples must be made to wedge the new world. Religious icons . . . people . . . they must be eliminated from memory. The bloodlines must be severed."

"The fathers . . . the mothers . . . the mothers with child and all the beautiful children," the King said, still smiling.

"To cleanse . . ."

He closed his eyes, as if tasting something wonderful. "Purge the pagans and their icons, and bring forth the Shek King."

"The cities will stand firm, but isolated. Damastra will be the first - a small but well respected state. The ruler will bow before you and the others will follow by example. Cowards in their decadence," said the Havasa.

He continued.

"They will demand protection and assurances of their positions. If this is provided, the cities will never sleep. The usurpers and their loyal must be removed from memory to usher in the new world. The bloodlines must be severed."

"And what of war, man?" asked the King impatiently.

The Havasa closed his eyes and breathed deeply, thinking.

"Some will resolve through show of might. Some will resolve through bloodshed. Sumat will test your will, for its ancient roots, like a tree, will be difficult to uproot. But it is modernized, and there are allies amongst them," he replied.

"You will send scouts to Kadasha and seek out Canstad, Ghezem, Menaphir. They are not of Sumati heritage and will be directed by profit. There is unrest in the city, and the Oam alienates his own people while filling the pockets of foreigners. They will turn for power in the new world."

"What of Damastra, Kundi, and Menakala?" the King asked.

"Patience, my King. Damastra will fall upon the might of Dimas armies. Your spearmen may fill the ocean, they are so great in numbers. You are a magnificent military leader, my King. All states will kneel before you. After Damastra will come Sumat. Sumat is a great city and will iconize your ascension as ruler of the new world, my King. Kundi, Menakala, and others past the great rivers will kneel before you. We will use Sumat as a symbol, for Damastra will surrender, but Sumat will not."

"Sumat will not?"

"No, my King," the Havasa replied, "and so, Sumat will burn."

PART III

CHAPTER 31

DIVINITY

"I dreamed of you the other night."

She looked down, then at him, smiling shyly, her beautiful, tender face brimming with youthful femininity.

"I dreamed you wore long, flowing white gowns and stood upon a moving animal . . . a giant animal. And you commanded those around you."

Aydan smiled silently, staring at the ground.

"When you spoke, somehow it echoed all about."

She looked at him.

"What do you think?"

He looked at her briefly then smiled and looked back down.

"I don't know . . . it sounds like a premonition. Maybe I will become a magnificent military leader," Aydan replied.

She giggled.

"You are a beautiful man, Aydan."

He looked away from her, his mouth tense, his face red.

He then looked back at her and smiled, staring into her eyes.

"I force myself, now, to look at you, because it is so scary to me."

She smiled, looking back.

"See? You say such things . . . things that weaken the strong . . . but in your words, you breed strength for yourself. How do you do that?" she asked.

"I am strong?" he asked.

She nodded, smiling.

"I feel you would never do anything just because I told you to. Even if you did, it would be your choice to do it. I don't know why you are like that."

"That sounds like stubbornness, Tima," he smiled.

She shook her head.

"It is different!" she forcefully proposed. "I know stubborn men! Yours is not stubbornness. You are loyal to your heart first. It is somehow within you."

She looked at her feet.

"I really do envy it, Aydan. I want to be loyal to my heart."

Aydan smiled at her.

"And what does your heart tell you?"

"It tells me . . .

"It tells me . . . that I am not happy, Aydan."

He frowned suddenly, surprised.

"Oh . . . but you are with me, and we speak freely. What saddens you?" he asked.

"I am unsure what it is, Aydan. I do not even know if it is sadness."

They sat in silence, both pondering, unsmiling.

"You are beautiful to me, but others are not. Others with different eyes. Their loyalties . . . are not so clear. Do you understand?"

"I don't . . . Tima . . . what others?" he asked.

She paused, then looked at him and smiled quietly.

"Are you about to cry, Tima?"

She nodded, still smiling.

"You can cry . . . if you wish, you can hold my hand so you don't feel so alone."

She wiped her eyes and sniffled, holding his hand.

"This is not such a happy place, Aydan," she said.

Aydan stared at her, trying to understand.

"Do you feel it?" she asked. "Close your eyes and search."

He closed his eyes. She squeezed his hand and did the same.

"Whisper to me, Aydan. Let our hearts whisper together."

"I . . . adore you, Tima."

She grimaced.

"My heart tells me that this does not matter, Aydan. You will never have me."

He suddenly squeezed her hand hard and frowned, about to cry.

"My heart tells me, it is your nightmares that haunt you . . . that tell you such things. You are mine, Tima."

She began to wear a sullen, worn out look upon her face.

They sat in silence, eyes closed, as Aydan held her hand tightly, sweat forming in between their skin. He waited for her, hearing every nuance of her breath, anticipating her response.

"Come with me, Tima. You can come with me."

She shook her head, tears rolling down her face.

"I cannot, Aydan. You will lead a wonderful life with your glorious heart."

He began to cry profusely and fell upon the ground, pressing his forehead into her hand.

"My . . ." he stuttered, "my . . . heart . . . it tells me that you are being a coward, Tima."

"Yes . . . I am," she replied.

"You needn't be . . ."

He looked up at her, the sun glistening off the tears in his eyes.

"You needn't . . ."

He stopped mid-sentence when she looked down at him. He looked up at her face, a face he had grown up with and adored further than he contemplated he ever could. He loved her smiles and knew the little expressions she made depending on her mood.

He stared up at her, his brow frowning, and saw something in her eyes. It was a separation, as if the Tima he had always known was now sleeping somewhere within her, and some new person had taken control of her body. He stared, trying to see her, but as if trying to block out the view, this new person kept moving in the way, separating them.

"What . . . are you doing?" he asked.

She was taken aback and looked confused.

"What do you mean?"

"You turn from this, though I know you do not wish it. Release your heart, Tima. Let it speak to me, as you always have."

She looked at him and cocked her head to the side, looking compassionately at him.

"That time is over, my love."

As he heard her end her sentence, he let go of her hand quickly and turned to lean back against the torn brick she sat on.

He sat there for a few moments, absorbing her presence. He looked at her feet, then her knees and thighs, her stomach and chest, and perused each arm and hand separately. Then he looked upon her face and hair, querying every inch. He frowned as he did and stared at her eyes once more.

"You disappoint me," he said tiredly, then turned and walked away.

He sat in the ghost of an old abandoned house. It was located some ways from the village and had shade in one corner. He sat in it and took a sip of water from his bladder.

The sun was scorching hot as the late afternoon eased on, and Aydan felt as though his head was spinning.

"How does the world end in such a brief moment?" he thought. "How is it possible that yesterday she was my wife, my love, my hope and dreams, and now . . . now . . . it is inconceivable."

He covered his eyes with his hands and began to cry, hunching over.

"If I were a man, a man with flowing robes who commanded the world, she would come to me. But I do not, yet she dreamed it. I do not understand!" he moaned.

He looked at the decrepit side of the house.

"Perhaps she will come to me . . . perhaps, it was a confusion. A momentary confusion. Perhaps my disappointment will awaken her, perhaps she sees reason at this very moment and searches for me."

He smiled.

"It is possible. It is possible."

"It is likely," he whispered to himself.

He contemplated their reunification, how they would hug, how her familiar body would bring him to his knees. He would look upon her face, and love her.

He frowned.

He imagined her face, and though it was her, she was no longer the same. He thought of it again, trying to force familiarity, but it did not return. His jaw began to shake as he thought of her face, trying to find what was previously there.

"What is going on . . ." he asked himself.

"Tima, Tima, Tima . . ." he repeated, over and over.

"What is happening?!" he screamed, terrified.

His head began to buzz, and he lay down in the frame of the abandoned house, closing his eyes. As he began to drift away, fantastical thoughts swirled in his head, dreaming of being awoken by her hands, her familiar feminine body.

As he smiled at the thought, he curled up and felt a sinking sensation in his stomach which he pushed away by diving towards the unconscious. He was already half asleep when he heard the whisper.

"Was there truly a dream, brother?"

Aydan awoke in the center of an ocean of sand, his eyes gracing the black horizon as the night sky filled the universe above. The wind was silent, but cool and present.

"I am lost, Samaye," he said, looking down, his finger already stroking his friend's hair.

Samaye's head lay in his lap, pale as it was the last time they spoke.

"I am lost, brother."

"You are never lost, Akin. Your heart is the center of the universe, a powerful entity, and it travels with you, always."

Aydan's eyes filled with tears.

"It matters not how anyone calls upon me . . . but when you say my name, I know who I am."

Samaye smiled weakly at him.

"You carry me with you, brother. You carry the essence of my life in you."

Aydan began to weep.

"I am so alone, Samaye."

Samaye looked up at the sky as Aydan's tears fell upon his face.

"Stare at the stars with me, brother."

Aydan looked up and saw the dark sky, trickled with an infinite sea of sparkling lights in random, beautiful patterns.

"What are they, Samaye?"

"I do not know, brother. But they are a part of us . . . a part of our world."

He looked down and grasped some sand in his hand.

"Like the sand, Akin."

Aydan shuddered, closing his eyes, feeling pain within.

"Please . . . say it once more, brother."

"Akin . . . Akin . . . you are Akin."

Aydan squeezed his hand upon a lock of Samaye's hair as he cringed, then opened his eyes and took a sudden, deep breath in.

"Akin . . ." Aydan said out loud. He looked up at the stars again.

"Not rifts in the universe for the ancient wars . . . but sand. The sand above . . ."

Samaye smiled.

"The sand above."

"As the sand below . . ." responded Aydan.

The weight of Samaye's head upon his lap was a comfort, knowing he was with his friend. He held a lock of Samaye's hair like a child, staring quietly above, trying to absorb the visceral view and spot the changes in the lights as they twinkled.

"There is a wind above, just as particles float upon the desert."

The landscape was perpetually dark, and though the moonlight shone over the sand, it could only be seen for some distance, vanishing into blackness. A black horizon was clearly cut in every direction, making the whole universe seem empty except for them, for them.

"This is not the place to be . . . amongst the dead," Aydan commented, still staring upwards, a cold breeze shuffling past his face.

"Not here, brother. A world awaits you."

"I fear it."

"Do you believe there exists a flower in the middle of the desert?"

Aydan pondered for a moment.

"No, Samaye, I do not. I believe the sands are as they are, with shrubs and weeds, and there are no magics touched by god."

"Do you believe you are touched by god?"

Aydan grimaced, and his tears again began to well up.

"Do you?" Samaye asked.

Aydan nodded, his face squinting in pain.

"Yes . . ."

"Then there is nothing to fear, brother, for everything you are is as it should be."

Aydan nodded, still crying, his face grimacing.

Suddenly, he flew into the air, staring at the skies. As he turned his head to see the ground beneath him, it moved like a blur, stopping above his village. He descended upon it from the sky, finding Bethelhurst sleeping in his cot. He slept on his chest, his mouth agape as he breathed in and out.

Akin stood beside him and looked at him with an overwhelming compassion in his eyes, tears still drying on his cheek. He kneeled down beside him and looked at his face.

"Don't you know that the sky touches you?" he whispered lovingly.

He stared at him, his head tilted sideways, observing his breathing.

"The world breathes with you, defa. Don't you see there are worse things in this world than an uncommon son?"

He stared, awaiting a response he knew he would not receive. He stood slowly and looked down at his father, sadness upon his face.

"You will always do as you wish . . . led by your fears. What terrorizes you, I do not know. I do not think you remember anymore either."

He placed his hand upon his father's cheek, feeling its warmth.

"I adore you, defa."

His eyes began to well up as he looked down at Bethelhurst, pain in his face, consuming him.

"This is the last time you will ever hear my voice."

The world turned black. He was in the center of the night desert once again, alone. His eyes tensed and he looked about him. Something began to surge within him, in his stomach, and became larger and larger.

Though it felt painful, it was powerful, like an explosion of energy resonating from the center of his body, filling every part of his system, slowly making its way to his extensions.

He felt his whole body heat up, rising upwards.

Suddenly, his head snapped backwards, his mouth flung open, and he began to roar. It was an alien sound, louder than anything he had ever witnessed. It was visible to him as something he could not describe, but it filled the air quickly and traveled upwards and downwards, blowing the sand around him away in a sandstorm.

The stars above blew like the sand below, distorting and pushing away. His arms extended behind him, his palms wide open, his whole body tense as the immense, lucid sound left him.

He collapsed suddenly, falling forward upon his hands. As he focused his eyes, there was nothing but blackness. He could see nothing around him, not even his hands or body. The sky was empty; even the night sun had vanished. He stood up, but could not feel the ground beneath him though he was supported in place.

There was no wind or noise - just silence. He opened his eyes and closed them, and could no longer tell whether they were ajar or not for the lack of difference in light. It was perpetual blackness, and he was weightless.

He did not know if he had closed his eyes and allowed his body to float in place as his mind became empty, silent, and quiet, like the universe around him. It was sleep, but he was fully aware of everything around him, as if he chose to sleep and could alter that choice at will.

The world changed, and as Akin slowly opened his eyes, the familiar wall in Jarvis's house emerged in view. He breathed out deeply, sinking into the cot.

CHAPTER 32
HUNGER

T wo men stood up on a dune upon the desert sands, the scorching sun beating down on them. There was a wind blowing particles across the sandy hills, dancing with the sparse hairs on their legs.

Their feet were weathered, the color faded, and they wore sandals of a military type, thicker and more rugged than domestic ones. Their lower extremities were vacant of hair having been stripped from endless days in the harsh desert.

One man pulled his tunic off, hung it on a spear stabbed into the sand, squatted, and began defecating.

"What do you think of what Toofa said?" he asked.

The other man stood, leaning upon a long spear.

"It matters not . . . if they surrender, I will still take my fill."

He smiled maliciously at the other man who grinned back.

"I have heard that if you break the treaties the Shek makes, he punishes you severely."

The other man scoffed.

"The King wants us to break these rules to strike fear into their hearts. It makes conquest easier. The diplomacy of these bureaucrats has no place in war - the King is a warrior."

The squatting man tensed as he released.

"What will you do?" he asked.

"Once we enter Damastra . . . whether it be peaceful or not . . . we will find a home with a great many daughters."

He grinned, an erection growing under his tunic.

"Two of us will guard the door while the rest take their turns. We will do fun things to them. I will sing as they scream."

The squatting man looked up at the other man and thought for a moment, then smiled.

"Sisters? That sounds good."

"Sisters . . . their mother if she is worthy," the standing man responded. "They exist right now, Hafa!"

He looked on the other side of the dune and kept smiling, a spark in his eyes.

"Right now, they travel back and forth, carrying water in their virtuous clothing. Beautiful, lovely young girls."

He knelt down and looked at Hafa.

"I can smell them, Hafa."

He closed his eyes, breathing in.

"I can smell their beautiful, soft cothas in the wind."

He placed his palm upon his lips and kissed it, then pressed his hand down on the ground, smiling at his friend. He slid his hand along the sand.

"The sands will lead us to our princesses, won't they Hafa?"

Hafa began to laugh eagerly and did the same thing, kissing his palm then pressing it against the sand.

He then arose and stretched, grabbed his tunic and threw it over his body. He looked over the dune. He was a slightly larger man than his friend, but both were muscular and lean.

They both began to walk to the top of the dune and disappeared over the climax.

On the other side of the dune was a large flat valley, and though it was filled with desert sand, the orange pebbles were barely visible. Instead, a plethora of men populated the area with gusts of wind traveling through their ranks. Some had tents, others lay upon mats, and thousands upon thousands of spears littered the landscape, poked into the ground, their shiny heads pointed to the heavens.

The two men descended to join the large gathering as others traveled up and down dunes surrounding the encampment.

"Do you miss Heena?" Hafa asked.

"I have all the Heena I need in the cothas of our conquered wives," the other man responded bluntly.

Hafa laughed.

"No, I am serious. Do you miss home?"

The other man stopped and looked at him.

"There is nothing like this. Home is a relic. We are conquerors . . . masters of the world."

He pointed to the mass of soldiers.

"We are brothers. The world has not seen an army as numerous or powerful. Don't you see? We have broken the barriers of the gods. I worship the Shek King . . . his bloodlust is greater than my own, but even he controls it better than I. That is why he leads us."

He gently slapped Hafa in the face.

"You forget about home. Home is our spears within the chests of our enemies. That is home. Heena is an old luxury not worthy of us."

Hafa nodded.

"I want to lick those daughters, Reima," he said. "I hope they do not speak our language so their words sound foreign when they scream."

Reima smiled.

"Foreign cothas!" he impulsively screamed.

"Foreign cothas!" Hafa screamed back.

As they approached a group of men, they turned to them.

"What were you shouting about?" one of them asked.

Reima stood close to the man and began to suck on his own finger, grinning.

"Foreign cothas, my friend."

"Aaaah . . ." the other man smiled.

The whole group began to make jovial sounds, some dancing slightly, wiggling their bodies, making licking noises.

Reima fell to the ground and leaned back on his arms.

"What do you think our spears are made of?" he asked randomly.

Some others kept joking amongst themselves. One man sat down opposite him, cross legged.

"I've not seen anything like it," Reima continued.

He pulled his spear down and slapped the side of the spearhead with his hand. It was a silver color, the size of his palm.

"Only the Shek knows for certain," the other man responded, examining his own spear.

"Where do you think the relic is?" he asked.

Reima shook his head.

"I think only the Shek's advisers know. He guards it, I have heard."

"Do you think he would have become King if not for the relic he found?" the other man asked.

Reima looked at the other man aggressively.

"Of course! The technology is just aid to his cause. He found the relic, sought to construct weapons of it, and it facilitated him. It matters not whether these weapons are special or not. It is his leadership."

"I wonder how old it is," the other man replied.

Reima continued to examine his spearhead.

"They say even he does not know where it came from or how old it is. Just that he led his people to it in the middle of the sands, and it stood, half covered, shining in the sunlight. And when he struck it, and heard it echo, he knew it was what he had been looking for."

The other man tried to bite the end of his spear.

"I've never seen material like this."

"They say it is ancient . . . from the wars of the gods. And so the Shek constructed weapons of it, and we are an army of men, armed by the gods. That is why we cannot be defeated," Reima responded.

"Do you think we will fight in Damastra?" the other man asked.

Reima smiled.

"When the King arrives to lead us, we will find out."

He leaned in close and whispered.

"But I assure you, I will kill something before that day is over."

CHAPTER 33
AURORA

Akin's dreams had driven his waking emotions for days. A depression had taken hold of him, for every time he saw Jarvis, it seemed a weight fell over him. He spent much of the time wandering the streets, silently taking note of the changes in the city.

At night, mothers and daughters were escorted by their sons and husbands to the thinning river to avoid the turbulent rushes that had taken form during the day. The desperation of the Mashaya farmers was visibly ignited as fights broke out amidst the huge crowds that surrounded the edge of the river from dawn till dusk.

Akin would sometimes sit in the distance and watch as the people would, like a swarm of insects, climb over each other to reach Mala's waterway.

Though it thinned, most concluded it was a normal trend, and that as time progressed, it would widen once more. The rich families suffered little, however, as they had prioritized access to higher parts of the river.

Even the local food shortages were supplanted by massive influxes of imported goods, and none benefitted more than the Sumai merchants. As months passed, for the first time in the city's history, Juma began to appear a dejected old neighborhood as more and more wealth was directed towards Kadasha.

Akin's own appetite for the dashas in the Mashaya neighborhood began to wane as walking its streets became both distasteful and dangerous. The Mashaya families had already begun to splinter as some formed limited partnerships with foreign traders through desperately unfavorable contracts, while others turned to crime.

Kadasha, on the other hand, had become more busy than Juma ever was, as never before was there such an immense focus placed upon such a small area of the city. The rich clamored over new and rare imports, and the poor were able to eat at cheaper prices than even the local farmers were able to provide for their limited access to arable land.

Jarvis had become increasingly isolated, speaking little as his workload increased, even as his health began to deteriorate. The impending approach of the Shek made his visits to the Oam an almost daily occurrence, especially after it was rumored that Damastra had surrendered without a fight.

Foreign information was readily available to the masses as trade blossomed, and it was heard that the Damastra king was publicly beheaded before his people by the Shek King and had professed his loyalty to the invader as the sword fell. Such was the nature of their agreement, Akin had concluded.

Mashaya and Sumai tension slowly dissolved after Jumali. Foreign traders prospered by selling their goods to the Sumati elite at exorbitant prices while local foods and goods became both less plentiful and demanded. However, since a large majority of the rich in Sumat were locals, Mashaya aggression no longer isolated itself to the Sumai and opened itself to anyone and everyone. Even amongst their own ranks, there were feuds, though murder was rare.

Their leader, Rafae, attempted to maintain control and manage the organization, but it was rumored that he too had begun to instruct his subordinates to seize shipments and orchestrate minor robberies around the city. Such events were done carefully, however, so as to not awaken the ire of the powers that be, and generally went unnoticed. And though they avoided large, noticeable crimes, keeping their presence hidden from those that would police them, the common people quickly learned just how much more dangerous the streets had become.

Akin would often sit in the maza, watching the beggars and passersby. Something had changed in the interactions of the people, even if only in a slight manner. Akin had spent much time in his past life watching the people as they walked and interacted and was convinced that if he were a beggar in the present, he would starve to death.

Since Jumali, and over the span of time since, people's gaze towards each other had turned a slight more aggressive. The poor were more ruthless in their approach to begging, and the rich seemed to appear surprised when approached and reacted defensively. Akin's own methods would be hard pressed to find success as rarely were the beggars looked upon or even acknowledged. It was as if a cloud had befallen the city, for even though in the past, life was hard, the hope of a brighter day did not seem so elusive.

The air of isolation that seemed to surround everyone in slight manners appeared amplified in Akin. It felt as though a pungent stink followed him around, for any interaction, subtle and irrelevant as it may have been, almost consistently left him feeling worse than he did a moment prior.

Sleep, too, did not come easy. He would lay in bed, aware that Jarvis was in the house, feeling as though he would like to say something to him, to share something with him, but somehow knew that it was pointless and had no drive to pursue it. After long periods of sleeplessness and running in obsessive, unsure loops, he would eventually close his eyes and drift away. The dreams were lucid when he slept in such manners, for it seemed the more he could not sleep, the more vibrant and mesmerizing his visions became.

He walked one day, amidst the crowds, past the main road to Kadasha and out the gates of the city. The river was hidden behind groups of people who fought for access. They seemed like parasites fighting to digest the last morsel of flesh, the river being the corpse they fed upon. He had seen insects feed on a dead animal long ago, and stared at it in awe as he did so at the river. In and out people jumped and pushed, and the angry noise was both constant and deafening. Nothing was discernable in the screaming and yelling, with parents scolding their children, pushing them into the small crevices of the crowds, ignoring their frightened crying.

It was mid-day, and just as the sun stared directly downwards at the people, so too did the intensity of their desires climax. This was the busiest time of the day, when the most people were awake and readily seeking to mine the blue gold.

Akin sat down in the middle of nowhere, watching the spectacle. The noises were so continuous, so loud, that it became a hum to him, resonating more peacefully in his ears than silence would. His back faced the sun, and a cloak covered the back of his body, protecting his flesh. He began to sweat, but even as the feverish shivers came amidst the intense heat that began to penetrate his skin, he relaxed even further.

The brightness of the sand that glowed in front of him was piercing to his state of mind, and he closed his eyes, pulling his hood further, narrowing his view.

The noises became a hum, continuous, and time began to bend like something truly tangible and wonderful. It stretched out the world, and though he knew he sat upon the golden sand, his emotions fell down a deep chasm. As he abandoned worry and closed his eyes amidst the free-fall, he suddenly realized he was not falling, but flying upwards. But then, even as he smiled with joy as he spread his arms wide apart, he again saw that he was neither falling nor flying. There was no direction, no force upon him, yet he moved and certainly traveled, for he felt the motion across his face, and emotions scraping the edge of the universe, as he discovered new pockets of awareness.

But he was not distant from the sands, or the people, or the water that they so desperately sought. In fact, the sounds began to bounce against his awareness and trigger sensational beauty within him, the heat of the sun causing the feverish aura to consume him, sending shivers up and down his spine into every part of his body.

"What . . . magnificence . . ." he whispered.

He isolated the sound . . . a sound that may have always been there. But as his mind gravitated towards it, it became louder as all the other sounds seemed to fade. It was not true, for he could hear them just as loudly as before, but the baby was there, as if right next to him, crying, wailing in despair.

Akin smiled, tears running down his face intertwined in salty sweat as he imagined the child. It was so utterly beautiful to him, that the sound was like a dream that could not possibly exist in reality. It had to be a figment of his imagination, for it was so real, so intense . . . the event of a creature so complicated and alive as the child, crying, overwhelmed him. He could not look upon it, but attach its sounds to his imagination, some beautiful creature that sought bread and water and so aggressively and sharply pursued what it desired, using its eyes and mouth, and even its hands, to alter the universe around it.

Blood coursed through its system, under its skin, and its muscles tightened as it relayed its passion with utter accuracy to the world around it, grasping for someone to care for it.

Akin took a deep breath in and supported himself against the sand, feeling ill. The sounds suddenly became loud, intense and coarse, knocking at his head as physically as a brick would. He wiped his face and straightened himself, closing his eyes once more.

He focused on the heat at his back which immediately shot through him again, the burning shivers sending his body into a disjointed state. Not cold, not hot, but as if dipped in boiling oil, and evaporating into the sky.

"What . . . is . . ." he whispered, suddenly moving his head, as if following the direction he traveled in his heart.

"I see you . . ."

He saw his mother's face, and though it was still, as if a single unmoving memory, he could move about her, exploring her in detail. Her face was unclear, but emotionally distinct.

"I am leaving, Aydan."

"No, you are not."

"I have to leave, my son."

"Why, maja?"

"My heart is not here."

Her face changed, and he saw it from above as a child, looking into the pit. She was worried and sad, but she did not reach out for him, and he did not reach out for her. They stood, looking at each other.

He turned his head and saw Bethelhurst's shadow in the desert night. He was hitting her, then picked up a tool and bashed her skull. She fell to the ground in a heap, dead.

He looked down and saw her lying on her cot. She looked at him and smiled, then took a knife and slit her throat.

He looked up and saw his own reflection. He stared at it as it stared back at him. It spoke as he spoke.

"You will never know."

He paused and stared at himself, examining the wrinkles around his eyes and the unique shape of his mouth.

"But you do know."

"Yes."

"She betrayed her heart."

"Yes."

He looked at his chest.

Akin quickly reached under his tunic and pressed his hand against his beating heart, immersed in sweat. His reflection opened its eyes, grimacing.

"You are a child of the universe," he simultaneously whispered and said to his reflection.

He saw an image of Tima smiling, unmoving like his mother, a frame frozen in time. Then his father, looking downward, hiding a smile under his nose.

Akin opened his mouth, his head tightening with intensity.

He saw Samaye's dead face, but it was not frozen. It lay unmoving upon his lap, but existed in real-time.

"Oh, God . . ." Akin whispered.

His reflection began to grimace further, opening its mouth.

Loud, deafening, the reflection began to speak in unison with his silent but intense whispers.

"More heart . . . more heart . . ."

His reflection gasped for air as did he.

"More heart in death through action . . ."

He saw Samaye's perished face in front of him, unfrozen as the others.

The tension that held his chest suddenly loosened, and he breathed in deeply, feeling the release.

Akin began to smile and cry, laughing, thinking about Samaye's face.

"You held your life in your palm, my brother," he whispered in tearful joy. "You died more fulfilled than any man I know."

He began to laugh uncontrollably, pure, sheer happiness enveloping him. He cried immensely as he laughed, tasting his salty tears mixed with sweat, feeling overjoyed at the sensation. His reflection smiled sincerely and fully at him, slowly fading away.

He continued to laugh and pulled his cloak off, tossing it behind him. The sun mercilessly attacked him with heat and sunlight, and he stood up, his entire body drenched in sweat, eyes closed, and smiled as it touched every inch of his skin.

He slowly opened his eyes and began to focus on everything around him: the people still fighting for the river, coming and going, and the gates of Sumat in the distance.

He leaned down and picked up his cloak, walking slowly and calmly back towards the city, smiling genuinely, looking at the sand around him and each person that walked past, tears still encrusted upon his face.

He stumbled once, losing his breath, and as his hand struck the earth to support him upon his knees, he laughed once more, breathing heavily. He stared at the sand, lost in thought, a sincere smile upon his face. The wind upon the grains danced in front of him, and as he saw some particles move across the skin of the back of his hand he leaned down, pressing his lips against it, kissing.

He retracted his head and looked at the back of his hand once more where a wet outline of his lips caught the particles, holding them to it. He began to laugh once more, crying in ecstatic joy. He ran his other hand across the wetness, smudging it, and took a deep breath in, watching the shape of the impression change. He closed his eyes and held his hand against his head and sat there for some time, collecting himself.

When he opened his eyes, he looked to the nearby gates of Sumat and peered into the city.

"Beauty, even in that," he whispered to himself, slightly smiling.

He arose once more and again continued to walk towards the gates.

Once in the city, like a blur, he noticed people walking towards him and past him in every direction. Though he acknowledged their existence, they were like particles isolated from him, moving at lightning fast speeds. They were not people, nor did they make noise or sounds. All he could feel and hear was the resonating angst in him, as though he had been asleep for years and was overwhelmed with the drive to act.

He ran up the street to Jarvis's house and did not even notice the guards at the entrance as he breezed past them.

"Jarvis!" he screamed.

Jarvis came out of his room and looked at Akin.

Akin stopped and looked at him, a large smile on his face.

Jarvis stared at him, suppressing his curiosity in favor of a confused dismay.

Akin stared at him still, widening his smile suddenly. He inhaled, but interrupted his breath, for at that moment, it seemed he was meant to say something, and so, mid breath, he began to speak.

"Let us go."

"Where?" Jarvis asked.

Akin smiled again as if reacting to being toyed with. He looked more intently at Jarvis, silently smiling.

"Ask your heart, my friend . . . and you will hear it. I am with you. Take nothing save a cloak, and we leave forever."

Jarvis frowned and took a deep breath in, suddenly holding back tears. He squinted tensely.

"What are you talking about? I . . . I cannot leave. They will kill me . . . they will kill you!" he replied.

He rubbed his forehead and closed his eyes.

"We will . . . find a way. We will find a way."

Akin walked up to Jarvis and held his shoulders in his hands.

"Come, Jarvis. I am leaving. I am leaving, right now!"

Jarvis could scarcely look at him, again trying to calm himself. Akin followed his face and eyes as he tried to distract himself, staring intently at Jarvis.

"You are my friend."

He grabbed Jarvis's hand and held it tightly.

"We travel together . . . always."

Jarvis stared at Akin's eyes. His eyebrows contorted as he felt a surge of pain fill his brain. Akin stared back at him sternly and sympathetically.

Jarvis swallowed.

"Two cloaks . . . I suppose."

Akin smiled.

"Yes! Two cloaks will be perfect. Smear them with some ungodly odor. It will help us blend in."

He began to laugh.

Jarvis returned to his room and quickly threw clothes all over the place, looking for the cloaks. When he found one, he pressed his hand against it and breathed, sighing. He closed his eyes and smiled.

"I can scarcely feel myself . . . though I am alive, somewhere . . ." he whispered.

They quickly left the house, carrying the cloaks. Jarvis looked back as they walked, feeling the surreal nature of their anticlimactic departure as the house became smaller and smaller. An unknown excitement, like a bright spinning light, seemed to be blaring in his chest, causing him to feel manic.

He suddenly laughed once.

"Wondrous," he said.

Akin looked at him and smiled.

"Are you ready?"

Jarvis took a breath in and nodded. They snuck into a corner and covered themselves completely in brown cloaks. They were of bad design, old, and of the types many of the poor wore in and around the city.

Before they exited the corridor, Jarvis grabbed Akin's arm.

"There is no return, Akin. Mahjidi to the Oam are forbidden to leave the city. If we are caught, they will give us to the priests. You will go first. If I am caught, you will still be past the gates, and I will see you in the next life."

Akin stared at him, then nodded calmly. He smiled slightly and tapped Jarvis's bristled cheek lovingly.

"Follow your heart, old man, and you are already free."

Without another word, they both left the corridor and proceeded to the gate.

The gate was filled with people. Two guards on each side stood with spears, half-watching the people, half-talking amongst themselves. The crowds were in full-swing, the afternoon having just begun, and the rush of citizens going to the river had saturated not only the gate, but the entrance to the city.

Akin and Jarvis joined in the line. Jarvis nudged Akin forward and waited a few moments to continue, leaving space between them. The crowd moved slowly, and they tried to remain as centered within it as possible. Though they smelled bad, the crowd was so thick that the plethora of odors had now become a normal part of the movement and went unnoticed. In fact, it seemed to encourage the people around them to interact less and focus only on moving forward.

The noise was loud. People yelled at each other to move quicker, and the general chaos of the crowd formed a promising subterfuge.

Even as Akin approached the line of exit, his heart remained tense. He was permitted in and out, but the true gamble was Jarvis. If he was caught, he did not know what he would do, as leaving without his friend did not seem a comprehensible path. Jarvis, however, had planned for that possibility, and respecting his wishes was an important factor to consider. He pondered these questions, and as he did, he failed to realize that he was now past the gates and in the free open desert. He turned and looked for Jarvis, biting his lip nervously, the tension causing his legs and arms to tighten as his stomach started to tingle.

Jarvis was not as nervous as he was determined. He skillfully walked with a common lack of grace that was normal for the old and poor. He did not make eye contact with anyone and kept his face sufficiently hidden, yet not absolutely covered. Even if noticed by a guard, the masterful manner in which he played the part would make him appear familiar yet irrelevant. Even the focus of the exodus became his motivation, and he thought only about water and begging and the wretchedness his beggar life.

As he walked past the same line of exit, he felt both excitement and relief. In front of him, the crowd began to disperse and widen, and as he stepped forward, he saw a cloaked figure staring back at him. Akin's familiar smiling face was one of the most beautiful things he had ever seen at that moment, and he was overwhelmed with joy.

He turned his head and looked at the guard behind him. He was leaning on his spear and laughed at something the other guard said. He had an apathetic demeanor about him, and Jarvis could sense the familiar comfortability the guard had with his position. He did not understand its significance, nor did he care of its effect. He was a representation of all the ugliness from the Oam down that had corrupted Sumat.

A scowl formed on his face.

He looked up at the gates. The city had been his home, and since taking his vow, he had never left the city or touched the open desert. He had tried to do what he could, but lived in constant fear though he often forgot how terrified he was.

He turned and looked back at Akin whose smile had now lessened as he stared concernedly at his friend. Jarvis looked at him deeply and then slowly began to remove his cloak. As he did, Akin's eyes widened in horror.

The people walking in and out initially ignored him, but as his face became visible, more and more people slowed their pace, starting to notice the familiar old man.

"You!" he screamed, pointing at the guard. The guard looked at him, initially surprised.

"Can you hear me?" he yelled.

The people around them became increasingly quiet. The guard looked at Jarvis, still not yet recognizing him.

"Yes . . ." the guard replied, embarrassed at the attention being focused on him.

"Your mother was such an ugly whore, that the only creature willing to father you was a three-legged dog!"

The entire crowd stood silently, along with the guard, stunned. The guard frowned and picked up his spear, approaching a smiling Jarvis menacingly.

"It's the Mahjidi!!!" a person screamed.

The guard stopped, both confused and surprised, trying to recognize the man.

"You . . . you left the city?!" the guard asked Jarvis, bewildered.

"That's right, you box of shit. I did."

"The drought! He has cursed us!!!" another person bellowed.

"You stupid old man!" the guard screamed, hitting him in the head with the edge of his spear.

Almost all at once, the crowd closed in on Jarvis, hitting him. He fell to the ground, bloodied immediately.

Another cloaked figure jumped on top of him, protecting him from the blows.

Underneath all the rage and the blunt end of the spear, Jarvis and Akin were beaten unconscious. As they lay there, almost passing into the darkness, Akin tried to see his friend, whose bloody face was lying sideways in the sand.

"Jarvis . . .

"Jarvis . . . are you all right?" he whispered.

Jarvis suddenly inhaled and searched for and grabbed Akin's hand, squeezing it. Akin immediately cried, smiling at him.

"Sometimes . . ." Jarvis whispered.

"Sometimes . . . it is better to tell someone to go fuck themselves . . . than get away."

Akin abruptly laughed. He then felt a strike against the back of his head and disappeared.

CHAPTER 34
LEVIATHAN

"I am trying as hard as I can, yua."

"Well you must try harder, boy."

He pressed the stone deeper against himself, pushing it inside, grimacing.

"Harder, boy!"

He began to cry and obeyed.

"I am trying, yua!"

The man chuckled and looked at his comrades, then back to the boy.

"You are a disgusting little thing, my lovely boy."

The boy wept.

"Why do you cry?"

"Because it hurts."

They chuckled once more.

"If you don't press it in, so far so I can see it no more, I will come and do it for you. You need not accomplish what I ask . . . all I ask is that you try. That is what a yua does, is it not?"

The boy nodded, still crying. The man's face turned serious.

"Now sit on it."

He began to cry harder, anticipating the pain.

"What do you think?" one man asked.

The yua shrugged and watched the boy as he painstakingly tried to sit, supporting himself with his hands, trying to press the stone further inside.

"Yua, it hurts!!!"

The man stared at him as the boy stared back. His eyes were swelled with tears, and he looked unblinkingly desperate. The yua returned a stare, unemotional, yet both understanding and acknowledging the agony the boy was in.

"Did you try your hardest?"

"Yes! Yes, I tried. I swear on my mother's life, I tried yua, I tried."

The boy lifted himself slightly. The man arose and screamed at him.

"Did I tell you to stop?!"

The boy shook his head fearfully and pressed down once more, clenching his teeth, his eyes closed.

The man slowly sat down, staring at the boy.

"Now you may stop," he said.

The boy fell over without rising and breathed deeply on the sand.

"Pull it out and bring it to me."

The boy slowly pulled the stone out, grunting as he did, and crawled over to the man, handing it to him. He examined it carefully and showed it to some of the other men sitting close, smiling. He stood, holding it up in the air.

"Nectar! We have nectar, and tomorrow it shall turn to gold!" he proclaimed melodiously. All the men began to cheer and scream as the boy lay on his side, his eyes wide, immobilized in pain.

As the men jeered and cheered, talking loudly, the boy squeezed his eyes shut as tears began to run down his face. A large man crawled to him and placed his hand on his side, comforting him. The boy opened his eyes slightly and looked up, seeing the heavily scarred face of a large and brooding warrior.

"I'm sorry . . ." the boy muttered.

The man smiled at him.

"What are you sorry for?" he asked in a raspy voice, his broken lip slurring his slow speech.

"I don't know," he said as he began to cry. "I am just sorry."

"Do you think of your sister?"

The boy nodded and cried at the thought.

"Safia . . . her name was Safia, yes?"

"Safia . . ." the boy bellowed, crying, thinking of his elder sibling.

"Do you know what ora is, my boy?"

The boy shook his head, crying. He held his behind tight in his hand, covering it and keeping it warm.

"Ora . . . is what the weak call strength. Ora is a seemingly impassable combination of fear and pain. Pain you cannot contemplate. You cannot survive it, you think."

He pressed his finger against his chest.

"It changes your heart, when you pass through the seemingly impassable," he motioned with his hand.

"Does it make it better?" the boy asked.

The man pondered the question, staring at the boy.

"It is . . . as it should have been. Your thoughts are impure until you witness ora. Until you suffer it. Then you understand."

"I . . . don't understand . . . yua."

"No . . . you do not. What I am saying is not familiar to you. But every man here understands. Every man here has a hard blackness coursing through his veins. Not in other camps, but this one. I am Sangis, the Man in Black."

"The Man in Black?" the boy asked.

"It is what they call me. Those that have seen me from a distance. It is what the people in your caravan knew me as."

The man grinned as he sensed woe erupt in the boy.

"Thoughts of your previous life grace you . . . they fill you with a soft pain, do they not?"

The boy nodded weakly, feeling needy of the man.

They sat in silence, the man's hand still on the boy's side. They watched the other men as they talked and laughed, some observing Sangis and the boy, others eating and drinking.

The boy's face dropped sharply, and he began to cry.

"Do you think Safia is all right?"

Sangis looked sympathetically at him, his eyebrows raised.

"Oh, my boy. I'm quite sure the things those men are forcing into her are far worse than what we are doing to you."

The boy lost his breath and stared at Sangis, his eyes unable to react to the shock.

"But as long as you do as you are told, she will live."

The boy began to cry uncontrollably loudly, drawing the stares of some of the others.

"It is better if she lives, is it not?"

The boy nodded profusely, confusedly, crying uncontrollably.

"Now come here and give me a kiss," Sangis said, grinning at him, leaning towards him.

As he pulled the boy in, the others began to cheer, their voices drawing the attention of others in the distance. Some of the other groups also began to cheer, and soon, spreading like wildfire, the entire Shek army was bellowing into the night.

Like an infectious disease, every camp that began to cheer triggered five around it. Thousands of thunderous war cries roared into the sky. They banged their spears against the ground, some against their shields, their bare skins of a thousand different shades like beasts in the moonlight, screaming for blood and carnality.

Even the King himself heard it, far off in the distance, in a tent surrounded by guards.

"My dear brother," the King smiled. "Do you hear them?"

He looked at a thin man in an austere hat who lay on the cot behind him.

"They cheer for you, my brother."

The man smiled.

"No, they cheer for you, my King. I am just a vessel of your prosperity."

The King smiled once more.

"You are a good brother, Amus. We will see the great walls of Sumat tomorrow. Are you ready?"

Amus took a deep breath in, reflecting.

"I have seen you defy the odds, my King. I have seen you do things I thought impossible. And now you lead the largest army the universe has ever seen. That I could be the one to light this fire is a blessing I will carry with me into the afterlife."

The King looked at him suddenly, seriously.

"You are prepared then?" he asked.

Amus also became serious.

"Yes, my King."

The King smiled.

"Good. You rest. You close your eyes and sleep now."

The King refocused himself towards the massive table in front of him. Upon it was a thin layer of sand, and in it was etched a large replica of the Sumati walls. On various sides, different symbols were beveled in, and he continued to make small adjustments, flattening out where and in what numbers these symbols remained.

He exited the tent and looked down upon the distant Dimas army. In the moonlight, the small fires and men were spread as far as the eye could see. He reached under his royal tunic to grasp his sword, sheathed and tempered masterfully. It was a unique item, made of the same material as the spears bestowed upon the men of the Shek. Its glow shone in the moonlight, and he held its black handle tightly with both hands.

He rubbed his thumbs against his fingers, the night wind passing over his hand.

"Streams of blood absorbed into the sand, and the last memory of a once great city forever bound to the lord of lords."

The wind blew disproportionately strong the next morning. Wrapped in their covers, the soldiers had awoken one by one, covered in sand. Like a ritualistic dance, thousands of men shook their sleepdress in the wind, ensuring no creatures had taken refuge overnight. As they did, waves of thin sand got caught in the wind, covering the entire valley in an orange haze.

A few hours away, a procession of highly armed guards draped in red stood watch in front of a newly erect tent, and in the far off distance, the gateway of Sumat stood visibly closed. The windy sands bouncing against the walls was the only motion visible outside the city which now seemed to hold its breath, ready for war.

Inside the Oam's palace, a group of men, followed by Amus, walked through the ancient corridors, eventually leading into the great hall of the Oam who sat upon his pedestal once again, his beard a triangular symbol of the Temple City.

The thin, bald man in red stood, again, between the visitors and the Oam. The hall was filled with the elite of the Iman Ir, other ministers, and Mahjidi. Two guards stood to the sides of the throne, spears in hand.

The visitors positioned themselves before the Oam's escalating throne, and the hall remained quiet for a few moments as all parties examined one another.

Unprovoked, the Oam spoke.

"What is it you hope to accomplish here?" he asked.

The rest of the Sumati elite looked surprised, for it was Sumati custom for the Jhazbin to make all introductory remarks.

A translator to the left of the visiting party bowed and spoke in a foreign dialect to them, translating the Oam's words.

Amus looked at the Oam unemotionally and began to speak. After he was finished, the Jhazbin motioned to the translator with his hand.

The translator bowed and began to speak.

"Your irrelevance, beckons irreverence, and if we are to speak, as we are to meet, it behooves me to say, I am filled with dismay, how irrelevant and irreverent you appear today."

The entire hall remained quiet. No one spoke as all looked silently forward, wondering if the person next to them held any secret information that would pacify their confusion. The Oam appeared flustered, looking down at Amus. He looked at the translator, it appeared, angrily.

"Is that precisely what he said?" the Oam asked.

The translator bowed.

"Yes, My Oam."

Amus stared at the Oam unemotionally.

"Your armies will never breach this wall . . . our walls. This is Sumat. It has been and will always be. Do you understand?"

He angrily motioned to the translator who obediently bowed and translated to the Dimas congregation.

Amus responded almost immediately. After he was finished, after an almost arbitrary pause, the Oam motioned to the translator again.

"I see the fear, you hold so dear, your wanton lust, is a thing of disgust, you may attempt to deceive, even conceive, of notions and motions from sands to oceans, for convince me not, of your sinful pride, it is the will of the Shek by which you abide."

The Oam swallowed, clearly disturbed by these strange happenings. He briefly looked about the room without moving his head but saw nothing but confusion in the eyes of the Sumatis who looked back to him for resolution.

"Now . . . I understand. I beckon you now, tell me what you want. What he wants."

The translator translated, and Amus responded.

"If you admit your small city is now in peril, we may begin negotiations upon that basis," the translator said.

The Oam scoffed.

"You see these men around you, diplomat? They are the defenders of this city, and behind them are a thousand more, spears in hand. I admit your army is formidable, but a negotiation to avoid bloodshed is in our mutual interests, for the outcome of war certainly favors the unbreakable walls of Sumat defended by the veterans of the Ir."

As he mentioned their name, the Iman Ir slammed their spears to the ground in unison and let out a brief chant, staring at the group from Dimas.

The translator translated for Amus. Amus took a deep breath in and closed his eyes. He then opened them and said something indiscernible under his breath. He immediately jumped forward, grabbing a spear from one of the guards, and in a few short steps, flew up the throne, lunging at the Oam with it.

The Oam stared at Amus at that moment, seeing fury in his eyes. Yet his face, screaming, hinted at humor as he stared intently at the Oam. It was as if he was grinning at him in that last moment, for the tip of the spear, inches from the Oam's face, paused. It was at that moment that the grin became more obvious, as if Amus was mocking him.

Immediately, the other guard and members of the Iman Ir lunged upwards to protect their leader. It was only as Amus felt a blade pierce his neck and follow through, as if in slow motion, that his eyes wavered and his smile turned into a scowl.

His body fell to the ground, spear in hand, as his head rolled down the throne to the feet of the Dimas congregation, littering the impeccable staircase with messy streaks of blood.

At that exact moment, a distance from the palace, deep in the sands, the soldiers stood to attention, staring upwards at their King who was surrounded by the warrior elite of the Dimas army.

"We attempted peaceful negotiation!" the King's Havasa screamed at the soldiers, others in the valley echoing his message. "We tried to find a way to avoid bloodshed!"

The soldiers screamed in reaction to his words.

"And look what they have done! We sent Amus, my King's brother, your beloved comrade and leader, to reason with the unreasonable people of Sumat!"

The soldiers screamed at the mention of Sumat.

"They murdered your beloved Amus in cold blood! During negotiation, as he offered peace! Terms! Compromise!"

The Dimas army began to lose control. They banged their heads, their bodies, their weapons against each other and themselves, screaming in anger. News of Amus's death had already spread across the encampment, but it was only now, in unison, that the mob became almost bewitched in bloodlust. The King stood some ways behind the Havasa as he spoke, two royal guards by his side. The commanders of the army stood in unison near them, a procession of Dimas leadership.

"Will you let these treacherous dogs darken the sands with their presence? Will you let the Untouched sit upon his throne, spitting upon the corpse of your poor fallen comrade? Will you let them spit at your King?!"

Unanimous and multi-faceted disagreements were screamed by the soldiers, some forming words, others simple yelling, their throats burning from excitement.

The King held his hand high over his head and the entire audience quickly calmed, quieting down into complete silence. The winds still blew, and their rough collisions upon the sands was all that could be heard.

The King concealed a slight smile, nearly unable to contain his euphoria as he looked upon the scene before him. He then lowered his hand, and as he did, all the commanders saw, as did the Havasa.

Daesius, leader of the Bahar, jumped forward, his golden robe flowing behind him, screaming.

"To Sumat, my brothers! Scream for blood, and you shall have it!" he yelled, banging his fist against his chest.

The whole army exploded, bellowing out, shouting, scrambling to collect their things. One by one, the individual groups jumped to attention, led by their chosen superiors who screamed and pointed in the direction of Sumat. Some walked, some ran, unable to contain themselves as they began their furious advance towards the Temple City.

CHAPTER 35
MIDAS

"They tricked us," Maerus commented, his brother sitting by his side. He dipped a flatbread into some dal and continued to speak, pre-occupied. He sat, hunched over his meal in full uniform, his head and arms caved in over the bowl and bread.

"I saw it in that man's eyes . . . he had no choice. He went mad at that moment, I will swear by it."

He shook his head as he spoke.

"There is no way to control the spiraling news of his death. The brother of the Shek King," he laughed cynically. "It will dishearten our men and empower theirs.

"He looks beyond the walls of Sumat already, as if we were nothing. That is the most disturbing thing of all."

He looked at his brother, an Ir just starting to embrace manhood.

"Legends will speak of this as a war of revenge. He, the martyr that sought to honor his brother. The whole world will believe he is a brave, righteous man."

He took a breath in and put his hand on his brother's shoulder, looking at his eyes.

"Do you see? The truth will be lost to everyone, including us."

"We know! We will not forget!" his brother defiantly replied, standing up.

"Sit down, Maicha!" Maerus beckoned, slapping his brother on the cheek as he did. "You remain calm."

He pointed to the food in front of his brother and waited for him to resume eating.

"You will know this now. And a year from now, when a thousand stares and words have graced you . . . whether we prosper or not, will you be sure we did not murder his brother?"

He slapped him once more.

"You listen to me . . . it is not just the peasants or the beggars that succumb to passionate simplicity. The seductive tale that is revenge far outreaches the accuracy of diplomatic manipulation. You will find even yourself bending what you know to be true to fit what you desire."

He placed his hand on Maicha's head, first calmly, then pulling his face forcefully close to his own. He pressed his forefinger into Maicha's head, staring at him.

"Never underestimate the tricks of the heart and the toll time can take on what you know to be true."

As night began to drape over the walls, dark shadows formed throughout the city. After days of scouting and preparation, the doors of Sumat were shut, the walls surrounded by guard towers and runners. Every hour, they scurried across the city pathways carrying clay pots with food and water, relaying messages, all under the quiet night sky.

Families had begun retiring to their houses earlier, rationing food and water everywhere they could. Shopkeepers and societies would congregate in private, keeping the noise level down, as ordered by the Ir.

The Iman Ir now commanded the entire city, moving from post to post all throughout the night, collecting information and discussing strategies amongst themselves.

Deep in the temple, the priests, draped in their robes, sat and watched in silence as the brethren and cousins of the Iman Ir held the heads of their chosen women down as they had their way with them. As if trying to escape their fears of the walls outside, they looked at one another, disliking what they saw, and took the toll of their angst on the girls before them, beating them while intermittently raping them.

Driven to exhaustion, some were unable to extract sufficient satisfaction despite orgasm and slumped down, half on pillows, half on the ground, staring at the scarcely human vessel before them. The men held their eyes half open, dazed and drunken, exhausted at having failed exacting their disappointment on the daughters of the city.

"This is lovely," Dispa, a young Ir, commented, his voice traveling quietly over the screams and moans. He spoke calmly and tiredly, as if resolved. "Only in the temple of Mala could I ravage this basla three times and still desire to do it again. It fills me with potency."

"It is by the grace of the temple that your phallus rises at all," his cousin yelled from across the room.

Dispa smiled weakly.

"Perhaps your mother will serve as a worthy replacement," he responded.

"I wouldn't replace a donkey with your mother," came the quick rebuttal.

Everyone simultaneously began to laugh. Many stopped in mid position, some pressing into their women, others leaning over, their hands wrapped around their necks, smiling and starting to giggle. As the infectious humor spread, everyone began to laugh uncontrollably loudly, as did Dispa.

Those that had been raped so severely that they could no longer move were carried, one by one, by slaves who remained hidden behind the priests. Upon their silent hand-gestured commands, the slaves ran into the room and carried off woman after woman, dragging them deeper into the crypts of the temple.

Far into its cavernous and old tunnels, the women were piled into cells and locked up, waiting to die or recover. Further down the circular corridor of doors were the prisoners of Sumat, and within one such cell, curled up on the ground, lay Akin.

Some silent, muffled sounds could be loosely heard from his cell, littered with the scuffling of feet and the occasional scream. He was unconscious, with a large wound on his forehead which was draped in dry blood. The sounds that echoed, however, soon began to irritate his mind, and slowly but surely, he started noticing the world.

As he tried to open his eyes, the dried blood that covered his face was somehow familiar, and he suddenly became aware that he was back in the cave. The suffocating darkness terrified him, but he was immediately filled with an overwhelmingly wondrous thought and began calling out, throwing his hands in the air, trying to feel around him.

"Samaye! Samaye!"

He paused and swallowed, still unable to open his eyes for the coagulated blood, and sat in place, frightened. He took a deep breath in and screamed in terror, releasing it explosively.

"Samaye!!!"

"Akin . . ."

Akin paused and frowned, his mouth still open, scared.

"Akin . . ."

"Who is that?" he whispered.

"Akin . . . awaken . . ."

Suddenly, Akin recognized the voice and clasped his chest as he frowned, trying not to choke. He grimaced, all at once understanding that if the voice he heard was that of Jarvis, then he was not in the cave, and nowhere near him lay the still breathing heart of Samaye.

He fell forward to the ground, his head resting on his hands, clutching his face in his fingers. His mouth ajar, he breathed quickly and deeply, inhaling the dust on the floor before him.

Jarvis remained silent, listening to Akin as he tried to collect himself and come to grips with his nightmare. Slowly, the memories began to familiarize themselves within him, and though the emotional knowledge that Samaye was close to him, that he could call out his name and receive a response still resonated through his body, every time he prepared to scream for him once more, he was simply unable to.

He wanted to, so desperately for the possibility that it would happen, but could not bring himself to do it again. Somewhere, a defiance rolled about in his head instructing him to invest in what was before him and not what was tantalizing but fantastical. The hope of hearing Samaye's voice would remain within him just one moment more if he called out, and like tearing the flesh from his own skin, he decided not to pursue it.

Though the choice was now made, he immediately began to cry, feeling the pain of the loss of hope. He ran his bare hand against the ground before him, feeling the unfamiliar texture, cementing within himself the awareness of being in a new place.

After a few moments, he wiped his face and started to calm his breathing, leaning up in place, kneeling.

"I cannot see, Jarvis . . ."

"Why?"

"The blood has dried upon my eyes. I cannot open them."

"Come to me . . . I will help you."

Akin began to crawl towards Jarvis's voice.

"Here . . . here . . . here, my boy."

As Akin touched Jarvis's warm arm, he felt calmed and clasped it tightly in his hand.

They both remained quiet as Akin leaned back against the wall. Jarvis was lying on the flat ground, his head slightly perched against the brick behind him, and both just breathed quietly in each other's awakened company.

"What a world this is, Akin . . ." Jarvis remarked.

Akin hung his head down effortlessly, his eyes still stuck shut.

"That I am not alone . . . that you are here makes the fear less pronounced," Akin responded.

He thought of waking in the cave so long ago and the terror that shot through him when he could see, feel and hear nothing. He felt eternally grateful that this time a familiar voice was within reach.

He had thought of cleaning his eyes, but it passed quickly as he could tell the room was barely lit. In knowing it was lit, he did not struggle to see, knowing that when his eyes would free themselves, he would then explore his surroundings.

"We are . . . imprisoned, aren't we?" he asked.

Jarvis tapped his thigh twice.

They both remained quiet.

Akin had a thought and took a breath in, as if to say something, then stopped, grinning. He paused for a moment and pondered.

"It was a beautiful sight," he said.

Jarvis did not look up at him, but instead stared directly at the wall in front of him.

"What was?" he asked.

Still grinning, Akin responded, raising his arms in the air to demonstrate his words.

"The beautiful sands, our feet upon their golden cheeks, and the great walls of Sumat . . ."

He paused arbitrarily.

" . . . behind us," he said, loudly and aggressively.

Jarvis suddenly choked mid breath and began to cough, trying to smile.

Akin still grinned, feeling successful.

They both remained still, thinking and smiling.

Jarvis looked at him.

"You should have known I had much disdain in my heart for these people."

He looked back at the wall.

"You should be more careful next time when you advise someone to follow their hearts without restraint."

Akin smiled large, his eyebrows raised, surprised at the critique. He remained still, smiling and nodding.

They continued to sit there, smiles upon their faces. Akin's smile was reactionary while Jarvis's seemed more initiative. Akin still held Jarvis's arm with his hand, locked in grip.

Jarvis looked at Akin once again, grinning. After a moment of examining him, he looked back at the wall.

"One might say . . . this is actually completely your fault."

Akin laughed suddenly. This triggered Jarvis, who also began to giggle. He looked up at Akin, seeing his eyes shut as he laughed, forcing him to squint as he giggled even harder, his eyes welling up.

When Akin heard Jarvis's subdued giggling, he too began to laugh harder, clenching his fist, feeling his own eyes well up.

"Some repression . . . may very well have done . . . a bit of good . . . for you and me," Akin pushed out in between breaths.

Jarvis shook his head, raising his finger up in objection.

"No, my young friend." He placed his hand on Akin's. "This is as it should be."

Akin felt the water that had collected in his eyes dislodge the hardened blood around them, and he quickly tried to stretch his lids and pull away at the dirt with his free hand. Soon one eye was freed, then the other, and he blinked over and over, trying to normalize his vision and rid it of the debris.

He looked at Jarvis and examined him. His tunic was torn and filthy. He squinted and frowned as he tried to examine him in the bare light.

"What is that?" he asked, pointing to a dark spot on Jarvis's chest.

Jarvis's smile slowly faded as he looked at his body.

"It is a wound," he responded.

Akin frowned and leaned his hand over to touch and examine it. Jarvis looked at him and shook his head, staring into his eyes.

Akin grimaced and straightened himself, looking at the wall before him. He looked down and covered his face with his hands.

Jarvis suddenly frowned, the edges of his mouth curved downwards extremely sadly, looking at Akin.

"I am sorry, my friend."

Akin shook his head, feeling tears.

Jarvis stared at him and swallowed.

"I have lied to you, and I am ashamed of myself."

Akin sucked in his breath and turned to Jarvis.

"What have you lied about?"

Jarvis's eyes filled with tears, but he did not move his gaze from Akin's.

"I . . . the entire pretense under which I approached you, comforted you, invited you into my home . . . it was not a kind gesture."

Akin frowned, staring at him. Akin immediately felt a hole well up in his chest, the feeling of betrayal being so vivid in his memory, he felt unearthed and loose.

Helplessly, Jarvis continued, swallowing again.

"I am so ashamed, Akin."

"Well, tell me already then . . ." Akin replied.

"When I saw you . . . I knew, unlike the others, that you were a foreigner. I have always had an eye for foreigners. Like a gold mine, they were always my muse in the square. I would always look at them and hope that they were my foreigner."

Akin, still confused, listened.

"When I was very young, I have the memory of being told that my fortunes would change when I encountered an Aizik man. I was told countless riches would come my way, that I would be prosperous and powerful, and things would alter for my desires.

"When I saw you, I immediately considered that you were Aizik. And you did not know, but before I even spoke to you I caught the edge of your marking, on the back of your neck, and claimed you for my greed. It was lust in my eyes, not philanthropy or adoration . . . nor following my heart. You were to be my inhuman charm.

"It was through that desire that I manipulated you into feeling welcome and staying with me that first day, and the days after.

"That I hid this from you is in itself a testament to the underlying hypocrisy of our relationship. You were to interact with me in complete sincerity while I carried a hidden agenda in mine."

He stared at the wall ahead of him.

"I know not what to say except say it as it is."

"The initial sensation of betrayal I feel, though potent, is temporary. In fact, I may attribute it to my desire to feel betrayed, for what reason I cannot say," Akin replied.

He looked at Jarvis.

"Perhaps you are giving too much credit to the effect this oracle had upon you, and too little to the whispers of your own instincts."

Jarvis looked at Akin, and Akin back to him.

"What I mean to say, Jarvis, is that I do not believe you have pursued riches from encountering me, and so, your conclusion that this was what motivated you is caused by a lack of faith in your own choices. Do you see what I mean?"

He smiled and placed his hand on Jarvis's arm.

"You are my friend, and I am yours. Whatever factors contributed to us meeting are as they should be, but do not determine the nature of our friendship. Feel angry about feeling guilty, nothing else. It is not your creation that causes you to hold yourself in such a negative light for something so natural."

"But . . . I have held it from you! I have lied to you!" Jarvis yelled back, immediately loud and angry.

"But that is because you viewed your action as perverse and sinful! Whatever prompted you to approach me lies in an influence ages old! You were a child - how could you control what it would implant in you? You have held this secret gamble in your heart with shame for longer than our relationship . . . do not apologize to me, for I am compassionate for your misunderstanding of your own intentions!"

Jarvis stared at him, his eyes wide, his mouth open, stricken.

"There is no shame in acting in accordance with what you were forced to believe, Jarvis. Be compassionate to yourself, and angry at those that both made you believe it and caused shame in you for believing it."

"I don't understand!" Jarvis screamed. "Angry that I believed in the bastard oracle?"

"Yes!" Akin screamed back.

"But it led to our friendship! How can I condemn it if I embrace its effect?"

"Do not condemn it, simply understand the incorrectness of it and its effect on you. You cannot change the past, but learn from it. Our friendship is not how you have suffered, nor the 'lie' you have kept from me. You have suffered your whole life, hoping and dreaming of an Aizik man to bring you happiness."

Jarvis grimaced, gritting his teeth, clutching his chest. Akin tried to support his head and shoulders as his body tightened. Jarvis grabbed Akin's hand and squeezed it, grunting.

"It is you that found this friendship, not the oracle. The oracle lied, and you believed it, and it was not your fault."

Jarvis moaned out in anguish, trying to curl up, his body tight. His face was tense and strained, his eyes shut tight, and he kept shuddering every few seconds, letting out angry grunts.

Akin held him and kissed his forehead.

"You are my friend, Jarvis, and you always will be."

Jarvis opened his eyes, welled with wetness, staring widely at the ceiling. His mouth was open, not tight like before, but weak, as he held unto Akin.

"I am going to die soon, Akin," he said, tears filling his eyes. Akin frowned sadly and pressed his head against Jarvis's. Jarvis looked at him and tightened his hold of Akin's hand.

"Endless predictions mouthed by frauds and charlatans like myself, and once every long while, their words intersect the world as it is," Jarvis said, closing his eyes.

Far off in the distance, the men who stood upon the Sumati guard towers could see clouds of sand bellow up into the sky. It was like a sandstorm, but slow moving and coupled with a buzzing roar. It stretched across the horizon as if the world were closing in on their small, miniscule position in the universe.

Some called to others, telling them to look, asking for explanations. Many of the veterans simply watched silently, their scarred faces containing old eyes, eyes that both knew and understood the impending crisis, but were too weathered to fear it.

"It is not a sandstorm. You know it is not a sandstorm," one veteran said to a clearly uncomfortable and edgy soldier.

"How do you know?" he asked as he looked out in the distance. "It could be a storm moving to the west."

The man smirked and pointed to the sky above the sand, leaning on his spear.

"A storm never ends so abruptly. There are layers of thinner sand, three times the height. This is a very flat storm indeed."

He looked at the young soldier and widened his eyes maniacally.

"And have you ever encountered a storm that chanted?"

The soldier stared at him then closed his eyes, trying to listen. Others were speaking, and he yelled at them to be quiet, his eyes still closed.

"Yes! Let us all listen, so there are no fools amongst us!" the veteran screamed.

Up in their towers, they heard nothing but the buzzing. But ever so slightly, the buzzing changed with certain small pauses, the sound changing pitch, with nooks and crannies and rounded portions. The buzzing was changing, inconsistent, and roared in the distance, seemingly louder than anything they had ever witnessed.

The young soldier began to shake, his arms and teeth shuddering. He tried to hide it, his eyes still closed, focusing on the sound.

"Embrace it, young man," the veteran advised. "It will only get louder."

Tents amassed within view of the Sumati gates, all of which were now closed, surrounded by guards upon guards. Throughout the city, watchers stood ready to bolt towards the nearest Iman Ir to relay information and updates from guard tower to guard tower. The Iman Ir were distributed all around the city, with the central congregation of them some ways from the front gate, in front of the temple, within the maza.

They wore their full dress, easily distinguishing them from commoners and other Ir. They talked amongst each other and barked orders to those around them. Though their average day to day activities usually consisted of hedonistic endeavors, their heritage made them hardened men, both willing to kill and die to protect their federation.

It was a hierarchy of bloodlines, for all the Iman Ir were brethren in some fashion or another. The common people were mechanisms for them to protect their city, for Sumat was certainly regarded by the Iman Ir as an ancient familial homeland that belonged to them.

As such, their families were kept in the most guarded of locations, away from the walls, and given the cleanest food and water while the rest of the populace was forced to ration all of their goods for the possibility of a long siege. Both the Iman Ir and their families had led such a long and consistent age of decadence that this battle was viewed, for the most part, as another day in the field, as all were assured that though there would be some difficulties and losses, Sumat would go on as it always had.

The disgruntled Kunda, both Sumai and Mashaya, held within their ranks outsiders and the poor, and both groups maintained little loyalty towards anyone save those they could transact with. Sumai had benefitted through local shortages but were still kept subservient by those that ruled over them while Kunda Mashaya, native to Sumat, dejected and ignored by the Sumati elite, focused on survival by any means, prioritizing resources over any sense of loyalty.

They continued to operate in whatever capacity they could, profiting from the limited food supply and investing in the knowledge that though the war may inflict wounds upon them, business would resume once the war was over, and they sought to maximize their positions when that happened.

Both Kunda operated under the principle of hoarding, disguising and hiding satchels of food and water, both for power in trade and to protect their holdings from the Iman Ir who could, and would, readily annex their supplies at a moment's notice.

They were accustomed to the irresponsibility of the ruling class but believed that the supreme confidence of those in power could not be so misguided that Sumat could actually fall, and for the most part simply prepared to weather the storm as safely and profitably as possible.

Those that were not already recruited within the Kin Ir were expected to fight when and if the situation arose, and though households for both Kunda prepared their sons, fathers, and husbands for war through blessings and rituals, it was Kunda Sumai that felt the brunt of the pressure for their foreign, and therefore inferior, bloodline. Though Mashaya had lost much of their economic prowess within the community, they were still deeply embedded within the Kin Ir and found ways to use the impending crisis to swell their ranks within the communal police force.

Even as war drums and chants from beyond the walls could be subtly heard, both Kunda were plotting their moves, trying to gather and capture as many resources as possible, preparing to distribute them at exorbitant prices once the siege was over. Mashaya, now a shadow of its former power, loosely organized thieves to rob and steal little batches of goods here and there while Kunda Sumai plotted larger coups, hiding whole loads of grain from the Iman Ir and using goods to bribe the local Ir for better footing in the forthcoming community.

The Iman Ir were well equipped machines of war. They each carried a bronze spear for both status and support, and though it remained more iconic than practical, it was traditional to have it cleaned and sharpened every morning. It was, therefore, still an effective war weapon, the pointed tip an extension of the Iman Ir's expected might. Around their waist was a leather belt that held their tunic to their bodies. Attached to the belt was a large royal sickle, bestowed to each by the Oam himself upon promotion to the Iman Ir. It, too, was sharpened and cleaned every day, its golden color shining as the men walked in the sunlight, rocking it back and forth.

Many of the Iman Ir were neither fit nor quick, but despite their long ritualistic indulgences, they appeared overpowering, both in confidence and strength. They were large men, produced through training but also eugenics, for the family line of the Iman Ir rejected males that were born as runts, often as babies or later in life when they performed under par. The outcasted brethren of the Iman Ir still held nobility but were not respected by the ruling class and spent their time toying with the poor as compensation for this lack of recognition.

Treated like women and children, these men also remained protected in their households as the siege began. Their positions were uniquely insulting as they could neither lead as Iman Ir nor join the ranks of the lesser Ir, restricted by their nobility.

At the front lines of the gates, the watchers in the guard towers observed the massive Dimas army as it sprawled out across the horizon, pitching tents and lighting fires. They took refuge in the idea that there was little to worry about until morning and settled in their positions.

Both Sumat and Dimas were old cities and as such relied upon the spear for their strength. The Dimas army boasted the Sand Spears, an ancient line of spearmen that was the staple of their might. Each member was trained to use their spear to both defend and inflict grievous wounds upon their enemies, contorting their bodies amidst tense battles to facilitate repositioning and striking stances. The Sumati Ir were a force of their own, specializing in defensive, piercing thrusts that utilized the city walls to their advantage.

Archers were mostly an ornamental addition to the war machine of Sumat, for most men found it easier to fling sharp, pointed spears at their enemies than learn the use of a bow. A dejected class, only a few dedicated men experimented with different wood to create bows that could reach enemies in the distance, albeit with little accuracy. Dimas had begun training a class of archers, as demanded by the Shek King, but their use in sieges such as the Sumati one was both limited and premature. The strong defensive structure of the city, with its guard towers and walls, was designed to protect its men from invaders, minimizing the effectiveness of projectiles.

In the distance, the Sumati guards could randomly hear chanting and loud talk. They watched little groups and figures walk about and every now and then caught glimpse of what they thought to be weapons shining against the moonlight.

As they watched the Dimas army organize their camp, they felt a layer of calm knowing that the time to fight was not yet upon them, and that the soldiers in the distance respected and understood this. It was almost as if they sought to find a common ground towards the armed men in the distance to make them appear less daunting. The harsh veterans, however, sat in complete disdain, eyeing the army in the distance rarely, feeling nothing but bitter hate and an absolute lack of trust towards them.

"It is death," one remarked under his breath. "We all die alone."

Sumat had engaged in a number of battles over the years. Since it was a centralized nation, it mostly defended its walls from marauders and competing states vying for their resources. Most battles were relatively short for the exquisitely practiced art of defensive offence that the Sumati war machine unleashed upon its opponents.

The walls themselves were far taller than men, and the hoarding of wood and stone for spears was a constant edict of the city, grown and implemented years ago. The purpose was to transform the city into a pointed spike, inducing massive losses to its foes while minimizing both a loss of resources and life to itself. Bel Tazim, an associate to the Iman Ir and regarded highly by the city's leaders, was a foreigner to Sumat who had grown to become its central tactician. Shunned by the Mashaya clan for his alien blood, he had encouraged and aided Kunda Sumai and was unofficially an influential leader in their cause.

At the center of the city, Bel Tazim remained locked in position, constantly organizing information he was receiving from the guard towers. He discussed and related his observations to the Iman Ir who then decided, in the end, what path to pursue. Though a resident of the city for a many years, and having provided the Iman Ir with a great many victories, he was still an outsider to them, and though they utilized his tactical mind, he always remained somehow alienated from them, valued for what he could provide and little else.

Weapon design and defensive stratagems were constantly calibrated, and Bel Tazim had contributed to many of these innovations. Every battle provided some insight towards a weakness that could be addressed or a strength that could be further improved. As a result, Sumat always kept an arsenal of armaments, water and food to last a prolonged siege, and was well prepared for anything that resembled the battles of recent past.

Bel Tazim had never encountered the Oam as foreigners were not permitted to advise him. It was primarily through his closest friend, Mihra, an Iman Ir, that his suggestions and observations were shared. Mihra had been the man who discovered Bel Tazim many years ago, befriended him, and fought to introduce him to the warrior class of Sumat. Through his own affinity for war and repeated successes, Bel Tazim had become an integral part of the war machine, and though he maintained his friendship with Mihra, he remained silently judged and shunned by others for his bloodline, or lack thereof.

At the threat of invasion, every day a ration of spears and grain was stored within the war house, a large enclosure that was heavily guarded at all times. Though the spears were tucked together within it, each food parcel was individually stored and wrapped to minimize the possibility of infestation or disease spreading from pack to pack. By the time the Shek King arrived at the Sumati gates, the basal had been filled for weeks, with items no longer fitting within it stacked outside.

These resources were reserved for the army and the penalty for theft was extremely harsh. Though this edict was obeyed, the Iman Ir, like most things in Sumat, had full rights to indulge as they pleased. It did, however, encourage the voluntary participation of the Ir and increased their desire to fight hardily. For though it was illegal, it was readily accepted that those that fought for the city hid their army rations and distributed it to their families. This permitted embezzlement facilitated a more dedicated and efficient armada, for as long as the Ir fought, and as long as they survived, their families would be fed.

Outside the gates of Sumat, Dimas scouts ran cloaked in dark robes about the city walls gathering intelligence for their leaders. This was done constantly as the Shek King valued information in battle above all else.

"If I ever have to fight a fair fight," he was quoted as saying, "I failed to interrogate my enemy enough."

The central kiosk where the Dimas leaders were congregated was lit with a multitude of fires. Above their heads, a large red sheet was hung taut extending from end to end with poles dug into the ground supported by a man at each corner. Perfect circles were pierced all over it to allow the smoke to escape, and above each hole, light and smoke emanated upwards as if some religious procession was underway underneath.

It was so bright beneath, where the leaders ate, that one could scarcely tell it was nighttime. Surrounding the kiosk, some ways away, stood a tight circle of guards, spear in hand. These were the lines of the ancient Dia, the royal guard that protected the King of Dimas. They always wore red and had illustrious helmets.

The men ate ravenously, feeding on bovin, breads and soup. The King sat at the head of the group, a long carpeted drapery under them. Behind him were two more Dia, quietly standing guard. His seat was slightly elevated, raising the carpet upon which he sat, cross legged. Upon his lap was a large shiny plate, and on it were large morsels of meat with bowls filled with vegetables and lentils. Breads lined one side of it, some soft, some hard, some thin and some thick. The plate itself was suspended just above his lap, a long cloth supporting it with two men kneeled far off to either side of him, holding it taut with rods in the sand. As he ate and pressed down upon it, the two men leaned away from each other, tightening the cloth.

"Tell me, my King," Samrit, a Bahar who was invited to dine with the King by Daesius, their leader, began to ask. "What do you envision tomorrow?"

The King eyed Samrit under his brow and continued to eat without responding.

"I don't," the King eventually replied, dryly.

Samrit looked at the others, still smiling, then refocused on his food. The King looked at him whilst no one saw and contemplated.

"Do your men sleep, Samrit?" the King asked.

Samrit looked at him and swallowed the morsel he was chewing on. The rest of the congregation kept eating, listening but remaining un-reactive.

"They do not, my King. They stand ready."

The King kept eating.

"I thought they were my men, Samrit."

The young officer looked both frightened and surprised and nervously replied.

"Yes, of course, my King. Your men. Your men."

"But you replied to my question and did not correct me. Are you here for sycophancy or for consultation?"

"Consultation, I hope, my King."

The King was becoming visibly agitated.

"Why have you invited this fool to my table, Daesius?"

Daesius continued to eat, quickly responding in between mouthfuls, still un-reactive.

"It is my mistake, my King."

The Shek again refocused upon Samrit, this time ceasing to eat. Samrit was visibly shaken, watching him.

The Shek King stared at him.

"They are my men?"

"Yes, my King."

"And you say they do not sleep?"

"No, my King. They are yours to command."

"Do you ever wonder where the steel comes from that forms the tips of your spears? Do you ever wonder why they pierce the bronze plating of your enemies?"

Samrit looked about but responded quickly.

"I do, my King."

"And your men?"

"They are your men, my King."

The Shek grinned slightly.

"Good, little Samrit," he said, waving his finger at him. "Now, do you wish to kill the Sumati?"

"Yes, my King," Samrit replied, this time strongly.

"Do you wish to spill their blood upon the sand?"

"Yes, my King."

Daesius began to wipe his face upon his tunic and quickly guzzled down his tonic. He turned his head and looked at Samrit just as the King had done.

"Then go spill it," said the King.

Samrit blinked and looked at him.

"Now? My King?"

"Now, you little bastard!" the King screamed.

Samrit jumped to his feet and ran out of the tent. The Dia made a hole for him to exit and closed it as he disappeared into the darkness. Daesius calmly arose and bowed to the King, also disappearing into the night.

The King refocused and continued to eat.

In the darkness, Samrit had collected his sling and flung it over his shoulder. He picked up a large, hard and round stone and held it in between both his hands, then disappeared into the night. He ran towards the gates of Sumat, barely seeing the sand in front of him, feeling the glow of the massive encampment behind him. The air was cold, and he slowed as he tired, but kept pressing on until he was only a few manlengths from the Sumati walls.

Once there, he stopped and dropped the ball onto the sand. It was etched with markings and drawings, all familiar to him. He leaned down and kissed it, then dropped one side of his sling to the ground and rolled the ball unto it. He picked the other side up and gently dragged the sling along the sand as he walked towards the wall. Few sounds, if any, were audible around him, and it appeared as though the guard towers above him were either vacant or filled with sleeping men.

He took a few deep, arbitrary breaths in and struck a hard stance, his feet apart both horizontally and vertically. His front foot remained positioned some ways from the wall, and he slowly lifted the sling which now contained the huge stone within it.

His training had made all his movements definitive and practiced. He recalled the difficulty with which he first tried to lift a Biha. A new Bahar recruit long ago in Dimas, he remembered Daesius inspecting him and instructing him. He was to use his knee for leverage, always bending it and utilizing his legs to lift the stone, using the arms only to hold it. He remembered how surprised he was when observing in actuality the difference Daesius's instructions made in the ease of carrying such a large weight.

The Bahar were created for one specific reason, and that was incursion. They were trained endlessly, created centuries ago by Aadmin Bahar, a war general who fought for The Last Light, the twelfth king of Dimas. Techniques had evolved over the years, but the Bahar remained loyal to their original calling, and each recruit was gifted with their own Biha once officially ushered into their lines. Samrit, like most, had spent years etching insignia into his Biha which was now a permanent part of him. He carried it with him everywhere, and its shape, weight and feel were so familiar to him that if anyone were to switch his stone with another's, he would notice almost immediately.

His Biha now rested within his raised sling as he stared at the wall before him, actuating something he had practiced a thousand times before. He began to turn, slowly at first, the sling soon catching speed as the ball rose in the air with it. As he completed one turn, he began to quicken his rotation, the ball becoming lighter and lighter as he was pulled from side to side. He used his feet to counter balance the weight of the stone as it pulled him and leaned almost completely against it as it tried to yank him harder and harder.

Eventually, he began spinning extremely fast. The movement had been something he had practiced many times, and he was skilled at compensating for the odd effects such a large weight was imposing on his body.

His eyes slowly escaped the dizzying twirl and began to focus on the wall before him, stopping in mid turn to observe it, then spinning once quickly to refocus back on it. His eyes became tense, his brow turning to a frown. He tensed his arms and began to mouth a count with his lips. As he pushed out an airy but quiet "sana", he released one side of the sling. As he did, the ball, now travelling extremely fast, flew with immense force at the wall before him. It struck the Sumati wall, loosening sand from its edges, causing a deep blasting sound to echo within. He looked at the wall which, though slightly marked by it, remained strong and still.

He quickly heard shouting from above and saw two heads poke out from the guard tower overhead. They pointed to him and screamed in a foreign dialect. He could hear even more movement on the other side as the edge of the city woke up.

Filled with adrenaline, he stormed forward and jumped to the ball, picking it up arduously, then ran back to his previous position. Up above, the guards were still screaming, and just as he ran away from the wall, a spear shot through a hole within it, barely missing him. It retracted back into the hole, and Samrit could briefly see eyes and men scurrying on the other side. The entire structure that was the thick Sumati walls was lined with horizontal and angled holes, just small enough to fit their specialized spears through in defense of the city.

He could see flickering movement on the other side as Sumati guards gathered their weapons and readied to defend. He dropped the stone upon his sling and once again picked up both ends of it, lifting. He began his motions, twirling, faster and faster. A soldier in the guard tower was pointing a throwing spear at him, trying to aim as he moved around and around. He let loose, and the spear flew down, just missing Samrit but striking his stone, ricocheting away. Again Samrit began to focus on the wall, eyeing the small, almost invisible mark his stone had made. He let go of one side of the sling once more, and the stone flew directly at the wall, smashing against it. He missed his previous spot, but struck the wall beside it, this time not as hard, but still forcefully.

He took a deep breath in and eyed the guard in the tower, then the holes before him. He closed his eyes for a moment then opened them and dashed towards the stone. As he did, the guards on the other side screamed, thrusting their spears through the holes. As he saw one poke outwards right in front of his face, he fell backwards while his body still flung forward, sliding upon his knees and falling on the ground. The spears retracted from their holes and were then shoved through the holes beside them, these ones angled downwards.

One pierced his arm, another slashed his cheek. Others poked the sand, missing him entirely. Others that hit air were swung sideways, slapping his body, cutting him with their tips. He screamed and tried to crawl forward to his Biha, placing his hand on it. Just as he touched it, he heard a distant howl, recognizing it to be the war horn of the Bahar.

Suddenly, he heard the Sumati walls echo thunderously. The spears all retracted, and he heard screams from the inside, followed by shuffling and movement. He lay there, blood gushing out of a series of wounds, his hand planted upon his Biha, his fingers resting in its familiar grooves. He breathed quietly and still, closing his eyes, feeling the cold wind.

On the other side of the city, an armada of Bahar slingmen had positioned themselves in spaced formation along the central length of the wall. Their fetchers, made up of slaves and prisoners, were already rushing to the wall to retrieve the stones. Most did so successfully while a few, the unfortunate targets of spears from the guard towers, fell to the ground, impaled. Behind the Bahar were spearmen, angrily screaming and pointing the tips of their weapons at the slaves. Shield bearers stood before the Bahar after every throw, protecting them from incoming projectiles with long, rugged barriers. Made of wood, they were used to defend the slingmen, and the shielders kept close watch over those in the guard towers, adjusting their positions accordingly.

Far behind the attack front stood Daesius, accompanied by a pair of spearmen. He stared at the giant moonlit wall, observing his men from a distance.

"One man for one free throw," he thought. "A better trade is hard to find."

CHAPTER 37
PRISMATICS

"Your Biha is your heart. Upon touching it, holding it . . . understand that you shall never part. You are forever bound. Your breath lays tied to it. If it should break, your heart will too . . . and like a war-torn lover seek another to fill its place, but never forget its touch and feel.

"When you thrust your heart towards your enemy, your chest gapes as it flies. Pain and love in your throw, all that you are and ever will be is contained in your heart, and when it strikes upon your foe with your life-force bound to it, it will penetrate, de-motivate, and bring them to their knees.

"To carry another's Biha is to bed his wife! Protect yours as you would your whore mother, lest she become an even greater whore, loving another man's touch!

"Henceforth, you receive your Biha. It is yours, it is your heart. You will touch it, feel it, and pray your love to it. It is a gift to you from your King, and you will gift him back by using your passions to destroy his enemies!

"Now, throw your heart upon the ground, and feel its hardness, hear its roar, and know that you are now men of steel and stone, boys and civilians no more. You are Bahar!!!"

"The first in line!" Daesius yelled at his men. "We are always the first in line! The biggest, strongest, protected, revered. The front line of all war, we throw our heavy hearts at our enemies, and with it pave a road for all of Dimas to follow!

"The first in line!" he screamed suddenly, standing upon a podium held by slaves, coupled with elite spearguards. His men, focused on the onslaught, screamed in acknowledgement.

Before him was a battlefield. Strewn along the length of the wall were bloodied bodies, some still moving, others crushed by falling Biha or the soles of slaves sent to retrieve them. His men stood firm in Khusara formation, lined parallel to the wall, facing it, sweating in the darkness, breathing heavy as they prepared to launch their stones once again at the wall.

Petrified retrievers were forced by threateningly sharp spears to run to the wall to bring back the now stained stones. Drenched in blood, not of the enemy but of fallen and impaled retrievers, the Sumati wall had splatter marks lining it now, the blood seeping into the sand beneath it. The crushing sound of bone caused ill many of the slaves while the Bahar men, trained to use the vulgar scene before them as a source of empowerment, seemed to thrive on it.

"Get me my Biha, you son of a whore!" Algo, an elite strongman of the Bahar screamed at his fourth retriever as he ran speedily towards the wall. "I'll eat your children!" he screamed angrily.

As the retriever navigated the spears from above and frighteningly approached the holes in the wall, he fell to the ground and crawled, rolling the stone closer to him. He eventually grasped it and started moving away.

"Hurry up, whore!" Algo screamed impatiently.

The slave ran to him awkwardly, Biha in hand. Algo grabbed the back of his head and tugged his hair back, forcing him to his knees before him.

"Did you not hear me?! I'll eat your children, fucker!"

He slapped him hard across the face and resumed loading his sling with his stone, proceeding with the attack hurriedly. He lifted his sling and began to spin, his huge arms swinging it both quickly and powerfully. He began to stare at the wall in a focused manner, much as Samrit had done, and after a few more spins grunted and let one side of his sling go. The ball of stone flew like lightning in the air, flying fast and ramming itself hard against the wall.

Directly on the other side, Sumati soldiers fell to their knees momentarily, recovering from the thunderous sound the stone made against it.

"Up!" Inaisi, an Iman Ir, screamed at them. "I want this bastard dead! Ready your spears and use alternate holes to aim! Get him! Get him!" he yelled.

Appearing fearless, he was a younger Iman Ir, lean and focused on the task at hand.

A Kin Ir ran to him and yelled something in his ear, trying to communicate over the loud sounds of the stones striking the wall. Inaisi ran to his left, moving the first few spearmen out of the way of the holes, staring out them, trying to observe. He placed his ear against the wall and closed his eyes, listening.

He ran back across the inside of the wall, tapping each spearman on the shoulder to get their attention.

"When you hear the slide or the scream of the man to your left, retract! I want to lose not one spear to this bastard Dimas scum!" he screamed.

"Aye, my Ir!" the men screamed back.

Suddenly, there was a loud shout at the start of the spearman line. Inaisi peered down and saw each man screaming, one by one yanking their spear out of the hole. Some did so too late, withdrawing not a spear but instead a wooden stake, the head dismembered.

"Retract in time, you bastards!"

On the other side of the wall, the scraping became louder. A very large man, both fat and muscular, carried a large shining steel shield and dragged it across the outside of the wall, stepping on skulls and bodies as he did. He leaned into his slow jog, pressing the sharp edge of the shield against the wall, trying to tear down as many spears as possible that remained protruded out of the holes.

Inaisi screamed at one of his men.

"If you lose another spear, I'm going to tear your fucking head off!!!"

The man bowed and threw down the splintered wood he held and reached down for another spear, readying to strike through the hole once again.

The hammering of the Biha against the outer wall of Sumat echoed through the nearby huts. Those very close to the wall could neither rest nor sleep, though the sky was black and calm. The screams of Sumati Ir and the banging of the walls was constant but disjointed and taxing to hear. The collisions created deep sounds that resonated throughout, lightly rumbling through the city, loosening age old dust and sand from crevices in the infrastructure.

"This has befallen a city, a city that proclaims itself the Temple City of Mala, filled with hypocrites and liars," said Begui, the head of a small Sumati household that had gathered in the center of their home.

"Do you look around? Do you see through your windows the other people, your friends, your cousins? Do they pray, do they surrender themselves to Her love?"

His four children all shook their heads. His wife and mother remained seated, all in a half circle watching him.

"Do you think we will suffer the same fate as them? We remain in our household, in our home, and it is surrounded by Her love. It shines in the darkness, and only the beautiful, the loving, the blessed can see it. Look outside my love . . . look outside . . ."

He motioned to his youngest daughter, Malaiva. She arose and looked out a nearby window and saw the dark huts.

"Look at the edge of our home. Look at the sand, look at the brick. It shines, it glows, it emanates strength and beauty. We are guarded, but they are not. Do you pity them?"

She turned to him and paused, then nodded.

"But they had a choice, my love."

He beckoned for her to sit back down.

"All the time in the world to capture Her glory, to glorify it and proclaim themselves Her children. It is only now, now when the threat is at their door that they believe every ounce of prayer will help them. Do you believe it will help them, Meeric?"

"No, bafa. When the bad men come they will kill them."

Begui smiled at his youngest son.

"It is not for us to decide what will happen to them, Meeric. All we know is that we differ from them because we remained faithful when there was no threat, so when threat is abound, Mala will gift her truly loyal with love. Do you understand?"

Meeric nodded, mesmerized by being corrected by his father.

Begui looked out a window, staring at the large wall at the edge of the city. Sounds jumped up and down it as if an ocean of chaos was trying to break in. He leaned against the edge silently.

"It is a currency, you know. More real than shel."

He turned to his family.

"Your mother knows this . . . has witnessed it. It is a real currency.

"Do you think one can amass a fortune working very hard for one night? Or does it take a lifetime of work to save one's wealth, to prosper and protect his family?"

He looked out the window once more.

"These dogs, these men who call themselves men . . . they cower like heathen rats now . . . praying for their families, trying to protect them. Trying to amass a lifetime of wealth this one night."

He knelt down looking at his family.

"I want you to understand and learn from me, Meeric. You will be a father someday, and when you have your children, you must pray for them. You must devote your love to Mala. She is God, She is your protector. There is no other option. No amount of shel will protect you."

He smiled and placed his hand on his son's shoulder.

"We are the richest family in Sumat!" he yelled, smiling, causing everyone else to smile happily.

He sat cross legged, closing the circle with his family and closed his eyes, beginning to pray. They all followed suit, placing the back of their hands flat against their knees, their palms facing upwards.

"Mala, She, my God, my Lord, my Queen. We feel Your presence, Your hands upon ours. Your endless embraces, welcoming us into Your lap. We surrender all unto You, like our parents, like our children, my mother and father, everything before and after.

"Mala, She, my God, my Lord, my Queen. Tell us, touch us. Will the harbingers breach the walls and siege the city?"

They all paused, then suddenly spoke together.

"Yes."

Begui's oldest daughter, Maramir, reached over to him and touched his hand for comfort. He quietly moved her hand back to her knee and pressed it there, her palm facing upwards.

"Through Mala, my love, all the hope in the universe resides. I am but a man . . . She is Mother to us all."

He continued.

"Mala, She, my God, my Lord, my Queen. Will the brutality of the harbingers dwarf the fear in your children's minds?"

"Yes," they all responded. The younger children began to cry slightly, reverberating terror in the hearts of the older ones.

Begui paused upon hearing his children, letting them weep for a period. Their hands shook slightly, repressing the yearn to reach out to touch someone near them for comfort.

"Bafa . . ." Maramir beckoned weakly, her face grimacing.

"Quiet, my love," Begui responded sternly. She bit her lip and dropped her head, trying to keep tears away. The banging of the walls in the distance periodically shook their hut, each subsequent jolt storming through her tender body.

"Mala, She, my God, my Lord, my Queen. Has this household remained loyal, worthy of Your boundless love?"

"Yes," they all responded, this time quicker, some through tears. Begui smiled.

"Mala, She, my God, my Lord, my Queen. Though others may suffer the hand of the wicked, though they may perish the means of the damned, will the engagement of heathen upon heathen escape us?"

"Yes."

"Mala, She, my God, my Lord, my Queen. Will you protect this house with your mighty hand?"

"Yes!" they all responded.

"As a brick survives the wind," Begui added calmly.

By the time the sun started rising in the distant skyline, the onslaught at the north side of the Sumati walls had dwindled down. The wind had picked up with the early sun, and the swirling sands made it harder to breathe for the already parched

Bahar. Only the top of the uppermost corpses remained visible, their skulls bloodied and dried as more and more retrievers were forced to brave the Sumati spears to retrieve the round Biha.

And though the siegers were tiring, the besieged remained in full force. Already, three lines of spearmen had oscillated positions, and those in the guard towers had exchanged shifts a number of times. The aggressive thrusts from the Sumati walls were as potent as ever while both the Bahar and the enslaved had slowed, softening the impact of the stones against the wall and slowing the speed with which they were retrieved.

The horn sounded, and Daesius, still positioned at the rear of the line, motioned for his men to retract. The accompanying spearmen rounded up the remaining slaves and marched them back to the encampment. The Bahar all regrouped around Daesius, some ways from Sumat, and fell upon the sand before him, exhausted.

"What a glorious initiation," he said, looking down at his men. Dozens of them lay parched, breathing heavily, their faces wrapped with cloth as their sweaty muscles glistened in the reddish light of dawn.

"The walls shatter from the inside, and with every thrust, we crumble them. Scream if you acknowledge!"

With a loud yell the Bahar obeyed, screaming triumphantly back at him.

"I wish to continue!" Algo screamed.

"You will continue when you are ready! Slaves are needed, and we round them from the outskirts of the city. Travelers and tradesmen, to retrieve your heart. Does that bring you satisfaction? To know we are satisfying your wish?"

"Yes, maisa!" Algo responded.

"We are Bahar!" Daesius screamed.

The men screamed in acknowledgement.

"The battle begins and ends with us! The walls crumble by our hands and hearts!"

Again, they screamed back at him, having heard the same words numerous times before.

"The first in line!!!" he screamed, with them following suit.

Their yells, though far from the city, were heard at the outskirts of Sumat, echoing worry within the base defenders. They had been fighting for hours, and still their roars seemed full of energy and force, as if the slingmen would return endlessly until Sumat was crushed to dust.

The meticulous planning of the Bahar siege led to minimal slingmen casualties, with few wounds and even fewer deaths. Though the Sumati guard towers were assigned to the best of the Ir, the shield bearers that protected the Bahar were trained to keep a watchful eye upon them and quickly adjusted their positions to protect the attackers.

As they left the field, the outer Sumati walls looked oddly sinister with bloodied circular blotches lining them, methodically spaced from each other with corpse upon corpse piled up beneath them. As sand carried by the wind struck the walls, it stuck to the splashes of still wet blood. The rest fell, gently covering the dead bodies. Along the now vacant Bahar line, there remained few casualties, though some shielders, spearmen and Bahar remained, their blood draining into the same sand that had begun to cover them.

The walls themselves stood tall and firm while the panels directly opposite the front of the attack were smeared with sweat and blood, and though barely noticeable, every impact of the Biha had created a series of small craters in the ancient brick. The compacted mudstone where the craters lay was shattered, containing small compressed bits that had turned into an orange dust. It had been thousands of years since the small particles were free to fly, and the passionate force with which the Bahar sought to release them freed them from their ancient prisons within the wall.

Lanam, a lowly Ir who tended the spears, leaned against the wall from the inside, feeling around it, asserting to himself that they were indeed strong, still firm. He pressed his ear against it and closed his eyes, feeling the cool silence of the brick. He was pushed aside by a spearman who positioned himself before a spearhole. All along the wall, spearmen followed suit, a hundred eyes peering out along the morning sands, trying to catch a glimpse of their enemy.

"Oyaff!" the men screamed as they held their carafes high, drinking deeply from them.

The Dimas leadership had congregated with the King to celebrate the start of the war and discuss strategy. They all sat calmly upon cushions as they sipped their drinks under the same red veil they ate below the night before.

"The Bahar have once again shone their bright light upon us, ushering in the demise of our enemies with the screams of their Biha that echoed all throughout the night!" Daesius yelled triumphantly, standing up.

"Fazaa!" all the men screamed.

The King motioned to him with his finger, and all subtly watched, still drinking and chattering, as Daesius approached him and held his lips close to his ear.

"The walls are strong, my King. Few casualties though the slaves perished in indiscreet numbers. Their defenses are slightly more sharp than we anticipated. The retrievers will not last if we are to continue as such.

"All attempts to circumvent the spears were met with expected success, all minor and somewhat inconsequential.

"The Biha were loud, and the expected result has been achieved. The city is certainly demoralized, though not fully affecting the soldiers. They fight with the vigor of the Iman Ir's voices in their heads."

Daesius subsequently returned to his seat, smiling and drinking, joining the others. The King sat silently, pondering, staring at them but gazing somewhere else altogether.

He tapped a wooden spoon against a bronze dish lightly, causing all the men to collect themselves, sitting in order, quieting down.

"We will proceed with the full assault. The Bahar, along with their commander, will rest during the day and continue at nightfall."

He turned to Bo Iri, one of his officers.

"You will organize a chaist during the day, rest in the evening and join the Bahar. Use Sumati speaking men with strong voices who will last through the night. I want their cries to scale the walls and grace the ears of every person in the city."

"Yes, my King," Bo Iri replied.

"Increase our range of collection - send marauders even farther into the wastes to collect travelers and tradesmen, their families and wives, and bring them here. Fill them with water. We require slaves as numerous as the stars. You will invest a small portion of your men in training them to retrieve the Biha. Smart tactics, for their longevity is one day - I want you to double that."

"Yes, my King," Halif, the master of wares replied.

He stood and held his drink in the air.

"We shall scale the walls, and may the dead amongst us, the blessed who perish today, drink and feed in the heavens!"

"Hauss!!!" the men screamed in unison, holding their drinks up.

The aftermath of the assault went as predicted. Wooden ladders were quickly run into the battlefield as soldiers flung them up against the walls and began to scale. A pathway lined the inside of the top of the walls, and spearmen rushed to defend, skewering with vigor anyone who neared the summit.

No one approached the base of the walls, and the spearholes remained mostly vacant. A few foolhardy Dimas swordsmen took the opportunity to peer through, trying to assess the inner workings of Sumat. Unbeknownst to them, a small regiment of specialized Ir were kept at the base, watching with intensity every light that shone from every hole. If one dimmed, they arose and quickly shoved a spear through, letting loose their war cry, impaling the inquisitive visitor directly through the eye.

Runners brought food and water to the front lines of the Sumati Ir, keeping them hydrated and energized. Bel Tazim's well implemented system of rotating spearmen along with rushing the exhausted to isolated cots on the other side of the city kept the defensive line not only filled, but explosive.

Even when a section of the wall was overcome and a series of Dimas soldiers stormed inside, catching their first glimpse of the grand city, their brethren could not scale the ladders as fast as the reserve Ir rushed up the stairs to meet them. Slowly, but surely, those within the city walls were slaughtered, and further intrusions repelled. It was through this give and take that the day progressed, with the Dimas army wearing down the initial front line as aggressively as possible, catching a rift in the defenses, then being pushed back promptly by the heavy arsenal that waited for them just beyond the walls.

Both sides suffered losses, and though the Shek's army suffered worse, the Sumati leadership had not predicted the ferocity of the assault or how quickly their spearmen would fall. The Iman Ir had declared with certainty that the defenses would not fail, that the reserves were just a careful precaution. Their necessity became apparent, however, as line after line slowly wore down, forcing the reserves to act as interim defenders while assignments were shuffled.

"Their weapons are carved of a strange material," Bel Tazim remarked as he inspected a Dimas spearhead.

"I visited Dimas before The Shattering and their weapons bore no major difference from ours. This material is completely different. It does not splinter, is light as a feather and pierces, does not flex when thrust."

He struck it against a table before him.

"It digs in and maintains its sharpness."

He turned to a runner named Nechaya.

"Do they have many of these weapons?"

"They are all of this type, Sai Bel Tazim," Nechaya responded.

He stood there, pondering for a few moments.

"You will instruct the gate guard to collect as many Dimas spearheads as possible and fasten them to ours. They are to be stored separately and provided to the leadership to distribute. Only the strongest, do you understand?"

"Yes, Sai Bel Tazim," he responded. He then bowed and scurried away.

"Is it superior steel?" Tindai, an Iman Ir, asked.

Bel Tazim held it up against the setting sun, staring at it.

"This Shek has brought more than diplomatic tricks with him to this battle," Bel Tazim responded. "It is like nothing I have ever seen. Have you any reports on its source?"

Tindai shook his head.

"I have heard nothing," he said.

He leaned against the table before Bel Tazim and breathed in deeply.

"They fight heavily, the Dimas soldiers."

"They fight as we predicted they would . . . a bloodthirsty army. They burn far too bright, and cannot last the course of this war," Bel Tazim responded, still staring at the silver spearhead.

He turned and looked at the weary Tindai. He was a veteran Iman Ir, his belly unshapely, his breath lost in the walk to the maza. His poor state of affairs was the result of years of indulgence brought about by his military position, a position certified by the very armor he now found troublesome to carry.

"Our city is a spearhead, my Ir. They will smash themselves against it, and as they split their wounds upon its blade, we will open the gates and galvanize their defeat."

Tindai looked at him, still breathing heavily.

"Sumat is a city of alchemy, my Ir. It purifies the weak and rewards the strong."

Tindai nodded and picked up a flask that sat upon the table and began to drink from it. Bel Tazim smiled and resumed examining the diagrams before him, placing the Dimas spear upon the table.

As dusk began to comb the surrounding area, the eager Sumati defenders stared from their guard towers and spearholes, watching the dwindling number of Dimas invaders as they left the battlefield, some limping, others exhausted.

Friends and family, the dead that lay along the pathway at the top of the walls, some with half their corpses hanging over the edge, were pulled back into Sumat. Their teary brethren, some overcome with anguish, sat beside their dead comrades holding their heads in their hands, weeping wholeheartedly.

They tossed the dead Dimas over the edge, feeding the blood soaked sand which was littered with bodies, both defender and imperial alike.

The retiring Dimas army was instructed not to seek out or mourn their fallen, for remaining in the open battlefield posed too great a threat. Instead, during the mask of night, a select few veterans took hoards of slaves out to the sands to dig trenches where the bodies were to be buried. The Sumati guards watched as huge trenches were dug along the outside of the city with slaves dragging and shoving fallen imperial soldiers into them.

Suddenly, a familiar horn blew and Sumat was immediately thrown into a state of panic as fresh spearmen rushed to the front walls. The first barrage of Biha that struck the wall seemed to shatter it from within, echoing a thunderous boom all across the city. People stared out their windows at the wall, every subsequent bang causing them to shudder, bracing themselves for yet another frightful night.

Bel Tazim, having fallen asleep in his chair at the center of the city, opened his eyes halfway, alerting himself to the sound. Begui sat in a circle with his family, their palms facing upwards laid upon their crossed knees, praying. The Oam sat far inside his palace, bathed in fresh water, with young women gently cleaning his skin, kissing his face and arms, massaging every inch of his body, pleasuring his manhood. He sat in the center of his illustrious pool, his gaze both relaxed and focused, as if in a trance, staring at the empty wall before him. Despite the sounds of the water and his distance from the battle, he stared, certain that the wall before him shook as the Bahar once again sieged Sumat.

As Bel Tazim slowly began to close his eyes to resume sleeping, he suddenly began to hear voices. This piqued his interest, and his eyes widened as he leaned upwards, listening intently.

"Gracious soldiers of Sumat. Your benevolent friend and King, the Dimas Lord, wishes for your safety. He instructs you to open your hearts to him, to share in his vision, that Sumat be a city free of corruption, that you be free to practice your life as you wish. The Oam has murdered the brother of the Dimas Lord. Join with him to avenge this insult and your efforts will be rewarded."

Bel Tazim began to laugh and slouched back in his position, closing his eyes.

"You laugh?!" a nearby Ir leader asked him, incredulously.

Bel Tazim responded without opening his eyes, still smiling.

"The Shek is a worthy opponent. I find his ingenuity humorous. Do not worry yourself. He will lose."

The gaze of those in the guard towers switched from the front walls where the Bahar were to the other side, trying to listen and catch a glimpse of the source of the sound. Those stationed on the other side stared down at a congregation of Dimas soldiers organized in lines outside the city. A man ran back and forth between them, speaking to them, then returning to a man stationed at the rear, guarded by two spearmen.

"Yours is a beautiful people. The Dimas Lord wishes to bestow riches and peace upon you. Aid his victory, and you will be rewarded. This pain, this suffering will end. The Oam's city is surrounded. Trade, food, water - it will all end. Join your Dimas brothers, aid the Dimas Lord and you will suffer no more at the hands of those that would suppress you."

The sound of their voices rang in unison, deep breaths in between, with the intensity of their toned muscles ringing through the air, like lions calling out into the night. They were all soldiers, ones that could speak the Sumati dialect, and did so with so much vigor that nearly every household in the city became aware of their speech. Townsfolk left their homes to go witness it for they had never seen anything like it before.

"We will not cease, we will not stop. Every member of every house that does not aid the Dimas Lord will feel his ire rather than gratitude. The city will suffocate. This is the new world army, one that has never retreated. We surround your city with men as far as the eye can see. We will break the walls and remove the usurper. Aid us, and you will be rewarded. You cannot remain neutral. Your families depend upon you.

"Your leaders lie to you. As you hear this, your walls suffer fractures. Our Royal Bahar create cracks like rivers in your ancient walls. They are crumbling. To protect their positions, to fight for their decadency, they give you hope when it is hopeless. You cannot stop the Dimas Lord just as you cannot stop the wind.

"Unleashed upon your city will be a torrent of never-ending pain. During the day your brothers will perish at the hands of the Lakta, the Hand of God, the Sand Spears. They will scale your walls like water rising and reach the very foot of your households. Every night from now you will witness the great Bahar legions, and you will hear their roar as your walls collapse. The Dimas Lord will unleash the Man in Black of the Aspyre, the Crylists, the Butchers of Vicha, the Ora Kana of the Mudbao, all sworn loyalty to the Dimas King. The tales you have heard are true, and it will be inflicted upon you.

"Release yourself from the curse that is not your own. Swear allegiance, organize rebellion, facilitate the victory of the Dimas Lord and you will be saved from the horrors that await those that refuse his kindness."

Bo Iri, at the rear of the chaist, listened intently and constantly instructed the runners to communicate what he wanted said to the men. They ran to the front of the lines and sentence by sentence repeated what was to be said. Each runner remembered one line and ran back to the commander to receive a new one. Once received, the men immediately began to speak in unison, gestured by a man at the front of the entire congregation who would give them the sign to proceed.

All instructions were delivered in Sumati as many members of the Dimas army had descended from local heritage and still spoke the language at home. Others were chosen to learn the language, while Bo Iri, a masterful linguist, was fluent in it. He was vocally gifted, and though he spoke softly, he was a tactful diplomat that knew a variety of languages. He had been an instructor in Dimas during the years preceding The Shattering, after which he resumed his post as an integral component of the military intelligence leadership.

As the chaist continued, repeated and re-stated throughout the night, the Bahar laid siege on the opposite side of the city. The runner slaves were now equipped with light armor and were provided incentives to perform their duty well. Some were promised food while others with family ties received protection for as long as they survived. The Bahar themselves found a steady pace, slamming their Biha against the Sumati walls ritualistically. The defensive spearmen found it harder to target the slaves who were now better fed and hydrated. They dodged and strategized their retrieval, waiting for the spears to thrust, diving forward to retrieve, then crawling away as quickly as possible. The guard towers were less useful at night, and though they were permitted to fling their spears at the attackers below, there was the constant scent of pressure applied to the entire defensive line in regards to conserving their limited armaments.

"One . . . house . . . long ago.

"A house with a family . . . though I had not yet seen them all . . . I met the father, and his eyes welled with tears as he stared upon the body of his wife.

"He stared at me . . . and though he was struck with grief . . . he still maintained his calm . . . trying to keep his tears retracted. He looked at me . . . he was . . . submissive. And I knew . . . immediately, I knew . . . there was something soft behind that doorway.

"I normally hold no interest in them . . . but this time, I pushed him aside and peered in. Upon the ground, kneeling, covered in white was his daughter. I had never seen something like that before. It was not that she bore any special beauty or tenderness. What it was did not matter. I was taken aback. I wanted her . . . I . . . wanted her in a way . . . I could not explain.

"That she could want me . . . I think . . . that this beautiful creature could want me. I turned to her father and asked for his permission. I told her that I did not want to take her . . . that I wanted it to be of her free will and that of her father's. He agreed, tearfully, frightened, as did she. I instructed Kanifta to end him, and he did once we departed. But that is not important, because she was never to know. It was not because of that that she failed me.

"I bedded her, and the first night was good. I later understood that it was more my blinded vision than her desire for me. She performed . . . she performed with strength and might, with drive and passion. I spread her legs, and she bent her head and pressed her body in all forms of strange, contorted manners upon my manhood. I drove a stake through her and she moaned in ecstasy.

"One night, after having her numerous times, I believe I had dried myself. I wanted more. I turned to her and held her, pulling her to me. She made a sound, and I looked at her, and after a moment she climbed upon me. But at that moment, that look she leaked . . . that look before she climbed on me. I don't know what it was. But a pain began to resonate within my chest. I took her from behind and as I pounded myself upon her, I began to weep. I stared at her back as she bounced back against me and knew she did not love me. Yes, I wept as I stared at her back . . . for it became apparent to me that she preferred showing me her back.

"Now I want you to close your eyes. I want to you listen to me as you close your eyes."

He slapped his hand in a puddle of red behind him and picked up a raw morsel from it, chewing it. He then ran his blood-stained palm across his face, closing his eyes.

"Think of the beauty, of any beauty, of all the beauty that could ever exist. Think of a green garden of flowers and all the water in the universe in an unending pool. Imagine driving your hands within it, pulling up the cool heavenly liquid and drenching yourself with it. Beside you are little children, beautiful little children and they laugh . . . they smile and hold you for you are their father."

He spoke slowly and tenderly, his deep voice and strong accent resonating against the silence and distant murmur of war. His words were littered with small indentations caused by the rupture in his lip, an old scar that added an intoxicating signature to his hoarse voice.

"Behind them, far behind them, is a beautiful woman. Not a girl, but a woman. She stands and stares at you with adoring eyes. You look at her, and her thighs are thick, welcoming. You stare at her and approach her. The children make way. You hold her head in your hands and stare at her face. You lean forward and press your tongue against her skin and lick her, and the warmth of her love exudes through her eyes into you.

"You lie with her, your face beside hers, and stare at one another."

He again drenched his hand in the pool and began rubbing it all over his body, eating another misshapen morsel.

"You see yourself in her - you see a reflection of embraces, and the endless years of prosperity before you, for she would never leave you, never abandon you. Your life for hers, and hers for yours. Bonded for life by some unspeakable and indefinable unquestioned loyalty that need not be communicated or confirmed, simply that she would spread her legs and climb upon you, and as you entered her you would feel the arms of the universe close over you, every fear and hurt and pain dissolving, making way for her embrace, her absolute acceptance and adoration . . . all the blue air, all the love in the universe, all the energy and hope that could ever exist, swimming within it. Swimming within it, forever . . . endlessly."

The men remained locked in position, their heads drooping or swooning, listening, some with erections, others holding themselves for support.

The man stopped talking, and all that could be heard was his chewing and his hand as it returned to the pool, over and over.

"Do you hear that?" he said, after a pause.

Some men shook their heads, others seemed to grimace slightly.

"It is the end of the dream."

The men remained fixated for some time, still breathing, but one by one their faces went from odd, captivated smiles to genuinely morose, childlike frowns. Some began to hold their heads, others fell to the ground, and some began to press blades against their skin. Slowly, they began to weep uncontrollably, some moaning in agony. The man stood up, standing at the edge of the sprawled group, his eyes shuttering as he moved towards them. He leaned down and yelled next to different men, directly into their ears, making them shake.

"Nothing," he screamed, his booming voice filling the tent, "good will come tomorrow."

He leaned down immediately and began beating one man, slamming his fist against his chest, then crawled to another, wrapping his giant hands around his neck, squeezing, staring at the man's face as he turned red. He screamed at them, gritting his teeth through his red mask as he continued moving from man to man, slicing them, beating them, thumbing their closed eyes.

Behind them, on the other side of the tent, a long wooden spike remained lodged in the ground. Impaled upon it was the little boy, his half-skinned body hanging loosely upon it. The blood from his disturbed corpse had drained down the pole and snaked its way into a depression in the sand where the pool of red flesh lay.

His muscles glistening in sweat and blood, Sangis arose, staring towards the fires in the distance through the lip of the tent.

"You are shameful, wretched men," he said. "All are superior."

The men moaned loudly upon hearing his words, their agonizing, woeful cries spreading to the nearby encampments, sending shivers down the backs of other Dimas soldiers.

"I loathe being positioned so close to those bastards," one man commented.

After some time, he looked to the tent of the Aspyre and saw them emerge. Their faces were shadowed, and they walked steadily, holding weapons in their hands, some screaming maniacally, others striking themselves. The Man in Black emerged as well, his white eyes shining brightly through a mask of coagulated blood that covered his face. He looked like an inhuman ghoul, and his demeanor matched it, for the Dimas soldier that watched them immediately became afraid that Sangis would catch his gaze and closed his eyes, pretending to sleep.

"Sometimes, I feel as if there are voices in my mind that tell me things I do not think, and they guide how I feel. I do not even know why. But I believe they are related to the life I have led ... what fear I would have, contemplating a dream, holding a loved one in my lap, not knowing if they were dead or alive. For the dream of Samaye ... the dream and nightmare, for the only moments I spent with my brother were in the shadows of life or the void of a false memory."

Akin held Jarvis's head in his lap as he spoke, his head leaned back against the cell wall. The lighting had faded as unlit torches riddled the jail passageway with only a few shining embers still roasting.

"What a wondrous life . . . memories of this moment will pass, and die with me. I wish for them to live on . . . I wish for people to experience the excruciatingly beautiful extreme thoughts that convert into emotions . . . transform in my mind in such piercing manners."

He stared down at Jarvis's head.

"You did not die in hiding, my friend. My very best friend."

He stroked Jarvis's hair as he looked at him.

"I must ground myself, for you are not alive, and this is not a dream. I fear awakening once more for the darkness in this place, unknowing reality from falsehood . . . believing my brother to be standing beside me."

He cupped his hands over Jarvis's face, feeling his features with his palms, leaning his head back once more, closing his eyes.

"That these moments would die with me, and all the anguish and love I have felt to exist no more . . . is a greater tragedy than death itself.

"Perhaps . . . perhaps in voicing it . . . in creating words and uttering it . . . even if no one hears it . . . it now exists outside of myself."

He grimaced, tears forming along his eyes.

"Akin's passion does not die if the dust retains his memory," he uttered between gasps.

Across the city, Bel Tazim had made an unlikely twilight departure from his fixed position in the town center. He visited his house during a gap in the Dimas assault, a gap he had predicted was likely to occur that night. Though the chaist still roared and the Bahar still sieged, his immediate stratagem was not required to manage the defenses which were already well in place. As the walls periodically rocked to the Biha, he opened a shiny container in one of his rooms and took out something wrapped in a soft, emblemmed cloth.

He left his house and proceeded to a large wooden enclosure. The central Iman Ir barracks, unlike the regular Ir house, was unwalled, and within it were only a few loose rooms and a large table at the center. It was lit very brightly, and he could already hear the laughter and gallivanting that emanated from within as he approached.

"Come, come, my brother!" Mihra exclaimed as he saw him.

Bel Tazim smiled and approached him, placing his palm on his neck, looking over the rest of the Iman Ir. A majority of them sat at the table, collectively eating and drinking. Maerus, who had never particularly liked Bel Tazim, watched him with prying eyes. The burly Tindai also attended, focused on the large portions before him. Inaisi, who excitedly joked with those seated next to him, had opted not to miss the meeting and instructed lesser Ir to manage the wall's defenses.

Mihra touched Bel Tazim's hand in response and held his goblet up to the rest of the table.

"To Sai Bel Tazim! The masterful strategist!" he yelled.

The other Iman Ir followed suit, some more enthusiastic than others.

"You have been very helpful in assisting us in defending our city, Sai Bel Tazim," Maerus commented. "May you live long, and continue assisting us."

Bel Tazim stared at him, his lessening smile a relic of Mihra's previous words. He bowed his head at Maerus slightly, then smiled through what seemed a slight grimace. He reached under his tunic and pulled out an aged goblet.

It was an old silver color, and the top of it had been bent. It bore marks of oxidation and was clearly a hand crafted cup from an archaic past.

He leaned forward and picked up a large carafe with Sumati ale, filling the goblet.

"And what is that, Bel Tazim?" Discha, another Iman Ir, asked.

"This, my friend, is a very special cup," Bel Tazim responded as he poured, still focused on filling it. "It was forged long ago by my ancestors. It is said to be so old that when they made it, they resided atop the highest mountain in the world and coated it with the essence of the heavens. This is why I hold it now, so many eons later, and may still drink from it!"

"That's very wonderful, Sai Bel Tazim, but it looks like a beggar's cup to me!" Discha joked, breaking out in drunken laughter with the others.

Bel Tazim smiled and nodded.

"Yes, I know. Such wonderful things often appear disguised as nothing. But sometimes, the entire universe can be contained in something we believe to be worthless."

"Correct, absolutely correct," Maerus interjected, snidely.

Bel Tazim took a deep breath in, then held the glass up.

"And so, I salute you, for your wondrous abilities and skills, and hope for the long and prosperous health of each and every one of you."

Everyone held their glass up in response, and as they did, he leaned his cup down, holding it in front of Mihra.

Mihra looked at it, then up at him. Bel Tazim stared at him as the others watched.

Mihra stood and grabbed his own cup, nearly pushing Bel Tazim's out of the way, stepping backwards, almost losing his balance. He held his cup in the air.

"To all my brothers!" he cheered as he placed his arm on Bel Tazim's shoulder.

Bel Tazim watched as Mihra pulled his cup to his lips and drank. He smiled and pulled his own aged cup to his lips and paused for a moment, then drank from it, closing his eyes.

As he opened his eyes, he felt Mihra's hand leave him as he sat down, resuming his meal with the rest of the Iman Ir.

"I leave you now, my Ir," Bel Tazim said, bowing his head. His words went mostly ignored, though some of the Iman Ir, such as Discha, acknowledged and briefly held their cups up once more as he departed. He flung the rest of the ale to the ground as he walked, wrapping his cup in the emblemmed cloth, carefully placing it back under his tunic.

CHAPTER 39

EON

Dawn brought with it the debriefing screams of the departing Bahar as they crossed paths with the oncoming Dimas force, ladders, spears and slaves en masse. Within the city, weary citizens pressed their cheeks into their hands as they leaned on their elbows, unable to do anything or go anywhere, their faces reeking of interrupted sleep and emotional fatigue.

"Run, bastards, run!"

The commanders screamed at their footmen as the war machine approached Sumat. The loud noise of their sandals striking the sand as they shuffled drowned out the screams and filled the soldiers with a sense of energy and excitement.

"I am running as fast as I can!" Hafa screamed, his back bent forward carrying a large ladder with a dozen other men.

"Faster, you bastard!" Reima responded, laughing at him.

They were both shadowed by the ladder and surrounded by hundreds of other men. Most carried spears like them while others were in full gear with shields and helmets. Reima wore a helmet while Hafa was bare with just a spear in one hand and the ladder in the other.

They both carried the ladder along with a group of other men extending both behind and in front of them.

"I see the walls!" Hafa screamed.

Reima looked up and could barely make out the top of the Sumati walls in the distance.

"When we strike it, do not stop until your palm touches the wall!" Reima yelled back.

Atop the wall, in the guard towers, the Sumati soldiers nervously watched as the stream of men steadily approached, their roar loudening. Before them was a seemingly endless number of them, all wearing different colors, uniformed eclectically. As the front line approached the walls, the Ir behind their holes stood ready, clutching their weapons tightly, while the guards above them prepared to repel the oncoming attackers with thin, pointed spears, firmly in hand.

One by one, the Dimas soldiers began to scream, a symphony of angry yelling that emanated from the front and like a wave carried itself backwards.

Both Reima and Hafa also began to yell, squinting their eyes as they heard the sound of metal on rock as the men smashed against the walls.

"Thrust!" yelled an Ir. The men followed suit, shoving their spears skillfully through the holes, impaling the men on the other side, then retracting just as quickly. Some spears were deflected by armor or missed entirely, stabbing the space between soldiers, while others wounded or landed devastating blows.

Both Hafa and Reima continued to push forward, pressing against the men before them.

"Not until you feel it strike the wall!" yelled a soldier.

"Push!" screamed Reima, his teeth gritted as he shoved the ladder forward.

Hafa started screaming as he put his full force behind it, his knees bending as he pressed. Suddenly, the ladder shook as they felt it stop with a jolt.

"Now!" screamed someone.

One by one, the soldiers grabbed each prong of the ladder and pushed it forward, the front men pushing it up, raising the front end against the Sumati wall. They did so in methodical unison, screaming with each raise. All along the wall, other ladders were also being raised, with small groups of men grunting together as they pushed. Behind them, excited soldiers stood ready, waiting to climb. Some jumped on prematurely only to be shoved off by others for preventing the ladder from being raised.

Behind each segment of the front line was an officer who watched each ladder as it was lifted. As the top feet of the ladders reached the summit of the walls, they yelled at their men who subsequently stopped raising it and stomped down on the lower prongs to ground it in the sand. Soldiers immediately stormed up, spear in hand, war cries bellowing out at the top of their lungs.

"Are you ready?" Reima asked Hafa, his teeth shining through under his helmet.

Hafa looked at him nervously then nodded once, tightening his grasp of the spear. Without hesitation, Reima began screaming and jumped on the ladder, climbing as fast as he could. Hafa followed, finding it harder to navigate its prongs than Reima who seemed to glide up it.

He watched as the soldiers below slipped farther and farther away, their yells becoming dimmer as he took each step. Soon, his gaze switched from those below to those above and looked forward to the ancient walls of Sumat and the impending summit that was soon to reveal itself. Ahead of him, men stormed like water over the edge, disappearing past the wall, entering the city.

As Reima reached the top, he placed one hand on the Sumati ledge and thrust himself upwards, squatting upon it as he landed, the point of his spear held close. Before him was a quickened battle filled with the Dimas dead. Those that had led the charge had already fallen, and it was only the few that preceded him that still stood, weapon in hand, trying to penetrate the Sumati defenders that stormed forward to confront them.

He jumped off the ledge and fell into the wall enclosure. Immediately, he threw his spear forward without hesitation and impaled a young Ir through the heart. He quickly jumped to the boy and retrieved his weapon, defending himself from an oncoming soldier who tried to strike him. He smashed the edge of his spear against the spearhead of the enemy's, pushing it aside, running his elbow straight into the Ir's neck, hearing a crack. As the Ir fell, clutching his throat, gasping for air, Reima stomped upon his head repeatedly, impacting it.

Hafa's feet landed into Sumat, and he looked over the grand city in the horizon, then down to the bloody carnage before him. He saw Reima who was now clashing spears with an equally formidable enemy, both grunting as they tried to pierce one another in some frenzied dance. Hafa ran to him and stopped, trying to find a safe opening with which to aid his friend. As he stood there, nervously trying to slow their movements in a predictable fashion, a blade pierced his shoulder, held by a screaming Ir who was lunging at him. The Ir bellowed at Hafa in a foreign dialect as he fell to the ground. He kicked the Ir in the ankle with his large leg, causing the man to shuffle and fall, then clutched his bleeding shoulder, grimacing.

He jumped to his feet and ran to the edge of the wall. Peering down, he saw the eager and untouched Dimas army as they screamed and waited to storm the city. Beside him, more and more men jumped into Sumat from the ladders, pouring in like drops of water. Ladders lined the wall, and as he observed the men, he fell to the ground. Ir in the guard towers fervently flung spears at the invaders, shouting as they did, targeting both those inside the city and those waiting to storm within. Leaning his back against the inside of the Sumati wall, he watched his fellow soldiers storm into battle only to be met by the severe resistance of the Sumati army. Peering along the long pathway that stretched across the inside of the wall, he noticed two large and uncommon legs land upon it in the distance. As he looked up, he saw a ghoulish creature, the largest man he had ever seen, covered in black, brandishing a large silver scimitar. The sight mesmerized him, and he watched as the man stretched his arms back and released a loud, deafening howl.

Both the Dimas and Sumati soldiers were interrupted as they witnessed his arrival, pausing for a split second to notice him. Behind the line of conflict, Sumatis were yelling at each other, some nervous, others angry, and in the distance he could see onlooker peasants running away from the front line, tugging frantically at their sons and daughters.

The Man in Black immediately began running forward. His family, the Aspyre, equally scarred in appearance, stormed behind him brandishing strange weapons of torture and mayhem.

Sangis raised his weapon high as he ran and swung it down as he encountered resistance, chopping through the center of an Ir's spear and severing a portion of his leg. The scimitar moved without interruption, and as the Ir fell, shrieking, Sangis looked down at him unemotionally. The man began to scream in terror as Sangis leaned down and began to chew on his face, tearing his skin apart toothily. The image of the large man, loosely draped in black, towering over the small Sumati soldier rattled those that witnessed it, the muffled screams of the dying Ir amplifying the horror.

"It is as expected," Bel Tazim commented upon hearing of the entry of the Man in Black. As he spoke, Sangis continued to relish torturing the man, ceasing only when he stopped squirming. When he arose, his face was covered in fresh blood, and the Ir himself was dead, his face mutilated beyond recognition.

"He performs ghastly actions, but he is just a man. Just a man like any other, with paint and blood and a heart that can be pierced. He is a godsend, not to be feared; the Dimas army will fall if the Man in Black, the undefeated beast of the Shek, is defeated."

Sangis stormed forward once again, clutching his scimitar, dodging a spear as a group of Ir targeted him. One by one, they took stance and threw their spears at him, aiming precisely. Some would land upon him, piercing his shoulder and leg. Others he would deflect with his weapon, and others he would dodge entirely. He seemed unaffected by his wounds and screamed as he neared them. As his mouth opened, his red stained teeth were revealed, drenched in blood and littered with bits of skin.

In the distance, a large congregation of heavily armed Iman Ir approached the city wall, escorted by an even larger regiment of Ir. They wore their golden helmets and carried silver spears, eyeing the screaming Sangis who was surrounded by empty space, gladly provided by both the Dimas and Sumati soldiers who readily avoided him.

Discha stepped forward, raising his shining spear, and turned to face his brethren and their escorts.

"Turn the tide today! The Man in Black is just a man, and when we tear down the legend of his ungodly immortality, so too shall the spirit of the enemy be vanquished!"

The men yelled back in agreement.

"He is just a man!" Discha yelled, turning to face the front line.

"He is just a man!" another Iman Ir screamed.

Suddenly, they ran forward, screaming. The defending Ir gave way and created a path for the legion.

As Sangis heard them, he turned and stopped, staring. He smiled in glee and began to cry out, reaching forward with his hand then retracting it quickly, yelling, "Come!" at them.

"Die, you whore!" another Iman Ir screamed as they neared him.

Sangis raised his weapon high and struck down with force just as the Iman Ir reached him, slicing through the shoulder and neck of an Ir, nearly lopping it off. The Aspyre jumped forward, clashing with the defenders, using their strange weapons to lock spears in position and pierce their enemies.

Sangis raised his weapon once more, freeing it from the twitching corpse of the soldier and swung it at Discha who tried to block it with his spear. In doing so, he slowed it but could not prevent the follow through which ended up in his shoulder. He fell backwards as Sangis pulled the scimitar back, raising it again. An Ir jumped in front of Discha and stabbed Sangis in the chest with his spear. Sangis reacted by grabbing the boy's neck and crushing it, grimacing as he threw his body back at the Sumati defenders.

The previously energized Iman Ir were now cautiously eyeing Sangis as they tried to surround him, pointing the tips of their spears at him. Others battling his deranged brethren, and all around the inner wall the battle continued to rage on between the Dimas and Sumati soldiers.

Sangis began swinging his scimitar wildly in front of him, creating a circular barrier that the men feared to cross.

"We must attack together!" an Iman Ir screamed.

They paused, still eyeing him, tightening their hold of their weapons.

Suddenly, one man bolted forward, and like lightning the rest followed, screaming as they tried to plough their spears into any part of Sangis that they could. He swung his blade downwards, forcing all the spears that were targeting his chest to the ground while the rest struck their targets, piercing his arms and shoulders and even his head. He fell backwards as a spear tore a line along the outer edge of his eye, all the way to the back of his head, scraping the very flesh aside, revealing bone.

He screamed angrily and swung his arm against the spear, dislodging it from his body and pressed up against the attackers, forcing their weapons deeper into his torso. He punched the man closest to him and pushed his head away, then quickly raised his weapon, striking a number of Sumati soldiers in the chin with the blunt end of it. They fell backwards, stunned, both Iman Ir and Ir alike.

Nechaya stepped forward, a small man hidden under the burly men before him, and unsheathed a small knife. The blade was coated with a red substance, and he leaned forward, quickly cutting into Sangis's leg with it once, then disappearing back into the crowd.

Sangis screamed again, swinging his scimitar wildly, trying to distance the men away from him. He began to stumble suddenly and fell backwards onto his knee, clutching his eye which was now bleeding profusely. An Ir lunged forward at that very moment, holding one of the Aspyre blades in his hand, and ran it down on Sangis, striking him right between his neck and shoulder. The blade cut so deep that the man could not retract it and instead stepped backwards, releasing it. Sangis himself arose, disoriented and stunned, walking backwards as he clutched his eye.

He turned slightly and tried to look at what was around him but could not focus. He stumbled to his knees once more and again tried to rise, stabilizing himself. He did not realize how close he was to the outer wall and tried to lean against it, missing the top of it entirely, falling over, stumbling downwards into the crowd of Dimas soldiers below.

The men stood, exhausted, and looked at one another slowly, almost unaware of the battle that raged beside them.

"We did it!" an Ir exclaimed loudly.

"The Man in Black is defeated!" another followed.

The Iman Ir stood still and looked at one another, not entirely certain of the outcome or what was achieved by it. Then they observed the smiling Ir before them who were screaming in ecstasy and of their own accord had begun jumping into the battle to push the Dimas horde from within the city walls.

"The Iman Ir have destroyed the Dimas champion!" others began to scream, relaying it along the battlefield.

The Dimas soldiers that braved the battle also became aware of the fall of Sangis, weakening their resolve. A young man whispered into the ear of the Shek King, giving him the news. He sat under his tent and stared forward upon hearing it, looking at his Havasa.

"The gamble is made then," he said nonchalantly.

Suddenly, horns blew all along the outskirts of the city. The Dimas soldiers quickly became alert to them and began to retreat. Some tried to fight their way back after being separated from their brethren, while others did not wait for space on the ladders and simply dove off the wall.

"Now! Now is the time!" Bel Tazim screamed.

Maerus shook his head as he walked about the table.

"I must disagree wholeheartedly. The rest of our brothers have still not returned, and such a decision cannot be made hastily. Look at their numbers! They still stand numerous as the stars at our gates!"

"It is not a hasty decision! It is a wise one, one that will continue to turn the tide of the battle in our favor and strike a blow the Shek will never recover from. We must stop the Dimas army here and now. If we permit them to retreat to safety and rearm, they may lay siege for weeks or months and starve us into submission. We cannot win a war of attrition - we must attack!"

"I will agree with Sai Bel Tazim here, my brother," Mihra commented. He sat, along with a few other Iman Ir under the roof of their barracks while Bel Tazim and Maerus remained standing, proponents of their own perspectives.

"Mihra, to open the gates, it is a risk we need not take," Maerus said.

"As he has stated, it may be a risk we must take. How long can we remain under siege? We have never encountered such a well-armed force so plentiful in number. We may outlast fickle barbarian raids for they lose interest and scurry away, but this is an imperial war. The Shek has brought the Red City to our doorstep and will not leave simply because our doors are closed," Mihra responded.

Maerus stared at him then closed his eyes and began shaking his head.

"There is something wrong . . . my friend."

He turned and looked at Bel Tazim accusingly.

"You . . . this man is a foreigner. Yes, you have aided us, you are very talented. But his heart, it knows not the true nature of Sumat. We must defend ourselves and not open ourselves to attack. I swear to you, it is a mistake."

Tindai leaned forward and placed his hands on the table.

"My brother, Maerus, I believe if we can broker peace with the Shek, we should do so. We are not welcoming them into our homes with arms . . . they retreat as we speak. We may catch them on their heels."

Bel Tazim looked to the wall in the distance.

"The time of action is quickly slipping away, my Ir. We must decide - risk this same onslaught day after day until we run out of food and water or strike a decisive, unexpected blow upon their entire army and secure a victory to protect our city. We need not destroy them, just make a thorough dent in their numbers. The Shek will move on, as all always have, and always will. We will strike a blow and retract. There is nothing to lose!"

He flung his arms up, palms facing upwards, pointing at the walls.

"They run now! They run upon hearing the horns of defeat! We may spear them from behind and force them to fight when they wish to flee. We will storm over them like the wind."

Maerus looked at him then back at the other Iman Ir. He sat down and shook his head.

The vast Dimas assault force slowly began to organize itself and retreat from the outskirts of the city. Those unfortunate enough to be stuck behind enemy lines were repeatedly gashed and tortured by the Ir. It was a clear symbol of defeat, for it was not even mid-day and still the Shek had signaled their retreat. As they walked back to their camp, the Ir in the guard towers watched them, leaning on their spears, their nerves still tense and at odds with resting.

The horns continued to sound methodically, and men who had not had a chance to even touch the outer wall became flustered, complaining repeatedly about the decision to retreat, citing their readiness to destroy the "Sumati dogs". Most veterans simply obeyed as if following the task list provided to them by their employer.

Suddenly, the ground began to rumble as a large echoing sound was heard. The men turned to face Sumat and initially could not pinpoint the source of it. Soon, however, they began to notice dust falling off the large stone gates and watched wide eyed as they started to open.

On the other side, every able bodied Ir had been assembled with full armor, fed and hydrated their fill, clasping their spears which pointed directly outwards. As the door became more and more ajar, the men became visible with hundreds of pointed spears standing in perfect formation.

A huge bang was heard from within the city that kept resonating outwards. Immediately, the men began to move forward, running towards the retreating Dimas army.

"Do we fight or run?"

"Run to where?!"

"We must fight!"

"We are to retreat! It is ordered!"

"Stand your ground! Fight, you bastards! Resume formation!"

The Dimas army was in complete disarray, with many of the men running away from the Sumatis while others planted their feet in position and held their weapons pointed at the oncoming force, while even others simply screamed and ran towards the attackers, brandishing their spears.

"I say, stand your ground!!!!" an officer yelled. The men around him quickly tried to organize themselves, and the rest of the force, upon seeing them, followed suit, planting their feet in the sand, pointing their weapons at the enemy.

"Stand your ground!!!!" other leaders screamed.

The men that had decided to charge the Sumatis were quickly cut down in the most brutal of fashions, with a multitude of spears piercing their bodies quickly and efficiently. Those Ir that engaged them hastily retracted their weapons and resumed running towards the Dimas force.

The Shek King sat under his tent and watched the battle unfold in the distance. Beside him sat a few commanders and his Havasa.

"What shall we do, my King?" one commander asked.

"Our force will hold most of them . . . we have sufficient defenses to beat off the rest," he replied, a shining excitement in his eyes.

The commander looked back at the war front uneasily.

"What of the Watermen, my King?" another asked.

The King turned to him quickly and stared incredulously.

"What?" he asked.

"I inquire about the Watermen of Vicha . . . I recall their camp but not seeing them in some days."

The King began to clap ecstatically.

"My dear Messim, you surely are full of providence."

Messim smiled with uncertainty.

"You speak of the Watermen, the hidden beasts, and here, I give them to you."

He pointed to the battle, and Messim turned to see it.

Suddenly, as the Sumati force ran forward, distancing themselves from their city, the sand behind them began to shift. In the distance, it was only through strange deviations in the sun's reflection that the shifting was visible. Soon, however, hundreds of black arms began appearing above the sand, and after that followed whole men, leaping out from under the sand, running straight towards the open city gates. It looked as if the sands were bleeding blackness, for the men who ran forward were dark in complexion, contrasting the golden sands and the sun that shone upon them.

PART IV

CHAPTER 40

DARKMEN OF VICHA

No one knew how the Shek King had tamed the northern "half-men", for the tales surrounding the disappearance of the ancient town of Vicha reeked of bizarre repugnance. It had been a small farming village, stretched far out to the north, isolated from its peers, welcoming few visitors. Still, Vicha was an established colony and boasted ripe vegetation and hunting due to its proximity to the northern marshes.

A small caravan, broken and in shambles, returned after its final visit to the town, raving of horrific half-men that had emerged from the swamps. Hamas, their leader, retold the story of Zazi, the town headsman of Vicha, who had organized an expedition to investigate the disappearances of some of the townsfolk whose lands were farther to the west.

When the caravan first arrived in Vicha, the whole village was in a state of tension as men were being organized with scythes and other farming tools that could be used as weapons.

"You visit us at an unfortunate time, Hamas," Zazi said as he welcomed him.

They stood in the village center surrounded by bush and vegetation. The entire area was conspicuously shaded due to the large amount of brush, and behind them was a large house that served as their town hall.

"What is wrong?" Hamas inquired, weary from their long trek.

Zazi shook his head.

"We are not sure. Come, let us quickly eat something, and I shall fill you in. Perhaps you can aid us while you are here."

He motioned to Hamas's caravan which was made up of mostly his family and a few other workers, both men and women.

"Come, all of you . . . come and eat and rest."

Inside the town hall, a large table was organized, and food was brought in for the people of the caravan. The members of his family sat together and began to eat while Zazi and other citizens of Vicha made them feel welcome, their smiles hiding an uneasy tension.

"My family adores coming here for your hospitality. There is nothing quite like the food of Vicha. When we begin to see the marshes, a feeling of joy always overtakes us," Hamas told Zazi, trying to distract him.

Zazi sat down, examining the table to ensure everyone had been taken care of. He sat beside Hamas, leaning in.

"You eat, I will talk."

Hamas nodded and began to bite into thick, green legumes coated with sauce, flavored by the large portion of fish that sat beside it, its juices flowing, creating a light gravy at the bottom of the platter.

"Months ago, there was idle talk of movement in the marshes where none should be. Mostly, it was children saying they saw something move in the water, or farmers hearing noises from within the wet bush. It was not taken seriously, but then Damia and his family failed to join us for Pardone many weeks ago. Some men were sent to investigate, and his house was found abandoned. A small makeshift shelter was discovered some ways from it, small enough to fit a child, but was also vacant."

Hamas looked confused and kept listening, his overwhelming hunger keeping him distracted by the food.

"The shelter had been slept in . . . it seemed like days. It was filthy. It was of concern but just a mystery like any other. However, soon after that, another family, the Maiazi, also located far to the west, disappeared. Their entire lot was found abandoned. And yesterday, yet another family failed to attend our feast. We have not yet investigated their land but are now going to perform a more exhaustive search. It is demoralizing for the whole village to be worried every Pardone that yet another of our kin will fail to join us.

"There is certainly a sinister element at work here, for these families are generational citizens of Vicha and would never abandon us without word. We believed perhaps Damia and his family simply left, odd as that may have been, but the Maiazi and Lycha would not have. The isolated shelter is also of concern and makes no sense."

"What are you going to do?" Hamas asked.

"We have organized and are going to first examine the Lycha farm. If we are fortunate, they are there and missed Pardone for some other reason. If my fears are correct, their home will be abandoned as well. We shall then proceed to the swamp and find the source of these illegal and immoral actions."

"But there is nothing to the north . . . just swamp," Hamas said.

"Yes, just swamp. This is why I hope to find our comrades. The perpetrators could not be far for the impassable terrain. Will you join us?"

Hamas immediately stood up and wiped his mouth.

"I am joining their small expedition. I shall be back shortly. Remain here, frolic about, but do not leave the town center. Is that clear?" Hamas said to his family.

"Yes, faiza," his son replied.

He walked out, followed by Zazi who smiled at members of the caravan. Hamas approached his large convoy which was stationed outside the town hall and retrieved a large sheathed sword. He pulled another one from another part of it and handed it to Zazi.

Zazi shook his head, pointing to a blade attached to his waist.

"Take this as well, my friend. It is forged in the sands of the south and will cut through anything we find," Hamas urged.

Zazi took it and wrapped it around his waist and shoulder, the sheathed sword hanging on his back. Both men, now armed, joined the others who began to walk towards the Lycha farm, disappearing into the thick trees.

As they maneuvered the thick bush, every step felt totally indistinguishable from the next to Hamas, yet the dense foliage seemed familiar to the men of Vicha. They navigated trees and bush, chopping at newly grown branches, clearing the thin path that was etched into the ground. The trek spanned almost an hour, the Lycha estate being relatively close to Vicha compared to the others.

They navigated a corridor of bush along a twisting trail and eventually entered a clearing. Before them in the distance was the Lycha house which stood forebodingly silent on the edge of the pasture.

The men continued on their way, a large, armed congregation of them, following the path through the farmland that the Lycha family had frequented for generations.

As they reached the front of the house, the first men to see it stopped, looking at the entrance. The door was eerily ajar, and as the one of them approached it, he saw half-dry red spots in the open doorway, pressed in the shape of partial footprints.

Zazi motioned for the men to surround the house and examine every side of it. With Hamas close by, both men, along with a few others, entered the house, feeling the handles on their weapons cautiously.

As they entered the main hall of the large, old house, all the men froze as they stared at the dining table. Upon it was a carcass, recognized by Zazi to be the body of Shenho Lycha.

The man had been beheaded, and though they eyed the area around the table, his head could not be seen. His hands lay on either side of him, palms facing upwards, and was centered on the table, directly in the middle of the large hall. Hamas stared at the corpse, wide eyed with disbelief while Zazi simply frowned, unable to emotionally comprehend what he was looking at. Others began to heave and left the room which stunk of rotting blood.

Items had been tossed about, and a pattern appeared visible to Zazi who immediately began running through the rectangular house from room to room, looking for others. He began to scream their names as he did and called out to the other men as he stopped somewhere within.

As the men approached, they saw before them one of the Lycha daughters. Sitting awkwardly against the wall, her head hung low with her arms by her side. Her legs were spread out in front of her, and she was naked, a streak of dried blood leading to her thighs.

Zazi leaned down and touched her chin, looking at her face. She suddenly breathed in and looked at him, then began to scream. He grabbed her with both hands and held her tight as she tried to continue screaming, her arms loosely hanging beside her.

"Shasen . . . Shasen . . . it is Zazi. It is Zazi . . ." he whispered calmly and soothingly to her. He leaned her back, still holding her, and looked into her eyes, smiling.

"It is me!"

Her eyes were welled with tears, and she stared at him silently, breathing awkwardly and quickly.

"They took them . . ." she whispered suddenly.

Zazi frowned, still looking at her.

"They took . . . who?"

"Ma and Danji," she responded.

"What do you mean?"

"They came with Shono . . . from the swamps."

She began to cry profusely, moaning.

"They took ma and Danji!" she screamed maniacally.

Zazi quickly turned his face sideways and closed his eyes. He then motioned to some of the other men who leaned down and began lifting Shasen.

"To the swamps then?" a man yelled angrily.

Zazi looked at him slowly and stared. He reached over and grabbed Hamas's knee for support as he leaned against it, losing his balance for a moment.

"What could it be?" Hamas asked.

Zazi shook his head and stood up, turning to the group. He paused for a moment then nodded, grasping the blade at his side tightly.

The men stormed out, running as fast as they could towards the northern swamps. Hamas followed with Zazi, one worried with the other still perplexed.

"Zazi . . . Zazi . . . what do you make of this?" Hamas asked as they walked, following the others.

Zazi looked at him, as if for the first time.

"I do not know . . ."

"They took the women?" he asked, incredulously.

Zazi did not answer, his brow tense.

"Who is Shono?"

"Their small boy. They would have followed him from the marshes," Zazi responded.

"Dark skinned boys were taken to the swamps. Women were used as hosts, taken to their lair, raped for days, then released to find their way back to their homes. They have adapted since the time of Vicha."

The Shek King continued.

"They care not about raising children and return when the boys are of a ripe age. They are given genus and forced to breathe through them. Genus are their weapons, long tubes with blades attached to the ends. They prevent the genu from being obstructed and when spun and retracted form a spike at the end."

"And what of Vicha?" Messim asked.

"The city vanished. A small, armed pilgrimage was sent to Vicha sometime later and found the town deserted. They found corpses in different places, fire pits, and a number of bloated women hanging from their necks within the town hall. This was a long time ago. Vicha has been lost somewhere in the north, re-consumed by the swamplands, and the Watermen no longer limit themselves to swamps. They have had to adapt, as you see, to a world of sand."

"So they fight for Dimas?"

Bo Iri approached the King from the side. He stopped and looked at him as the Shek looked back and nodded. He then bowed and left, turning around.

The casual focus the King was giving Messim made him uncomfortable, as before them in the distance was the grandest battle he had ever witnessed. The Dimas army was fighting hard against the Sumati spears, with men on both sides falling, bleeding into the ground. It was only as screams began to emanate from Sumat that the Ir began to turn and notice the border of holes in the sand behind them and the dark men with strange spears that continued disappearing into the city.

"They are in our city!" an Ir screamed.

"Stand your ground! Fight the Dimas horde!" yelled another.

Suddenly, the loud, familiar voices of the chaist began to fill the battlefield.

"The Butchers of Vicha are upon your wives and daughters. They feed on your sons and desecrate your homes. The war is over. Lay down your arms and you will be protected."

The chaist kept repeating the same message over and over. At first, most of the Sumati men did not even register the words, but soon it was penetrating their minds, and they began looking at one another as they fought, seeking aid as their morale began to plummet. The sounds from within Sumat became more and more terrific, with the screams of women and children echoing about, some of fear with others more sudden and desperate.

The Sumati surrender started with one man who fell to his knees, placing his spear upon the ground before him, bowing down. Upon seeing him, others followed, and the infectious despair and hope terrified those still fighting. In fearing they would be the last ones standing, they too fell to their knees, bowing in submission.

Those Ir unwilling to surrender were quickly cut down, their comrades hiding shamed looks as they remained bowed to the Dimas soldiers before them. The force that kept fighting was soon decimated, and as the Dimas men looked across the battlefield, seeing nothing but bowed men, they began to cheer, screaming in excitement and angst as they raised their weapons in the air, hugging one another.

The Shek King arose, smiling as he looked at the open gates of Sumat and the bowed Ir before his enormous army.

A runner approached the King, watched by the Dia guards.

"Liem, commander of the Sand Spears, requests your orders, my King. The Sumati army has surrendered; all others are vanquished."

"Tell him the sky is burning and the sands are parched," replied the King.

CHAPTER 41

DAGGER IN THE SAND

T he last flickering embers of the torches that lined the hall underneath the great temple had died out long ago, and Akin sat upon the hard ground, grasping his friend's cold hand.

"It is dark," he thought. "So dark, as it was so long ago."

He did not feel the same terror as he had when he was younger. Perhaps, he thought, because this was not such an enclosed space. Perhaps it was because he had his friend beside him.

"That was such a fortuitous day," he thought. "The day I looked back upon Jarvis, and it was as if all the wind in the skies had energized his soul. Without regret he dropped his veil."

He could not remember seeing anything or anyone else at that moment. Only the memory of Jarvis and the sun upon him, glowing like a deity upon the earth, and a blur of motion all around him. It was as if at that moment, something within him exploded and surged outward like a flood. Akin had felt it and been mesmerized by it . . . it pulsated within him even now.

"Everyone had felt it," he thought.

Like a grand, visionless explosion of energy that knocked everyone before him to their knees, as ripples in water humbles those insects that clutch to its surface as if it were stone.

"Perhaps providence, then, that such a grand effect would drain him of his spirit, and be recalled . . . die, for the intensity of the release," Akin thought.

He thought of Jarvis's corpse and felt good thinking that it was as it should be . . . that this was the path of freed spirits. That Jarvis had spent his whole life forced backwards, and because of that, the impact of his resurgence turned him into something more than human, escaping him, taking his soul and spirit with it in a grand burst of passion. He smiled and felt his eyes well up as he imagined his friend soaring to endless places, exploring the universe limitlessly.

"But what of me?"

He suddenly began to breathe heavy and leaned forward, his eyes clutched tight.

He thought of his angry face in the baseless dark of the cave and the rage with which he kicked the door and yelled at Samaye to do the same.

He thought of running up the uneven steps to Jarvis. He imagined his face and eagerness. He knew they were the same. Lightning from within that struck those closest, energizing them. It could not be contained once felt.

"We are the hands of effect," he thought in a blur of thoughts.

He felt the inside of his hand against Jarvis's and envisioned a thousand men standing tall, holding their palms out to the air before them, creating ripples in the wind, jolting and energizing all those before them, forcing them to their knees. Understanding and awareness, with empathy and love, unstoppable and uninterruptable thoughts gracing each and every one of them, adoration for those that affect them, then filled with the desire to open their palms likewise and return it two fold.

He ran his hand along Jarvis's face and felt love for the memory that was his friend.

"What a beautiful memory his body is," Akin thought. "But he is not dead. Alive and living for his breaths that shake the world still. All those that saw him, that beat him, that knew of him or will ever know of him. His presence lives like the air in everything he touched. Immortality in the change he effected that altered the world.

"What a glorious life I have led," Akin thought. "Opening my heart and all the fires that followed. The passion within . . . the spirit of desire . . ."

This is why Bethelhurst was dead to him. He had tried to open his palms to his father so many times. But Bethelhurst's influence dies with time.

"In truth I sought to welcome the future, for it always brought about revelation. He tried to reverse that, to always return to some safer, more stagnant time.

"That is the difference," he thought, "between fear and truth. Fear expires whilst truth lives on forever, propagating itself."

Huddled in a circle, Begui and his family sat in the center of their home, praying. He eyed them while they kept their eyes shut, maintaining a vigilant standard upon them. His daughter Maramir squeezed a peek through her shut eyes, and as soon as Begui noticed it, he lunged forward, slapping her across the face.

"Faith, child! If you open your eyes, you scream doubt! If you doubt, the hordes will flood into our household!"

"I'm sorry, bafa," she muttered without crying as tears rolled down her cheek. She closed her eyes upon being struck and kept them closed.

Outside their house, it sounded as if some hellish portal had opened up underneath Sumat, darkening the skies amidst the late afternoon. Defiled screams emanated from nearby huts as men ran back and forth through the streets. The sounds of doors breaking and children calling out for help were quickly silenced with singular grunts and muffled whimpering. The sudden and immediate silencing of the screams of a young boy shook the whole family as they held their hands together tightly, pressing their eyelids shut with a similar vigor.

Begui watched his family intently and slowly arose, walking to their door. He grasped the latch and unlocked it. He looked back as he did, watching nearly all of them tense as they heard the noise.

"Do you see? Mala protects us. You maintain your faith, you hold together as a unit of love and adoration, and our house remains protected by an unseen force. We must offset Maramir's infraction, and I offer this act of trust upon Her."

"I am sorry, bafa," she muttered.

"Be quiet, child," he soothingly replied. "We have amassed a fortune in our lifetime, and though it can be lost in one moment, I believe if you truly ask for forgiveness, She will grace you."

A lump of pain began to develop in her stomach as her father finished speaking, and she began to cry.

As he heard her weep, he closed his eyes and smiled.

Suddenly, the door kicked open, and Begui swung around to see two dark men standing at the entrance, looking intently inside. As they saw the women on the ground, they smiled suddenly, largely.

"Get out!" Begui screamed. "You have no right to enter here. Be gone, bastards!"

He swayed his hand at them, shooing them away angrily. The family held each other tightly, still not opening their eyes.

The two men looked at each other. One man suddenly lunged in and grabbed Begui, tossing him to the ground. As he grunted and screamed, the other held him down. Though the family remained still, grasping each other, terrified, they kept their eyes closed. Maramir, however, could not contain herself and opened her eyes. As she did, Begui immediately caught her gaze.

"What have you done?!" he screamed.

Her eyes widened in horror as he clamored for breath. One of the men suddenly reached into his mouth and pulled out his tongue, leaning down, biting into it. The other approached the family circle, grinning.

"What have you done?" Maerus asked, staring down the still empty maza. Within the large and dense households, past the circle limits, he could hear the screams of city folk and spotted small incursions of dark men as they spread like liquid from house to house, advancing on their position.

Bel Tazim stood silent and motionless before the war table, staring in the same direction. His gaze was dry and blank. He slowly and carefully pulled a large sword from his side and placed it on the flat surface before him, displacing all the meticulously placed battle figures.

Maerus stared at him angrily, though as if he still sought tactics from the man.

Bel Tazim continued, carefully removing a small sharp blade that was sheathed in a leather belt around his waist and placed it on the table as well, followed by the belt itself. The blade was triangular with two open loops above a small bronze handle, meant to protrude out between two fingers, held within a fist.

"Have you nothing to say?!" Maerus screamed.

Bel Tazim picked up the small blade and held it tightly in his hand, dropped to his side, continuing to stare outwards, directly to the edge of the town center. His brow became increasingly focused as a few dark men became more visible, leaving a hut, spotted in blood, breathing heavily. They walked casually and soon entered the square. Others began to simultaneously ooze out of the residences.

Still some distance away, Bel Tazim held the blade tightly. Maerus stared at him and the blade, both angry and eager.

As he lifted it, Maerus stared intently. He slid the sharpness across the inside of his left palm, then his right, and dropped it on the table, stained. His hands began to drip blood, and he slammed them together symmetrically, kneeling down. As he did, he bowed his head and raised his hands in the air, separating them, displaying his torn hands to the oncoming horde.

Maerus stared incredulously at Bel Tazim.

"You bow . . . to the Shek?"

Maerus's face scowled hard, as if his cheeks would consume his eyes, his mouth widening while remaining closed.

"You fucking traitor!"

Bel Tazim grinned slightly and turned his head to face Maerus.

"I was never a brother to you, Maerus.

"But you were the only one that knew what I saw."

He breathed in, his smile gone.

"I pray in your next life, you heed your instincts more readily, my friend."

He looked forward again, watching the black men as they started to run, as if in slow motion, just as they saw the leadership enclosure. Bel Tazim bowed his head once more and Maerus, awestruck and horrified, still staring at the Sumati war planner, turned to see the black men almost indifferently as they ignored the bowed Bel Tazim and leapt upon him.

CHAPTER 42
MYSTIFIED

Silence echoed throughout the halls under the great temple. A decaying air surrounded certain cells while flames slowly flickered out causing sporadic spaces between luminance and darkness. The previously busy and somewhat jubilant circular room where the elite congregated in magnificent orgies under the obedient gaze of the Manu priests was silent as well. The scent of dried blood and other human secretions smeared the floor and illustrious furnishings.

It had all come to a grinding halt a few hours earlier when the temple was sieged by the Shek's forces, and one by one, anyone outside of a cell was dragged to the top of the temple and flung to the ground beneath. Their wails could not be heard deep within, but those waiting in line, unable to fathom the fate that soon awaited them, broke out into sweats and tears, pleading to their jovial invaders for mercy. One by one, they flew from the top ridge of the stairs, and as the sun dropped from the sky and night began to manifest, they could scarcely see the ground beneath them. Even as they fell, they sought to see the earth beneath, as if knowledge of it would somehow lessen the terror of the fall, if even for the few seconds it took for them to strike it.

What proceeded outside of the temple was beyond measure, for the atrocity that took place, encouraged by the roaming officers, would be the subject of ghastly tales in the annals of ancient lore for years to come. Sane family men, twisted by what they both saw and were surrounded by, seemed to become possessed by diabolical spirits that released some wanton lust within them that even they found surprisingly pleasing. Torch upon torch was lit, creating eerie shadows that danced against their backs as they pursued rapture vivaciously.

Akin, unbeknownst to the world outside, lay flat upon the ground of his cell, still holding his friend's cold hand. His head was slightly propped up against the wall behind him, and as it was in pure darkness, his eyes opened and closed randomly. The bucket of water remained tipped over somewhere in the darkness, now worthless to him. His thoughts had been forced into a lull, and he pondered little as he just lay there. Memories of past were out of reach, and the intensity of the surrender that had filled his whole body had simply numbed him. His mind had been slowed, all dimensions outside of the present eluding him. He lay there, waiting for his breaths to stop, as if calmly watching for the sun to drop in some distant horizon.

Soon, however, the lull was interrupted by quiet voices in the hall. In some foreign dialect, men spoke to one another, and as they did, they walked from cell to cell, closer to Akin's.

He heard them pause a few cells away.

"What is your name?" one man asked.

"Horath," came the reply, quiet and masculine.

"What is your crime?"

"Theft."

The man spoke to the other in the foreign dialect. Suddenly, a footstep was heard, followed by piercing as the man in the cell grunted, then fell.

They continued walking and stopped at the cell beside Akin's, then continued to his.

As he looked up, three men stood in front of him. One man was dressed well and stood behind the other two. The one in the front was shorter and beside him was a large soldier carrying a bloody spear.

"What is your name?" the man in the front asked.

"Akin."

"What is your crime?"

"I committed no crime."

He translated to the man in the back. The man stepped forward and bent his knees, crouching before Akin's cell, staring at him. He said something in his dialect.

"Your name is Akin?" the other man asked.

Akin pressed his palm against his chest.

"Akin," he said, firmly.

The kneeling man smiled and threw a blade into the cell. Again, he spoke in his language.

"In my mother's tongue, you are my blood then, are you not?" the other man translated.

Akin still lay there, quiet. The kneeling man spoke again.

"Mark your palms with the blade and carry your comrade with you. You may leave the city."

Akin slowly crawled to lift the blade and looked at the man. He motioned with his fingers as he ran his forefinger along the inside of one palm, then the other. Akin followed suit by quickly slicing his palms with the knife, then pressed them together, following the motions of the man.

He slowly stood and reached under Jarvis, lifting his body up into his arms. As he did, the soldier opened the gate, and the three men proceeded onwards to the next cell, letting Akin leave. He walked slowly, finding Jarvis's weight uncomfortable, but continued automatically, as if in a trance. His hands stung under Jarvis's sandy clothes, but he scarcely registered the pain.

It was the view before him that began to pulse against his mind. Cells to the left of him were filled with the bodies of women, and as he stepped in the puddles of blood that had amassed beyond them, he felt his toes become sticky with it. As he entered the large, round room, he felt ill when struck with the stench of some decrepit, ungodly aura. He pressed on, slowly and alone, following the small, newly burning torches that sparsely littered the floor.

As he exited the temple, he felt as though he was in a waking dream. He had not seen the sky in many days, and the last time, it had been burning brightly. Now, it was dark, and below him he could see random fires raging throughout the city. The very steps he stood upon were alien to him, for only priests and royals were permitted to walk upon them. But there he stood, atop the stairs that led into the depths of the temple, looking down upon a city clouded with death.

One by one, he stepped down with Jarvis's weight upon him. As he neared the sandy floor beneath, he began to see others with bloody hands carrying the deceased, walking silently towards the city gates. To the left of the long staircase was a pile of bodies, and Akin stared wearily at it. Naked, bald priests' bodies were strewn up on stakes, and their once revered robes were scattered about.

He could hear grisly screams emanating from the city as organized rape parties took place. He could see small homes with flickering lights where men were lined up, eagerly awaiting their turn with a Sumati girl or woman who had been spared for just this purpose. Out of the corner of his eye, he would briefly witness solitary women bound to beds or furniture, screaming while man after man thrust against them. Drool began to drip from his mouth as he walked, exhausted, staring at the torment before him while simultaneously wishing for the visions to cease making imprints in his mind.

He had joined the ranks of the walkers who were all carrying corpses out of the city. Being in line with the group provided him some calm in the face of his natural apprehension, and he began to stare downwards as he walked, trying to ignore the events that transpired around him.

Soldiers that came and went, drinking, eating and screaming, mostly ignored the long line of walkers, for they wore the mark of the Shek. It was clear, as Akin saw house after house, that the city was being destroyed, burnt to the ground and dismantled, with the people either being eradicated or used as slaves. Familiar locations had been warped oddly in the night hue with flames and fallen slabs of brick revealing hollow crevices where houses used to be. He looked down at his friend's face as if to share a moment and see his reaction, and in seeing his silent, closed eyes, Akin felt Jarvis was exactly right.

He nodded gently in his fatigued state, as if acknowledging Jarvis's response.

"Where decency . . . is dwarfed . . . by something else," he whispered quietly, almost incoherently.

The invading army had demonstrated a loose sense of organization, for Akin and the walkers periodically passed piles of corpses that seemed to be depots for victims of the onslaught. When he noticed small hands protruding from under larger ones, he looked down, disassociating. The stench was stronger as they approached these hills of bone and flesh, but the smell of blood followed them through and through for the small streams of red that were invisibly flowing along the ancient crevices in the night.

Once again, the blood was surreptitiously black and seemed to shelter all those that walked about from the true carnage that surrounded them. It was only as they neared fires that the stained sand revealed its true nature, a brownish red grit that seemed to be stamped everywhere in some fashion or another, echoing some tantalizingly vulgar knowledge.

As he caught sight of the large Sumati doors, he became frightened, for beyond was blackness that suddenly reflected a cold homelessness to him. Sumat was no more, and he could not return here. He looked about and knew it to be true, for nothing would remain when this incensed machine was done with it. And beyond it was desert, alone, for his friend and companion was dead, and once again Akin felt uncomfortably adrift.

Tears began to roll down his cheek as he crossed the gateway. The last glimmering reflection of light that bounced off the inside of the walls soon faded as he stared outwards upon fires in the distance, with hundreds of men walking to and fro between the city and encampment. The walkers kept walking and soon reached a large and widely spread graveyard of sorts. Within it were hundreds of Ir, impaled upon the ground. Some were strung up upon spears, others beheaded. A large pyre was burning to the left of them, and in succession, bodies were being flung into it as Dimas soldiers sat around while others danced about it.

One by one, the dead that the walkers held were laid down on the ground. Some simply thrown while others gently placed as the carrier knelt down and began to weep or sing, offering blessings to their loved one for the afterlife. Akin looked about, one of the last remaining walkers still standing, and looked down at his friend's face.

He grimaced and began to cry, leaning down, kissing Jarvis's cheek.

"You are with me, I know it," he stuttered within tears.

He began to walk, farther and farther from the people, directly into the darkness, carrying Jarvis with him. There was firelight in a great many directions, and Akin chose the darkest of them, void of people or life, disappearing from view, the ancient city fading behind him.

CHAPTER 43

TABRIL

Fatigue seemed to permeate as a visible foe, a lucid enemy that Akin could touch. Thirst and hunger were not a sensed priority, and it was only the weakness in his knees and arms that he constantly worked to overcome. He became methodical, still waking from a nightmare, thinking like an animal, his analysis and thoughts limited to the present and the pursuit of immediate survival.

He buried Jarvis in the moonlight, eons from Sumat. Hours seemed to pass as he walked beyond the point whereupon he could no longer hear anything behind him. Once again, he was alone with just the sound of the wind and the night sun above him. But he worked systematically, moment by moment, sitting in silence beside his fallen friend, then taking what clothing he could to drape over himself. He then proceeded to walk in what seemed a constant direction. He looked back every two or three steps to ensure the line he left behind him was straight and had draped a mask of cloth around his face, leaving only his eyes visible. He limped slightly, both due to fatigue and random pains that shot through his body, moving in some automated manner.

"Days? Or this night?" he thought. "It could be just over the horizon now, for the distance I have already trekked."

Tabril was a small depot, so small it could not even be considered a village. A single well surrounded by a few old houses stood in the middle of nowhere, a small station for travellers who came to and from Sumat in a northward direction.

"In droves they will arrive. Days from now. I must quicken my pace."

Akin had planned to make Tabril their first abrupt stop, and though his original plan had not eventuated, he hoped the encampment still stood and was inhabited by people who knew little of the war to the south. Soon, survivors from Sumat would spread everywhere, and the freedom to drink, rest and eat would become thinned by sheer numbers, overwhelming what little could be provided in the arid land.

"A few days, perhaps a week. They will fall in sooner, possibly, but not in great numbers. Ten days from now and it will begin."

He walked briskly, still limping slightly, but determined. His head nodded with every bend of his knees, and he began to sing, keeping pace.

"What world, I may have fallen upon, brought upon, sung upon. What world I leave behind, for my children and theirs, fields of green."

He took a deep breath in and exhaled louder.

"Skies of blue and darkish hue, that I fell upon, I think of reaching and ascending my place. Oh, what world shall I leave behind for my children and theirs, gardens of green."

He suddenly stumbled and fell, then raised himself, kneeling. He stared outwards in front of him, his eyes wide. He saw the bloody blade in the Temple of Mala, in that dungeon, half buried in the sand. He knew it would stay there for the rest of time, and as the temple itself fell, it would be buried along with the bricks. But the stain of his blood would remain there forever. He turned his hands and saw the large wounds in the moonlight.

He suddenly curled his body downwards, still on his knees and began to cringe, breathing heavily.

He began to gasp, losing his breath.

"What further blessings will you carry my life with in death? My sweet . . . sweet . . . lovely . . ."

He suddenly turned around and arose to his feet, looking behind him.

"Jarvis!"

He began running backwards, trying to follow his trail, but stumbled and fell. He arose again and frantically began running and kept on until he could breathe no more.

"Jarvis!" he screamed. "My friend . . . I am sorry . . ."

He began to cry in place and fell to the ground, lying on his back.

"I left him . . . I left him . . ."

He arose again and began to crawl on all fours but could not maintain movement. He gasped for air and fell upon the sand, breathing for dear life.

He closed his eyes.

"I am sorry, my friend.

"Do you float about me? Are you smiling?"

He thought about Jarvis's body, lost somewhere in the desert, and again began to cry.

"I am sorry."

He began to feel dizzy, distancing his conscious mind from the world.

"You are with me. You are all inside me," he whispered incoherently.

Like a soft warm embrace, sleep came. It was inviting and enticing, as if the solution to all the worries and pain in the world. He nearly smiled as he felt it consume him.

"And the world . . . will move on without me. Nothing is real any longer. No ghosts or demons, or voices in the night. It is just my mind, now, and this beautiful feeling."

"No."

Akin opened his eyes suddenly, almost completely aware.

"Tabril . . . is in the other direction."

He leaned up and sat, looking at the scraggly line he had created in running back along his tracks.

"I must go soon. I must go now, at a reasonable pace, and recover."

He stood and started walking forward again, looking back periodically to ensure he was traveling in as straight a line as possible.

Tabril was as he had anticipated; a haven, a temple surrounded by sand, but only to him for it was made up of nothing more than a few sparse huts, barely visible in the night sky. He had unknowingly planned the trip from Sumat to it a hundred times in his semi-conscious states, staring out past the city, memorizing the moon and sun and their positions to it. It had just been a fleeting thought, nothing more than adventure in his mind for the worst of possible scenarios, but he had not assumed some usefulness would be derived from his meanderings. Unbeknownst to him, the now vanished line he had created in the sand was curved and bent, not leading but following some guided knowledge he had within his own mind. Whether it had been the stars or moonlight, somehow the path was known to him.

He approached the dark huts slowly and navigated around them to find the main entrance to the enclosure. As he did, he sat down staring at their shaded entrances and breathed deeply, resting. A well graced the front and was centered to the three huts which stood quietly before him.

He sat awkwardly, feeling calmed that he had arrived. He could tell they were inhabited for the marks in the sand nearby and a solid rope that descended into the well. He closed his eyes and fell backwards, asleep, drowning out the breeze.

A hazy world surrounded Akin upon awaking, as if a daystorm had struck down directly above his head and had penetrated deep into it, surrounding his vision. He knew outside his sight the sand and huts were of a natural stature and pigment but could not see them as such. They moved, it appeared, as if enlarging and shrinking, and he found it difficult to either walk or lie down. It had begun when he saw the graves, he remembered. Or so he thought. Something around that time, and his sight gave way to strange perceptions and feisty manifestations.

He would attempt to lean against the stone surface of a hut and discover himself on the ground a moment later, losing the moments in between. He could not clearly recollect how he had fallen and barely felt the impact of the hard floor against his side. He had missed, he remembered. He missed the wall and simply fell. And then he lost time.

At some point, he had huddled against the sand in the middle of all the huts, hugging his knees to his chest. He closed his eyes and tried to normalize his mind, for even when they were closed, it was as if he was moving. He hummed, sang, and even prayed to the gods he knew. But neither the names of the ethereal beings, whether they be Mala or Vespa, nor the demon lords Saal, Begum, or Aisca provided clemency from his despair.

The strange vibrations were amplified by the complete lack of noise or interaction, for surrounded by this small, ghostly encampment, he was still alone, more pronounced, it seemed, every time he bounced from one hut to the other, looking for some sign that he was still alive.

He had leaned over the well, staring down into it for a time, considering the ease of losing his balance in just one small step. It was the end of all things, he had concluded. He had no illusions about the world outside of himself; this was not the world, but only that which he saw, which followed him around. He was locked within an alternate universe, and the sole inescapability of it kept making his mind feel a pressurized madness in repeated pulses. Thinking about the lack of ease built upon itself, and in noticing his discomfort, it became worse and worse.

And even as the joy of ending it piqued his interest, it remained fantasy, he acknowledged, for he was terrified of death. He was more terrified of death at that moment, more than he had ever feared it, even though he desperately lusted ending the chasm of unease.

It was an unknown that terrified him more than not being able to walk or think properly. His mind was shaking, and he could not escape it, and though the vacuum of that state petrified him, the unknown of death scared him further. He imagined it to be worse, more hellish, more tortuous, even though he had no idea what such a state could possibly entail.

He stared down the well as if indulging in a fantasy of freedom, like being the king of a grand country or having all the women in the universe lusting after him. Some focal point that would release whatever demon had invaded his body, or at least distract him from it.

Memories of the past began to compress, as if another lifetime, or stories of someone else's life. He no longer felt bonded to any particular person or moment, for the fear within appeared to take precedence, making clear to him some truth he had been ignorant of his entire life.

"Peace at this very moment . . ." he whispered to himself, tearing up.

Nothing else mattered, he thought.

"Nothing else matters.

"Nothing else has ever mattered, and I walked and talked and ate and shat . . ."

He began to weep.

"How will I find my way back now?

"I am Aydan."

He shook his head suddenly.

"No, Akin. Akin. Fuck that. Akin."

He remembered the distant memory of Samaye, and as he did, he wept, tears falling down the well, half his torso leaning over it awkwardly.

He took a deep breath in and fell down on the sand beside the well. The day had splintered into odd fragments, and though it was not night, he could not tell what time it was. A twilight in the afternoon, it seemed, for the sky was red but dim.

"Maybe death when nothing else matters. I cannot escape it."

Like waves of suffocation, his mind became worse and worse, then lessened despite his inability to control it. Moments without it were filled with terror for the fear that it would return. And it happened a thousand times an hour, it seemed. And every time it did, it asserted to him that some fundamental change had happened, that something had broken in him, that he could never and would never find himself again.

"There . . . is a storm within my mind. It rages behind my eyes but no one can see it. It is deafening and suffocates me. I can eat, I can sleep. But every waking moment . . ."

He held his forehead in his hand, grimacing.

"Personalize it, Akin. It is within you, it is no ghost or demon."

He took a deep breath in once more.

"Every waking moment . . . I try to find peace where there is none. The peace has fled from my soul. My bitter, bruised soul is naked without peace, the peace that came with me into this world."

"It fled," he thought.

"If it fled, and it came with me into this world, then I chose it not, nor did it choose me. We have parted ways, and I am frightened, like a lost lover. I must find peace . . . and make it my own. I must find my own peace and grow it like a flower. I must own it, not be gifted with it."

"I must earn it," he thought.

And just as suddenly as some resolve grounded him, his breath became faint as his mind collapsed on itself. It felt as though his heart was falling and he could not catch it, not in some sad manner, but as if his entire being or reason for existence had suddenly lost interest in this world. He touched the sand and felt the granules but did not feel anything familiar, not in the touch nor the sight of the yellowish orange matter that had surrounded him his entire life.

"The peace I came with was mine," he thought. "I should not have to rebuild it. But now I must, simply because that is my path."

"I believe this!" he screamed as another wave of woe engulfed his mind.

He immediately arose and looked about, blinking to straighten his vision.

"Though I am not thirsty, I must be, and so I will drink."

He mechanically grasped the rope around the well and shook the bucket, pulling it up. He counted to himself, one by one, as he lifted it. As it neared the peak of the hole, he placed it on the ledge, stabilizing it. As he let go of the rope and dipped his hands in it, it fell to the ground, spilling into the sand. He stared at it and began to cry, grimacing sadly.

He fell to the ground beside it and closed his eyes. He became quickly frightened and opened them again, looking at the bucket.

He arose once again and dropped it into the well, shaking it so it gathered water.

"I must be thirsty," he muttered to himself, tears still glistening on his cheek as he pulled the bucket up a second time.

As evening wore on, all the progress he made between each episode of dread was instantly demolished, and he felt just as helpless as he did the first time it came. And though he tried, he found it impossible to remember just how he had felt the last time it had resolved itself. It was as if he had to find his way out of the same maze each time anew even though he had navigated its exact corners just minutes earlier.

"I've walked this road before," he whispered to himself. "Yet I retain no memory of it."

He dreaded night as it emerged, but for some strange reason the confusion and fear that seemed to emanate from within his bones subsided as he tired.

He breathed a sigh of relief. It was sudden, but he noticed his stomach was in pain. He did not understand why, initially, then concluded he must have been hungry. He had tried to eat some dried grains during the day but found it difficult.

He arose off the ground and found his body to be aching with wear. He slowly limped to one of the huts and looked for something to eat. There were a series of pockets etched into the hard brick of a wall, and within them were assortments of different grains and fruits, all dehydrated. They were not plentiful, but it was more food than he had seen in some time.

He stood and stared at it, trying to decide what he desired eating. It was a simple decision, yet he found it to be not only taxing, but he could locate no desire towards either crevice and was perplexed by the problem. Such conundrums were never of issue – he would know if he was hungry or not, and if so, what he felt like eating. But it was as if he had no capacity to make the decision, whether it be for appetite or health. It began to trigger the same sensations that had plagued him all day, and he immediately began breathing hard as the fear that the unease had not left him began to take shape in his mind.

"No, no, no, no . . ." he muttered to himself desperately.

He opened his eyes and stared at the food again despite the chaos in his mind escalating, causing strange vibrations and uncomfortable tension in his body.

"I must be hungry," he said. "I must be hungry, I must be hungry, I must be hungry."

And there, at that moment, for a brief instant, he felt something. He felt an attraction towards the dates for they were sweet, and he felt that their sweetness on his tongue could provide him some satisfaction.

As he bit into the dried fruit and felt the sugars against his tongue, he recognized the sensation of sweetness, yet it felt as though it stopped there. Whatever flutter his heart would previously have shared with him, it was quiet now, as if the fact that the date was sweet was acknowledged, but irrelevant.

He chewed it mechanically and felt as though he had forgotten how to eat. Small decisions like deciding when to swallow a chewed portion were made almost consciously, for somehow his body was not tending to itself as it had in the past.

He lay down on a cot as night wore on. His mind would not turn off, and though the hazy visions had lessened, his body was uncomfortable, and he felt as if his blood was randomly heating up and cooling down.

As he closed his eyes, he tried to imagine the small group that had lived in Tabril. It felt as though he had spent the whole day aware yet unconcluded about their whereabouts, and he wondered if they had been sitting around a fire in the morning and greeted him with warmth and love, whether his mind would have cracked as it had.

He had found the graves, he remembered, shortly after he had awoken. Fresh graves for their protrusions from the sand were still distinct. Perhaps only a few days since the people had all simultaneously perished. He imagined a man slitting their throats and placing them in the graves one by one, then lying down in one himself. Perhaps a blade would be found in one of the graves, confirming Akin's thoughts.

If soldiers had come through, there would be no graves. Was it poison? Was the water of the well sickly? Had he drank water before his vision was corrupted?

He could not remember. Had his affliction struck the entire encampment and caused their demise? Would he awaken from sleep if he slept?

He thought of Samaye in the moonlight, like an angel staring at him, and felt tears well up under his eyelids.

"How far . . . I've fallen since you left me . . ." he muttered in agony.

CHAPTER 44
A FAMILIAR LIFE

The morning was an abhorrent awakening to Akin. What baseless fear had taken seat within his chest the day before found itself fully functional as he awoke. At first, he had completely forgotten about it, and during those brief few moments, it didn't exist. But as if birthing it from his own mind, as he thought of it, it emerged, and sank him. It might have been worse than his first encounter with it, for his hope that it had left forever the night before was now shattered, and once again that same maze appeared before him, still unfamiliar. Behind him, as he briefly looked, was something faceless, so unspeakably dreadful, that he had no choice but to walk the puzzle arduously, arbitrarily trying to stabilize himself.

Each time it came, he believed it would never leave. And each time it came, eventually, it left. Within the hazy spectrum of episodes, he would try to eat and rest, telling himself that a physical recovery from the prison of Sumat and the trek to Tabril was of utmost importance, and that with physical recovery his vigor in battling this mental curse that had befallen him would strengthen.

"The secret to life is to simultaneously know it is a dream while reacting to it as if it is real. The unknown end keeps the latter in check.

"Great thoughts, pivotal thoughts . . . they come to me from somewhere, do they not? While I am lost? Then I am still here, somewhere. But I cannot feel myself. If this is a dream, at this moment, I wish to know it so this anxiety is less pronounced."

But terror, Akin concluded, was part of the dream.

"Amidst such angst . . . that twists my insides at this very moment. Tension I cannot escape that precedes every thought with fear. This is part of the dream. I cannot accept that it should last forever. And I do not think that it should. But if it should last longer than I expect . . . I must live because I am too afraid to die. I fear death more than the terror."

Certain thoughts persisted through waves, and his decision to live, though flayed by the unbearable feelings, meekly held on as a subtle but accessible goal. It wedged some light, though unseen much of the time, into the darkness, and served as something permanent that wasn't twisted by Akin's instability.

He felt more comfortable, it seemed, when he worried about real threats to his well-being. The already scarce food, for example, and where he could get more. When he contemplated digging for hidden stores or looking for shrubs nearby, it was as if the demon within him kept quiet. But when it was time to rest or recover, the endless dread would suddenly manifest. Accordingly, he tried to keep tasking himself, but found very little needed to be done, at least in the short term. There was enough grain and dried fruit for his limited appetite and plenty of water in the well. He was physically exhausted as well, and in forcing action, his sickly state was exasperated, further weakening his resolve.

He searched for weapons for protection in the case that soldiers or survivors of Sumat found their way to him. Tabril mostly had farming equipment, but the winds had slowly encroached on their crops, leaving them graveyards in their own right. The unpleasant view of small shrubs that may have once been green choking against the weight of little pebbles of yellow was somehow embedded in his brain as a dismal symbol of hopelessness.

He twisted a blade off its trencher and sharpened it, tying it to a naked broom. He held it to him and used it as a walking stick as he navigated the encampment, examining, putting things in order.

The houses were abandoned but left intact. It was as if the entire encampment had woken up one day, a day like any other, and everyone suddenly died. Akin contemplated digging into one or two of the graves to get an idea of what had happened, but every time he approached them or even thought of them, he felt the uneasiness bubble within him.

The nights were calmer as he sat in front of the small fire, a position that was familiar and naturally seemed to distract him from all else. He would sometimes burn it during the day to mimic the sensation which worked only marginally. It seemed anything that provided him any sense of calm made him increasingly nervous in retrospect for the fear that its effectiveness would wear off, and that any haven from the unease would quickly become obsolete.

No matter how long he waited for sleep to come, it never came while he did. Non-specific thoughts rummaging around with the desire to simply drift away kept his mind buzzing with a persistent awareness. Only when he had forgotten about it, sitting in front of the fire, would he eventually fall to his side, his body giving out in exhaustion.

"The gates of Sumat. The grand city, full of infrastructure."

He stared at them, massive and impregnable.

"And suddenly, the city was no longer there."

He heard the voice booming from the sky, but it was not alien to him. He listened to it as if it was his own. Before him the city crumbled into dust as people screamed and ran. Brick by brick dissolved into little particles, and it was only as it began to sink into the sand beneath, absorbed by the red river, that he realized he was looking into the city from the outside.

The gates stood tall, disconnected from their parent structure which had long expired into the wastes. A thousand years, it seemed, and only some base foundation deep in the ground was all that remained of the houses, the dasha, the maza, even the magnificent temple of Mala.

And in front of the gates, facing the expired city, but looking back towards Akin, was Jarvis. He stood, and time was not still, for the wind blew at his disguise. His face was still shrouded by cloth, and only his eyes remained visible, staring directly at Akin.

Akin knelt before his friend.

"Come . . . walk to me . . . face not the city, and come to me," he begged.

Jarvis stood, staring at him.

"Look! Before you, there is no city. Only the gates bidding you farewell. Come to me!"

Jarvis's gaze turned to face the city, then back towards Akin.

Akin stared, and under Jarvis's guise he noticed the cloth parting slightly as Jarvis's eyes squinted. Akin suddenly gasped and smiled in ecstasy, covering his mouth with his arm, catching drool.

Jarvis began to walk towards him and away from the gates which, like the city, began to crumble with a roar.

Akin awoke suddenly, gasping for air. It was still pitch black in the hut, and the fire outside had burnt itself out. He stumbled outside and began to meander around in the darkness.

"Jarvis! Jarvis!" he called out, spreading his hands wide.

He suddenly stumbled over something and scrambled to feel it out. It was a body, still warm. He leaned his head down quickly to hear the heartbeat of the figure and slid his hands underneath, picking the person up.

He ran back to the huts frantically and dropped the person to the ground by the well. He quickly flung the bucket in and shook it around, pulling it back up. He placed it on the sand beside the well and pulled the person's head in his lap. It seemed to be a young boy, and he reached into the bucket, cupping water and placing it against the boy's lips.

Akin rocked back and forth, visibly excited.

"You are safe, and drink . . . water. No need to lose yourself. Live . . . live!"

He reached in and grabbed another handful, spilling half on the way to the person's mouth.

"I cannot see if you are drinking, but you must drink. You must live, live . . . live!"

Suddenly the boy coughed and turned sideways, his body twitching against Akin.

"No, no, no, no, no . . ." Akin whispered soothingly. "You will live, just breathe. Breathe with me. There is food, shelter, water, rest. You rest with me."

As he tried to turn the person back, the coughing subsided, replaced by an incoherent voice. Any words were mutterings, and just as Akin felt small breasts under his arms, her voice began to break, oozing something more feminine than boyish.

Akin stared downwards, confused by this change in sex, trying to categorize it in his mind. He leaned down and kissed her forehead, feeling her short, almost bald scalp with his palm.

He reached over to her arm and clasped his hand in hers, closing his eyes.

She continued to mutter and raised her fingers to Akin's cheek, feeling it with the back of her hand.

"Are you hungry?" he whispered gently to her.

She did not respond and kept muttering. She tightened her grasp of his hand and held onto his leg with the other. He leaned back and sat there for a moment with her head in his lap. He felt an erection grow under his tunic and adjusted her to avoid it. She soon stopped speaking and seemed to fall into a deep sleep.

He leaned down to hear her breathing once again and then picked her up, taking her into the hut. It was still pitch black, with the moon hidden somewhere in the horizon. He laid her down on the cot and placed a bladder next to her. He then lied down beside her instinctually, hugging her waist and winding his body against hers, pressing his nose against the back of her neck.

When he awoke, he was greeted with the warm feeling of another body and squeezed himself against it. He heard her murmur and opened his eyes, seeing the woman in the light for the first time.

Her head was roughly cut with spots of uneven hair. Her body was frail and thin and she was fair skinned. He unwrapped his arms from her and leaned his legs off the cot, turning to sit. As he did, he paused for a moment, and that familiar chaos swarmed in, collapsing the foundation of his mind. He felt his heart tense as his breathing quickened. He took a deep breath in and arose, straightening out his tunic. He turned to look at her again.

Her lips were tender and feminine – petite and beautiful. Her frame seemed fragile, and he felt immediately attracted to her, wanting to touch and feel her body, as if to calm himself. It was a mixture of desire, for the night he shared holding her to him had left a comforting memory in his mind, and waking up to the smell of another was some unaccustomed gift he seemed to cherish.

He leaned down and sat upon the floor beside the cot, lifting the cover sheet from her legs. She was wearing a man's tunic which exposed much of her thighs and legs, and he ran his hand along them, leaning his head down on the cot. He reached down and felt his manhood thicken, grasped it, and began to pleasure himself, holding her thigh.

She awoke later in the afternoon. Akin had been tending to the fire, readying some bread with water and crushed grains. He heard a shuffle from within and the drop of the bladder to the floor. He arose carefully and walked to the entrance, peeking his head in.

The woman was sprawled out on the cot, lying on her stomach. Her legs were exposed, and he felt himself getting aroused again.

He bent his knees and sat on the ground at the entrance to the hut.

"Are you awake?" he asked.

She did not respond but slowly opened her eyes. She looked at him wearily and saw the bread in his hand. He quickly leaned forward and gave it to her which she immediately began eating.

"I'm sorry if it isn't very good," he smiled.

"It is good," she replied. She looked at him as she chewed and smiled back briefly. "It's very good."

He sat and watched her eat and drink. Her small chewing mannerisms entranced him, and every time she opened her mouth to take another bite, he wished to travel with the bread, into her mouth and down her throat. Even the view of her fingers clasping the morsel made him flutter inside, feeding a drive that seemed to occupy his previously unsafe psyche. His body and mind seemed to synchronize, focused on only his desire and growing obsession with the tender creature before him.

After drinking some water, washing down the last dry morsel, she lay back down and quietly motioned for Akin without looking at him. He crawled to her and touched her hand. She held his and tugged, turning her back to him, pulling him. He rose with her turn and lay down next to her, spooning her as he had the night before. She pulled his arm around her waist and pressed her body into him, closing her eyes. He too closed his eyes, mesmerized by the fact that she had felt his erection and accepted it, pressing herself against it.

When he awoke hours later, he felt calm. The sickness within him seemed to have been tamed, and in sensing her hold his arm against her body, he felt somehow cared for by the beautiful woman.

He squeezed himself against her and gently rubbed his hardness against her behind, not specifically as a sexual act, but a mixture of intimacy. She pressed back against him and moaned gently, turning to face him.

They made eye contact, it seemed, for the first time, and as they did, she smiled at him. He stared, unsmiling, visualizing her features and absorbing her face. She leaned forward and kissed his lips sensuously, whimpering slightly as she did. He felt a shiver run through his body and smiled shyly, pressing his head down against her.

"I'm Arraki," she said quietly, running her hand in his hair. Akin smiled, still hiding his face.

"I'm Akin. My name used to be Aydan, but now I'm Akin."

"Aydan is a beautiful name," she replied.

Akin shrugged.

She tightened her grasp of him and sighed.

"Did you come from Sumat?" he asked, his mouth muffled by her body.

"Come here," she said, pushing one thigh underneath him, pulling him in between her legs. He obeyed and pressed himself against her entrance, moaning quietly, hugging her tightly. Her legs lay spread on either side of him, loose in the air with her heels gently touching his lower back.

He raised his head to look at her and observed her open mouth, breathing deeply as he pressed against her. She squinted, almost painfully as he did. Upon seeing her face, he leaned in and pressed his lips against hers, diving his tongue into her mouth. She quickly reached down and grabbed his manhood, squeezing it in her palm.

"Oh, my god . . ." she whispered, quickly lifting her tunic, aiming him inside her.

He paused nervously and looked at her inquisitively.

She leaned her head up to his ear and whispered.

"Be one with me, my love, and all the world will love you."

As she ended her sentence, she rubbed him lovingly, pressing him against her soft skin. She leaned her body up slightly, pushing him inside, and as he felt her entrance, he moaned, pressing down on her.

As he penetrated Arraki, a warm feeling overtook his entire body, and he became manic in his movements, losing himself completely in the moment. She held his body and moaned as he repeatedly slid in and out. He clasped his hands against hers and squeezed them tightly as he tensed his body against hers, quickening his pace, feeling ecstatic.

"Give me your love . . ." she said to him in between breaths, her face grimacing. He looked at her and stared into her eyes, pressing himself harder and harder against her, his face scowling as his body tensed.

He closed his eyes, dropping his head as he continued to press against her. She raised her hands and tilted his head upwards, looking at him. He opened his eyes and looked at her. As he did, she raised her body again, pushing him even deeper into her, and as she did, he moaned. He began to quicken and did not lose contact with her eyes. Even as he climaxed, though he felt pressed to shut them, he kept them open, staring down at her, squinting as she looked up at him welcomingly.

He gyrated his hips against her roughly as he orgasmed, his hands clasping the sides of the cot tightly. He reached back and wrapped his hands around her thighs and leaned down, resting his head against her shoulder and his body against hers, breathing heavily.

He kissed her neck and pulled her tunic to the side so he could kiss her breast as well, holding it in his hand. They lay there for some time, entangled and mostly naked, still connected to one another. Holding each other, they adjusted every few moments and eventually fell asleep, doused in sweat, with Akin still inside her.

When he awoke, it was still daytime. Upon noticing that he was alone in the cot, he quickly jumped up frantically and ran out of the hut looking for Arraki. She was crouched down in front of the small fire, holding a poking stick in her hand.

"Arraki . . ." he said, almost out of breath.

She turned to look at him and smiled, opening her arms to him. He lunged at her and embraced her, causing both of them to fall down. He quickly spread her legs and pulled his tunic up, pointing himself inside her. She hugged him and kissed his forehead as he grinded his body against hers.

"Did you come from Sumat?" he asked. They were both lying in front of the red embers of the now dead fire just as darkness began to descend.

"Sumat . . ." she replied. "I don't want to think of Sumat. As my hair grows I'll forget all about it."

"What happened to your hair?"

She turned to him quickly and glared.

"You complain already?"

Taken aback for a moment, he soon found humor in her question.

"Does it sound like I am complaining, my Asa?"

She turned away again, relaxing against him.

"What is an Asa? A bald donkey?"

"No . . . it is indescribably lovely. But it is a good thing."

He paused for a moment.

"I am not complaining. What happened to your hair?"

She turned to him again.

"Why?"

"Simply because I am interested."

"Do you know what they did to the women? When you found me, I was half dead from carrying a corpse I could not carry. When I heard the screams I took a blade to my scalp, and here before you, you have me . . . a bald, poor donkey."

Akin stared at her and ran his hand along her face.

"Why do you speak like that? Your head is beautiful to me . . . it is beautiful to me that you did what you did, else you would not be here."

She placed her hand in his hair lovingly.

"I am glad I am here, with you," she said.

He leaned forward and kissed her, wrestling her tongue against his.

They fell asleep outside of the hut that night which was uncommonly warm.

Akin awoke early and brought a sheet to cover Arraki with from inside the hut. The sun had only begun rising in the sky beyond, and he explored the horizon in every direction, circling the entire encampment, failing to see any movement or approaching people. He made note of the rising sun and which of the three huts was closest to it, calculating directions to get his bearings.

He knelt down beside Arraki and whispered in her ear.

"Arraki . . ."

She murmured and turned, opening her eyes slightly, looking up at him.

"Yes, Asa?"

He smiled and almost cried upon hearing her first words.

"It is time for us to go."

"Go where?" she asked.

He pointed in the direction of the rising sun.

"What?" she asked.

"I have packed bladders and food . . . enough to sustain a trek to the East. To the blue Desta."

"No, Akin. We stay here."

He smiled and looked at her.

"We cannot stay here, Asa. More will come from Sumat, and there is nothing here. It is dead."

She shook her head and grabbed his arm.

"There are none from Sumat . . . no survivors. Nothing. The soldiers have moved on, this is our home now, Akin. I will not leave it and you will stay with me. We have water, the crops will grow. This is home now."

"Arraki, we cannot stay here. The crops will not grow, I know this. Once the sand encroaches as it has, it is too difficult to irrigate. We cannot stay here."

He paused, silently, thinking.

"I do not even want to stay here," he said.

She quickly and immediately slapped him. He stumbled backwards, holding his face. An angry look suddenly replaced his tenderness, and he stared at her.

"Do not strike me, Arraki . . . do not ever strike me."

She looked apologetically and crawled over to him.

"I am sorry, my love. We can go wherever you want, but later. Once my hair grows," she said.

He looked at her confusingly.

"Your hair? What does that have to do with this? We must leave while we are free to do so . . . while our stores will supply us. There are no caravans passing through; we will end up as the poor bastards that preceded us, dying of starvation or worse."

"Worse? What is worse? You would hurt me?" she asked.

"What?!" he asked incredulously.

"What would you do to me if we ran out of food?"

Akin arose quickly.

"I don't know what you are talking about!"

"What would you do to me if we ran out of food? Rape me? Eat me? Kill me?" she yelled at him.

"Are you out of your mind? I am saying we go together, right now, and we can survive!"

"Not until my hair grows back!" she screamed, louder than before.

"That doesn't make any sense, Arraki!" he screamed back. "What does your hair have to do with this?"

"We go nowhere until it is long again!" she replied.

"You are beautiful as you are, you stupid woman!"

She jumped to her feet and again slapped him in the face, trying to hit him repeatedly.

All at once he pushed her back, causing her to fall on her behind. He stared at her sternly.

"You fuck me and kiss me and now you will leave me," she muttered.

He looked up at the sky, thinking, then walked to the hut, picking up the supplies he had gathered.

She followed him quickly, screaming at him.

"I'm not going anywhere! And you can't take the food!"

She struck him in the arm, and he immediately slapped her face in response, causing her to fall to the ground, crying.

"Asa! You call me Asa? You lying bastard . . . you felt me . . . you sinful boy. I know . . . I know . . . you're not a man, you're a dirty little boy. You had found me and you pleasured yourself to touching me? Pathetic . . . pathetic boy . . ."

He continued walking towards the sun that had still barely risen.

"I don't want your food! Take it all! You fucked me anyway! If I am with child I will split its head on the rocks or drown it in the well in your honor, you bastard man! I don't want a dirty boy in my womb."

"Half the food sits there for you, you crazy woman," Akin whispered to himself, trying to drown out her voice. "I have done my part."

She sat in silence for a few moments, watching him slowly walk away.

"What if the soldiers come, Akin? Will you leave me here alone?"

He shook his head suddenly, as if to interrupt the thoughts she was triggering and continued to walk towards the sun.

"You're the coward, Akin! You're the one running from me! You will never be happy, because you are a boy! You will never be a man because you are too stupid! You use women, you used me! You are a filthy jhimha! Not a man, a jhimha!"

"I am a man," he whispered under his breath, "and I would have cared for you."

"Shameless!" she screamed at the top of her lungs. Her voice was barely a distant echo by that point, it being the last thing he ever heard from her.

CHAPTER 45
THE SAIFA

Akin walked and walked, saying nothing, the scratches and voids in his body slowly re-energizing through plentiful water and his satchel of food. He followed the path of the rising sun during the morning and kept pace against it in the evening as it fell to the west.

He ate sparingly, uninterested, with some numb and methodical automation taking over his actions. The only thing he maintained some interest in was his direction in comparison to the sun, the one necessary detail he needed to remain vigilant about.

The walk had proceeded dismally, his hope in whatever Arraki could have been fading with the footprints he left behind him. Yet, as he walked in silence, some strange calm seemed to form a base underneath his wandering thoughts, and though he understood not where it was coming from, he welcomed it. It seemed to urge him forward, gently strengthening his interest in the fantastical destination before him.

As night began to fall, he decided to stop, rolling out a khalla over a patch of flat sand. He had packed the desert bed in Tabril, and it formed a pocket around its wearer, protecting them from both the sandy wind and creatures of the desert. He placed his bladders beside him along with the makeshift blade and any other gear he was carrying.

As he made himself comfortable within, settling in for the night, he wrapped a travelling veil around his face to keep himself warm. Only his eyes shone through, staring upwards at the panoramic sky that buzzed with twinkling lights against black.

He had thought of Arraki randomly during the day, recovering from what odd and unnatural events had transpired at dawn. And though he understood not why what happened, happened, it seemed to be of less relevance now. It was as if he had traveled worlds since then, and though only a day had passed, he felt completely severed from the conflict. The distance, he concluded, and the silent space within it had not only created physical barriers between him and what he left there, but an irreversible emotional segregation as well.

"What were you, Arraki?

"Did you even exist?"

He continued staring upwards, his arms crossed against his chest snugly.

"It feels as though the last bastion of what fear I carry with me still resides in Tabril . . . in your aggression.

"Shameless?

"Why is it shameful to seek humanity to ground you?"

He reached up and felt his cheek, massaging where she had struck him. As he did, he felt the prickly ends of new hairs across his jaw and began to run his fingers about his calloused face, examining old scars and bruises. He gently flicked his finger up and down his lip, the torn skin long since healed. He thought of when he fell against the stone so many years ago, dazed out of his mind, and how he felt saved by Kaius with no knowledge of how insane the man really was.

He began to laugh under his breath, thinking of the man.

"What was it he said? Be polite? Ask me for bread and water . . . politely?"

He shook his head in disbelief.

"Are these the men that become kings and gods? Is the Shek an incestuous rapist who believes his member is the guiding light of the cosmos?"

He shook his head again, this time in disdain.

"How irrelevant I am . . . just a man like any other. And yet I witness the strange doings of strange people . . . no one speaks of it! I remember it. Kaius is etched in my mind, and I randomly wonder what Heina is doing. So many are corrupted and strange, and here I find love in my heart. I lay alone in the middle of nowhere, and I feel love for the sky above me. What has happened?"

He pondered the last images he witnessed in Sumat and thought of the suffering of any one individual who could not escape the wrath of the invaders.

"Those last moments, horrifying . . . it seems a waste . . . unfair, somehow . . . that no witnesses remain."

He imagined a young girl in the worst of situations: bound, looking past the man who was upon her at the line of men waiting.

"After she dissolves, my stars," he said, staring at the sky. "After it is all over, neither the men nor her body will tell the tale. They will speak of the event, but no one will know the event. They will not know her . . . and the intensity of her thoughts and feelings at that moment are preciously valuable for the unconscionable vigor with which she felt them."

He tensed his eyes shut and tried to imagine and touch the girl in his imagination, feeling and sharing in her last moments.

He opened his eyes and stared upwards, natural tears forming around them as a result of the tension.

"I will imagine it . . . someday, my love. I will do justice to your memory so that it survives."

He turned to his side, burying his head, and thought of his village, visualizing its colors and smells and the familiarity of the gravel that paved its roads. He thought of Bethelhurst and wondered what reaction his father would have upon seeing him.

"Not spectacular, to say the least. Subdued . . . I see your old face now. Grayed over the years, but still you."

Thoughts of the village sparked an excitement in his mind, for he suddenly became aware that he was now walking nearly the same path he had stumbled down in the opposite direction so many years ago.

"Does the ghost of an old me still peruse these windy lands? If I look up now, will I see Akin limping, half dead, towards the city of Sumat?"

He lifted his veil and looked forward, then all around him, seeing nothing but the darkness.

As he returned and closed himself in his cocoon, he felt a sinking sensation in his heart. The pain of those past events became lucid to him, and as if it was only yesterday, he became aware that he would also be passing Samaye's body, as though in the visible distance about him he was buried somewhere. He remembered Samaye's pale frame, and like an old wound he was suddenly struck with the immense feeling of loss for the life that could have been had his brother been with him from then till now.

Suddenly, he caught the tail end of a memory and frowned as he pondered it carefully and intently, trying to pull it into his awareness.

"What was it you said to me?"

Immediately, he drifted into a visible recollection, feeling hot, sticky air and sweat all about him. His breaths were short and strained, and he was laid back against some small, sandy dune that formed an unlikely pillow. He held unto his friend's arm, warm to the touch and pulsating with life. His eyes remained closed, and he felt his awareness trickling away as sleep came to take him with warm, soft care and whispers of peace.

Samaye also lay unmoving, and Akin felt him put his hand on his forehead, speaking.

"Water, my brother. Water for the rest of your life."

Akin opened his eyes and breathed in deeply, shifting in position, staring up at the night sky. He suddenly felt scared of being alone in the desert, leaning up, looking about at the suffocating emptiness around him.

He pulled his knees up and sat upon his khalla, covering his eyes with his hands, breathing in and out.

He thought of when he was sick in Sumat . . . when the water from the river and an unconventionally cold night had converged to stricken him with illness . . . how he tried to hide his cough as he dug himself in, alone, in some uncomfortable crevice. He thought of how he felt tears as he vomited that day, throwing up, wishing he could somehow reconstitute the food that came for the dire effort that went in attaining sufficient shel to purchase it. He remembered, vividly, how it looked upon the brick, and how he tried to think of a way of eating it again.

"But the loneliness does not subside."

He suddenly felt overwhelmed, as if a gate had opened in his mind. He could see through it, almost visibly. But the path was just emotion, pure and heated . . . and unlike the previous moment, it was straight and directed . . . clear.

He breathed in, his eyes wide, watching, following, riding and travelling with it, feeling the awareness tear all preconceived purpose away from his insides, all for one focused point and movement in a very specific direction.

His fingers began to create streaks before him, as if his soft movements were within water, alternating currents, and it was as if the previously empty air revealed itself to be moving, thick, full of force and direction.

He could not stand, but tried to do so, unable to carry the weight of the universe upon his back. He looked upwards, and it was as if the stars themselves were dancing in a circular fashion, moving just above him, spiraling, churning around his position. The sand below was no longer attached to the ground and seemed to levitate, float, and as he gently moved his hand downwards, it was as if it too swam within the speckles of dust. The stars above, the sand below, and the water wind which he breathed in all created some unclear spectrum of weightless force that simultaneously pressed against him, lifting him. He looked at his knees which were firmly planted against the sand below . . . and yet he could not sense his own weight upon them.

He began to cry, to laugh, to laugh heartily and overwhelmingly. He could not contain the joy that began to flow out of him, from his fingers and limbs, joining the dance of elements before him. He laughed and laughed, not humorously, but for some tender and real happiness, like fluid in a tightly shut jar reverberating against its closure, unable to stop. He moved his arms back and forth, trying to physically empty himself, to push more of the hazy glow out of him. It twirled about like smoke, disappearing into the aether, thickening it.

He raised his hands and stared up at them. In the far off distance, the stars still twinkled, and the miniscule movements that his fingers made as a natural consequence of his inability to keep them perfectly still continued to create wispy lines before him. He took a deep breath in and suddenly screamed in celebration, staring at the most profoundly beautiful thing he had ever seen in his entire life. He stared, wide eyed, his open mouth smiling, and closed his fingers into a fist. He closed his eyes tight and felt nothing but the insides of his palms as they heated up within his tightly clasped hand. He grunted and tightened his whole body, forcing all his energy into his hands, crushing them shut.

All at once, he released and opened his eyes, staring at his now naturally curved palms. They slowly dropped in front of his eyes as he stared, observing their automatic need to curl in. He wondered why they curled, for he knew he elicited no action out of them at that moment, allowing them to be as they wanted to be, unmolested by his own force. As he stared at them, it was as if he began to see something familiar in the natural shape, the lines, the color.

"So utterly beautiful," he whispered, tears forming in his eyes. "There you are, Akin . . . there . . . you . . . are."

CHAPTER 46
DUST

Thoughts seemed to direct themselves in the days that followed. He awoke with inklings of the dread and fear as if they had taken to hiding within his heart, and he slowly worked to excise them with some newfound drive. Energy seemed to perpetuate force underneath his mind, giving him vigor in reasoning with the instability that shadowed him.

It was as if his fear of survival, one that seemed to always plague him, was somehow now irrelevant. He could think of visiting the Desta Ocean and felt little fear of who he may encounter or if harm should find him along the way. It was as if an understanding or choice had taken place in his mind, and through that choice he could no longer fear the repercussions of the world before him. It simply did not enter the equation. It was as if his death, should it occur untimely or violently, was "as it was", and was a straight and directed part of the world. He did not want to die . . . he wanted to live a long and explorative life. He wanted to see different people and experience different souls, different men and women and tell stories to different children. But if that should not occur, if he should cough and die at that very moment, he accepted it, avoided that possibility, and continued on his way. That was his path. Survival was a goal now, but its opposite was no longer the driving force under every impulse he generated. It was parallel to his mindset, not the basis of it.

He wondered what Bethelhurst would say to him if he saw him. Was his father even alive? Likely. Would he be angry? He always seemed to be able to maintain a timeless disappointment in Akin but forgave the strangers about him quite readily.

"Father, defa, I have returned. But I will not stay. I have chosen to become a Saifa."

"A Saifa? Ha! What credentials do you have? Were you born into it? Did some priest bestow upon you that title? Or did you conjure it up yourself?"

"I felt it to be true."

"Gone for years now, and you return, not to help your father, to receive my blessing . . . to receive my blessing in your new foolish venture?"

"I did not return for your blessing, Bethelhurst."

"You call me Bethelhurst? I am your father! You will refer to me as such."

"You are a familiar, Bethelhurst. I call you father out of formality, but since you provide no such luxury to me, it seems inappropriate for me to do it for you."

"You are a foolish boy, and have always been one."

"My motivation escapes you, Bethelhurst, but I believe I am free of trying to convince you of my intentions. I believe after this, I shall doubt myself due to my vestigial vulnerability to your bold objections, but will always find my way out of your convoluted distortions."

"Convoluted?!"

"Convoluted. You have lived, and shall likely die as someone else's man, but not your own, and certainly not as a father of relevance to me. I cannot be an instrument of those around me – you are bound to that life. You make yourself as relevant as an irrigation blade."

"Incoherent, foolish, stupid boy. There is pride in minding the fields, to bring life and provide food in this world."

"You pursue nothing with passion, Bethelhurst. And without passion, without belief and strength, you are a chamber pot. Worthy of other people's needs. They live while you bow to them."

"Why did you return if you have such disdain for your heritage?"

Akin laughed suddenly.

"If cowardice is my heritage, I openly reject it. I usher in a new heritage, starting with my line, severing yours."

"A Saifa . . ."

"That is correct, Bethelhurst, a Saifa. A truth teller. I speak to you now because it is the truth in my heart. It is the truth as I see it. And no one shall ever receive anything else from me, but just that. The truth as it is seen by my eyes."

"And what a wondrous life you have before you, Aydan."

"My name is Akin," he replied, sternly. "You have tried hard enough to fill my head with lies surrounding what I am . . . do not try to make me forget who I am."

"Your name is Aydan . . . of my Kunda. I am Bethelhurst, your defa."

"You are Bethelhurst, that is for certain. How he dies is your prerogative."

Akin paused to open his bladder and take a sip of water. He stared outward before him, at the sun, then behind him. He liked looking behind him, seeing his tracks and witnessing the distance he had travelled.

"We never forget home," he thought. What a surprise it was to him that as he ran through fictitious conversations with his father in his head, he was able to predict Bethelhurst's responses with such uncanny accuracy.

"Perhaps, like those who loved us . . . others unfortunately embed themselves within us as well, and we must extract them slowly, precisely."

He wished to forget how to predict his father. It was a part of his mind he did not wish to store or have knowledge of. He wanted to replace it with color and the smell of grass. He wanted to be surprised and unrehearsed when he met him, unprepared for anything negative or positive. He just wanted to receive the interaction in as natural a state as possible, without any fear or apprehension. He wanted to be surprised by Bethelhurst's cynicism, just as he would a stranger's.

Akin's anticipation began to grow. He began seeing changes in the way the sand presented itself, and he allocated it to the familiarity of the Aizik village. He knew that he was nearing it based on the number of days he had walked, but could not know exactly when he would land upon it. It would rely on some familiar icon or signs of human activity to guide him to it.

The trip had been totally void of life, a welcomed change from what he was used to. Though he drank his fill at the random waterhole, he saw no prints and encountered no strangers. It was almost like a pilgrimage for him, and though he was nearing the village, he did not feel apprehensive about it ending. His life would be a trip, he felt, from one place to another, in slow, purposeful steps, without the complications of worrying about the unknown.

He recognized a familiar hill in the distance. It was the Facci, a large protruding rock that people from all over the land would touch on their pilgrimages to Visium. Said to be touched by every person that had ever visited the land, it was the first priest, Aysa, who pressed his palm against it upon witnessing Vespa as she departed. He bowed as he did, absorbing her presence, and every person since followed suit.

As Akin approached it, he looked at it. Sand had gathered around the large stone, and he could see no footsteps in either direction, as if it was just a common boulder one would stumble upon in the desert. He pressed his palm against it and felt the coolness of the stone, then sat down, leaning his back against it.

So many years since he had touched it last. He was just a child, and it was only a brief memory. So sacred, monumental – people would line up to touch it. And here he was, leaning against it as if it was the side of a house.

He looked about again, expecting to see life in some direction, but saw nothing and no one. The quiet was strange and eerie, but he did not dwell on it and proceeded to eat some grain and drink some water.

He covered his face more thoroughly as he approached the village to prevent himself from being recognized. In the distance, he saw the mud brick huts, and the familiar view increased his urgency to get there. His pace quickened, and though he could see no movement in either direction, which was strange to him, he kept walking faster and faster.

His anticipation was matched with worry and some odd tingling in his system, an urgency of sorts, as he got closer and closer, for he could see no motion, anywhere.

He slowed, and inquisition took precedence over any form of excitement as he caught view of the inside of his village. He ran to the entrance and stared.

In every direction within, the familiar placement of the age-old huts remained standing, but all was covered with a layer of yellow dust. He stared incredulously and ran inside, peering into every doorway and window he could see to find some element of life. The huts of neighbors, cousins, Gorav and Manik, their children and family were nowhere. When he turned to see his own house, he fell to his knees as some immediate and intense discomfort struck his stomach.

He stared at it, old and decrepit, its corners softened by winds and sandstorms. He slowly arose and walked to it, stepping inside, feeling the familiar hardness of the floor. As he saw Bethelhurst's cot, he cringed, angst shooting through him harshly as he felt soft tears form from under his tense eyelids. One of the legs had fallen, and it was leaning on its side, the familiar frame and base now covered in dust. He sat down, staring at it, and crawled over to it slowly, placing his palm against the frame, then the base where his father had laid his head.

He began to weep silently, holding the stitched fabric in his fingers, squeezing it. He could not fathom where his father was, nor where the entire village had disappeared. The utensils and pots were still there, sitting on their sides, disorganized. It seemed everywhere he looked, he was mesmerized by some painful emotion, yet the pain felt familiar, as if he was discovering a lost part of himself, a part he loved, that he immediately had to say farewell to.

He stared at his father's cot as if it represented Bethelhurst's last moments on this earth. He imagined him falling, dead, and the bed simultaneously breaking, leaving him alone and breathless in his hut, surrounded by the empty houses. But that was not so – Bethelhurst may have still been alive, moved somewhere with the rest. The bed may have broken long after his departure. Yet, as Akin stared at it, nothing but compassionate sorrow flowed from him.

He crawled on his hands and knees to the adjacent room, and upon seeing his cot, he broke down, holding his head in his hands, weeping. There it stood, just as the last memory he had of it, in the exact same position. He crawled to it and climbed in, hearing it creak under his weight.

He curled up into a ball, holding his knees to his chest, pressing his head against his khalla.

He stared out his doorway and expected people to walk by his view. No one did, and though he logically had anticipated this, he was not prepared for it. The deadness of the village was not registering in his mind, and he hesitated closing his eyes for the fear of discovering a plethora of silent people staring at him as he opened them.

It was as if he could hear murmurs and the day to day activities of people in the distance, but as he tried to legitimize these sounds, they became quieter and quieter, then no more perceivable than the wind.

He closed his eyes and relied on his ears to guide him. He had slept in this bed for so long, and it seemed many lifetimes ago that this was called home. The familiarity had ripped through him suddenly, but now it was as if it distanced itself from him, creating new memories, ones that would override his past ones. He lay there and pondered these thoughts, wishing to retain his childhood impression of this place. But the creaks of the bed were crystal clear now, and in hearing them, it was as if his mind was purposely letting go of the memories of what his cot had sounded like every night he used to fall asleep.

He sat upright slowly and stared at the room, flashing images of that last night in his face, then looking at the floor where his father had struck him. He arose and gathered his pack, touching the wall, feeling it, staring out at the town before him.

He walked into the other room and stared at his father's old cot. Tears began to roll again, and he knelt down, pressing his palm against it, closing his eyes.

He sniffled, sucking inwards, opening his eyes.

"You fucking idiot," he said under his breath, shaking his head. "I would have taken care of you too, you foolish old man."

He sat down beside his father's bed and leaned his back against the uneven wall. He looked around the room, then at the basin and brick stove. There was no more wood within it, but staring at it reminded him of food and the smells that used to emanate from it every day after the fields. There was some odd form of coldness here as though Akin was trying to connect to something that had no interest in reciprocating the effort. He stared and stared, trying to feel familiar, but as each moment progressed, it was as if his mind was naturally accepting that this was no longer his house, and that the bed in the other room resembled the one he had used his whole life, but was no longer that bed. It was, like this house, like the entire village, someone else's life now.

As he walked the rest of the village, his heart was filled with a weighty sadness. The well was dry, and no bucket or rope was anywhere to be seen. Everything triggered memories in his mind. Memories of people he knew in life, and old forgotten ones, like Jacub who had disappeared long before he did. Their memories still haunted this place, somehow imprinted in the brick and organization of the town. It was still emotionally unfathomable to him that the entire world that existed here, so strong, full, and in control, had suddenly vanished without any record or trace. No one would ever know what happened here, for those that had escaped would be scattered, and past their lifetimes the Aizik village would remain some story told once every few years, lore, like the mysterious huts found randomly in the desert from ages past. Even Akin would disappear someday, but perhaps the traces of his love and passion would remain in the people he touched, in the words he spoke.

He thought of the prison in Sumat and the words he came to while he held his friend in his arms.

"Fear expires, while truth lives on forever."

"Immortality . . ." he thought. "Perhaps I am the most selfish person that ever lived. Greedy for it. Like my lovely Samaye. Greedy for love and truth so that we may live on forever. Perhaps it is in my blood, and the path found me."

He found himself naturally walking as his mind buzzed, leaving the village and heading to the fields. He had spent most of his life in the fields with his father, and the path was found easily by him though the grass had long since died off. The trail was still there, a slight indent in the floor of the earth where all the farmers would walk back and forth, day after day.

It occurred to him as he walked that it was possible Samaye's body was somewhere nearby, and in thinking it, he became aware of his close proximity to all the events that had transpired surrounding their friendship. It was strange, because though it had all happened in and around the Aizik village, it was as if he carried them with him, and they were closer to his memories than to this place. He was certain Samaye felt this as well. That he would have felt completely detached from both here and even his own body, and found Akin's heart and mind a more familiar and desirable home for all that remained of him in this world.

Akin smiled.

"But I cannot hold you to me, my friend. You will emanate from me and jump from person to person, rock to rock, and continue like the wind. Endlessly."

There it stood, tall and dry before him. He smiled and walked to the tree, pressing his hands against it as if he was hugging an old friend.

Surrounding the Gimba was nothing. The fields were dry dirt, sandy, and no other trees existed in any near proximity. It was just as he had remembered, albeit surrounded by far less lush an environment. It angled just as it used to, and he sat down under it, cushioning his behind with his sleeping pack.

He closed his eyes and imagined the world around him as it used to be when he was younger, much younger than when he left. When the fields were filled with men and women and children, and it was green all around. Water was plentiful for the irrigated river, and celebrations in festivals and weddings used to grace his life every week.

It was the colors he dwelled on at that moment, and the smiles and lack of worry.

He took a deep breath in, and as he breathed out, he opened his eyes.

"The worries existed . . . even if I did not know it yet."

He thought of the pit and shook his head, staring outwards at the dead fields.

"I cannot return to a lie."

He looked at the dirt beside the tree and felt it with his hands, leaning down, pressing his cheek against it.

"How many times have I sat here?" he thought to himself.

"But I can accept the truth."

He walked back to the village as the sun began to drop, and in the oncoming dusk, the empty town looked menacing. Walking back from the fields always led to more noise, fire and light as it approached dinner time, and the village was always filled with a familiar havoc. But like a bad dream, as he walked the same path and stared down at the huts, their darkening hue reflected the skies without argument.

He entered the village once again, and it was almost as if the view of the dead huts struck him just as the air turned cold. He decided rather quickly that he did not want to spend the night there and felt more comfortable out in the open sea of sand than alone in the center of this empty place.

He felt strange walking into a nearby hut to look for food or bladders, for he half expected someone to interrupt his trespassing. However, after the first few houses, his bonded fear that people still lived there was overshadowed by new sounds and sights and his desire to pillage what useful tools he could find for his oncoming trip.

He found blades and kept only the ones he could safely sheathe, small pieces of light wood here and there and bladders that may or may not work, for they were empty. He could not spare water to test them and pocketed as many as he could. Food was hard to come by, though he did find covered bowls with scraps in them and quickly pressed all the bits together in his food sack after checking for rot.

When he entered the home of Kunda Medura, he was more explorative and felt good to be there. Medura had been a rich household with beautiful daughters, and their Kunda was far above Akin's in status. He had therefore never actually been inside their hut before, and being able to do so now seemed to quench some age-old fetish, bringing back memories of his yearning to be a part of their glorious life.

But as he stared about it, he realized that all they were and all the status they had held was now over. When he was a child, they seemed like wondrous princesses. But in lieu of his experiences, they were just villagers slightly richer than he. He had just witnessed the generational ruler of a timeless city, the Untouched, dethroned . . . a god who was worshipped and feared . . . a deity who's aura seemed to engulf residents like Akin even though most had never even laid eyes upon him. And here, in this tiny speck of a place, these princesses were just women, women just like Arraki, and they had run away just like the rest of the people . . . just like his father. There was nothing but variation in the rise and fall of kings and queens, and so little separated the peasant from the god for it seemed in such a slight, brief instant, all were equated.

Akin, at that moment, may have been superior to the Medura sisters, for he was the only resident in their house, while they were either dead or displaced. His life had led to this switch in hierarchy, and though he wished them no ill-will, it felt good to be the freest man he knew.

As he stepped out into the moonlight, he looked upwards, seeing through the roofs of the empty houses the familiar view of the night sun. He stared and smiled and imagined the envious creature staring back at him. He raised his palm up, covering the image of the creature from his eyes, then uncovered it, as if to surprise it. He dropped his hand to the side and continued staring upwards, his smile fading.

"Breathing life into a reflection does not make anyone less alone."

He continued staring upwards, absorbing what it was that he saw.

"You are a reflection in a pond, and I am alone."

Akin resumed walking about the village, running the tips of his fingers against the mud-brick walls.

Upon returning to his own house, he looked about and felt more detached from it. Bethelhurst's bed still struck a chord in his heart, but the rest, familiar as it was, was distancing itself from the past and entering the realm of the present. He looked about like a scavenger, seeking utensils and food just as he had the other houses, save more carefully and without breaking anything. Most of the bits were unfamiliar to him, but when he spotted a spoon or bowl that he had used as a child, he placed it carefully and tenderly elsewhere, as if to bury it along with the hut itself. After he had excavated what he could, he methodically placed everything in order, keeping his last memory of the place untainted and intact.

He pulled the legs off Bethelhurst's cot so it would not slant and put the base directly on the floor with the legs beside it. He fantasized about his father returning someday to find his home the cleanest and most organized, never knowing it was his son who had put it together again. But he knew his father was gone, and again tears formed in his eyes as he pondered his defa's fate. He would be older now, weaker and perhaps less aggressive for his frailty. But he would be alone, Akin concluded. All alone, whether still alive and soon to die, or in the earth already from a lonesome death at some point in the past.

It was the last moments of his father . . . that last breath that seemed to haunt him over and over.

He held his head in his hands and sighed.

"Either it has already happened or it will happen soon enough," he whispered to himself in the darkness of the hut. "And it was his choice. Respect his choice . . . as I must respect my own."

He arose and took one last look at his home, then exited, looking down the street of the Aizik village. It was one of the main paths in the village, and though he had always entered and left through one entrance, this time he went the opposite way, for he was not going to the fields. This time he was going East, towards the great ocean.

EPILOGUE

"The elder minded Banek opened his eyes to a brightness he had felt just once before. The whiteness of what he saw was hardly describable. There were no markings and no decrepitude. Even the clothes he wore were perfectly woven, of a fabric he had never touched before. The air he breathed tasted like no other, and his body noticed neither cold nor heat. The land bore no sounds, yet it did not feel silent. There was a thickness about this place, as if his fall would be cushioned by the very brightness that surrounded him.

As he stood, he felt his eyes watering, for the lighted realm seemed to brighten. It shone brighter and brighter, and within moments he could scarcely hold his eyes open, no matter how hard he tried. He wiped his eyes one final time and closed them tight, shutting out the brightness.

The light still shone, and through his closed eyes, he saw blood. He could tell it was blood because of its dark reddish color. But this blood shone as it became brighter. As moments passed, it was no longer red, but a yellowish hue. The yellowish color began to gather shape, and became a round ball of flame. It was then that Banek heard the voice.

'This is your world, yes?' the voice asked.

'This is what I know my world to be,' he answered.

'You existed as Banek in this world.'

'Banek was my name.'

'And here now, do you stand before me as Banek?'

'That I do, Lord.'

'Why do you call me Lord, Banek?' the voice asked.

'Because I would listen to you, Lord. Because I hear nothing, yet you speak to me.'

'And so, I could be Lord, or could I be something of your creation, Banek?'

'If you were my own creation, Lord, I would believe you still to be the Lord,' Banek responded.

'And so you believe you may create me then, Banek. An entity of such perpetuity that is the Lord, exists within your creation?'

'I feel this to be true, my Lord.'

There was a brief silence after Banek's response. He could see the radiant ball of flame becoming larger and larger. He saw an endless ocean, and then a beach. He stood on this beach now, void of any life, and stared at a miniature building made of sand near the encroaching tide. The day was darkening, and there was a cold breeze.

'Do you remember this place, Banek?' the voice asked.

'I do, Lord. I visited here as a child.'

'Do you remember this construct?'

'I do not, Lord.'

'As a child, Banek, you created this in the sand. You spent a great deal longer than other children constructing it, for you engineered a way for the rising waves to pass around it, without destroying it. In creating it, you devoted yourself entirely, and were forced to leave as the day became darker.'

'I was a meticulous child, Lord, but did not have the knowledge or skills to preserve a construct of sand.'

'Yet, you believed that you could protect your creation from the encroaching waves,' the voice said.

'I did, Lord.'

The day became dark and the wind grew chilly as rain began to fall. The waves moved forward and devoured the little house, revealing mangroves and swamp. The water rose with vines, and he was now outside a wooden hut.

'Do you recognize this place as well, Banek?' the voice asked.

'I do, Lord. It is Taiga, and I lived here as a young boy.'

'You lived here alone, did you not, Banek.'

'I did, Lord. With my parents, but alone.'

'Most of your boyhood memories are isolated ones, are they not?'

'They are, my Lord. I recall many nights spent building creatures of wood as playthings behind this house.'

'Were they more than playthings, my dear Banek?'

He felt his heart stutter.

'My Lord, I suffered from loneliness as a child. In such times, I created creatures to provide me with company. I recall spending whole days creating them, naming them, and conversing with them.'

'At night, before you slept, you covered your creations with oil so that they may be spared from rot,' the voice stated.

'I did not want to lose my friends, my Lord.'

'But you did.'

'I did, Lord.'

The night turned black, and Banek was again staring at the ocean.

'What do you regret, Banek?'

'I regret many things, my Lord. I regret mistreating a child named Loki. I regret harsh words I spoke to those that are no longer with me. I regret losing the life of my dog, Nanu. I regret my failure in removing the suffering from innocents in the world.'

The voice paused.

'What about your pain, Banek?'

'I have not suffered, Lord. I am blessed.'

'But you know your pain is greater than most.'

'Yes, Lord, but unlike most I am not an innocent.'

'Explain yourself to me, my dear Banek,' the voice requested.

'Lord, I am more capable than most. I am more knowledgeable than most. The loss of my attachments is the root of any sorrows I have suffered. Yet, I pursued them till my own breath was ended.'

'What did you pursue until the end?'

'Naya, my Lord.'

'But Naya was not with you,' the voice said.

He paused. Banek's head slowly fell as he felt tears gather about his tightly shut eyes.

'No, my Lord. Her body did not outlast her soul.'

'You suffered, Banek. You still suffer as you speak to me, whom you call your Lord. I ask you, why do you not regret your suffering?'

'Because I am blessed, my Lord.'

'How are you blessed, my dear Banek?'

'My Lord, my eternal Lord. I believed, with every entity in this creation that is yours with which I have bonded, that our bond would be as eternal as the souls that contain us. With such bonds in such a decrepit world, how could one such as I not feel blessed?'

'But how do you contain such a belief?' the voice questioned.

Banek immediately answered.

'My Lord, with a love as absolute and boundless as the love that I have felt in this world, there exists no expiry large or long enough to leave content my eternal soul.'

The voice paused once again.

'My dear Banek, my beloved, what if the soul you speak of is not eternal? What if those you showered in such love did return nothing?'

Banek looked up, as though looking above the heavens that he stood in.

'My Lord, if such is the nature of reality, then I stand defiant of all things, and state in my eternal will that I accept nothing less than the eternity of my love, and a universe vast enough to contain it.'

'You stand defiant to me, Banek?'

'My Lord, you cannot exist if my love is not eternal.'

The voice smiled.

'My dear, beloved Banek. It is in this defiance of the imperfect world that I have created for you that you have found me.'

'Found you, my Lord?'

'You have found me, Banek. You have found me, for eternity has survived the perils of your impure world.'

Banek began weeping. He knelt down and bowed his head down, holding his face in his hands.

'My Lord, was my love to my beloved Naya pure?'

'Banek,' the voice gently but sternly replied, 'my paragon, my apotheosis, my quintessence, your love for your exalted Naya is so vast, so grand, so eternal, that it gives me permission to venture the belief that even I may exist.'"

"Sa! Sa!" a man cried out. The children began to slap their thighs with their hands.

Akin sat before the group, the reflected blue hue of the ocean against the moonlight at his back, looking at them, smiling slightly.

"I told you, san . . . the ocean is blessed," a mother warmly instructed her small son.

"What a wondrous tale, Saifa!" another man yelled. "Do you have another?"

"Is Banek dead?" a child asked.

Akin shook his head.

"Banek is in your mind," he responded. "Just as he came to mine. There is no missing what exists in your memory. It remains in your heart. His story now survives in all our hearts."

The group remained seated against the center fire, still pondering Akin's tale, with some randomly clapping or thanking him. Some asked him questions of Banek, of the house made of sand, and of the ocean itself. He answered what he could with what he knew, and shared his perspective on the rest.

The group, made up of an eclectic number of different people from different places, spoke variations of the Sumati dialect, and some asked for clarifications from him. They offered him portions of different foods, foods he had never seen or tasted before. He enjoyed their hospitality and felt thankful for being so well received by the strangers.

Later, as night wore on, just as noise and movements used to settle in the village every evening, the camp wound down with families retreating to their erected tents. Akin sat alone on the beach while others smoked and laughed some distance away.

He stared out at a body of water larger than any he had seen before. He thought of Arraki and wondered if she would find love in this life, eternal love like the love Banek spoke of.

He did not know where the story had come from, though he knew it emerged from him. As he told it, he could not predict what would come next, yet what followed over and over seemed to flow naturally as if he was reciting something already known.

He closed his eyes and visualized the ocean before him, just as Banek had seen, and saw nothing but water in every direction.

"And in some other land, I am just a memory in the wind."

Printed in Great Britain
by Amazon

62382967R00302